D1409862

THIN ICE

Center Point
Large Print

Also by Irene Hannon and available from Center Point Large Print:

Lethal Legacy
That Certain Summer
Trapped
Deceived
Buried Secrets
Hope Harbor

This Large Print Book carries the Seal of Approval of N.A.V.H.

Men of Valor • 2

Irene
Hannon

CENTER POINT LARGE PRINT
THORNDIKE, MAINE

This Center Point Large Print edition is published
in the year 2016 by arrangement with Revell,
a division of Baker Publishing Group.

The text of this Large Print edition is unabridged.
In other aspects, this book may vary
from the original edition.
Printed in the United States of America
on permanent paper.
Set in 16-point Times New Roman type.

ISBN: 978-1-62899-865-8

Library of Congress Cataloging-in-Publication Data

Names: Hannon, Irene, author.
Title: Thin ice / Irene Hannon.
Description: Center Point Large Print edition. | Thorndike, Maine :
Center Point Large Print, 2016.
Identifiers: LCCN 2015042520 | ISBN 9781628998658
    (hardcover : alk. paper)
Subjects: LCSH: Women police chiefs—Fiction. | Murder—
Investigation—Fiction. | Large type books. | GSAFD: Mystery fiction. |
Christian fiction.
Classification: LCC PS3558.A4793 T49 2016b | DDC 813/.54—dc23
LC record available at http://lccn.loc.gov/2015042520

To Dr. Avis Meyer,
with fond memories
of my days at the U News.

Thank you for pointing me
toward journalism.
It led me to a road less traveled . . .
And that has made all the difference.

Prologue

What was that odd shimmer in the night sky?

Christy Reed crested the hill on the undulating rural road and peered at the eerie dome of light above the trees in the distance. On a chilly, clear November evening, the heavens should be pitch black save for the stars strewn across the inky firmament, not tainted by unnatural illumination.

The road dived again, the woods snuffing out her view of the mysterious glow. But the twinge of unease that had compelled her to head to her sister's tonight instead of waiting until tomorrow intensified.

Pressing on the accelerator, she swooped through the dip in the road and shot up again.

At the peak of the next hill, her twinge of apprehension morphed to panic.

Flames were strafing the night sky—in the vicinity of her sister's house.

Please, God, no! Not again! We can't take any more trauma!

Smashing the gas pedal to the floor, she plunged down the hill.

Only then did she notice the police cruiser at the bottom, angled sideways, blocking access to the narrow road that led to the Missouri farm-house her sister called home.

She flinched as the harsh, flashing lights strobed across her retinas. They screamed emergency. Disaster. Tragedy.

All the things that had changed her world for-ever six months ago.

Fingers clenched around the wheel, she sped toward the vehicle, screeching to a stop beside it.

As a uniformed officer emerged from the shadows and circled around to her side of the car, she fumbled for the auto window opener. Lowered the insulating sheet of glass. Inhaled the smoke-fouled air that leached into the car.

The coil of fear in the pit of her stomach tightened.

"Can I help you, ma'am?"

"I need to get down that road." Her last word hitched.

"Do you live that way?"

"No. My s-sister does."

Twin furrows dented the man's brow. "What's her name?"

"Ginny R-Reed."

"Hold on a minute." He pulled his radio off his belt and melted back into the shadows.

Christy closed her eyes and clung to the wheel, shudders coursing through her.

Please, Lord, let there be some simple reason Ginny wasn't answering her phones or returning calls all evening! A dead cell. An emergency at work. Anything that's not connected to this fire.

"Ma'am?"

She jerked her eyelids open.

"There's a fire at your sister's house. I'll move my vehicle so you can get through. One of the officers at the scene will meet you."

Her knuckles whitened as she struggled to suck in air. "Is she okay?"

He shifted from one foot to the other, the leather of his belt squeaking as he rested one hand on his gun. "I don't know. But they're doing everything they can to contain the fire so they can get inside."

"You mean she's still in the house!" Hysteria goosed the pitch of her voice.

"They aren't certain of that. Give me a minute."

Before she could respond, he jogged toward his car—putting as much distance between him and her questions as possible.

Because he didn't have the answers . . . or because he didn't want to deliver more bad news?

Please, God, let it be the former!

The instant the cruiser moved aside, she yanked her wheel to the right and accelerated down the woods-rimmed road.

The glow grew brighter as she approached, and fingers of fire stabbed the night sky above parched leaves not yet willing to relinquish their tenuous hold on life.

Her lungs locked.

This was bad.

Really bad.

Though she tried to prepare for the worst, her first full look at Ginny's small, two-story clapboard farmhouse across a field of shriveled cornstalks destroyed the fragile hold she had on her composure.

The whole structure was engulfed in flames.

No, no, no, no, no!

Another uniformed officer appeared in her headlights, waving her to the shoulder before she could turn in to her sister's driveway.

Swerving to the right, she bumped onto the uneven ground, flung open her door, and scrambled from the car. Despite the crisp chill of the late fall evening, the air was hot.

Too hot.

"Ma'am?"

She tore her gaze away from the fire to focus on the officer. Flashes of light darted across the woman's face, giving her a macabre appearance.

"Why don't you wait over there?" She inclined her head toward an ambulance parked halfway up Ginny's driveway, off to the side. The paramedics were standing idle and silent at the rear door, watching the blaze.

Waiting for a victim to treat.

Meaning no one had yet rescued Ginny.

Unless . . .

Was it possible she wasn't here? Maybe she

had been called in to work for an emergency.

Please!

Christy squinted toward the garage at the rear of the house . . . and her stomach bottomed out.

The door was open—and Ginny's car was inside.

Her sister was here.

But where?

Lifting her head, she scrutinized Ginny's second-floor bedroom. The window was cracked open, as usual. Even on the coldest nights, her sister liked fresh air. There was no movement from inside, but maybe . . .

She grabbed the woman's arm and pointed. "That's my sister's bedroom! She might be in bed. Can't you get a ladder up there and . . ."

"Clear the collapse zone. Now!"

At the sudden barked order, the firefighters who'd been struggling to quench the hungry flames dropped their hoses and scattered.

Seconds later, a shudder rippled through the house. The siding buckled. Then, spewing sparks high into the black sky, the second floor collapsed into the raging inferno below like an ancient Viking funeral pyre.

Christy stared in horror at the consuming flames, the world around her receding.

No!

This wasn't happening.

It couldn't be.

11

But the roar of the voracious blaze and the surge of scorching heat against her face mocked her denial, searing the ghastly truth across her mind.

No one could survive a fire like this.

Ginny was dead.

Despite the waves of heat rolling off the collapsed house, a numbing cold gripped her. Tremors convulsed her body. Blackness nipped at the edges of her consciousness.

And somewhere in the distance, screams ripped through the air.

Again.

And again.

And again.

Christy squeezed her eyes shut and pushed her hands against her ears, trying to block them out.

But she couldn't.

Because they were her own.

1

Two Months Later

"You settling in okay?"

At the question, Lance McGregor swiveled in his desk chair. Mark Sanders stood on the threshold of the cubicle, holding two disposable cups of coffee. His new FBI colleague held one out.

"Thanks." Lance leaned forward and took it. "Still adjusting to St. Louis in the winter. When does the January thaw hit?"

"Don't hold your breath. I was referring to the job."

Lance took a sip of his brew and gestured to the warren of cubicles in the center of the St. Louis FBI office. "This bullpen arrangement will take some getting used to. Ditto for the suit and tie."

"You'll get there."

"I appreciate the encouragement—especially in light of the source." When Mark responded only with a raised eyebrow, Lance tipped his chair back and grinned. "Since you're a former member of the Bureau's Hostage Rescue Team and the current leader of this office's SWAT team, I suspect you'd prefer to be in field dress chasing bad guys too."

"You've done some homework."

"I like to know the players."

"A skill that would have served you well as a Delta Force operator."

Touché.

"I see you've been checking me out too."

"SOP for new agents—especially ones fresh out of the academy. For the record, you came out rosy instead of green."

"Nice to know."

Mark took a sip of his own java. "If you're interested in the SWAT team, let me know. It's an ancillary duty, so don't expect any perks for volunteering, but we can always use members with your background. The Delta Force operators I've met were the kind of guys I'd want watching backs when lives are on the line."

Despite Lance's valiant attempt to hold on to his grin, it slipped a hair. "Thanks. But my first priority is to get the lay of the land."

"Makes sense." Though Mark's words were agreeable, the slight thinning of his eyes told Lance the man had picked up on his sudden discomfort. "If you want to consider it down the road, the door's open." Raising his cup in salute, he strolled off.

Lance waited until he disappeared, then pivoted back to his desk, mouth flattening. His new colleague's offer was flattering, but the SWAT team wasn't in his future. Sure, he'd handle trouble if any came his way as a special agent. But he was done seeking it out. Done having to watch people's backs 24/7. Done trying to be Superman.

Because even Superman had his Achilles heel—and if you played the odds long enough, you were bound to lose. Mistakes happened.

And sometimes they were deadly.

A bead of sweat popped out on his forehead, and he scrubbed it away. Enough. He was past this. History couldn't be rewritten. It was over. Finished. He'd made his peace with that and moved on.

But if that was true, why had a simple invitation to join the SWAT team twisted his gut and short-circuited his lungs?

Blowing out a breath, he raked his fingers through his hair. This was *not* a complication he needed three days into his new career as a special agent.

The phone on his desk rang, and he grabbed for it, checking the digital display. A call from the receptionist might not provide much of a distraction, but it would do a better job redirecting his thoughts than reviewing eye-glazing case files—his lot since reporting for duty.

"Hi, Sharon. What's up?"

"Do you have anything urgent on your desk?"

"Not unless sifting through old 302s qualifies."

A chuckle came over the line. "I figured Steve would give you a pile of evidentiary interviews to read. I think it's his version of hazing for the new agents in the reactive squad. Kind of an endurance contest."

"If it is, I'm failing."

"Maybe I can rescue you. You ready for a real case?"

"More than."

"Don't be too anxious. I might be handing you a fruitcake."

"Better a fruitcake than files. What have you got?"

"I have no idea. She won't tell me. Won't give

me her name, either. Just said she needs to talk to an agent."

"Okay. Go ahead and transfer her."

"I jotted down her number from caller ID in case you need it. The fourth digit is a nine."

Meaning there was a strong chance she was calling from a pay phone.

"Thanks."

"Good luck." The line clicked. "Ma'am, I'm putting you through to Agent McGregor." Another click as Sharon exited the call.

Lance leaned back in his chair. "This is Agent McGregor. Who am I speaking with?"

Silence.

"Ma'am?"

A beat of silence passed. Two. Three. He heard an indrawn breath. "A situation has come up that merits FBI involvement—but I can't discuss it by phone."

Still no name.

"Would you like to come to our office?"

"No! That would be too dangerous." She sounded agitated. Scared, even. But she was lucid. That was a plus. "I'd like to set up a meeting on neutral territory. I want it to look like friends getting together, in case anyone's watching."

He tapped the tip of his pen against the tablet in front of him. Paranoia—or valid caution? Too soon to tell. "Can you give me a clue what this is about?"

More silence.

He waited her out.

"I think it . . . it could be kidnapping."

He sat up straighter. "Have you called the police?"

"I can't do that. Please . . . I'll explain when I see you. Besides, this would fall under FBI jurisdiction."

"Is a child involved?"

"No."

He doodled a series of concentric circles on the blank sheet of paper in front of him. The woman was articulate, and she sounded intelligent. Yes, she could be a nut—but the mere mention of kidnapping warranted further investigation.

"All right. Where would you like us to meet you?"

"Us?" He could hear the frown in her voice.

"I'd like to bring another agent along." That was the usual protocol in a situation this filled with unknowns.

"No. Just you."

The tension in her words told him she was getting ready to hang up. Better to agree to her terms than lose her. He could always call for support if he needed it.

"Okay. Where?"

"I was thinking a Panera. They're busy, and the noise level should give us some privacy. But please wear casual clothes. A suit would draw too much attention."

The lady had thought this through.

He put a dot in the middle of his circles to complete the bull's-eye. "Which one?"

"It doesn't matter."

"Brentwood." The central corridor was a reasonable choice. Besides, it was the only Panera he'd visited to date. Why not make this easy on himself?

"Fine. I get off work at five. I'm available after that."

He'd have to bail on dinner with Mac, but his older sibling would understand. Police detectives didn't keep regular hours, either.

"Let's make it seven. I need to go home and change first. How will I recognize you?"

"I'll be wearing jeans and a dark green sweater. I have longish auburn hair."

"Got it."

"I'll see you at seven."

The instant the line went dead, he punched in Sharon's extension and got the source number. A quick check of the crisscross directory confirmed what he'd suspected—the call had come from a pay phone.

The woman wasn't taking any chances.

A ping of adrenaline prickled his nerve endings. At least his first case was intriguing.

And even if the meeting led nowhere, a

clandestine rendezvous was a whole lot more exciting than reading old case files.

Pummeled by a gust of icy wind, Christy whooshed into the crowded Panera, muttering an apology as she jostled the elderly gent who'd stopped to remove his gloves.

He steadied himself on a trash bin topped with a stack of empty trays. "No problem, young lady. Mother Nature is pitching a fit tonight, isn't she?"

"Yes." His amiable comment deserved a reply, but she wasn't in the mood for smiles—or chitchat. Not when she was getting ready to meet an FBI agent . . . and tell him a story he would undoubtedly find farfetched.

But the letter in her pocket was very real.

And very, very scary.

The door opened again, giving her an excuse to move away. She took it.

From the edge of the dining area, she surveyed the room. There were only a few empty tables, and she claimed one in the center, beside the fireplace. An older couple, two teens doing home-work, and a woman engrossed in a bestselling thriller occupied the adjacent tables. None of them seemed suspicious. Besides, no one other than the FBI agent knew about this meeting. And as far as she could tell, no one had followed her here.

She shrugged out of her jacket, draped it over

the back of her chair, and perched on the edge of the seat. Wrapping her fingers around the computer case in her lap, she held on tight.

What if she'd made a mistake by going to the authorities?

The knot that had been lodged in the pit of her stomach since she'd made the call tightened. If this decision turned out to be wrong, the consequences would be dire. That much had been clear.

Yet she wasn't equipped to deal with a kidnapper. She needed the kind of resources law enforcement could provide.

Talk about being caught between the proverbial rock and a hard place.

She pried one hand off the case and tucked her hair behind her ear. She could have hung up while the operator transferred her to McGregor. In fact, she almost had. She could also have severed the connection at any point during her conversation with the agent. He didn't know her name, and using a pay phone had allowed her to keep her options open.

But the man had sounded confident and professional, with a subtle take-charge, I'm-in-control manner that reeked of competence.

All of which had convinced her to take the leap.

Now it was too late for second thoughts. He'd be here any minute. All she could do was hope she hadn't misjudged him.

And pray she wasn't making a fatal mistake.

So that was his auburn-haired mystery caller.

From his seat at a corner table that offered a panoramic view of the eatery, Lance did a quick assessment as the woman claimed a table. Early thirties. Slender. Five-five, five-six. Model-like cheekbones. Flawless complexion. Full lips. Classic profile.

In other words, the lady was gorgeous.

And very nervous.

It didn't take an FBI agent—or former Delta Force operator—to recognize that the taut line of her shoulders, the clenched fingers, and the lower lip caught between her teeth spelled *tension* in capital letters.

He took another sip of his coffee and scanned the crowded restaurant. Thanks to that striking hair, he'd spotted her the minute she stepped inside the door—and no one had followed her in. Nor was anyone watching her . . . except him. Whatever worries she'd had about someone seeing them meet appeared to be groundless.

But he'd give it ten or fifteen minutes to be on the safe side.

By 7:05, the woman was jiggling her foot and checking her watch every thirty seconds. She had to be wondering if she'd been stood up . . . and he was tempted to put her mind at ease. But he'd learned long ago not to let pretty women influence his judgment on the job.

Off the job . . .

His lips twitched. As his older and younger brothers would be the first to remind him, he wasn't immune to the charms of an attractive female in his personal life.

Then again, neither were Mac and Finn.

Must be in the McGregor genes—though Mac's newly engaged status meant the St. Louis dating field was his until Finn showed up on his next leave.

At 7:12, the woman rose and reached for her coat.

His cue.

After one more sweep of the café, he slid from behind the table, left his jacket draped over the chair, and wove among the seated diners.

"Don't leave yet."

She gasped and spun toward him, her face a shade paler than when she'd entered.

"Sorry. I didn't mean to startle you." He leaned closer and dropped his voice. "I'd show you my creds, but I know you want to keep this discreet. I'll do that once we're seated."

She gave a stiff nod and rested one hand on the table she'd been in the process of vacating. "Is this all right?"

"I claimed a more out-of-the-way spot." He indicated the corner table he'd just left.

She frowned at it. "How long have you been here?"

"Long enough to scope out the place."

After a moment, she pasted on a smile, slipped her arm through his, and raised her volume. "It's good to see you again."

He could tell her she didn't need to follow through with the friends-getting-together act for the benefit of anyone who might be watching, since no one was. And he'd get around to that in a minute.

But why not enjoy the sweet scent tickling his nose and the pressure of her graceful fingers on his arm until they got back to his table?

Too bad the trip was so short.

Once they arrived, he indicated a chair at a right angle to his and held it as she sat. After retaking his seat against the wall, he again scanned the interior.

Still clear.

No one appeared to be the least interested in their meeting.

Redirecting his attention to her, he pulled out his creds and laid them on the table. "You weren't followed here. Or if you were, no one followed you in."

Her artificial smile faded as she cast a nervous glance around the room, then skimmed his ID. "Are you certain?"

"Yes."

She exhaled, and some of the stiffening in her shoulders dissolved. "I didn't think so, but

I'm glad to have that confirmed by an expert."

"Did you want to get anything to eat or drink while we talk?"

"As long as we don't need to keep up a social pretense, I'll just grab a cup of water."

Before he could offer to get it for her, she slipped out of her seat and headed toward the drink dispenser.

He watched as she wove through the crowd with a lithe, natural grace. Like that ballet dancer he'd dated in Washington, DC. The one with the legs that went on forever.

His gaze dipped. Hard to tell for sure, with those jeans—but he had a feeling this woman might give the ballet dancer some serious competition in the legs department.

Which was not the most professional train of thought under the circumstances.

Get your act together, McGregor. You're here to talk about a possible kidnapping, not troll for a date.

Check.

By the time she retook her seat, he'd reined in his wayward musings and was ready to concentrate on business.

"Now that you know my name, would you like to share yours?"

Instead of responding, she lifted the cup to take a sip. When the water sloshed dangerously close to the rim, she flicked him a glance, wrapped both hands around the clear plastic, and tried again.

The woman was seriously spooked.

She leaned close enough for him to catch another whiff of that pleasing, fresh fragrance. "My name is Christy Reed. I'm the director of youth programs for a municipal recreation center in St. Louis County." She named the city.

Based on what he could remember from his review of local maps, that was one of the closer-in suburbs. Not far from the location of the public phone she'd used to call him earlier.

"You mentioned kidnapping during our phone conversation."

"Yes." She swallowed. Crumpled a paper napkin. "Look, I'm taking a huge risk by trusting you. But I need experts on this. I can't lose my sister twice." Her voice rasped on the last word and she averted her head, bending to pull her laptop out of the carrying case.

Lose her sister twice?

What was that supposed to mean?

She angled the laptop his direction, a shimmer of tears in her eyes. "This is just a cover while we talk." She lifted the lid. "That's why I called you."

He glanced down. An envelope was lying on the keyboard, addressed by hand to the woman beside him. Next to it was a blank sheet of paper. Both had been placed in plastic bags.

Like she was preserving evidence.

He sent her a quizzical look.

She scooted her chair closer and locked gazes with him. "Two months ago, my sister, Ginny, was killed in a house fire. She was my only sibling, and we were very close. More than ever after we lost our parents eight months ago in a car accident."

Whoa.

Christy Reed had lost her whole family in the space of six months?

That was serious trauma. Enough to account for the smoky whisper of shadows under her eyes. Enough to etch those faint lines of strain at the corners of her mouth.

Enough to push some people over the edge.

Was she one of them?

He studied her. "That's a lot to deal with in a very short time."

"Tell me about it." She rested her left hand on the table beside the computer and clenched her fist. "I try to take it day by day, and I pray a lot. Some days are easier than others. Yesterday wasn't one of them. Not after this arrived in the mail." She touched the corner of the plastic-encased envelope.

"Why was that a problem?"

Her throat worked again, and she moistened her lips. "Because that's Ginny's handwriting."

The letter was from the sister who'd died two months ago?

He checked the postmark. The note had been

mailed January 5 from Terre Haute, Indiana. Four days ago.

But dead people didn't write letters.

"I had the same reaction." At her quiet comment, he turned his head. Intelligent eyes the color of burnished jade met his, steady but anxious. "This is what was inside." She flipped over the sheet of paper.

He read the short, typewritten message.

I took your sister. If you want her back, do not tell anyone about this or call the police. Just wait for further orders.

A typical kidnapping note.

Except this wasn't a typical kidnapping scenario. Not by a long shot. For one thing, kidnappers didn't wait two months to initiate contact. For another, this victim was supposed to be already dead.

"I know this doesn't seem to make sense." Christy drew a shaky breath. "But it could if my sister didn't die in the fire."

He frowned. "Are you telling me they didn't find her body?"

"They found *a* body. It was burned beyond recognition." Her voice choked, and she swallowed. "Everyone assumed it was her."

"Wasn't there an autopsy?"

"No. Ginny was a wildlife biologist in the Mark Twain National Forest. She lived on the outskirts of Chandler, a small town just south of Potosi, and the local police didn't see any need for an autopsy after an investigator from the state fire marshal's office ruled the fire accidental."

"What was the basis for that opinion?"

"My sister's house was old and drafty, and she supplemented her furnace with electric heaters downstairs and in her bedroom. According to the investigator, it appeared the one in the bedroom had been too close to the curtains. The window was open, and he reasoned that the wind blew the fabric against the heater, which started the fire. The frame house was old, the wood dry . . ." She lifted one shoulder.

No matter the apparent cause, an autopsy should have been done. *Would* have been done by a larger police department.

And it could still be done—if necessary.

Lance folded his hands on the table. "Other than this note, do you have any reason to think the body found in your sister's house belonged to someone else?"

"No. That's why the whole thing is so confusing. But this is Ginny's handwriting. The backward slant, the curlicue at the end of the *s*, the tail she always added to her capital *R*'s . . . her penmanship is distinctive."

"An expert forger could replicate it."

She sucked in a breath. "You think this is some sort of hoax?"

"It's possible."

"But . . . why would someone do that?"

"Good question—except look at the flip side. If this isn't a hoax, someone went to a lot of effort to make it appear your sister died in a fire, including providing a body. Why would someone do *that?*"

She shook her head, her distress almost palpable. "I have no idea."

"Did your sister have any enemies?"

"No. Ginny was the sweetest, gentlest . . ." She groped for her water, lifting it with both hands again to take a sip. "Sorry." She set the cup back down. "Everyone loved Ginny."

"Was she married?"

"No."

"Was there an ex-husband or boyfriend or ex-boyfriend in the picture?"

"No. She didn't date much, and she lived alone."

"How old was she?"

"Thirty."

He shot her a skeptical look. "Thirty years old and no significant ex-love interests?"

"She worked long hours, often in the woods communing with nonhuman species, and lived in the middle of nowhere. There weren't many opportunities to meet eligible men."

"Even so, most people don't make it to thirty without logging a few failed relationships—and those often leave bad feelings in their wake on one or both sides."

"Ginny never dated anyone long enough to generate hurt feelings when she stopped seeing them."

"As far as you know."

Her chin lifted a notch. "We were close. If there was a man in her life, she'd have told me. Not everyone is interested in putting notches on their belt, Agent McGregor. And not everyone ends relationships with bad feelings. It's dangerous to jump to conclusions about others based on personal experience."

Ouch.

Still, whether or not he liked her inference, it did tell him two things.

There was nothing wrong with her mind. The FBI might get its share of fruitcake calls, but this woman was a clear, analytical thinker not inclined to flights of fancy—or overreaction.

She was also becoming defensive, which would get them nowhere.

Better to ease off and circle back to this topic later or she might shut down.

He took a sip of coffee and set his cup off to the side. "Why don't you tell me about the fire?"

Her posture drooped, and she dropped her chin to stare at the melting ice in her cup. "It happened on a Friday night. I'd been planning to drive out on Saturday to spend the weekend with Ginny. But when she didn't answer her phone or return my calls, I got worried and went out after work.

The whole house was in flames when I arrived about nine forty-five. I got there right before it . . . collapsed."

Christy Reed had watched the tragedy unfold.

The lady beside him had had some very tough breaks.

Out of nowhere, an urge to weave his fingers through hers swept over him, the impulse so powerful his hand was already halfway to its destination when he caught himself, forcibly shifting direction to grab his coffee cup instead.

Keep your mind on the case, McGregor, not the woman. You're here to investigate, not console.

He took a sip of his coffee and set the cup down. "Any particular reason you'd worry because your sister wasn't responding to your calls?"

"Yes. Ginny was having a hard time dealing with our parents' deaths. She wasn't eating or sleeping enough, and it was beginning to impact her ability to function at work. She finally resorted to taking over-the-counter sleeping aids. That worried me, even though she was responsible about it."

"Did you tell this to the police?"

"Yes. Since she was found in bed, they concluded she must have taken some pills and slept through the fire. Otherwise, she should have smelled the smoke and called for help. As it was, a passing motorist sounded the alarm after he spotted flames on the roof. But it was too late. Ginny never made it out. At least I didn't think so, until that came." She touched the edge of one of the plastic-encased documents.

He pulled a notebook out of his pocket. "I'll get copies of the police and fire investigator's reports tomorrow morning."

She leaned down, removed a manila file folder from her laptop case, and handed it to him. "Done. I asked for copies of everything . . . never knowing I'd need them for such a bizarre reason. I assumed you'd want them."

Nope. No problem with this lady's brain.

He opened the file and gave the brief, straight-forward reports a quick read. It was hard to fault their logic or the conclusions. The pieces all added up to a typical tragic house fire.

Or they had, until now.

Unless the note was, indeed, a hoax.

He was back to the line of questioning Christy hadn't liked.

"I asked before if your sister had any enemies." He approached the topic with more caution this go-round, choosing his words with care. "If the note turns out to be some sort of sick joke, it would suggest this is more about you than her. Do *you* have any enemies?"

"No." Her answer was immediate—and firm. "And I'll save you from asking the next question. I've had one serious relationship in my life. It ended four years ago, but we parted on friendly terms. It's hard to fault a man for choosing the divine over the human."

He squinted at her. "What does that mean?"

She gave him a wry look. "He was Catholic, and after a lot of soul searching, he decided he had a calling to the priesthood."

A former boyfriend who was a priest.

Not a likely suspect.

He closed the file. "I'm sorry if I offended you with my earlier questions on this subject—but romantic relationships gone south are often the impetus for crime."

"I can understand that." She fiddled with the edge of her napkin and exhaled. "I owe you an apology too. My personal remark was uncalled for—and unkind. I'm not usually snippy."

"Apology accepted." No need to admit she'd come close to pegging him. "Considering the stress you're under, I think you're remarkably composed."

"Not on the inside." She touched the back of his hand, her fingers cold and not quite steady. "So can you help me with this? Since Ginny was a federal employee and that note crossed state lines, I assumed it fell under FBI jurisdiction."

He tried to focus on her question rather than her touch. "Yes, it does. And yes, I can help. My first priority is to have our handwriting experts in Quantico compare this envelope to a verified sample from your sister."

Once again she reached into the computer case. "I assumed that would be a first step, so I pulled notes and cards she sent me over the past few years. I also included a poem she handwrote for my thirtieth birthday. I don't have much else. She was more into email and texting."

He gave the documents a fast perusal. He was no expert, but he agreed with Christy. The handwriting appeared to match.

"May I?" He lifted the plastic-bagged documents.

"Yes." She watched him slide them into the file. "The instant I realized what they were, I put them in the bags. On my end, no one but me has touched them."

"We should be able to pull some prints from your sister's cards too. All federal employees are in the automated fingerprint database. Any others we find can be run to see if they belong to some-one with a criminal record."

"How long will that take?"

"I'll courier the material to Quantico tomorrow and ask for priority analysis. We should have a response by Friday if I press."

"What if I hear back in the meantime from the person who wrote the note?"

"Call me." He extracted a business card and set it on the table. "However, I'm not expecting that to happen. The fire was two months ago. Unlike most kidnappers, this person doesn't appear to be on a fast track."

"What's next if your experts decide that's Ginny's handwriting?"

"We'll need to exhume the body buried in her grave and do an autopsy—including a DNA analysis—to verify it's not your sister."

"This whole thing is surreal." She massaged the bridge of her nose. "Have you ever run across a case like this before?"

"No—but every situation is unique." No need to tell her he was so new to the FBI that he had no personal basis for comparison. "We'll figure this out. And you made the right choice in coming to us."

"I hope so." She didn't sound convinced.

"Ms. Reed, the FBI is committed to confidentiality. You don't need to worry about leaks on our end."

"But if you start investigating and asking questions, word could spread to the wrong people —especially if you get too close."

He couldn't dispute that.

"We'll do everything we can to keep that from happening."

Based on the apprehension in her eyes, his less-than-absolute reassurance wasn't what she'd hoped to hear. But it was the best he could offer.

Because sometimes, no matter how hard you tried, things went south.

Swallowing past the sudden constriction in his windpipe, he opened his notebook. "Why don't you give me your contact information, including address and cell phone?" After she complied, he pushed the card on the table toward her. "If you need to talk to me—day or night—use the cell number. Don't hesitate. That will always be the fastest way to reach me. Now let me walk you to your car."

He held her coat, then followed her out to a dark blue Mazda, scrutinizing the parking lot as they walked. Nothing seemed amiss.

At the car, she turned to him. "Just in case anyone is watching, can I give you a hug? So this looks like a social meeting?"

"No problem." At all.

She stepped toward him, and he pulled her close.

Nice—but over too fast.

"Thanks again for meeting me tonight." Without waiting for a response, she slid behind the wheel.

He moved aside while she backed out, shoving his hands in the pockets of his jacket as her taillights receded into the night.

Only after they disappeared did he return to his own car, a thrum of excitement pulsing in his veins.

His days of reading boring 302s were over. He had his own case now.

And it was a hot one—in more ways than one.

2

Watching the phone wasn't going to make it ring.

Christy blew out a breath, plucked the cell off her desk, and shoved it in the gym bag on the floor beside her. Lance McGregor had promised to call when he had any news, and unless her instincts were way off, he would. The tall, clean-cut agent with piercing blue eyes and a professional, buttoned-up demeanor struck her as a man who kept his word. Exactly the kind of integrity she'd expect from an FBI agent, based on the image the Bureau projected.

Yet she had a feeling the well-broken-in black leather bomber jacket Lance had worn Wednesday night at Panera, which sent a subtle don't-mess-with-me message, suited his personality better than the suit-and-tie image the FBI cultivated. It was the kind of jacket favored by a man who knew how to exert pressure and get results. Who didn't quit until he finished a job.

The very kind of man she wanted on Ginny's case.

Unfortunately, whatever pressure tactics he'd applied must not have worked at FBI headquarters. At five forty-five on a Friday, there wasn't much chance the handwriting analysis would arrive today. Or tomorrow. Or Sunday.

It was going to be a long weekend.

She rose from her desk, grabbed her gym bag, and headed to the ladies' room. Back-to-back coaching sessions should loosen the tension between her shoulder blades—and tonight's students would require her full concentration.

But she'd keep her phone handy, just in case.

Ten minutes later, as she emerged still tugging the hem of her lightweight wool sweater down over her leggings, a muffled chirp sounded deep within her bag.

Jolting to a stop in the hall, she fumbled with the zipper. The bag slipped from her shoulder, and she dropped to one knee to root through the contents.

Naturally the phone had sunk to the bottom and wedged itself in a corner.

By the time she had it in hand, the call had rolled to voice mail—but according to caller ID, it was Agent McGregor.

Yes!

"Ma'am? Are you okay?"

She looked up. One of the evening maintenance guys had stopped mopping and was watching her with concern.

"Yes. Thanks." She scrambled to her feet and hoisted the bag back onto her shoulder. "I, uh, dropped my stuff when the phone rang. It startled me."

"Well, if you're coming this way, be careful of the wet floor. I don't want anybody falling on my watch." He went back to work.

Drumming her thumb against the phone, Christy eyed the ladies' room. Not sufficient privacy for a return call. Anyone lingering after hours could barge in. And since the city had adopted the cube mentality permeating corporate America, her so-called office wasn't an option, either. Nor the conference room pod.

That left her car.

After a quick detour to grab her coat, she hurried down the corridor toward the front door, trying not to break into a jog under the wary scrutiny of the maintenance guy.

Once in the parking lot, though, she picked up her pace, dodging around a mother holding tight to the hand of a tiny girl toting a dance bag. The tot had to be a student in the popular introduction to ballet class she'd added to the program roster last fall.

Too bad she couldn't pop in and watch for a few minutes. The youngsters' innocence and enthusiasm was always a balm for the soul—and she could use some balm tonight.

An icy gust sliced through her, and she popped the locks, shivering as she slid behind the wheel. After once more digging out her phone, she tapped in Lance's number.

He answered on the first ring.

"Agent McGregor? It's Christy Reed. Sorry I missed your call." Her words came out in a rush, her breath forming a frosty cloud in front of her face. "I couldn't get to my phone fast enough."

"No problem. I meant to touch base with you earlier, but my whole squad was pulled into a bank robbery and everything else came to a standstill. I did hear from Quantico a couple of hours ago, though. Our handwriting experts are certain the envelope was addressed by your sister."

She closed her eyes.

Ginny was alive.

"Are they sure?" Despite the penetrating cold, her palms began to sweat.

"Yes. They also found her prints on the envelope—along with a number of others. One of those was on the greeting cards too, which suggests it belongs to you. They ran all the prints through the database, but nothing came back."

"Translation?"

"They don't belong to any current or past federal employees, military personnel, government contractors with clearances—or anyone with a criminal history."

She fixed her gaze on the pool of illumination from an overhead light, one of the few bright spots in the parking lot. "So what happens next?"

"I've already been in touch with . . ." A siren

sounded, and garbled voices spoke in the background. "Hold a minute."

She shivered again, trying to tune out the all-too-familiar emergency sounds.

"Sorry about that." A thread of weariness wove through his words.

"You sound like you're still in the thick of th-things." Great. Now her teeth were beginning to chatter. She should have started the car and cranked up the heat before returning his call.

"I am. But I wanted to bring you up to speed. I've spoken to the County ME's office. The body will be exhumed Monday and an autopsy done Tuesday. We should be able to determine if it's your sister through DNA or dental records. Do you have any personal items she might have used?"

"The fire destroyed everything at her place, but she kept a toothbrush at my house and I have the items from her car—including a hairbrush. Will either of those give you what you need?"

"Toothbrushes only work about 50 percent of the time. Let's hope there are some hairs in the brush with the roots attached. Do you know the name of her dentist?"

"Yes."

"I'll call you back after this winds down to get that information and arrange to pick up the brushes. Sometime tomorrow, probably."

"What if the autopsy confirms the body

isn't . . ." She swallowed. "That it's not Ginny?"

"Then we assume the note is real and treat this as a kidnapping."

She flexed her numb fingers. "I still can't get a handle on the motive. It's not like I'm rich or have anything valuable enough to be ransom-worthy."

"If that's the case, this could be personal. A vendetta of some kind."

"That gets back to the enemies question."

"True." More background noise, followed by a muffled exchange. "I need to go. But I plan to track down my boss and discuss this with him before I crash for a few hours. I'll call you tomorrow, and we'll talk next steps."

Her fingers tightened on the phone as she fought back a wave of panic. "If the results from the autopsy verify it's not Ginny, you'll launch a full investigation, right?"

"Yes. And I'm very cognizant of the kidnapper's warning. That's one of the reasons I want to discuss strategy with my boss. We need to come up with a game plan that puts your sister at the least possible risk. Will you trust me on this?"

A man she'd met two days ago was asking her to put her sister's life in his hands.

For some strange reason, she was willing to do that.

"Yes." A police radio blared in the background. "I'll let you get back to your bank r-robbery." Her teeth were chattering worse than ever.

"Are you okay?"

This man didn't miss much.

"Yes. I came out to my car to return the c-call. I thought it would be more secure than my office. But it's f-freezing."

"You're still at work?"

"For a while yet."

"Long day."

"Not as long as yours."

"No argument there. Go back inside where it's warm and I'll talk to you tomorrow."

The line clicked, ending the call.

Taking a deep breath, she tucked the phone back in her gym bag and shouldered open the car door. A blast of frigid air whipped past, and she turned up the collar of her coat as she hurried back toward the building. She had a few minutes before she had to meet her first student. Time enough to chase away the chill.

But she could think of a much more appealing way to warm up.

His initials were LM.

Christy pushed through the door, shaking her head. How inappropriate was that? Yes, Lance McGregor was handsome. More than. Even the small, jagged scar on his left temple didn't detract one iota from his appeal. Any red-blooded woman would find him attractive. And unless she was mistaken, she'd caught a glimmer of interest in his eyes too.

Too bad she hadn't met him under different circumstances.

Given the situation, however, she had no intention of fanning the spark of mutual attraction.

Right now, she wanted him focused on one thing and one thing only.

Finding Ginny.

Christy Reed was a world-class figure skater.

Or she had been, fourteen years ago.

Quite a discovery at nine o'clock on a Saturday morning.

Bagel in hand, Lance felt around on the kitchen counter for his mug of coffee as he stared at the screen of his laptop.

His quick Google search for her sister had produced a meager handful of hits, most related to quotes from Ginny in a few newspaper articles about bats and some disease called white-nose syndrome.

But Christy Reed was a whole different story—though she'd gone by her more formal name in her skating days.

He took a fortifying gulp of the dense brew and scrolled through the hits for Christine Reed. There appeared to be hundreds, all more than a decade old. By contrast, Christy Reed merited less than a dozen callouts, all from within the past few years and all related to her position at the rec center.

Dropping onto a stool, he scanned her skating bio. Bronze and silver medals in the US championships, bronze in two world competitions, one of the top finishers in a grand prix event. She'd even made the Olympic team.

But she hadn't competed.

A broken tibia that required surgery had sidelined her two weeks before the big event.

Could the timing have been any worse?

He took another swig of coffee and continued to read.

The fall had not only kept her out of the Olympics, it had ended her competitive career. Despite pressure from her coach and others in the skating community to continue on the circuit after her recovery, she'd elected to retire. After performing for several seasons with an ice show, she left the skating world behind to attend college.

It was an impressive resume—but also one filled with broken dreams.

To train for years in the hopes of earning a coveted spot on the US Olympic team, to reach that goal, then to have it snatched away days before the big event . . .

Wow.

What a crushing blow.

He scrolled down, studying the accompanying photos. He might have a lot of questions for Christy based on this new information, but those skimpy skating outfits answered the one he'd been pondering since they met.

Her legs were seriously great.

Taking another bite of the doughy bagel that would have tasted a thousand percent better ifhe'd bothered to toast it, he clicked on the embedded video montage of her medal performances.

In the first one, a younger version of Christy was wearing a toga-like outfit, her upswept hair decorated with flowers as she glided effortlessly over the ice.

She looked like Aphrodite.

He leaned closer to the screen. Man, those legs were . . .

Pound! Pound! Pound!

He jerked upright at the sudden banging, sloshing the coffee in his mug.

Pound! Pound! Pound!

As the assault continued, he shot an annoyed glance toward the front door and stood. Ignoring the rude summons didn't appear to be an option.

Half-eaten bagel in hand, he padded barefoot across his empty living room and peered through the peephole. Frowned.

Why was Mac here?

Clamping the bagel in his teeth, he used both hands to flip the lock and pull the door open.

Mac gave him a head-to-toe scan. "Pardon the cliché, but what cat dragged you in?"

He pulled the bagel out of his mouth. "Good

morning to you too. If I'd known you were coming, I'd have dressed for the occasion."

A blast of wind sent flurries scuttling into the room, and Mac motioned toward the door. "Could we continue this inside?"

In silence, Lance swung the door wide and stepped back.

Mac edged past, brushing a tenacious flake off his eyelash. "I came over to take you to breakfast even though you bailed on dinner Wednesday and haven't bothered to call since."

He banged the door shut. "What? Am I supposed to check in with you every day? Isn't that carrying the big-brother routine a little too far?"

Mac folded his arms. "You get up on the wrong side of the bed or what?"

Hmm.

Maybe he *was* being a tad less than gracious.

He shoved his fingers through his hair. "Sorry. I'm short on sleep."

"Late night?"

"Late enough."

That earned him an eyebrow arch. "Don't tell me you're already giving the locals competition on the social scene."

"I wish. I was working."

"I thought you told me on Wednesday morning that things were slow. As in catatonic."

"They heated up."

"Yeah? What's cooking?"

"A bank robbery on Thursday. I clocked four hours of sleep in the next thirty-six. Plus, I've got my own case now."

"Sounds like your first week turned out to be immersion by fire."

"You have no idea how accurate that is."

"You can tell me all about it at breakfast. Go get ready."

He held up his bagel. "I'm already eating."

Mac gave the lump of dough a disparaging once-over. "You call that breakfast? Buddy, I'm taking you to the best pancake place in town."

That did sound better than a bagel—or one of the fast-food drive-throughs that had become part of his morning routine since arriving in St. Louis.

"They have great eggs and bacon too." Mac propped a shoulder against the wall and grinned. "Not to mention huge cinnamon rolls."

His weakness—as his older brother very well knew.

"Sold. Give me five."

"Take your time. I'll get a cup of that coffee I smell and amuse myself." Mac pushed off from the wall and strolled through the bare living room. "Nice décor."

"Hey! Cut me some slack. I just got here."

"So had I when you critiqued my place on your first visit—but at least I had a couch and a lamp."

"None of my stuff was worth moving except

for the bed, and I haven't gotten around to shopping for furniture yet. You think Lisa might help me out with that?"

"My fiancée is busy planning our wedding, being a police chief, and keeping me company."

"Fine. I'll handle it."

"But she might work in a quick shopping trip if I mention the situation is desperate." Mac stopped and gave the room another perusal. "Which it is."

"Tell her I'll buy her lunch."

"Make it the Woman's Exchange, and you'll have a deal."

"That sounds like one of those froufrou places for ladies who lunch."

"What can I say? She loves their chopped salad."

Chopped salad.

Sheesh.

Still . . . He surveyed the empty room. Lisa had done a great job with her own house. It was comfortable and homey without being fussy.

"Fine. I'll take her there." He'd just have to stop somewhere for a burger afterward.

"I'll tell her to expect your call." Mac continued toward the kitchen. Paused again. "Is that 'Clair de Lune'?"

Lance frowned. "Who?"

"Not who. What. A piece of music by Debussy."

He tried to place the name.

"The famous classical composer?" Mac offered the prompt in a wry tone.

Oh yeah. He'd heard of that guy. And it made sense. Classical stuff was popular in figure skating . . .

Figure skating!

He lunged toward the kitchen, trying to overtake Mac.

Too late.

"You've got to be kidding me." His brother came to a dead stop in front of the computer as Christy executed some whirling dervish kind of spin. "You're watching figure skating?" Mac sent him an incredulous look.

He leaned over to close the window. "It's research for the case I mentioned on Wednesday that deep-sixed our dinner."

Mac studied him. "Seriously?"

"You don't think I watch figure skating for fun, do you?"

The oldest McGregor sibling strolled over to a cabinet and pulled out the single clean mug. "Why not? Lisa enjoys it, and I've watched a few competitions with her. What's not to like? Skaters are great athletes—and the women's costumes are very . . . captivating."

No kidding.

"So does this case you're working on have any similarities to that Nancy Kerrigan situation back in the nineties?" Mac poured himself some coffee.

He ran the name through his mental index. It

sounded sort of familiar, but he couldn't place it.

"Who's Nancy Kerrigan?"

"A top US skater who was assaulted by one of her rivals' cohorts a few weeks before the Olympics. The guy took a swing at her knee with a police baton."

Oh yeah. That rang a few distant bells. "I don't remember the details. It happened two decades ago."

"I didn't either, but Lisa filled me in. Despite classy videos like that one you had running"—he swung his mug toward the blank screen—"things are not all sweetness and light in the skating world. It's as competitive and cutthroat as any other professional sport." He sipped his coffee. Grimaced. "This is worse than SEAL sludge. Get dressed so we can go rustle up some decent java."

"I'll be ready in five."

"You said that ten minutes ago."

"This time I mean it."

"You never answered my question about your case. Any similarities?"

"Not that I know of."

How could there be? Christy's skating career had been over for years. She was no longer a competitive threat to anyone—and nothing short of an Olympic medal would be worth maiming or killing or kidnapping for.

Yet as Lance headed down the hall to his bedroom and dug through the packing boxes of

51

casual shirts and sweaters, the question he'd asked Christy about enemies resurfaced. She'd claimed neither she nor Ginny had any.

But every instinct he'd honed during his Delta Force stint told him she was wrong.

One of them did, indeed, have an enemy.

A very formidable one who had gone to a great deal of trouble to wreak havoc in the lives of both sisters with a meticulously planned and executed crime.

Lance buttoned his shirt. Pulled a sweater over his head. Savored the familiar adrenaline rush that kicked in whenever he was on the hunt.

What a change from a few days ago, when he'd been a desk jockey drowning in the minutia of old files, wondering if he'd ever get to put any of his Quantico training to use, itching for a case to crack.

Well, he had one now.

And he had a feeling solving it was going to take every bit of his Academy training—along with a few of the tricks and techniques he'd picked up during his high-octane Delta Force days.

3

"Let's try the axel once more before we call it a day, Lauren." Christy glided over to the twelve-year-old as the girl bent to adjust one of her laces.

The petite blonde straightened up and huffed out

a breath. "I don't know why I can't nail that one."

"You're getting there. The harder jumps take longer to master. Try putting a little more speed into the approach, and snap your hip around as fast as you can on takeoff to start the rotation immediately. Stay pulled in longer and tighter too. Your muscle memory is kicking in from other jumps and telling you to release sooner, but remember, you have an extra half rotation with this one."

As Lauren moved off for the setup, Christy watched for strays who might wander into the center area reserved for figure skaters. Teaching during public sessions wasn't ideal, but it was affordable for students who otherwise wouldn't have the opportunity to learn some of the finer points of the sport. Like her, back in the early days when she'd skated for the sheer joy of it.

No problem with wobbly interlopers or speedy games of tag today, though. Attendance at the Saturday morning session was sparse. The snow that had begun falling as she left the house—not to mention the forecast of significant accumulation—must be keeping most people home.

Christy watched as Lauren began her approach . . . leaped into the air . . . and double-footed the landing.

The youngster skated over, shoulders drooping, and Christy gave her arm a squeeze. "Don't be discouraged. We'll keep plugging away, and one of these days everything will click. Have you been practicing between lessons?"

"Yes. Mom brings me during the week."

"Excellent. The more ice time you clock, the quicker you'll improve." She swiveled toward the viewing area, spotted the girl's mother, and lifted a hand in acknowledgment. "I'll watch till you join your mom. See you next week."

As the girl skated to the side and stepped off the ice, Christy began circling the rink, keeping an eye on the viewing window. Sixty seconds later, Lauren appeared beside her mother. She gave them a final wave, checked her cell for any messages, then reset it to audible.

With the public session winding down, only a handful of people remained on the ice. Given the forecast, she ought to go home too—but the comfort of these predictable, familiar surroundings calmed her. Why not stay for a few more minutes?

Decision made, she picked up speed. Switched to back crossovers. Did a layback spin. Began to set up for a double salchow jump.

At a sudden chirp, though, she came to an abrupt stop in a spray of frosty crystals, pulled off one glove, and dug out her phone.

Lance.

"Good morning." She glided over to the edge of the rink and stepped off onto the rubber mat. "I hope you got some sleep last night."

"Yes. But first I discussed your case with my boss. I think it would be helpful if we got together again. Will today work?"

She moved toward the locker area. "Yes. Where and when?"

"Let's do the Panera in Kirkwood, near your condo, in forty-five minutes. That way, you won't have far to drive in the snow. And bring the brushes we need for DNA comparison, plus the contact information for your sister's dentist."

"It's all ready to go."

"Great. See you soon."

Pocketing her phone, she sat to remove her skates. Strange how just listening to Lance McGregor's steady, confident voice quieted the butterflies in her stomach—and reassured her that calling the FBI had been smart.

But if the kidnapper found out she'd ignored his instructions?

The butterflies took off again.

Doing her best to corral them, she tugged off her skates. Wiggled her toes. Rotated her ankles. The thick leather might protect and support, but it was also confining and restrictive.

Kind of like fear.

Except there were two types of fear—the kind that immobilized and victimized and the kind that empowered and spurred into action.

She'd chosen the latter.

Soft cloth in hand, she wiped the moisture off

her blades and slid the skates into their carrying case.

Maybe following instructions, leaving the kidnapper in control, would keep her sister safe.

Maybe.

But from everything she'd ever heard about crimes like this, kidnapping victims were often killed whether the family followed instructions or not.

She zipped the case closed and stood. Far better to put her trust in Lance McGregor and the FBI than in a person who torched houses and substituted dead bodies for living ones.

Besides, they had a lot more experience dealing with criminal minds—especially sick ones.

And this person was sick.

Christy was ten minutes early.

But he'd beaten her by fifteen.

As she pulled into the almost deserted lot, Lance watched from his corner seat beside the plate glass window. The heavy snow was obviously keeping most St. Louisans at home, and that suited him fine. If anyone was following her, they'd be easy to spot.

She parked near the door and slid from the car, her snug leggings flattering her lithe form. Resisting the temptation to watch her as she walked toward the entrance, he surveyed the lot instead.

No cars followed her in.

In his peripheral vision, he saw her enter . . . pause . . . scan the back corners. Once she spotted him near the front, he rose, keeping an eye on the lot.

Only after she joined him, leaned close to whisper "In case anyone is watching," and gave him a hug did he shift his attention to her—and return the embrace.

"Did you have any problems with the snow?" He tipped his head toward the window as she slid into a chair.

"No. Not much stops me on the weather front."

Or on any other, unless he was reading her all wrong. The lady had spunk.

"Have you had lunch?" The effects of the mega breakfast Mac had fed him five hours ago were beginning to wane.

"Not yet."

"Why don't we eat? If we keep meeting at Panera and never order anything, it's going to look suspicious."

"Are we being watched?" A spark of fear darted through her eyes.

"No. But I'm hungry, and I hate to eat alone." Not entirely true. He was used to eating solo meals, ingesting the food as fast as possible, a weapon at the ready. It was better not to be distracted when an RPG or sniper bullet could appear out of nowhere.

But those days were over.

And a distraction like the woman across from him was welcome. She was a far better meal companion than an MP5.

"In that case, I'll join you."

He rose. "What would you like?"

She stood too. "I'll go with you. I need to look at the menu."

By the time they placed their orders, collected their food and drinks, and returned to their table, the place had emptied.

"I brought the items we discussed." From her tote, Christy retrieved a small gift bag with fancy tissue paper stuck in the top and set it on the table. "The dentist's contact information is in there too. I guess I didn't need to go to all this trouble, since no one's watching us, but I didn't want to take any chances."

He slid the bag to the side, glancing out as a lone, snow-covered car rolled by, its windshield wipers struggling to fight off the onslaught.

Driving home was going to be a bear.

"It never hurts to go the extra mile in a situation like this. And consistency is important. Now that we've started the friends pretense, let's keep it up. It may come in handy as we move into the investigation."

She stopped dousing her salad with pepper from the packets she'd collected at the condiments counter. "Your boss gave the green light to proceed?"

"Not officially. He wants to have the results of the autopsy in hand first. But based on what we know, that's where this is headed. If the dental records or the DNA samples in here"—he indicated the gift bag—"match the body, someone is faking a kidnapping. That's a crime. If they don't, we can assume the kidnapping is real—and we'll run the DNA sample from the body through the national missing person database."

"What if you don't get a match there?"

"We might never know who it is."

Christy crushed the empty pepper packets in her fist. "This whole thing is crazy. Why would someone go to such effort—and take such a risk—to disguise a kidnapping with a fire and a fake victim, only to undo all that effort two months later?"

Lance wiped a glob of mustard off his fingers. "That's the $64,000 question. It all comes down to motive. What would someone have to gain from this?"

She rested an elbow on the table and watched the snow accumulate outside the window. "Not anything valuable enough to make all this worthwhile. Like I told you yesterday, I have some money, but not a lot. My parents left their estate to Ginny, but it didn't amount to much."

"You didn't inherit anything?"

"Some sentimental items. Nothing of great dollar value."

He could guess the reason for that—and it led directly to the subject he wanted to discuss.

"Since romantic or financial motives don't seem to be panning out, let's talk about other reasons someone might go to such extremes. Jealousy. Anger. Vindictiveness. Personal vendetta. Revenge."

She was shaking her head even before he finished ticking off the list. "None of those fit—for either of us."

"That might be true today, but what about in your past? I doubt Nancy Kerrigan is the only world-class figure skater who made enemies."

Her fork froze in midair, but she remained silent.

"I did some googling this morning on you and your sister. I didn't find much on her, but I discovered a bunch of stuff on Christine Reed. Any reason you didn't tell me about your skating career?"

She appeared to be puzzled by the question as she lowered the fork back to her tray. "I didn't see how it could possibly be relevant to this situation. That was years ago. A different life I left behind when I was eighteen."

"Some people carry grudges for a very long time."

"But there were no Tonya Hardings in my competitive circle, and I wasn't an imminent threat to any of the top skaters when I left the circuit."

"Because of an accident."

"Yes."

"Tell me about that."

She picked at the crust on her whole grain roll. "If you googled me, I'm sure you already know the highlights—or lowlights. It happened during a training session eighteen days before the Olympics. I'd had a bad case of the flu and shouldn't have been pushing so hard, but with the Games that close, every minute of practice counted. Long story short, I got dizzy, fell while trying to land a triple jump, fractured the tibia in my right leg, and ended up in surgery. End of story—at least as far as the Olympics were concerned."

"From what I read, it didn't have to be. It sounded like everyone encouraged you to keep competing."

Christy picked up her fork and rearranged her salad. "Leaving the circuit was the right decision."

"Why? You'd invested years of training and appeared to be on a roll."

She forked some lettuce. "Depends how you define *roll*. I did well in some important competitions, but I was never the top finisher. Could I have been if I'd stuck with it? Maybe. Might I have made the team again four years later? Maybe. But the training was grueling, and I would have been twenty-two before I got my next shot at an Olympic medal. Since I retired from competition, only three women over twenty-two have medaled at the Olympics."

The odds were against her and the work was hard, so she'd given up?

Not ringing true.

He might not yet know a lot about the woman sharing lunch with him on this snowy day, but his instincts told him she wasn't a quitter. Athletes good enough to make the Olympic team didn't shy away from hard work or let long odds deter them.

There was more to this story.

"What aren't you telling me?"

She finished chewing. "I did have other reasons for my choice, but they were personal."

"Why don't I toss out a theory?"

She watched him in silence as she stabbed another forkful of salad.

"Since your parents left their estate—such as it was—to your sister, and you seem okay with that, I'm assuming the costs associated with your skating were significant. You felt you'd already gotten your share of their material assets."

"More than my share." She set her fork down and lifted her soda in salute. "You have excellent deductive skills. Not that I'd expect anything less from an FBI agent."

"I'm also assuming the costs were a burden for your parents, and that the financial strain played a role in your decision."

She set the cup down, fitting it into the circle of condensation. "That was part of the reason."

"You want to tell me the rest?"

The lights in the café flickered. Steadied.

She picked up her fork. "We better hurry and finish before they shut this place down and throw us out." But she didn't dive back into her salad.

"Is that a no?"

She exhaled. "Are my reasons for quitting pertinent to my sister's disappearance?"

Not likely—but he wanted to know anyway.

"You never can tell. Anything that might help us get a handle on what's going on is worth exploring."

She gave up all pretense of eating and folded her hands. "Okay. Here's the short version. Mom and Dad got a little financial help as my standings rose, but most of the day-to-day expenses fell to them. My dad worked full time, plus he and Mom both took on part-time jobs. They put a second mortgage on the house and took out loans. Coaching, costumes, choreography—the costs kept rising exponentially as I moved up in the rankings."

"Are we talking serious debt?"

"Yes. And it got worse when I was fifteen. There isn't a world-class training facility in St. Louis, so I had to move to Colorado Springs with my mom. That was both expensive and disruptive to the family. Ginny needed Mom as much as I did at that stage in her life, and the separation was hard for both of them." She picked up her fork and detached the yolk from a piece of egg in her salad. "It started to eat at me that my skating dominated everyone's life."

So guilt had played a major role in her decision. He could relate.

Guilt was a powerful motivator.

Beyond that, though, was it also possible she'd simply reached a mental snapping point? Years of fierce competitive pressure, coupled with high financial stakes—after all, victors claimed lucrative endorsements while losers went away empty-handed—could make a person cave, couldn't they?

No.

Not this woman.

Christy was strong. She had to be to survive the loss of her entire family in less than nine months. To find the courage to ignore the kidnapper's threat and contact the FBI.

There was more behind her decision to stop competing.

He wiped some mayo off his fingers as he composed his question, but she spoke before he could voice it.

"You're thinking there was another reason I left competitive skating."

He looked over at her. His training had taught him to read faces, but he was coming up blank with hers—though she'd clearly read his.

"Yes."

"You're right. But you won't find it on Google. It's in here." She touched the region of her heart. "While I was recovering from surgery, my dad had a heart attack. Worse than mild but not debilitating. Still, he had a long recovery ahead, including rehab. He needed my mom, and as soon as I was physically able to be on my own, she went home."

Christy took a sip of her soda, watching the snowflakes cling to the plate glass window for one brief moment of intricate beauty before dissolving. "For the first time in years, I wasn't getting up at four thirty to go to my first training session of the day. I wasn't running nonstop between the rink and school. I wasn't falling into bed at eight o'clock so exhausted I needed two alarm clocks to rouse me the next morning. I had a chance to think. Evaluate. Pray. In the end, I decided everyone had sacrificed enough. Sure, there was a chance I could win a medal at the next Olympics, but there were no guarantees. I could work for four more years, make the team, skate an Olympic program—but one bad fall, it was all over."

"How did your parents react?"

"They were stunned. Everyone was."

"Did you tell them why you'd made the decision?"

"Some of it. Mostly I told them I had an offer from an ice show that was too good to ignore and that a slower pace appealed to me—both of which were true."

But not the whole story.

Bottom line, she'd given up her dream to make life easier for the people she loved.

"I'm impressed." To put it mildly.

"Don't be." She pinned him with a fierce look. "And don't you dare feel sorry for me. I had very rational reasons for my choice. Dad's heart attack was a wake-up call. I realized I was ready to be a daughter and sister instead of an Olympic-medal seeker. I was ready to give instead of take. To repay some of the debt. To reduce their stress. To go for a gold medal in life instead of on the ice. And for the record, I never had a single regret. Not one."

Her resolute tone conveyed her absolute conviction.

Must be nice to make a tough choice that left no regrets in its wake.

Fighting back a wave of melancholy, he lifted his soda and took a long swallow.

"Back to the money issue and Ginny's inheritance. Are you certain she didn't have some significant savings? Maybe your parents left her more than you realized."

"No. I went over the numbers with her financial advisor. My ice show earnings allowed me to pay off my parents' debt and gave me the funds for college, but medical expenses after my parents' accident ate up their limited savings. My dad . . ." She stopped. Cleared her throat. "He lingered in a coma for two months, and their insurance wasn't great. Ginny only bought her property two years ago, and there's a big mortgage on it. So no, there's no significant money to pay a ransom demand."

Cash wasn't the motive. Someone who'd planned such a meticulous crime would also have researched the potential payoff.

"Is there anyone at all from your skating days who disliked you? Who didn't seem stable? Who made you nervous or uncomfortable?"

"No."

"Anyone you keep in touch with?"

"I exchange Christmas cards with my last coach, who's retired. But my only direct contact with the world of skating these days is some coaching I do on the side. Most of my students are recreational figure skaters, but I have a couple who are showing promise and are in the early competitive stage."

If there was a connection between Ginny's kidnapping and Christy's skating, he wasn't seeing it. Besides, if someone in the skating world *did* have a grudge, why wait more than a decade to exact revenge?

"Based on everything you've told me, I think

we should concentrate on more current relation-ships. But that discussion can wait until we get the autopsy report. We won't dig in until we have that in hand. In the meantime, I'd like to put taps on your home and cell phones in case the next contact comes that way."

"No problem."

"I'll get them ordered. Also, assuming there's no DNA match, I want to be ready to move quickly. It would be helpful over the next few days if you could compile a list of people your sister knew—friends, neighbors, boss, co-workers—with a notation of the connection."

"I can do that . . . but how are you going to position the questioning?"

She was still worried about tipping their hand to the kidnapper—and he couldn't blame her.

"First, before we show up at anyone's door, we do our homework. If there's suspicious activity in someone's background, we'll know about it. In terms of positioning, we'll come up with an excuse that makes it appear the investigation was initiated by us rather than you."

She frowned. "How will you do that?"

"My boss and I already talked about this. We could say the family requested a DNA sample prior to burial, since there was no autopsy. With all the work being done now with genetic markers for inherited health risks, a request like that wouldn't be out in left field or raise red flags.

Testing in a private lab can take a couple of months, which works with our timing. Our story would be that when the sample being tested wasn't from the assumed victim, the lab notified us. We're making some inquiries on a nonpriority basis, very low-key."

"But even if it appears I followed instructions, the person who sent the note could panic—which would put Ginny at risk."

That was true. To some degree, every kidnapping investigation was a gamble.

"It's possible the kidnapper will give us a clue the next time he contacts you and we won't have to do a lot of questioning."

She pushed aside her half-eaten lunch. "Why do I think that won't happen? This person is careful and thorough."

"He's also human. That means he could make a mistake."

"You think it's a man?"

"In all likelihood. This doesn't have the MO of a typical crime committed by women." He wadded up his napkin. "You ready to head out?"

"Yes." She downed the last of her soda and slid from the booth.

Once they'd put their coats on and discarded their trash, Lance followed her to the exit, reaching around her to open the door. "Ready to take the plunge?"

"No. But why delay the inevitable?"

In other words, accept the hard realities and get on with it.

Not a bad philosophy for snowstorms—or life.

He pushed the door open, and she dived into the blizzard.

"Looks like everyone is hunkering down at home." He took her arm as the wind buffeted them, juggling the gift bag as he surveyed the half dozen cars on the lot.

"I can see why." The wind snatched her words, sabotaging any attempt at conversation.

They covered the remaining distance in silence. She unlocked her car as they approached, and the instant he pulled her door open, she slid inside.

No good-bye hug today.

He stifled his disappointment and leaned down. "Where's your windshield scraper?"

She reached behind the front seat, grabbed it, and started to climb back out of the car.

"Stay put. I'll take care of it."

Without giving her a chance to protest, he went to work on the windows. No sleet, just a thick layer of snow, making the job quick and easy.

When he returned to the driver's side, he passed the scraper back. "Will you be okay driving home?"

"Yes. I don't have far to go." But a touch of uncertainty crept into her voice as she surveyed the few cars creeping along the obliterated street,

70

their headlights barely piercing the swirling cascade of snow.

"Why don't I follow you?"

Her eyebrows lifted. "You must have better things to do on a Saturday afternoon."

"Not this one." He turned up the collar of his coat. Even the thick sheepskin lining didn't provide sufficient warmth in this wind. "I'm headed home too, where I plan to hibernate until the plows make a dent in this. I don't mind a short detour."

She hesitated . . . but in the end shook her head. "No, I'll be fine. Thank you for the offer, though—and for cleaning off the windows."

Should he push?

No.

Christy was an independent woman who might not take kindly to any suggestion that she was less than able to take care of herself. And he didn't want to fall from her good graces—for reasons that had nothing to do with professional decorum.

"No problem. Be careful, and call me if you have any problem. Deal?"

"Deal."

He waited until she began inching toward the exit, then slogged through the snow toward his car. By the time he'd cranked up his heater and was cleaning off his own windows, her taillights had been swallowed up in the gray shroud.

Too bad she hadn't let him follow her home.

That considerate deed might have earned him an invitation for a cup of coffee . . . a far more appealing prospect than going home to his empty apartment.

Perhaps this was for the best, though. If she *had* issued such an invitation, he'd have been tempted to cross the line he'd always drawn between his professional and personal life.

Strange.

Staying on the appropriate side of that line had never been a problem before Christy Reed.

He tossed the scraper onto the floor of the backseat, slid behind the wheel, and turned the defroster on full blast. He'd need a clear line of sight to navigate in this treacherous weather.

He also needed to maintain a clear line of sight with this case. Be careful not to let an alluring figure skater fog his professional vision.

So for now he'd go home to his bare apartment. Rev up the laptop for more research.

And try to think up some legit excuse to call Christy tomorrow.

This stupid snow was messing up his plans.

Nathan slammed the heel of his hand against the window frame. Yanked the shade down. Muttered an oath.

If this kept up, he'd be stuck here. The second letter wouldn't go out until next weekend.

And he didn't want to wait.

He'd been waiting long enough.

At a sudden scuffling noise behind him, he turned and scowled at the woman gripping the walker in the doorway. "What are you doing up this late?"

Instead of speaking, she rubbed her stomach and pointed to a box of crackers on the counter.

"You had enough at dinner. Go back to bed."

Her lower lip quivered, and Nathan swallowed past his disgust. If she thought that teary ploy was going to get her any sympathy, she could think again. How could he feel sorry for someone who'd created her own mess?

Besides, she was pathetic. Her body was scrawny. Her hair was a tangled mess. Her raspy voice grated on his nerves. Plus, with all her health issues, she was high maintenance.

But she did serve a purpose.

If he didn't have much control over the rest of his life, at least he had control over her.

And he knew just how to make her suffer.

"You don't need anything else to eat. Go back to bed."

When she didn't retreat, he took a step toward her.

Fear flared in her eyes, and she shrank away. Repositioned the walker. Shuffled back the way she'd come, all the while casting anxious glances over her shoulder. Wondering if he was going to hurt her.

He watched her until she disappeared, savoring the heady rush of power. Fear was a glorious thing—as long as you were on the giving rather than the receiving end.

But she didn't have to worry tonight.

Tonight, his plans to make someone *else* suffer were top of mind.

Nathan waited until he heard her door close, then grabbed a beer from the refrigerator. As he took a swig, a faint rumble sounded from outside.

He crossed back to the window and lifted the shade. In the distance, strobing lights pierced the gloom and the scraping noise grew louder.

The snowplows were on the job.

Yes!

He took another swallow of beer. Maybe he wouldn't have to delay tomorrow's trip after all.

After gulping down the rest of the brew, he lowered the shade and tossed the bottle in the trash. Soft sniffling came from behind the door opposite his bedroom as he moved down the hall, and he paused a moment to relish it.

He had her exactly where he wanted her.

Lips curving up, he continued to his bedroom. Removed the chain from around his neck, fingering the key. Inserted it into the lock.

Once inside, he reset the lock and crossed to the desk. The letter lay on top, ready to be mailed. He picked up the keychain beside it, palming the attached pewter Arch. Her welcome-to-St.-

Louis gift. The one he'd carried everywhere for a whole year.

Until she, too, had abandoned him.

He flung it back on the desk and lifted the faded photo. A half dozen nameless faces of long-forgotten people mugged for the camera—but he'd never forgotten the name of the one person in the picture who'd mattered to him.

Moving to the bed, he studied the image. Her hair was different now, and she seemed more sophisticated, but he'd had no difficulty recognizing her that day in the parking lot last year as she'd walked past him. None at all.

He shifted his gaze to the face tucked in one corner of the shot, slightly separated from the rest of the group, then examined his reflection in the mirror over the dresser. No wonder she hadn't recognized him. He wouldn't recognize himself based on that photo. He looked like a different person.

He *was* a different person.

But even if a resemblance had remained, she wouldn't have known him. She might have been his angel . . . his lifeline . . . but he'd meant nothing to her—even though she'd let him think he did.

His stomach clenched into a hard, painful knot. Who knew how different his life might have turned out if she hadn't abandoned him? If she hadn't ignored his pleas for help? Instead of being stuck in the same dead-end job as his old man, he might have been somebody.

Flexing his fingers, he took a deep breath. Let it out. Getting angry only led to trouble. Out-of-control emotions were bad. In fact, real emotions were bad, period. But fake emotions . . . they came in handy. As did traits like charm. That one had proven to be very useful on the job—and off.

Calmer now, he rose and walked over to the TV. Shuffled through his collection of classic DVDs. *Psycho* sounded good. Or *Silence of the Lambs*.

Psycho. It was hard to beat Hitchcock.

He put the disk in, grabbed the remote, and got comfortable on his bed.

And as the snowplow once again rumbled past on the other side of the street, he smiled.

Tomorrow was going to work out just the way he'd planned.

4

"I see you made it in despite that second dump of snow yesterday. Any problems?"

Christy looked up from the copy machine as Bob Harris approached. "No. The road crews around here did a great job, as usual."

"I'll pass that along." The city administrator stopped a few feet away. "The storm played havoc with the Monday morning rush hour yesterday, though—not to mention everyone's weekend plans. Did you manage to do anything fun?"

She pulled out a stack of copies and tapped them into alignment, praying he kept the conversation light and friendly. She wasn't up to dodging a date today. "I had some lessons on Saturday, but I didn't set foot out the door Sunday, even to go to church. What about you?"

"My weekend was pretty quiet." He shoved his hands in his pockets.

Uh-oh. She knew that posture. He was getting ready to move into personal territory.

Summoning up a bright smile, she grabbed her originals and eased back a step. "It was quiet around here today too. A lot of residents must not have wanted to risk a trip to the rec center in case Mother Nature got grouchy again."

"I guess not." He edged closer. "Listen, I was wondering if you might want to get together for a drink after work tonight. Celebrate the fact we're not still snowed in." He gave her a hopeful grin.

She stifled a sigh.

So much for the subtle evasion tactics she'd been employing for the past three weeks.

But blowing him off wasn't an option, either. Bob was a nice guy. Attractive, fit, early forties. Also newly divorced and lonely. He had to be missing his kids, missing the house he'd called home for fifteen years, missing female companionship—even if his marriage had been on the rocks for a while. No surprise he'd be trolling for dates.

Too bad he'd parked his boat in her pond.

"I'm not a drinker, Bob." She maintained a pleasant, conversational tone. "And like I've told you, I don't think it's smart to date people at work."

"I don't think a drink qualifies as a date."

"Close enough."

He studied her. "You're serious about not mixing work and dating, aren't you?"

Maybe he was finally getting the message.

"Yes."

"I wish I could convince you it won't be a problem. We're both adults. We can keep business and pleasure separate." His brow wrinkled. "Unless you're seeing someone new? I made some discreet inquiries before I approached you, so I know you weren't involved with anyone a few weeks ago."

Yes! The perfect out.

"As a matter of fact, I have met someone." Her relationship with Lance McGregor *was* new. Plus, they were pretending to be friends.

Also close enough.

Bob's face fell. "I was afraid of that. Well, you can't blame a guy for trying. Be careful on the roads tonight." With a lift of his hand, he wandered back down the hall.

Sighing in relief, Christy swung around, stepped forward—and almost ran into Sarah Marshall.

"Whoa!" The rec center community liaison grabbed her arm to steady her, then leaned sideways to watch Bob disappear. "Let me guess. He was hitting on you again."

"Good guess."

"How'd you ditch him this time?"

"He asked if I was seeing someone, and I said yes."

The other woman's eyes lit up. "Are you?"

"Uh-huh." She checked over her shoulder and lowered her voice. "But it's not a dating thing."

Sarah gave her a puzzled look. "Then what kind of thing is it?"

She chewed on her lower lip. If there was anyone she'd trust with her story, it was Sarah. How many evenings over the years had her friend dragged her home to dinner in the raucous house she shared with nine-year-old twin boys and a teddy bear of a husband? How many times had she provided a shoulder to cry on during the past few difficult months? How many times had she gone out of her way on one of the tougher days to share a funny story or a homemade treat?

Too many to count.

Yet Christy held back, the kidnapper's warning echoing in her mind.

Strange how she'd take a chance on her sister's life with a stranger like Lance McGregor but wasn't willing to do the same with the woman who'd been her friend since her first day on the job three years ago.

Go figure.

As the silence between them lengthened, Sarah scrutinized her. "Hey, is everything okay? You seem majorly stressed. And what's with those dark circles under your eyes? I thought you'd gotten past the sleepless nights."

So had she . . . until a certain letter arrived a week ago.

"Let's just say I've run into a major glitch in my personal life."

Sympathy softened her friend's eyes. "You've already had more than your share of those in the past few months." Sarah cocked her head. "So should I assume that meeting this man you mentioned to Bob wasn't a good experience?"

"Meeting him was good. The reason for it—not."

Sarah latched on to the first part of her response. "Does that mean once the reason is resolved, there might be some potential for romance?"

"You're not going to rest until I'm married,are you?" The hint of a smile whispered at Christy's lips.

"Nope. You've been to our house—look what you're missing." Sarah stopped and held up a hand in mock horror. "Wait. Erase that image of chaos central from your mind. Marriage is so much more than that."

"If I was anxious to get married, I could always take Bob up on his offer. I have a feeling dating him might lead to the altar."

"You can do better."

An image of Lance popped up in her mind. "Yeah, I think I can—at some point." Once Ginny was safe.

"In the meantime, if there's anything I can do to help with whatever is going on, all you have to do is say the word." Sarah touched her arm. "You know that, right?"

"Yes." The word came out choked, and she blinked to clear her vision. "Thank you."

"You're welcome. Now why don't you cut out for the day? It's almost five. And pick up dinner at a drive-through. I know fast food isn't your style, but indulge for once. Grab a high-carb meal, take a hot bath, and go to bed early."

"I like the sound of that plan."

"Then stick with it. You could use some . . ." Sarah pulled her cell off her belt, rolling her eyes as she put the phone to her ear and listened to the caller. "Got it. I'll be there in three minutes." She sighed and punched the end button. "The senior club is arriving early because of the snow. Like an hour early. Can't miss casserole night, ya know. Gotta run. Be careful going home." She called the last over her shoulder as she took off at a jog down the hall.

Hefting the stack of paper in her arm, Christy wandered back to her cube. Sarah could be right. A quiet, relaxing evening might be just what she needed—topped off with a mug of hot chocolate. If she was lucky, that calming regimen would help her get to sleep before two in the morning.

She dumped the copies on her desk for sorting tomorrow, grabbed her coat, and headed for the exit, nodding to some of the casserole-toting seniors as she passed them in the lobby.

The lot had been cleaned and well salted, thanks to the hard work of Bob's road crew, and the streets were in excellent condition. Much better than rush hour last night.

Fifteen minutes later, after a quick pass through the Golden Arches, she was pulling into her attached garage. After dumping her work tote and bagged dinner on the kitchen counter, she went to retrieve her mail, glancing around as she walked down the short front path to the mailbox. It appeared the condo association had risen to the challenge of the storm too. Every town-house walkway had been thoroughly salted.

She grabbed her mail, riffling through it as she hurried back to her door, head bent against the bitter wind.

But she stopped cold when she came upon a letter addressed in a familiar hand.

The kidnapper was back in touch.

● ● ●

Yawning, Lance stood, stretched, and pulled his suit jacket off the hanger on the hook in his office.

"Calling it a day?" Steve Preston paused as he passed the cubicle.

Lance resisted the urge to check his watch as the reactive squad supervisor pinned him with a keen look. The lean, late-fortyish man might have more than a few flecks of silver in his dark hair, but he hadn't slowed down one iota from his street- agent days, according to office scuttlebutt.

Nor did he cut the agents in his squad any slack.

"I can hang around if you need me." It had to be at least five thirty, and with all the extra hours he'd put in last week on the bank robbery, not to mention his evening and weekend meetings with Christy, he'd assumed it was okay to leave at a normal hour once in a while.

Maybe not—though Mark's informal briefing on office protocols hadn't included that as a faux pas.

"Relax. It wasn't a trick question. You've had plenty on your plate for the past few days. Sitting around fiddling your thumbs after hours won't earn you any brownie points with me. I'd rather you take advantage of normal days and leave on time so when I really need you, you're up for it."

"Good to know."

"What's the latest on the possible kidnapping case?"

"The body was exhumed yesterday. We were on the ME's docket for today, but another high-priority autopsy ran a lot longer than he expected. I talked to him a few minutes ago, though, and he did take a quick look at the remains. They're in bad shape, but he's confident the teeth are in decent enough condition for him or an odontologist to establish an ID from dental records."

"That's a plus. Waiting for a DNA ID would slow things down. Keep me in the loop."

"I will."

He started to walk away. Turned back. "Did Mark talk to you about the SWAT team?"

Why did that have to keep coming up?

"Yes." He strove for a conversational tone, maintaining his nonchalant expression. "I told him I want to get acclimated before I think about taking on anything else."

"No problem. Just wanted to make sure you know you'd be welcome if that kind of duty appeals to you. Now go home before the phone rings."

Great advice—but too late. As Steve disappeared around the edge of the cubicle, Lance's cell began to vibrate.

If fate was kind, it would be Mac calling to give him a hard time about something.

He scanned caller ID. Smiled.

Even better.

He put the phone to his ear. "Hi, Christy. I was going to call you later with an update." From home. Here, anyone in the open-office environment could tune in to their conversation . . . no matter if said conversation was business related.

"I got another letter."

His good humor evaporated as he snatched his overcoat off the other hook in his office. "In the mail?"

"Y-yes. I just found it." Her voice was shaking.

He picked up his pace, stopping only long enough on his way out to grab some evidence bags and gloves. "Are you home now?"

"Yes."

"I'm on my way."

"Are you wearing a suit?"

"Yes. But my leather jacket is in the car." He hoped. Near as he could recall, he'd tossed it on the backseat yesterday in case his duty vehicle got stuck in the snow and he had to dig it out. "You didn't open the envelope, did you?"

"No."

"Good. Sit tight, and expect me in less than half an hour."

He strode toward the back door, swiped his badge, and jogged to his black Chevy Cruze, shoes crunching on the salt. A quick glance confirmed that the jacket was in the backseat, and he made the switch in the parking lot before sliding behind the wheel.

The Chevy might not have as much power as he'd like, and the snarl of rush-hour traffic hadn't yet abated, but with a heavy foot on the pedal and some creative twists of the wheel he made it to Christy's condo in twenty-two minutes.

She opened the door as he reached for the bell. "I was watching for you. Come in."

A gust of wind at his back seconded the invitation, and he moved into the small foyer, wiping his feet on the mat by the door.

"Sorry to drag you out on such a miserable night." She shut the door and rubbed her upper arms.

"Not a problem. I've dealt with far colder weather than this. Where's the letter?"

She led him to a small but spotless kitchen and motioned toward the counter, where the envelope rested near a bag emblazoned with the Golden Arches. Based on the aroma emanating from the sack, her takeout dinner hadn't yet been con-sumed.

He shrugged out of his jacket and pulled on a pair of latex gloves, leaning close to read the postmark.

Springfield, Illinois.

Their guy was moving around.

"May I?" He crossed toward a knife block on the counter. At her nod, he chose a small paring knife, carefully slit the top of the envelope, and bowed it open. A single, folded sheet of paper was inside.

Positioning one of the evidence envelopes

underneath to catch anything that might fall out, he withdrew the paper and opened it.

The message was again typed and brief.

In case you're wondring if I really have her, here's proof. Poor thing—she looks scared, doesnt she? If you want to see her agin, don't call the cops. Wait for further orders.

Below the note was a laser-printed photo of a thirtyish woman, her blonde hair pulled back into a messy ponytail. One eye was black, and there was a fresh cut on her chin. She was sitting on what appeared to be a dirt floor, hands bound in front of her with crude rope, back against a concrete wall. The image wasn't the best quality, but it was clear enough to make a definite ID.

Christy leaned in to see. Gasped. Groped for the edge of the counter.

Setting the document on the evidence envelope, he turned his attention to the pale woman beside him. "Why don't you sit for a minute?" Without waiting for a response, he pulled out one of the stools at the counter and urged her down.

She collapsed onto the seat as if the stiffening in her legs had dissolved, never taking her gaze off the letter on the counter. Shock rolled off her in waves.

Strong as she was, this had thrown her. Big time. Without weighing the pros and cons, Lance reached for her hand. That tactic wasn't in any agent protocol rule book, but he wouldn't have been nearly as successful as a Delta Force operator if he'd always played by the rules.

"Christy." He waited a moment, then tried again in a firmer tone, giving her fingers a gentle squeeze. "Christy."

With obvious effort, she dragged her attention away from the photo.

"I take it that's your sister."

"Yes. I . . . I suppose I should have expected something like this, but . . ." She turned back to the note, her fingers tightening on his. "Seeing the photo makes it much more real. And she's . . ." Her voice choked. "She looks hurt and scared."

Lance slid onto the stool beside her without relinquishing her hand. He didn't relish making his next request, but she knew her sister better than anyone. If there was a personal clue of some kind in this shot, she would be the one to spot it.

"I want you to take a very close look at this." With his free hand, he slid the envelope with the sheet of paper on top toward her. "Tell me if anything in this picture seems out of character or suggests your sister was trying to send a message of some kind."

A pulse was hammering in the hollow of her throat, and her respiration was shallow, but she leaned close and did as he asked, scrutinizing the image for a full minute.

In the end, she shook her head. "I don't see anything unusual. If there's a message, I'm missing it—but I doubt there is. She looks too terrified to be thinking rationally."

He couldn't argue with that.

With one more squeeze, he released her hand and slid the note into one evidence sleeve, the envelope into another. Then he removed his gloves and tossed them in her trash can. "The quality of the image isn't great, but the lab can blow it up and do some analysis. They might find a relevant detail or two that will give us some useful information or clues about location. Do you have any recent photos of your sister?"

"I have a couple from when I took her out to dinner for her birthday in early September."

"Why don't you email them to me? The lab might find them helpful for comparison purposes. The address is on my card."

"I'll do that before I go to bed." She twisted her fingers together on the counter. "Did you hear anything from the medical examiner?"

"Yes. I was planning to call you this evening." He gave her the same information he'd passed on to his boss. "But based on this photo, I think we can safely assume the body doesn't belong to your sister. The ME should be able to verify that tomorrow."

Her gaze strayed back to the evidence envelopes. "So ever since the fire, some crazy person has been holding Ginny captive. And hurting her." She closed her eyes, a spasm of pain rippling over her features.

Not necessarily.

But Christy needed comforting, not unsettling speculation.

"We're going to do our best to find her as fast as we can."

"I know—and I appreciate that." She motioned toward the envelopes holding the latest missive from the kidnapper. "I'm sure you noticed the different postmark. Do you think this guy's hauling Ginny around with him?"

"It's possible. But he also might have stashed her somewhere and is traveling to different locations alone to do the mailing, hoping to keep us off-balance. Did you have a chance to put together a list of Ginny's acquaintances?"

"Yes. I was going to email it to you tonight. I'll send it along with the photos—but there's no one suspicious on the list."

"We'll check them out, anyway. If nothing else, one of them might offer us a lead."

"When will you start talking to them?"

"As soon as we run some background. I'd like you to put together a similar list for yourself."

"You still think this could be about me rather than Ginny?"

"I'm not ruling anything out. This case isn't following any typical pattern. Our guy disguises the kidnapping and lets you think Ginny's dead. He gives you a chance to mourn. Two months later—about the time a lot of people begin to come to grips with their grief and loss—he contacts you to say she's alive. Your world is thrown into turmoil again. He gives you instructions but makes no demands. Now he's stringing you along. This sounds like a very deliberate strategy to make life as difficult as possible for you."

She stared at him in horror. "I can't believe Ginny or I could have an enemy that vindictive and malicious and have no clue about his identity."

Lance stood and picked up his jacket. He didn't want to freak Christy out, but she needed to face facts. "I think you better start believing it, especially if you're right and everyone on the lists you give me comes out clean. The fire and kidnapping wasn't a random act of violence. Since money isn't a motive, we have to assume this is personal. That means we're looking for someone whose life intersected with yours or your sister's in a very negative way at some point."

"So how do we find him?"

"We dig deeper." He slid his arms into the sleeves of the jacket and picked up the evidence envelopes. "Before you send me those lists tonight, think hard about anyone you or Ginny crossed paths with who might have even the slightest reason to harbor a grudge. Stretch it if you have to. This person isn't thinking normally, so a trivial incident to you could be a trigger for a troubled mind."

Her knuckles whitened as she looked up at him, her eyes too big for her face, her skin devoid of color. "Okay. But I still don't think I'll come up with much."

"Anything is better than what we have now." He lifted the envelopes. "I'll send these in for processing tomorrow morning and call you after I get the results of the autopsy. Now I'll let you eat your dinner." He motioned toward the fast-food bag.

She wrinkled her nose. "I can't deal with that kind of food tonight. The best I'll be able to manage is soup. Have you eaten yet?"

"No."

"Take this." She grabbed the bag and held it out.

"I can't take your dinner."

"It will end up in the trash if you don't—and I hate to waste food. Please. It should be edible if you nuke it."

He hesitated. "You'll eat some soup if I agree?"

"I'll try."

Not the definitive assurance he wanted; Christy was on the thin side already. But his stomach *was* rumbling. Plus, accepting her offer would save him a trip through a drive-through.

Someday soon, he was going to have to stock his kitchen and prepare a real meal.

He took the bag. "Thanks."

"It's the least I can do after all your off-hours work on this case." She followed him to the door.

He pulled it open but paused on the threshold. "I want you to be careful until this is resolved."

The little color left in her complexion seeped out. "You think this guy might come after me?"

"Anyone who'd do what he's already done isn't predictable. I wouldn't put anything past him."

A shiver passed through her. "I'll watch my back."

He was tempted to offer to do that for her . . . but the FBI investigated, it didn't provide security for ordinary citizens. Even vulnerable ones.

And Christy *was* vulnerable. The woman standing inches away might be strong and resilient and able to take care of herself under normal circumstances, but this situation was far from normal. As was the person who had the sisters in his sights.

A chill snaked down his spine, and he crimped his fingers around the top of the bag. "If you get suspicious of anything, don't hesitate to call me—day or night."

"I will." She shivered again as a gust of frigid air invaded the house.

Get out of here, McGregor. The woman's

freezing in this open doorway, and your business is done.

But she seemed so forlorn . . . so alone . . . so worried.

So in need of a hug.

Not a smart idea, buddy.

Ignoring that warning, he reached out and pulled her close.

"Just keeping up the pretense." He spoke the words into her soft hair, breathing in her sweet scent.

For a moment, her body stiffened—but an instant later she relaxed into the embrace.

In the end, he was the one who pulled away. Reluctantly.

She wrapped her arms around herself and gave him a tentative smile. "Thanks for that. I needed a hug tonight . . . even if it was just for show."

It was more than that.

But he kept that to himself. He'd pushed it too much already. "Get inside where it's warm. And set the lock."

"Okay. Good night." With that, she stepped back and closed the door.

He continued down her walk to the street, juggling the envelopes and the food bag. The burger wasn't going to last past the next block, no matter how unappetizing it might be cold. He was starving.

Yet as he slid behind the wheel, put the car in

gear, and took one last look at the welcome light spilling from Christy's condo, food wasn't the only sustenance he craved.

Her dinner might fill his empty stomach, but it wasn't going to satisfy the unexpected hunger in his heart.

It was the same guy Christy had shared lunch with at Panera last Saturday, in the middle of the snowstorm.

Who was he?

Nathan lowered the binoculars and sank down behind the wheel of his car as the tall dude drove away from her condo. He was new in her life . . . but how new? Had they met before or after the first letter?

Hard to say. It wasn't as if he'd been following her all that much before then. Just on significant days. After the letter, though—that was supposed to change. Watching her had been high on his agenda.

Too bad that plan had fallen apart.

Nathan twisted the key in the ignition with more force than necessary. Of all times for Dennis to fall on the ice and break his ankle. Having to fill in for the guy several nights a week on the evening shift was a bummer. He might be able to track Christy's travel remotely, but knowing who she saw once she got there required eyes on the street.

And his eyes were now stuck at work on a lot of nights until long after she went to bed.

Checking his side view mirror, he pulled away from the curb. He could call in sick—but doing anything out of pattern would be a mistake. It might raise suspicions—and jinx the promotion that was within touching distance. All he could do was follow her when his schedule permitted.

As for this new guy in her life . . . the timing was fishy. Had she gone to the cops, despite his warning?

Doubtful.

The dude didn't look like a cop. He wore regular clothes, for one thing. For another, the two of them acted real cozy. That fancy gift bag he'd carried out of Panera on Saturday had been a present. And he'd held her arm as they crossed the snowy parking lot like he didn't want to let go.

Plus, the way they'd looked at each other a few minutes ago . . . Yeah, the two of them were involved. He'd seemed about ready to kiss her, and she hadn't been in any hurry to break off that hug.

The guy was a boyfriend, not a cop.

Nathan braked as a stoplight turned from yellow to red, tapping a staccato beat on the wheel. A boyfriend could be a problem. Even if she hadn't told him about the note, he might get in the way. He was hanging around her too much.

One more challenge to deal with.

But he'd manage. He'd pulled off his grand plan masterfully so far. This was the home stretch— and the finish line was in sight. Another couple of weeks, he'd have the payoff he'd been looking forward to ever since Christy crossed his path last year.

He turned the corner and drove toward his apartment, staying within the speed limit, using his turn signal, abiding by the law. He knew how to follow rules.

But he liked making them better.

People who made the rules ran the show. Did what they wanted. Took what they wanted. Lived how they wanted.

Killed who they wanted.

He squeezed the wheel, a muscle twitching in his cheek.

Power was everything. It gave you control. Kept you safe. Made you a big shot. A somebody.

He could have been a somebody. *Would* have been a somebody, if things had been different.

If everyone hadn't abandoned him.

They were all to blame for his menial life and menial job—especially the person who'd brought light into his world when he'd most needed it. At the moment he'd been tottering on the brink, Christy Reed had walked into his life, holding the key to his future.

It had seemed like a miracle.

He snorted. Some miracle. More like a curse.

Because in the end, she, too, had deserted him, leaving him to face his demons alone. To make the wrong choices and start down a path that had led to a point of no return.

She was paying the price now for her abandonment, though—better late than never.

The light changed to green and he eased forward again, staying a safe distance back as the car in front of him slid on a hidden patch of ice and fishtailed out of control. Only after the gray-haired guy reined in the vehicle did Nathan accelerate.

He shook his head. People who weren't capable of handling bad weather should stay off the roads.

Of course, some people were forced to deal with treacherous conditions.

Like Christy.

Thanks to him.

The corners of his mouth lifted. Toying with her had been so, so satisfying. Watching her suffer had been better than downing a few beers—and the high lingered a lot longer.

But those games were about to end. In less than two weeks, his master plan would be completed.

And then Christy wouldn't have to wonder about Ginny anymore.

Because he would take her by the hand and reunite her with the sister she'd loved and mourned.

5

"I have news on the kidnapping." Lance stopped in the doorway of Steve's office. "Is now a good time?"

Steve slid the file he'd been reading into a folder and motioned him in. "No time's good for a kidnapping. Solving a kidnapping—different story. What do you have?"

"The ME said the dental records were conclusive. No need to bring in an odontologist." He sat in one of the two chairs across from the man's desk. "It's not Ginny Reed. I just called her sister with the news." He'd have preferred to deliver it in person, but he'd promised to notify her as soon as their suspicions were confirmed.

Steve rocked back, fingers linked over abs that would be the envy of men half his age. The man must do some serious working out to be that fit on the cusp of fifty. "This one's on the bizarre side."

"It's not like anything I studied at the Academy, that's for sure."

"Or encountered in Delta Force, I'll wager."

"No. That was a whole different ball game—and a whole different enemy. However, a fanatic is a fanatic."

"You think that's what we're dealing with here?"

"I'm beginning to wonder. Based on everything I've learned from the victim's sister, it doesn't appear . . ."

Steve lifted a hand and glanced toward the door. "Mark!"

His colleague backed up and stuck his head in the office.

"You have a few minutes?" Steve waved him into the empty chair on the other side of his desk.

It wasn't a question.

"Yes." Mark detoured into the office and took the chair.

"Lance was briefing me on the case he's been working, which is now officially a kidnapping. He's going to need some extra hands on this. I'd like you to be available." Steve motioned toward him. "Give Mark a topline, then answer the question I asked before I interrupted you to pull him in."

He complied, ending as Steve had directed. "Based on interviews with the victim's sister, ransom isn't a likely motive. There's no significant money to be had. So I think we could be dealing with a fanatic who has some serious mental issues."

"Given the extreme lengths this person has gone to, a vendetta or revenge seem strong possibilities for motive—except for the sister's claim that neither of them have any enemies." Steve steepled his fingers.

"But people can have enemies without ever knowing about it." Mark exchanged a look with their boss that Lance couldn't interpret.

"That's why I called you in on this." Steve tipped his head toward Lance. "You want to tell him about your first big case here?"

Mark crossed an ankle over a knee. "In a nutshell, my wife was being targeted by a man she'd ticked off who thought he was doing God's will. He made more than one attempt to take her out. For the record, she wasn't my wife at the time."

The parallels on a personal level were closer than either of these two men knew.

"How did you track him down?"

"By taking a lot of disparate pieces of information and shuffling them around until they began to fit together. But it was a race to the finish. Literally. A few more minutes, Emily would have died."

Not the kind of close finish Lance wanted for this case.

"The problem is, at this stage we don't have many pieces to shuffle around. Quantico has the newest letter and photo, and we'll run the DNA through the missing person database once we have it, but an ID on the body might not end up being that helpful. I've got a list of friends and acquaintances for the victim and her sister, but Christy—I mean, the sister—claims everyone will come out of a background check smelling like a rose."

"She could be wrong. Let's get the checks done ASAP, see who's worth interviewing. Fill Mark in on the ruse we developed to explain the reason for our questioning this long after the fact." Steve leaned forward and pulled the file folder toward him.

His colleague rose.

The meeting must be over.

Lance stood too but paused before following Mark to the door. "The sister's obviously worried that if the kidnapper finds out we're looking into this, even if he doesn't think it was at her request, the victim could be in imminent danger."

Steve transferred his attention from the folder back to him. "That's a valid concern. Do you have an alternate investigation technique?"

"No. I'd just like to keep this as discreet and low-key as possible."

"That would be SOP in a case like this."

"Right." Lance felt as if the word *rookie* was stamped across his forehead—in green, not rosy, letters. "I just wanted to make certain we were all on the same page."

"Tell the sister we've discussed this and everyone involved is aware of her concerns." He opened the folder, but as Lance started to turn away, the squad supervisor added a final wry comment. "Now you have a legitimate excuse to call her again sooner rather than later, in case you were having trouble coming up with one on your own."

Great.

Steve was living up to the reputation he'd earned in his street-agent days as an astute observer of human nature. According to Mark, the man's acumen was almost legendary in the office.

He could see why.

Lance didn't respond to his supervisor's comment.

Instead, he made a fast exit.

Mark grinned as he emerged. "Don't say I didn't warn you. Steve is a force to be reckoned with."

"No kidding. My buddies in Delta Force were sharp, but they wouldn't get anything past that guy."

"Former HRT operators, either. You want to grab a conference room and divvy up the list of contacts?"

"Yeah. Give me five. I want to refill my coffee. You need a top off?"

"I'm still nursing the venti Americano with two extra shots of espresso I grabbed on my way in this morning."

"Late night?"

"Long night. We have a three-month-old who

hasn't yet figured out that dark is for sleeping and daylight is for crying. Last night was my turn to entertain Little Mary Sunshine—every hour, on the hour."

"Ouch."

Mark smiled. "I don't mind. She's a sweetheart. Now go get your stuff or I'll be pulling out my wallet to bore you with a bunch of pictures."

"I wouldn't mind seeing one or two." Lance eased away as he responded.

"Yeah, right." Mark chuckled. "See you in five."

Lance continued to his cube, pulled up Christy's email, and began printing out copies of her lists. Funny. He wouldn't have pegged Mark as the softhearted family-man type. The SWAT team leader might be an FBI agent now, but the distinctive macho, special-forces aura lingered. The HRT guys were as tough as they came.

You just never knew about people.

He gathered up his copies. Odd that he'd never given much thought to the whole family gig himself. After all, the McGregors were a close bunch. Mom and Dad were the best, and despite the grief they gave each other, he couldn't be closer to his two brothers. But settling down in suburbia with one woman? Not so much as a blip on his radar screen—and none of the women he'd dated had tempted him to put that notion there.

Of course, he'd never dated anyone like Christy Reed.

Copies in one hand, coffee in the other, he headed for the conference room.

It was way too soon to be entertaining any white-picket-fence notions about the appealing figure skater. He had a case to solve. That had to be his first priority.

But afterward . . .

He smiled.

With someone like Christy by his side, maybe suburbia wouldn't be so bad.

Mevlida Terzic shuffled down the hall, scooting the walker ahead of her inch by inch, taking care to avoid the frayed spots in the carpet that liked to snag the wheels. She couldn't trip again. Neven didn't like it when she got sick or hurt—and keeping him happy was important.

But a seventy-eight-year-old body that had been through as much as hers didn't always work right, no matter how hard she tried to stay healthy.

After skirting the last worn patch, she pushed into the kitchen, picking up her pace as her stomach growled. Lunch had been a long time ago—and the peanut butter and jelly sandwich hadn't kept her full for very long. Not like cevapi on a sliced lepinja. Oh, the wondrous beef sausages and flour-dusted bread of her homeland! Now there was a lunch.

She continued toward the refrigerator. Nothing like that would be waiting for her tonight. But perhaps Neven had left her a little treat, as he sometimes did when he was gone for the evening. A small act of kindness, yes—but surely a sign his heart was good, deep inside, in spite of all he'd been through. As for his eruptions of anger . . . who could blame him? He had reasons to be cross.

And she was one of them.

Pain that went deeper than bone and muscle ricocheted down her arm and through her body as she reached for the freezer door. But that was nothing new. Pain was a daily burden now—of body and spirit and heart.

With a shuddering sigh, she inspected the stack of frozen dinners, labeled by day. Today was Wednesday, wasn't it? Yes, it must be. That was the dinner on top, and Neven was very organized.

Balancing herself on the walker, she leaned forward and pulled it out. The words on the label were gibberish, but she recognized the photo. Salisbury steak. That was one of the tastier meals, even if no prayer had been said over the butchering. But halal was forgotten these days, like so much else. Still, it was more appetizing than the food in the homeless shelters that had been her lot until Neven rescued her. She had her own room here too, instead of a cot among many.

It was a better life than before.

Wasn't it?

Yes. Of course it was.

Dinner in hand, she crossed to the microwave and slid her food inside. As the turntable began to rotate, she shuffled to the other side of the small kitchen to retrieve a knife and fork.

An apple turnover, covered with plastic wrap, was on the counter above the utensil drawer, her name written on a piece of paper beside it.

Mist clouded her vision, and she reached out to touch the plate. It wasn't jabukovača; apparently no one in this country had ever heard of the beloved apple-stuffed phyllo dough of her youth. But Neven had tried, bless him.

See? He was a good boy, despite his faults. She should be grateful he'd taken her in—even if her life was much calmer when he was away from the apartment, like tonight.

The microwave pinged, and she removed a knife and fork from the drawer. Step by painful step, she retrieved her dinner, placed the apple dessert beside the microwave container, and lowered herself into the chair.

Picking up her fork, she stared down at the patty of meat, the slices of carrot, the pasty mound of mashed potatoes. It was sustenance, yes—but nothing like the dinners in the old days, when laughter rang at her table and food was plentiful and family and friends knew no fear.

A sob caught in her throat, and she groped for a paper napkin from the holder in the center of the table.

Ah, Mihad, how I miss you and those happy days when the world stretched before us with such promise! My heart pines for your stories about the patients who came from far away to benefit from your gift of healing . . . for our evening strolls in the park where happy music always played . . . for the beautiful home you built and furnished for me because you said a lady deserved the best.

But most of all, I miss your gentle touch, and the tender way you called me "pile moje."

My wonderful Mihad—you were my dear one too.

A tear leaked out of her eye, and she wiped it away as the food cooled in front of her, the gnawing hunger that had awakened her from her nap subsiding to a dull ache.

But she had to eat. The food might be better since she'd moved in with Neven, but it wasn't plentiful. Skipping meals wasn't smart.

She picked up her fork as another tear slipped down her cheek. Thinking about the past wasn't going to change anything. That life was gone. As dead as Mihad. And Daris. And beautiful Sonja.

So much death.

The yearning for escape swept over her, like it always did when she thought of the old days— and of all she'd lost. She needed oblivion. A place where life's hard edges softened. Where pain faded.

There was no escape, though. Neven had seen

to that—and he was right. Running away was for cowards. She needed to be strong. To learn to survive without a crutch.

Except it was so very hard.

Oh, my Mihad, if only you were here!

A tear dropped onto her food. Another. She closed her eyes to stem the tide. Wiped her nose. Drew a quivering breath.

Eat, Mevlida. You must eat.

Gripping her fork, she opened her eyes . . . and gasped.

Neven stood in the doorway, one shoulder propped against the door frame, watching her with an expression of . . . pleasure?

Shock rippled through her.

No.

Surely she was wrong.

No one smiled at another's tears.

She blinked, and when she looked again, the small smile and the odd glitter in his eyes were gone.

She must have imagined his reaction.

Nevertheless, a cold cloak of foreboding dropped over her shoulders.

The silence lengthened, and she searched for words. "You no . . . work?"

He pushed off from the door and strolled closer. "No. I'm only filling in at night a few times a week while the other guy recovers. I told you that already."

Had he? It was possible. Her memory wasn't what it once was.

"I forget."

"You forget a lot."

Not enough, though.

Not nearly enough.

"I old."

"Yes, you are." He moved to the refrigerator and withdrew a beer, counting the cans as he always did.

She summoned up a smile. "You eat?"

"Yeah."

Tugging the apple turnover closer, she dipped her head toward the plate. "Tank you, Neven."

With a muttered oath, he slammed the beer on the counter.

Her hand jerked, and her fork clattered to the floor.

How could she have made such a stupid mistake?

He stalked across the room to loom over her. "That is not my name. I'm Nathan. Nathan! How many times do I have to tell you that?"

She cowered, pulling herself into a protective tuck. Not that he would hurt her physically. That didn't happen very often. But the flush on his face, the anger in his eyes, the feeling of barely leashed violence—they always sent a rush of fear through her.

Just like the fear from all those years ago.

"I sorry." She whispered the words.

"That's one of my rules, old woman." Fury nipped at his words. "How many others have you forgotten?"

His angry words muddled into an incomprehensible jumble in her mind. Even after all these years, the language was so hard to understand.

He leaned close. Into her face. "What's my name?"

"Natan."

"Say it again."

"Natan."

He glared at her, his face inches from hers. "You remember that. I worked very hard to become an American. To erase my past. To get rid of my accent. You may still be living in the old country and using the old language, but I want no reminders of that life. Do you understand?"

"Yes." Not all of it, but enough.

After a moment, he straightened up. "Finish your dinner."

She leaned down, fingers of one hand gripped around the edge of the table for balance, and fumbled on the floor for her fork.

When she retrieved it, his gaze flicked to her trembling hands, and that odd light came back into his eyes. "Eat."

Bending to her food, she scooped up a forkful of potatoes. Forced herself to swallow them. Tried not to gag.

He retrieved his beer and stood over her,

watching in silence as she choked down her meal.

At last he sat at the table, picked up the apple turnover, and took a big bite. "No treat for you today. Mistakes must be punished."

She said nothing as he finished it off, grateful he'd taken it. The food tasted like cardboard anyway. All she wanted to do was return to her room, fall into the nothingness of sleep . . . and pretend that tomorrow would be a better day.

Because that was the only way she could face another dawn.

6

Christy positioned the cursor over the download prompt, tightened her fingers around the can of soda, and clicked the mouse.

A few seconds later, the Quantico-enhanced image of Ginny that Lance had sent to her home email filled the screen.

She cringed.

This was much harder to look at than the small version at the bottom of the kidnapper's last note.

Closing her eyes, she coaxed her lungs to inflate. Deflate. Inflate. She'd promised Lance she'd study it as soon as she got home. And she would—in a minute. What choice did she have? Since none of the fingerprints on the latest missive had turned up anything in the database, and Quantico's analysis hadn't extracted any clues from the photo, she was their last hope. If she didn't spot a helpful detail, they were back to square one.

The can crinkled beneath her fingers, and she loosened her grip, forcing herself to look at the screen again.

Unfortunately, while the lab had managed to clean up the image slightly, the clarity had degraded in the enlargement. Everything might be bigger, but it was also more blurry. In terms of searching for clues, a smaller version of the enhanced photo might be more helpful.

But after all the effort the lab had expended, she'd start with this.

Beginning at the top, she worked her way down inch by inch—praying she'd find some detail, however small, that might help the investigation.

By the time she got to her sister's bound hands near the bottom, though, all she had to show for her efforts was a growing sense of despair.

Her gaze lingered on Ginny's hands. Christy might have been the figure skater in the family, but her sister had always had more graceful, expressive fingers. And she'd always played up that asset with bright nail polish—not that it stayed on long in the woods. Despite frequent touch-ups, Ginny had difficulty maintaining a manicure. Chips seemed to be . . .

Wait.

She leaned close and squinted at the blow-up.

Was that . . . ?

Yes.

There were remnants of polish on Ginny's fingernails.

Christy frowned.

How could that be? No manicure lasted two months.

Unless . . .

Had the kidnapper taken this shot soon after the kidnapping?

She rose, pulled her phone from the charger on the kitchen counter, and scrolled down to Lance's cell number. Maybe her discovery wasn't critical. Maybe it could wait until morning. But *she* couldn't—and he'd said to call him anytime.

He answered on the third ring, a hum of voices and laughter in the background. "Christy . . . what's up?"

Great. She was probably intruding on some social engagement. He might even be on a date.

Her spirits bottomed out.

"You sound occupied. I don't want to interrupt anything."

"You're not. I'm just having dinner with my brother. Let me find a quieter spot."

His brother.

One piece of positive news, anyway.

Her spirits took an uptick as she waited for him to resume the conversation.

He was back on the line in less than half a minute. "Sorry about that. There was a large birthday party next to us, and they were in a very celebratory mood. Is this better?"

"Much. Anyway, I've been looking at the picture you sent of Ginny, and I saw something that seems odd."

"What?" His tone morphed from friendly to focused in a heartbeat.

"She's wearing nail polish. Or the remnants of it."

Dead silence.

"Lance?"

"Yeah. I'm here." He sounded puzzled. "Tell me why this is important."

Right. He was a single guy. How much would he know about nail polish?

She explained the issue.

"I get it now. That's a very astute observation."

A surge of warmth boosted her spirits another notch. "But what does it mean?"

"He might have taken the photo early on. The fresh injuries would support that. While I have you on the phone, why don't you take another look at the picture in light of this discovery? See if there's any other indication it might be an older shot."

Christy walked back to the table and dropped

into her chair. Once more she scrutinized the screen inch by inch.

A second shock wave passed over her as she stared at Ginny's hair and did some quick math.

"I found something else. Ginny's natural hair is light brown. She's been dying it blonde for years. About a week before the fire, she had a touch-up. After two months of captivity, brown roots should be visible. This isn't the clearest picture, so I could be wrong—but I'm not seeing any roots at all. This appears to be a fresh dye job."

"One more piece of evidence to suggest the photo was taken not long after the abduction." A couple of seconds ticked by. "I'll tell you what. Let me think about this and run it by my colleagues tomorrow. I'll also ask the lab to home in on the hairline and see if they can confirm what you think you're seeing."

A tingle of unease slithered through her nerve endings. "I'm getting a bad feeling about this, Lance. If she was okay, why wouldn't he take the picture now?"

"Let's not jump to any conclusions. He could have a lot of reasons. This guy has been throwing you curves from the beginning. Using an old picture could be another ploy to unnerve you."

"If it is, it's working."

"But if it's not, it's a mistake. It means he didn't realize how much information was in that photo. And if he made one mistake, he can—and

116

probably will—make others. That will work to our advantage."

"I don't see how this one does."

"No piece of information is wasted in an investigation like this. And speaking of information, a colleague and I are working through your lists. Yours is very short . . . and I don't see many friends listed."

"I don't have many—and none from childhood. Skating and school took up every minute of my waking hours. In college, I was on a fast track to catch up. I only started making friends after I entered the workforce . . . and I choose them carefully."

"Not a bad strategy. I also don't see any male names on the friend side."

She played with the mouse. Was his implied question prompted by personal—or professional—interest?

Both, she hoped.

"The men I associate with are nothing more than acquaintances."

"Any who might be interested in being more than that?"

An image of Bob formed in her mind. Her contact with him had been so limited on the job that she hadn't bothered to put him on the co-worker list—but he *had* asked her out.

"There is one guy at work who's been trying to get me to agree to a date, but I finally convinced him I wasn't interested. He seemed disappointed but took it in stride."

"You didn't put his name on the list."

"I hardly know him."

"We should at least run some background on him."

She bit her lip. "I hate to cause him any trouble. He got divorced not long ago, and I think he's having a hard time adjusting. I suspect the poor guy is just lonely."

"He'll never know we ran a background check —unless we find some negative information. What's his name?"

"Bob Harris. I don't have an address, but I know he lives close to work."

"Got it. I'll let you know if we find anything as we check out the people on your lists. In the meantime, keep hanging in there."

She tightened her grip on the phone. It would be far easier to do that if he was there to give her a hug. Even a fake one, like yesterday's, would do.

But wishful thinking wouldn't make it happen.

She took a steadying breath. "I will. Now I'll let you get back to dinner with your brother."

There was a brief hesitation before he responded. "Okay. But call me if anything comes up."

"I will. Enjoy your meal."

She pressed the end button, staring at the photo

of Ginny on her computer screen as she leaned back in her chair.

The old photo.

Lance hadn't offered any theories—beyond unnerving her—as to why the kidnapper might have taken it early on.

But she could think of one that made her sick to her stomach.

And as she shut down her computer, she had a feeling even a hug from a certain handsome FBI agent wouldn't be enough to chase away the new anxiety that was creeping into her bones.

"You aren't going to bail on me again, are you?" Mac skewered him with a don't-even-think-about-it look as Lance slid back into the corner booth that gave them both a clear view into the restaurant.

"Nope." He inventoried the plate of toasted ravioli between them and took two. "I see you put a dent in these during my brief absence."

"I was hungry. Who's Christy?"

Lance dipped the ravioli in marinara sauce and took a bite. "These are great. How come the rest of the world doesn't know about them?"

"They were invented here. So was the ice-cream cone, at the 1904 World's Fair. You can tuck that in your trivia file. Who's Christy?"

He should have known Mac wasn't going to let that rest. Too bad he hadn't answered her call with his usual clipped, official "McGregor."

A blob of sauce fell onto the table, and he wiped it up with his napkin. "A professional acquaintance."

"Right."

"I'm serious."

" 'Christy . . . . aaaahhh.' " Mac did an exaggerated replay of his greeting.

No way had he sounded that . . . smitten.

Had he?

Mac supplied the answer. "If your tone had been any warmer, you'd have melted that butter." He gestured toward two pats on a plate beside the basket of bread.

"Let's not get carried away."

"I'm not the one who seems to be getting carried away." Mac paused while the server deposited their plates of pasta, but he didn't let that minor diversion deter him. "Is she another agent?"

"No." Might as well give him the basics. His brother could be like a dog with a bone once he latched on to a topic. "She's the figure skater you saw on that video in my apartment. The one involved in my case."

Mac raised an eyebrow.

"Our relationship is purely professional."

"If you want my advice, keep it that way till the case is over." Mac dived into his tutto mare.

Lance glared at him, doing his best to suppress a surge of irritation. Typical Mac. Always the big brother, dispensing words of wisdom. "That cream sauce is a heart attack on a plate, you know."

"Maybe. But I'll die happy." He speared a shrimp. "I'd ask you about the case, but I don't want you to breach any confidentiality protocols."

Lance toyed with his vermicelli. Truth be told, Mac had sound insights—and he wouldn't mind having him weigh in on this. Between his SEAL experience and his newer career as a homicide detective, he might be able to offer a few helpful ideas—or at the very least confirm that the train of thought he was following was on track.

"Can I ask you a theoretical question?"

"Theoretical, huh?" One side of Mac's mouth quirked up as he continued to shovel in the pasta. "Sure."

He relayed the gist of his conversation with Christy. "I'm not liking the old photo angle."

Mac stopped eating. "I wouldn't be, either. I can only think of a couple of reasons your guy would do that—and neither one is pretty."

They were on the same track.

Either Ginny was in very bad shape . . . or she was dead.

Tomorrow he'd make sure her DNA was put into the missing person database . . . in case a stray body turned up somewhere.

"That's what I was thinking."

"Did you share your theories with the skater?"

"No. She's already freaked—and there's a chance it's not as dire as it appears."

Mac sent him a dubious look. "I hope you're right, but I wouldn't count on it." He grabbed another piece of bread. "You pulled a tough one for your first case."

"Tell me something I don't know."

"Any veterans in your group you can call on for help?"

"A very sharp former HRT operator."

"You want my opinion? Take advantage of his experience. I know it's not easy to go from special forces to rookie, but don't be too proud to ask for advice. I learned a lot from Lisa when I was a greenhorn working that bones case with her."

"I'll keep that in mind." He dug into his own pasta. "Speaking of special forces, have you heard anything from Finn lately?"

Twin creases appeared above Mac's nose. "An email over the weekend. I got the impression he was headed out on a mission and might not be in touch for a while. Sounded like the Middle East. Again."

"Par for the course for an Army Ranger. I don't like that he's still in the line of fire, though."

"That makes two of us."

"He sound okay otherwise?"

"Like he's been sounding for the past few months. Cryptic. Serious. No joking around."

"I wonder what's eating him?"

"I don't know—and he's not talking. I tried a little subtle digging but got nowhere."

"We'll have to corner him on his next leave."

"He did hint he might make it in for my birthday."

"Yeah?" Lance claimed the last piece of bread. "That's only six weeks away. We'll give the runt a talking to then. If we double-team it, we might wrestle some information out of him."

"It's worth a try, I guess. I've had a bad feeling ever since . . ." He stopped and pulled his phone off his belt.

The ensuing conversation was short and cryptic, but Lance got the gist of it.

"You're going to bail on *me,* aren't you?"

Mac pulled out some bills and tossed them on the table. "Sorry. A double homicide takes precedence over dinner with a brother."

"You managed to finish off most of your food, at least." Lance inspected his brother's plate as Mac scooped up a few stray noodles and took a final swig of iced tea.

"A skill I picked up as a SEAL. It's come in handy on this job too." He slid from the booth. "Good luck on the skater case."

"Thanks. I can use it."

"Hey—you'll do fine. You might be new on the job, but you're a fast learner, and there's not a thing wrong with that brain of yours, despite all the ribbing I give you. Just take it a day at a time."

He grinned. "And good luck with the figure skater too, once you get this solved. You may need a *lot* of help on that one, if the lady is as classy as she looked in the clip."

Before Lance could respond with a witty comeback, Mac took off toward the exit.

Just as well, since he didn't have one.

Because his brother had nailed it. He *would* need help wooing Christy, if that's what he chose to do when this was over. She *was* a class act. She was also strong. Steady. Smart. Solid. Any one of the tough blows she'd been dealt would have caused a lot of people to fold, yet she was still carrying on. Not only surviving, but forging ahead.

And he suspected her faith had a lot to do with that.

He forked another bite of pasta but didn't eat it.

The faith situation was an issue. On more than one occasion, she'd mentioned the importance of prayer in her life. How it had sustained her through the trauma of the past year and played a big role in her decision to leave competitive skating. Difficult as it must have been given all the ups and downs in her past, she'd managed to hold on to her belief in a loving, caring God.

Too bad he hadn't been able to do the same.

But all the stuff he'd seen and done in The Unit? Faith-busters—even for a guy who'd been raised in a faith-filled household.

For a woman like Christy, who clearly put God at the center of her world, that could be a deal breaker.

Expelling a breath, Lance set his fork down and signaled to the server for the bill. So much for the nice, relaxing evening he'd expected to spend with his brother.

On the upside, though, this case was in the early stages. Maybe a solution to the faith issue would come to him before it ended.

Unfortunately, that might take a miracle—and he'd seen far too few of those . . . no matter how hard he'd prayed.

7

"They're all Boy Scouts—or Girl Scouts." Mark dropped into the extra chair in Lance's cube and waved the folder in his hand. "My topline review turned up zip. Not one name on the Ginny Reed friend/acquaintance/co-worker list is connected with anything that suggests fanaticism or criminal inclination. How'd you fare?"

"Not much better. In general, Christy's people all sound like normal, law-abiding citizens."

"Doesn't mean someone couldn't go off the deep end, though. That's what happened in my wife's case. In hindsight, there were signs the guy was slipping—but no one who knew him ever suspected he had murder on his mind." He lifted the edge of the file on the desk. "What do you mean, 'in general'?"

No surprise that Mark hadn't missed his caveat.

He pulled out Christy's acquaintance list, glancing at the name he'd added after his phone conversation with her last night. "The only person who set off any alarms was a Bob Harris—one of Christy's co-workers who's been hitting on her. After he and his wife separated, the ex got a protection order against him. It's still in effect."

"What kind of order?"

"HRO."

"Harassment versus abuse. Not quite as bad."

"Bad enough to put him on the top of my list for questioning."

"Makes sense. Anyone else on your radar?"

"No."

"Then we might want to give the victim's list priority. Her friends and co-workers all sound squeaky clean, but they might pass on a tip about some connection her sister doesn't know about."

"Agreed. Sounds like a road trip to the Potosi area is in our future—or mine, anyway."

Mark leaned back. "Maybe not, if we want to keep this low-key. Our guy in Rolla is sharp, and if he has time, we might want to ask him to do the interviews. Agents from St. Louis showing up would be a bigger deal, and the news would have a higher probability of getting back to the subject."

"Good point. As long as you think he's up for the job, I can give him a call. This has to be handled with a lot of discretion."

"He'll be fine. I've worked with him on a couple of higher-profile cases."

"I'm also going to call Quantico and try to push the DNA analysis. If we can ID the body, that will give us a definite link to the kidnapper."

"You might get lucky. The database is a lot more comprehensive than it used to be." Mark rose and handed over his file. "I'm available if you need another set of hands or eyes."

"As a matter of fact . . ." Lance shifted in his seat. He had to position this carefully, since Steve had already discerned that his interest in this case was more than professional. "Christy Reed and I have fallen into a role-play of being friends. It was her idea the first time we met, in case the kidnapper was watching. She didn't want to run the risk of him thinking she'd gone to the cops. We've continued that whenever we've gotten together. I'd prefer not to blow that cover until I have to. It might prove useful."

Mark folded his arms. "You want me to talk to Harris."

"If you have time."

Mark pursed his lips. "Your ruse isn't bad. Go

ahead and give me what you have on him and I'll drop by later today."

Lance opened his file and pulled out a few sheets of paper. "Thanks."

"Not a problem. I'll let you know what I find out."

As Mark exited, Lance swung back to his desk and picked up his phone. He might be new, and he might not have much pull, and the ME might be swamped—but it couldn't hurt to keep pushing for fast results. Then he'd talk to the agent in Rolla.

And unless one of those efforts panned out, Christy was going to be back to waiting for the kidnapper's next move—fretting, frustrated, frightened . . . and as much a hostage as Ginny might be.

Which could be exactly the intent.

Friday night—and he was free for the weekend.

Perfect.

Nathan smiled, dropped into the chair in front of his computer, and pressed the start button.

While he waited for the laptop to boot up, he pulled on his thick leather gloves and removed the wire mesh over the small box on the floor. Why not amuse himself for a minute or two?

The mouse tried to elude him as he chased it, but to no avail. He toyed with it, teased it, then wrapped his fingers around the quivering body.

The critter squirmed, but after going through this drill dozens of times, he was used to their tricks.

Holding it in front of his face, he slowly tightened his fist until the rodent's eyes bulged. After a few moments, he reduced the pressure and let the mouse gasp for air. He repeated the process several times, always stopping short of finishing it off.

He had a different end in mind.

Once he tired of the game, he angled sideways and dropped the mouse into a galvanized bucket of water. As its legs began pumping, he leaned back to enjoy the show.

In less than a minute, the mouse slowed.

Soon after, it gave up the struggle—like any creature did when confronted with insurmountable odds.

Except humans.

A lot of them fought to the end.

His smile faded as the mouse went limp and sank to the bottom.

Daris would have fought longer if he'd had the chance. His brother might have been only fourteen, but he'd been tough. Even after those soldiers had ganged up on him, he'd punched and kicked and struggled with every ounce of his strength—until two quick, sharp retorts reduced him to a crumpled, lifeless heap.

The finality of those bullets hadn't stopped his mother from rushing into the fray, though. She'd pushed through the crowd, half crazed, and flung herself at the men, beating on them, flailing at them, cursing them for what they'd done to her oldest son. But they'd only laughed and grabbed her arms. Ripped her clothes. Dragged her into the alley.

Her gut-piercing screams had followed him as he ran as hard and as fast as he could.

They still did.

Nathan sucked in a sharp breath. Crushed the memories. Wasn't he always berating the old woman for living in the past? He needed to focus on the present.

On Christy Reed.

He turned his attention to the screen, scrolling through until he had the information he needed. Then he pocketed the ziplock bag containing the third letter and considered the mouse. He could leave it somewhere for the old woman to find, as usual. On her pillow. In the refrigerator. Inside one of her slippers. Her screeches were always amusing.

But he wouldn't hear them tonight.

Better to save that tactic for another day.

He fished the mouse out of the water and thumbtacked its tail to the corkboard above his desk, letting it dangle next to the autographed photo of Christy. The inscription was engraved on his memory, but he read it again anyway.

"To Neven—I'm glad our paths crossed.

Wishing you happiness and great success. Your friend, Christy Reed."

He snorted.

What a joke.

She wasn't glad their paths had crossed. How could she be, when she'd forgotten him so easily?

And she wasn't his friend. She'd never been his friend. Friends didn't desert each other.

Did she have any clue what havoc that deception had wrought?

Probably not.

But she would.

Soon.

One more letter to send after tonight, and the end of this game would be in sight. The final payback. A chance to make her suffer as he'd suffered.

In the meantime, he had preparations to . . .

A clatter sounded from the kitchen, and he frowned. What was the old woman up to now?

He shot to his feet and marched down the hall, stopping in the doorway. She was upright, clutching her side, but the walker had tipped over and lay on the floor. Beside it was a broken glass.

Her frightened gaze sought his, and a rush of power surged through him. This was what he was born for. To be in control. To make the decisions. To hold people's fate in his hand. Maybe that chance had passed him by in the bigger world, but in this apartment, he was in charge.

The key to using fear to your advantage, however, was to keep people off-balance. Leave them wondering if—and when—you might strike. And he'd been hard on her at dinner the other night.

Time to turn on the charm.

"Ah, Baka, did you hurt yourself?" He gentled his voice as he walked toward her.

She peered at him warily. "No, no. I okay."

"Are you certain?" He righted the walker and positioned it in front of her. She flinched as he reached toward her, but he just patted her shoulder. "What happened?"

"It . . . fall." She gestured to the broken glass and clutched her rib cage, wincing as she drew in short, shallow puffs of air. "I try to . . ." She made a clenching motion with her fingers.

He got the picture. She'd tried to grab for the glass, knocking over her walker in the process.

"Did you fall against the counter?"

"Yes." Her expression was guarded. "I . . . okay."

That was a lie. Lines of pain scored her face. She must have bruised or broken a rib—and dealing with an injury wasn't on his agenda for the evening.

Suppressing a surge of irritation, he patted her shoulder again. "Well, if you're hurting tomorrow, you let me know, okay?"

She gave a slow nod, the taut line of her shoulders relaxing a fraction.

"Are you finished with dinner?"

Again, she dipped her head.

"Let me walk you back to your room, then. And I'll get you something to help with any discomfort."

Calling up his most solicitous manner, he took her arm and guided her down the hall. After assisting her into bed, he brought her a glass of water and two Aleve.

"Hvala . . . no, no!" Her eyes widened with fear again as she handed the glass back and switched to English. "Tank you."

He let the language lapse pass as he adjusted her pillow. "You're welcome. Now get some rest and we'll see how you are in the morning."

He shut the door of her room behind him as he left, pausing in the hall. The monthly government checks she signed over to him were nice, but sometimes she was more trouble than she was worth. Once he was finished with Christy, he might have to reconsider their arrangement. There had to be easier ways to get the power rush than by dealing with a decrepit old woman.

Maybe that promotion at work would come through. Having other people to order around might satisfy his craving for power.

In the meantime, he had places to go and things to do tonight.

Sitting in a cold car on a frigid evening wasn't on his list of top ten ways to spend a Friday night.

Lance tugged the sheepskin collar of his jacket as high as possible and hunkered down behind the wheel. Mark had warned him that new agents often got stuck with the less desirable assignments, and doing night surveillance in the winter on a bank robbery suspect's girlfriend definitely qualified.

He could think of a lot better uses of his time. Like sitting beside Christy on that comfy couch in front of the fireplace in her living room, sharing a bowl of popcorn while they watched some chick flick.

Chick flick?

He shook his head.

If Mac or Finn ever got wind he was thinking along those lines, he'd be dead meat. They'd have enough ribbing material for the next ten years.

His cell began to vibrate, and he pulled it out, watching his breath cloud the chilly air as he answered. "What's up, Mark?"

"I hear you drew the short straw."

"Yeah."

"Cold duty."

"I've been colder."

"If you put in time in the Middle East—and I'm assuming you did—that goes without saying. I wanted to let you know I talked to Harris today."

Lance zeroed in on a guy ambling down the street. This wasn't a strolling kind of neighborhood—especially in the winter. Maybe that anonymous tip they'd received was going to pay off.

He leaned sideways to keep the guy in view. "What's your take?"

"Same as the victim's sister. I think he's lonely and trolling for dates. He seemed freaked by a visit from the FBI and immediately started explaining what happened with his ex-wife. According to him, she requested the protection order after he started parking across the street from the house so he could get a glimpse of his kids, who he misses. She claimed his presence was harassment. Sounds to me like he got a raw deal."

"Divorces can be nasty." The guy stopped across the street from the girlfriend's apartment and flicked a lighter.

"You got that right. Once I told him my visit had nothing to do with his ex, he calmed down. He admitted he was disappointed by Christy's rebuff but appears to have accepted her explanation that she's met someone else."

Lance straightened up.

Had she?

If so, why wasn't the guy on her list?

"Any idea who that might be?" Mark prompted when the silence lengthened.

"No. I'm thinking it was just an excuse." He hoped.

"You might want to double-check with her."

"Yeah." In the second floor of the apartment

135

building, a shade was lowered. Raised. Lowered halfway.

The guy crossed the street toward the front door. Bingo.

"I need to go. I think we're about to see some action here."

"Okay. Good luck."

Lance kept his eye on the guy as he called in reinforcements and pulled out his Glock. At least this cold surveillance gig would be short-lived—and hopefully the last one for this case. If all went well, they might wrap it up tonight.

Too bad they weren't making similar headway with the kidnapper.

Instead, they were stuck in a holding pattern, waiting for his next directive—and the guy didn't seem to be in any hurry to issue it.

Given the meager clues they'd uncovered, however, the kidnapper's lackadaisical pace worked to their advantage in some ways. The longer this dragged on, the more time they had to dig up some leads.

One day soon, however, the situation would escalate. The kidnapper would either tire of his game or they'd uncover a worthwhile clue.

Far better for that escalation to happen on the FBI's time frame than the kidnapper's.

But until they got a break, this guy was in charge —like it or not.

Not.

• • •

The pain medication was wearing off.

Mevlida groaned as she shifted in bed and peered at the illuminated clock on her nightstand. Three in the morning. Eight hours since Neven had given her those blue pills after her fall.

And she needed more.

But he kept all medicine in his room, and waking him in the middle of the night could be risky.

Better to lie here awhile and see if she could fall back to sleep without the pills.

Fifteen minutes later, however, the pain was worse—and intensifying.

What should she do?

Mevlida kneaded the edge of the blanket with her fingers. He'd been so kind last night, like in the early days two years ago, after that nice therapist at the rehab center had helped her find him. Perhaps his good humor had survived the night.

Raising herself carefully on one elbow, she eased her feet over the side of the bed, positioned her walker, and struggled to her feet.

For a full minute she stood motionless, waiting for the pain in her ribs to recede before she began her slow shuffle across the small room and down the hall.

Outside his door, she wiped her damp palms down the soft flannel of her nightdress. Dabbed a tissue at the beads of sweat above her upper lip. Clutched the walker.

Maybe this was a mistake.

Maybe she should try to get through the night without the pain medicine.

All at once, a cough rumbled deep in her chest. She tried to suppress it, but it refused to be contained—and with each hack, searing pain sliced through her midsection.

Moisture gathered in her eyes, and a tear spilled out. Waiting until morning was impossible. She needed the pills now.

Pulse fluttering, she knocked lightly on Neven's door.

No response.

Was he ignoring her—or sound asleep? He'd been working a lot of extra hours, helping to fill in for the injured man. He might just be very tired.

She knocked harder—and the door clicked, opening an inch.

Her jaw went slack as she stared at the slight gap. Neven never left his room unlocked. Even when he went to get a drink or use the bathroom, he locked the door. From her first day here, he'd made it clear she was never to set foot into his space. Nor had he given her any opportunity to do so, since he kept the key on a chain around his neck.

So why was the door unlocked tonight?

With a tentative push, she opened it a few more inches and peeked inside.

Neven wasn't there.

In fact, the bed hadn't been slept in.

Mevlida leaned on the walker, taking shallow breaths as her respiration slowed. Where could the boy have gone? Sometimes he stayed out late on weekends but never past one or two.

His absence could be a blessing, though. If he wasn't here, she might be able to get her pills without disturbing him.

But . . . what if he came home and caught her in his room?

A parade of possible consequences passed through her mind—none of them pleasant—and a sudden, cold sweat left her shivering in the chilly apartment.

But spending the rest of the night in pain was even less palatable.

She'd have to take her chances, move quickly, and hope wherever he was, he'd stay there for a few more minutes.

Pushing the door wide, she let her eyes adjust as the dim light from the hall spilled inside, then scanned the room. Her gaze skittered past the deer rifle propped against the wall. The one he used to hunt on the property some acquaintance owned out in the country. There was a chest of drawers on her immediate left . . . a neatly made bed . . . a nightstand . . . a desk in the far corner, in shadows.

The desk might be the most likely spot for the pills.

Gritting her teeth against the pain, she shuffled toward it.

Once there, she rested a hand on top as she flipped on the floor lamp beside it. Much better. Now she could see the . . .

She gasped.

Clutched her chest.

A dead mouse was pinned to the corkboard above the desk, beside a photo of an ice-skater.

Dead mice she was used to, thanks to Neven's cruel games. But this one, hanging next to the picture of that pretty girl, felt . . . sinister.

Clutching the walker, she dropped her gaze to the empty cage on the floor . . . the water bucket . . . and another dead mouse duct-taped to a board, its paws and ears missing.

Her stomach churned.

Disposing of the nuisance rodents that were far too plentiful in the apartment was one thing.

Torturing the little creatures was another.

Out of the murky waters of her past, a memory from a summer's day in the old country bobbed to the surface. They'd all gathered for Friday lunch after noon prayer, as usual, and Neven had wandered out to the yard to play. When she'd gone to summon him for the meal, she'd found him squatting beside a quivering baby rabbit he'd cornered in her backyard, poking at its belly with a pointed stick.

At her harsh rebuke, he'd let the animal scurry away and turned to her with an innocent expression. "I was just playing with it, Baka."

Tormenting a helpless animal hadn't seemed like play to her, but he'd been only . . . what? Six, seven. Maybe eight. No more than a small child. Too young to know better, perhaps.

At least that's what she'd told herself.

But now . . .

Mevlida looked from the mutilated dead mouse to the one hanging on the bulletin board. All these years, she'd attributed his callous behavior to the trauma he'd endured. But . . . had he been prone to meanness long before that?

As she examined the photo of the skater again, a chill ran through her.

Gripping the walker, she surveyed the items on the desk. A pistol was front and center. Beside it was a photo of a group of young people, Neven among them. Schoolmates, perhaps? The girl in the picture on the bulletin board was in it too.

She picked up the chain with the Arch on the end. It was for keys—yet it held none. And that envelope . . . why was it in plastic? She couldn't read the name, but the letters looked the same as the signature in the signed picture.

What did it all mean?

What was her grandson up to?

She had no answers.

But she knew one thing . . . it wasn't good. She could feel it in her bones, that same ominous sense of foreboding she'd experienced on that terrible day in the village, when the family holiday they'd anticipated with such joy had turned to tragedy.

The day reports of soldiers in the streets had reached them.

The day Mihad had disappeared.

The day Daris and Sonja had died.

The blackest day of her life.

Was she once again to be plunged into darkness?

A feeling of panic, of overwhelming helplessness, swept over her, just as it had on the day her perfect world had crumbled. Her hands began to shake. Shudders coursed through her body. The acrid taste of fear soured on her tongue.

Choking back a sob, she switched off the lamp, maneuvered her walker to face the door, and moved toward the light in the hall as fast as she could, ignoring the pain caused by her labored breathing.

Once in the hall, she shut the door tight. Neven must never discover she'd been in his room. Who knew what he would do?

Who knew what he still might do?

For years, she'd made excuses for him. Believed he was good at heart. But she could ignore the truth no longer. There was darkness in that boy. She might deserve his wrath, but why had he targeted that pretty young woman in the photo?

A car backfired in the parking lot, like Neven's often did, and she picked up her pace. He couldn't find her hovering in the hall.

Once back in her room, she closed the door and lowered herself to the bed, trembling in the darkness.

Waiting.

A few minutes later, she heard his key in the lock. The front door opened. Clicked shut.

She didn't hear his tread in the hall. She never did. The boy had learned to move with stealth. But though her eyes were closed, she sensed when he opened her door to look in. Knew, also, the instant he realized his door was unlocked—because he came back to her room. Crossed to her bed. Stood over her.

A faint aroma of onions wafted her way. He must have stopped at some fast-food place on his way home.

She tried to keep her respiration steady under his scrutiny, despite the pain. In. Out. In. Out. Keep. Breathing.

After several eternal seconds, he retreated.

The door clicked softly shut.

She exhaled and opened her eyes—to find him standing above her.

Panic clawed at her throat.

"So you're awake."

Don't admit anything! Pretend you were asleep!

She groaned and blinked, giving him a muddled look. "I hurt."

He leaned closer, resting a hand on either side of her. "Have you gotten out of bed at all?"

"No. I . . . hurt."

He studied her in the dim light while her heart hammered. At last he stood. "I'll get you some more pills."

She lay quivering while she waited for him to return, sheet bunched in her fingers. When he reappeared, she took the pills he offered, holding the glass with both hands as she washed them down.

"Go back to sleep now." He left her, clicking the door shut behind him.

She stared at the dark ceiling and released a quivering breath.

Sleep?

There would be no more rest for her this night.

She had too much to think about. To process. To plan.

Neven was family. The only family she had left. And family had been everything in the old country. They had stood by one another, shoulder to shoulder, heart to heart, loyal and true.

But where did loyalty end? How many sins should love overlook—and forgive? When did a stranger's welfare take precedence over that of a family member?

Such difficult questions.

Another shiver passed through her, and Mevlida pulled the covers higher under her chin. Neven meant that girl harm, she was certain of it. But how much harm? Was he playing upsetting but harmless pranks on her, as he did here? Or was he planning to hurt her—like he'd hurt that defenseless rabbit so many years ago?

She didn't want to believe that could be true.

But ignoring reality didn't make it go away, as she'd learned to her deep regret. In fact, closing your eyes to the truth could be deadly. You had to be ready for what life sent your way. Prepared to take action.

This time, she would be.

Maybe she couldn't bring back the people she'd loved and lost, but perhaps she could find a way to warn that girl to be careful.

Neven must never know of her disloyalty, though. If he found out, her life would become even more intolerable.

The wind howled outside her window, rattling the glass, and she burrowed deeper under the covers, into the warmth.

But the icy chill in her heart remained.

8

"Christy!"

Guilt tugging at her conscience, Christy turned as Bob waved at her from the far side of the rec center lobby. She should have sought *him* out, not the other way around. She owed the man an apology for adding more hassle to his already stressful life. According to Lance, he'd been freaked to find an FBI agent at his door. Who wouldn't be?

As for Lance's query about the met-a-new-guy excuse she'd given Bob—thank goodness their Saturday conversation had been by phone. Despite her explanation that it had been nothing more than a kind brush-off, her blush would have tipped him off that the excuse actually had legs . . . and they were attached to him.

Tightening her grip on the skates in one hand and the bulging satchel of summer youth program proposals in the other, she summoned up a smile as Bob approached. "Hi. I see you're working late too."

"Par for the course. Besides, there's not much to go home to these days."

The perfect opening.

She looked around. No one was in the lobby

except a maintenance guy, and he was busy mopping, buds plugged into his ears. Still, she lowered her voice. "About that . . . I didn't mean to cause you any aggravation."

He waved her apology aside. "No sweat . . . once I realized my ex hadn't sicced the feds on me. But I did want to say I'm sorry someone's hassling you."

So that's the excuse Lance's colleague had used for the visit.

It was true too—even if *hassle* didn't come close to describing the terror and confusion that had kept her awake more nights than she could count since the kidnapper's first letter.

Lifting one shoulder, she managed the facsimile of a smile. "I'll get through it—but I appreciate your understanding."

"Despite what Diane tells anyone who will listen, I do have a few empathetic bones in my body." His features tightened for a moment, then he dipped his head toward her skates. "Heading to the rink?"

"Yes. Skating is about the only thing that feels normal and predictable these days."

"Normal and predictable are good. Better than I realized until recently."

"You'll get there again."

"Maybe. But it will be a different normal."

She couldn't argue with that.

"Anyway, I won't hold you up." He took a step

back. "I just wanted to apologize for bugging you about a date when you had all that other stuff going on."

"I was flattered by your interest." True enough —even if the interest wasn't reciprocated.

"Thanks." With a lift of his hand, he started to walk away—then paused and turned back. "And I'm happy you met someone new—even if it killed my chances." After offering her a crooked grin, he strolled down the hall.

She exhaled, some of her tension evaporating. At least he was being a good sport about her rejection and the awkward visit from the FBI. And with her conscience appeased, she'd be able to give her full attention to tonight's student. She might even hang around afterward and lose herself for a few minutes in the motion and the music.

Two hours later, agenda accomplished, she arrived home tired but less tense—and ready for a hot meal. An omelet, perhaps? That would be fast, easy, and filling.

But all thoughts of food fled when she retrieved her mail.

Because tucked among the ads and the bills was another envelope addressed in her sister's hand.

"What do you think about this one?"

Lance stifled a groan as his future sister-in-law dragged him toward yet another couch in the vast sea of furniture. This shopping trip was worse than a visit to the dentist.

"Lance?"

He gave the tan leather couch a fast once-over. "It looks fine to me."

Lisa planted her hands on her hips. "You've said that about everything I've shown you."

"That's because I like everything you pick out. You have excellent taste."

"Resorting to flattery, are we?"

"It's the truth. Besides, if I'd known what to buy, I wouldn't have bribed you to come with me in the first place."

"But I can't help you if I don't have a handle on your tastes. You must have some preferences."

Not about furniture.

When it came to women—different story. He knew exactly what he preferred in the female gender. Tall, leggy, blonde, blue-eyed . . .

He frowned.

Wait a minute.

Christy didn't fit any of those parameters. Except for the legs, of course. On that score, she—

"Lance!"

He jerked back to reality. "What?"

"I need to know your taste—in furniture." Lisa's eyes twinkled as she tacked on the last two words.

Had she read his mind?

Maybe.

A former Chicago homicide detective turned

police chief was apt to have solid intuitive skills.

He forced himself to think about furniture preferences. "I like quiet stuff. Not a lot of patterns, no real bright colors. Homey but not froufrou. Clean lines, no knickknacks, no modern art. A few pictures are okay, and I wouldn't mind a bookcase. Some polished wood would be nice too."

Huh.

That pretty much described Christy's living room.

"Now we're getting somewhere." Lisa gave a satisfied nod and consulted the clipboard she'd been toting around the massive furniture store as she dragged him from item to item.

Lance scanned the store and shook his head. The choices were stupefying. How in creation did anyone wade through the clutter and pick stuff to create a room like Christy's?

He sneaked a peek at his watch. Only seven? It felt like they'd been here for a day and a half rather than an hour and a half.

"I think we should go with a fabric couch—one with a nubby texture, sort of like a Berber carpet —and pair it with a leather chair." Lisa tapped her pen against the clipboard as she pondered her scribbled notes. "That will give the room a masculine feel. We saw a couple of pieces that would work. We can accent them with some jewel-tone throw pillows, and—"

His phone began to vibrate, and he grabbed for it. Maybe the person on the other end would be speaking English instead of whatever lingo Lisa was spouting.

When Christy's name appeared in the window, he reined in his smile and gave his personal shopper a sober look. "I need to take this. Business."

"Fine. I'll scout out some end tables."

Pressing the talk button, he shifted away from her. "Hi. What's up?"

"I got another letter."

The impulse to smile vanished. "Let's follow the same drill. Set it on the counter and don't open it. I'll be there as soon as I can."

"How soon?" Christy sounded spooked.

"Twenty to thirty minutes."

"I'll be waiting. Sorry to interrupt your evening again."

"Believe me, I'm grateful to have an excuse to cut this one short. My brother's fiancée took me furniture shopping for my apartment. I'd rather be getting a root canal."

"That's a very stereotypical male comment."

"Some stereotypes are accurate. I'll be there as soon as I can."

Sliding the phone back on his belt, he went in search of Lisa.

He found her on her hands and knees inspecting the drawer in an end table.

"Look at that." She pointed to the inside, her tone indignant. "For this price you should expect dovetailing. Your budget might be modest, but we can do better." She rose before he could extend a hand to help her.

A twinge of guilt tugged at his conscience. "You know, I really appreciate you taking the time for this."

She brushed off the knees of her jeans. "I sense a 'but' coming."

Leave it to Mac to find himself a smart, insightful lady.

"But there's been a new development on a case, and I need to follow up."

She squinted at him. "Was that Christy?"

Just how much had his big brother told his fiancée about this case?

"Uh, yeah. She's the sister of the victim."

"Also the figure skater you have the hots for."

Mac and his big mouth.

His older sibling was going to get an earful the next time they talked.

"I'll admit she's a nice, attractive woman. But for now, our relationship is 100 percent professional."

"That's smart. So what do you want to do about the furniture?"

He rubbed his neck as he surveyed the display floor. "I trust your judgment. You did a great job with your house. Could you just pick out some basic living room stuff? As long as the room's not empty and looks like a guy's place, I'll be happy. And a small table for the breakfast area would be nice too. I'm tired of sitting at the counter."

"What if you don't like what I order?"

"I'll like it."

"You're giving me carte blanche to spend your money?"

"Yeah. Have at it."

"Fine. But you still owe me lunch."

"I know. At the salad place." He leaned over and gave her a quick hug. "You pick the day."

"Thursday. Noon. Be there."

"This week?" A hint of panic crept into his voice. He needed more time to psyche himself up for his ladies-who-lunch experience.

"Yep. And you know what? You might like it."

Rabbit food? Not a chance.

But a deal was a deal.

He sighed. "Fine. I'll be there."

"Try to contain your enthusiasm."

"Hey, it's not the company. I'm just more of a steak and baked potato kind of guy."

"Not the healthiest diet."

"Better than that tutto mare Mac was chowing down when I met him for dinner."

"Usually he eats healthier meals."

"Thanks to you."

"Guilty as charged. Okay, go ahead while I

shop for your cave. I'll email you the grand total and delivery dates."

"Just don't break the bank." He began to back away.

"I'll keep your budget in mind."

With a wave, he jogged toward the exit, already switching gears.

And hoping the kidnapper's latest note held more helpful clues than the previous ones had.

Twenty-four minutes after she and Lance ended their call, Christy's doorbell rang.

Reining in her pulse, she smoothed her hands down her leggings, adjusted the hem of her sweater, and crossed her foyer. Hand on the knob, she peered through the peephole.

So much for trying to make her heart behave.

Even the distortion from the fisheye lens couldn't detract from Lance's rugged good looks —and his off-duty attire added to his appeal. That make-my-day leather jacket and those worn, nice-fitting jeans should carry a blood-pressure warning.

She pulled back, fanning her face. Oh, for pity's sake. You'd think she was some teenager on a first date.

But she was thirty-two years old, and this was no date. The man was here on serious business.

Life-and-death business.

With that sobering thought dampening any

romantic notions, she pulled open the door and ushered him in.

After a quick greeting, he moved past her, leaving a woodsy, masculine scent in his wake. "Is the letter in the kitchen?"

"Yes. It's stiffer than the last one. I think there's something inside." She followed him to the back of the condo. "The postmark's from Columbia, Missouri."

He fished some latex gloves out of his pocket and reached for the same knife he'd used on the last letter. Once again, he positioned the note over an evidence envelope. After carefully slitting the top, he bowed it and looked inside. Then, in silence, he slid the contents onto the evidence envelope.

A folded piece of paper lay on top of two sheets of cardboard held together with small pieces of tape.

Lance opened the note and angled it so she could read along with him.

Did you like the pixture I sent you, Christy? Here's something even better. As for that new boyfrend—you can give him presents in fancy bags if you want to, but keep him out of this or you'll never see your sister again.

Her eyes widened. "He saw us at Panera? How is that possible?"

"Good question—and I'll get to it in a minute. Let's see what's inside his package first."

He set the note on the counter, picked up the cardboard, and felt the surface. Instead of cutting the tape, he used the edge of the knife to separate the two stiff sheets and tipped the opening toward the evidence envelope.

Ginny's gold locket slid out.

The one she never took off.

Christy's breath hitched.

"Is this your sister's?" His gentle tone wasn't enough to mitigate the shock.

"Yes. Mom and Dad gave her that on her s-sixteenth birthday. She always wore it. Even when she had to have her appendix out, she refused to take it off."

"What's inside?"

"Photos of our parents."

Again using the tip of the knife, he opened it.

A black *X* was slashed across each of the photos.

The lump in her stomach hardened. "What is that supposed to mean?"

"He could be rubbing in the fact that you're alone to emphasize the importance of playing along with him if you want to keep your remaining family member alive."

"Or . . . ?" There was something he wasn't saying; she could feel it.

"I don't know. I want to think about this. Does that lead to your garage?" He motioned toward a door off to the side of the kitchen.

He was avoiding her question—and she

doubted pushing would get her an answer. "Yes."

"I'd like to take a look in there. Do you have a flashlight?"

"Yes. Why?" She crossed to the sink and pulled one out of the cabinet underneath.

"I have a theory I want to test."

She followed him to the single-car structure, waiting on the threshold as he circled to the back of the Mazda, got down on one knee, and felt around under the wheel well. He repeated the drill on the other side. The next thing she knew, he was lying on his back and scooting under the car.

No wonder the leather jacket was scuffed.

A moment later he stood, a cigarette-sized device in his hand. "GPS, attached magnetically. Our guy's been following your movements on a laptop or PC."

Her stomach bottomed out.

The kidnapper was tracking her?

"Why would he do that?"

Lance bent back down, and when he stood, his hands were empty. "He could be trying to make sure you're following his instructions to leave the cops out of this."

Another *could be*.

Meaning Lance was mulling over other possibilities.

"Let's go back inside where it's warmer." He rejoined her.

She gaped at him. "Are you going to leave that thing on my car?"

Taking her arm, he urged her into the kitchen and closed the door behind them. "If I remove it, he'll know you found it."

"But if he didn't want me to know about it, why mention the incident at Panera?"

"He could be getting cocky. He might also be trying to freak you out by letting you know you're being watched. Based on his note, it appears he bought the boyfriend ruse. I'm also thinking he didn't hear anything about the visits our Rolla agent is paying to the people on your sister's list—none of which have produced any leads yet, by the way. Would you have checked for a GPS device if you hadn't contacted law enforcement?"

"No. I'd have assumed he knew about the bag because he was following me."

"That's why we need to leave the device on the car. We want him to keep thinking you're in the dark about it—which will help keep him in the dark about our involvement. But GPS has its limits. It will tell him where you go, but it won't tell him who you see or what you do once you get there. That means he had to be in the vicinity of Panera the day of the snowstorm."

"There were only a few people in the café, and they were there when I arrived."

"He must have been in the lot. No one followed

you in—but with GPS, he could have shown up later and parked. A car did roll by while we were eating."

Her brain began to shift into analytical mode. "Do you think he could be staying somewhere in town?"

"Yes. The letters have all been mailed from within easy-driving radius of St. Louis, on the weekend. Convenient for a guy who lives and works here."

A surge of hope buoyed her spirits. "Do you think Ginny is here too?"

"Not necessarily."

Her spirits deflated, and she wrapped her arms around herself. "Do you think he's outside now, watching the condo?"

"It's possible."

A shiver rippled through her. "This is getting creepier and creepier."

He touched her arm. Even through the wool of her sweater, she could feel the steadying warmth of his fingers. "Keep hanging in. We'll get this guy eventually. Every time he communicates, we learn new information. Patterns begin to emerge."

"But any of these letters could be the last one." A touch of hysteria raised her pitch. "We could run out of time."

"If he follows his usual routine, we have a week to dig for clues before the next one arrives. I've been putting pressure on the lab at Quantico, and

I think we'll have the DNA results on the body tomorrow. If we get a database match, that will be a powerful lead. And our guy in Rolla could turn up a significant piece of information in one of his interviews." He slid the envelope, note, and locket into evidence envelopes. "I'll send these to the lab tomorrow—and I'll have one of our Evidence Response Team techs swing by here tomorrow night and dust the GPS for prints on the off chance our guy was careless. They can also check the manufacturer and serial number. Sometimes those help us determine who bought the device."

As he jotted some notations on the envelopes, she curled her fingers around the edge of the counter. He was getting ready to leave—and she didn't want him to. Not yet. Not when the kidnapper might be sitting outside her house this very minute, watching her every move.

"Have you had dinner?" The words were out before she could stop them.

Based on his raised eyebrows, the out-of-the-blue question surprised him as much as it did her. "No. I was planning to grab a burger on the way home." He stripped off the gloves.

She tucked her hair behind her ear, taking a quick mental inventory of her fridge. Somehow she doubted an omelet would satisfy the tall FBI agent.

"I, uh, was going to throw together a quick

stir-fry. After all the times I've intruded on your evening plans, the least I can do is feed you dinner."

He hesitated, his expression unreadable.

Maybe he thought she was carrying the boyfriend ruse too far, crossing a personal/professional line.

And maybe she was—because her invitation had been prompted by a far deeper emotion than simple guilt over interrupting his evenings. Perhaps he was picking up on that . . . and her feelings weren't reciprocated.

If he was trying to figure out how to decline without hurting her feelings, she needed to give him an out. It was her fault he was in this awkward situation.

"On second thought . . . heartier fare might suit you better." She kept her tone light and casual. "You strike me as a meat-and-potatoes kind of guy."

"I must admit I never turn down a steak."

"In that case, since I can't offer you a steak . . ."

"But there's more to life than steak, and . . ."

When their comments overlapped, she stopped speaking.

Grinning, he continued. "And I do like a little variety in my menu. Stir-fry sounds great. Much better than fast-food stuff."

As if to reiterate that he was staying, he slid his jacket off.

Wow.

She tried not to stare at the snug, long-sleeved black tee that accentuated amazing abs and the kind of biceps only acquired by serious weight work.

How many hours a week did this guy spend at the gym?

"Where would you like this?" Lance held up his jacket.

She coaxed her lungs to reengage as she took it. "I'll hang it in the coat closet."

"If you'll point the way, I'd like to wash up."

"Down the hall. First door on the right."

They went their separate ways, and as Christy dealt with the jacket, she glanced toward the front door.

Was the kidnapper out there watching—or was he at home, keeping tabs on her movements via computer?

Both possibilities were stomach-churning.

Worse, no matter where he was, the odds were high he was plotting his next move. Planning how he could create more chaos. He might even be thinking about putting her in his cross hairs.

Now that was a chilling thought.

But at least for the next hour or two, she didn't have to worry about her safety.

Because she had a feeling that in a one-on-one battle with Lance McGregor, the kidnapper would find the handsome and very buff FBI agent an unbeatable adversary.

9

Staying for dinner was a mistake.

Lance rinsed his hands in the bathroom sink and tugged the towel off the rack, Mac's and Lisa's warnings echoing in his mind. Not that he needed them. Mixing business and pleasure was never smart. From day one in the military, he'd kept work and play separate. Personal feelings could compromise judgment—and during his years with The Unit, a lapse in judgment could have been deadly.

The same would be true in his FBI career.

So why had he accepted Christy's invitation— especially after he'd looked into her eyes and known it was prompted by more than good manners and gratitude?

He folded the towel, hung it back on the rack, and stared at his reflection in the mirror.

Was it too late to back out?

And if he did, what excuse could he give that would get him off the hook without hurting her feelings, tipping his own hand, or sabotaging his chances with her once this was over?

He leaned on the vanity. You'd think a Delta Force operator who'd had to strategize under the toughest battlefield conditions would be able to come up with an escape plan.

Then again, he'd failed on that score in the not-too-distant past—with tragic results.

A muscle spasmed in his jaw, and he gritted his teeth. After eighteen months, why couldn't he let the memories and the soul-sapping guilt go?

You know why, McGregor.

Exhaling, he closed his eyes.

Yeah, he did.

Because of Debbie—and Josh.

He owed Debbie an explanation . . . and an apology. And until he found the guts to take care of that piece of unfinished business, he wasn't going to be able to put the whole mess to rest. Nor would he be able to pry his personal life out of hold and move forward with it, as he'd moved forward in his career.

Propping one shoulder against the wall, he noted the clear glass bowl of shells on the vanity—the souvenir of some pleasant vacation by the sea, perhaps. A reminder meant to stir up happy memories.

But some memories were best left buried.

At least that's what he'd tried to tell himself all these months, over the protests of his conscience. Through sheer force of will, he'd managed to keep them at bay, to convince himself he was coping fine for the moment and that he'd get around to dealing with all the bad stuff someday.

Then a beautiful figure skater entered his world, and suddenly someday wasn't a fuzzy spot on a distant horizon but looming just ahead.

He reached up and kneaded the back of his neck. Christy might be new in his life, but he had a feeling she could be here to stay. She was nothing like any of the women he'd dated. All the others had been easily forgotten the instant he ended a phone call or dropped them off after an evening of partying.

Not Christy.

From the time he opened his eyes in the morning until he closed them at night, she either dominated his thoughts or hovered around the edges of what-ever else he was thinking about.

As for his dreams—she played a starring role in those too.

At this point, he was having difficulty imagining a future without her.

But there could be no future until he laid the past to rest once and for all.

He gripped the edge of the vanity and studied the solemn man staring back at him in the mirror.

Maybe it was time to take a trip to Virginia.

A muffled clatter of pots sounded in the vicinity of the kitchen, pulling him back to the present. Since he didn't have Superman's ability to rewind the clock to before she'd issued her dinner invitation, his best strategy might be to chow down quickly and make a fast exit. In the interim, he'd keep the conversation light, simple, impersonal. Ask some questions about her skating career, her hobbies, her work. Talk about recent movies, travel, books. Share a few laughs. That should get him through a stir-fry. It wasn't as if this was a multiple-course meal.

Armed with that plan, he joined her in the kitchen.

She gave him a tentative smile, almost as if she knew he'd been having second thoughts about staying. "This won't take long. I've already got the rice cooker going."

"Can I help with anything?"

"That depends. Do you cook?"

"Does adding milk to cereal or dropping a bagel in the toaster count?"

Her lips twitched. "I might have to assign you to cleanup duty instead."

"I can do that."

"I'll keep that in mind—but in the meantime, you don't have to be a cook to chop and dice. How would you like to use that knife for something other than opening envelopes?" She gestured to the wooden rack on the counter.

"I'm good with knives. Just tell me what you want done."

Once she got him started, he launched into topic number one—her job—and by the time savory aromas from the stove were setting off a rumble in his stomach, any lingering tension between them had dissolved.

"If you'd like to set the table, you'll find glasses, utensils, and paper napkins over there." She motioned toward the cabinets beside the sink while she set two plates on the counter and began dishing up the stir-fry.

"Ah. A job that doesn't tax my kitchen skills."

"You did fine with the chopping."

"Don't get too carried away. In general, it would be better—and safer—to assign me to cleanup duty."

"I'll keep that in mind next time."

Next time.

He liked the sound of that . . . once this case was over.

After finishing the table, he got them each a soda. She joined him in the dining area, heaping plates in hand—his piled higher than hers.

"Sorry I couldn't offer you steak, but I do make a mean stir-fry." She set the plates in each place and slid into her chair.

"This looks great. You might even convert me." Not that he'd ever admit that to Lisa after turning up his nose at her ladies-who-lunch place.

He took his own chair, picked up his fork— and froze when Christy bowed her head.

The lady prayed before meals . . . just like he and the rest of the McGregor clan had done during his younger years.

When she lifted her chin and found him watching her, she bit her bottom lip. "I'm sorry if that made you uncomfortable, but I'm used to offering a blessing at meals."

Did he look uncomfortable?

Maybe.

How long had it been since he last thought about saying a prayer before a meal, unless he was home for a visit and his mother or father initiated it?

Too long to remember.

"You didn't make me uncomfortable." He broke eye contact to scoop up a generous mouthful— and to hide that stretch of the truth. "We always prayed at meals when I was growing up. I just got out of the habit."

"How come?"

He chewed slowly, buying himself a few seconds to compose an answer he hoped wouldn't offend her. "It was hard to feel God's presence in some of the situations I was in during my military career."

Her eyebrows rose. "I didn't realize you were in the military. What branch?"

"Special forces."

She stopped eating. "As in SEAL or Delta Force?"

"The latter."

"Wow. I'm impressed. How recently?"

Uh-oh.

A direct answer would lead her to the obvious conclusion: he was an FBI rookie. Might be better to go with vague. If he was lucky, she wouldn't press the issue.

"Very."

She poked at her stir-fry, a hint of wariness in those green irises. "How long have you been with the FBI?"

So much for luck.

He braced. "I finished the Academy in December. I've been in St. Louis since the first of the year."

"You mean . . ." She bit her lip. "Is this your first case?"

He looked at her straight on, his gaze never wavering. "Yes. But I'm well trained and I have plenty of experienced agents to call on if I need help—including a former Hostage Rescue Team operator." He swallowed, then forced out the words he didn't want to say. "However, if you'd rather have a different lead agent on the case, I can talk to my boss."

Several eternal seconds ticked by while the food congealed in his stomach.

At last she forked a piece of chicken. "I expect God knew what he was doing when your receptionist directed my phone call to you."

He let out the breath he hadn't realized he was holding. "I appreciate your confidence."

"I've read about you special forces guys. You're a formidable bunch—on and off the battlefield, I suspect. And your earlier comment about God makes a lot of sense now. War is tough enough for ordinary soldiers, but I imagine you've seen a lot of very bad stuff. I'm sure God can seem far away in those kinds of circumstances. And in the midst of trauma, it can be hard to feel his comfort or hear his direction."

The voice of experience.

Christy might never have been on a battlefield, but she'd known personal tragedy and loss and grief—yet she'd held on to her faith.

"So how did you manage to do it?" The question was out before he could stop it.

If she considered his query too nosey, she gave no indication. "I didn't always succeed. I felt abandoned by God, first after my parents were killed, and again after the fire. But whenever I get depressed or discouraged, I think back to the lesson I learned after my career-ending fall: even if it seems God is ignoring us, he's listening. And when the time is right—his time, not ours—he offers us the guidance we need. Knowing that, believing it with all my heart, has always been a great source of comfort and strength." Her voice was steady, her resolve absolute.

"I envy you that."

"It's yours for the taking if you want it."

"I wish it was that easy."

She speared a piece of broccoli. "I never said it was easy. Most things in life worth having require effort. Maybe you should recultivate that habit of prayer you had growing up. It would be a start, anyway."

"Maybe." But he had a feeling it would take a

lot more than a few words spoken from the heart for him to reconnect with the Almighty.

As if sensing his skepticism—and resistance—Christy switched gears. "You mentioned family. Does that mean you have siblings?"

"Yes." He dived back into his meal. This was a much safer subject. "Two brothers—one older, one younger." He filled her in on their background.

"Talk about an accomplished family." She offered him another piece of bread from the basket she'd set on the table before they began eating. "SEAL turned homicide detective, Delta Force operator turned FBI agent, and Army Ranger. You all make me feel like a slacker."

He buttered his bread. "Are you kidding? We might know how to fight, but none of us would have had the discipline to be an Olympic athlete, even if we'd had the talent—which we didn't."

"I can't speak to the talent part, but from everything I've read about special forces soldiers, discipline is their middle name. Have all of you been to the Middle East?"

He chased an elusive piece of carrot around his plate. "Our missions were classified, so I don't know exactly where Mac and Finn have been. With the current state of world affairs, though, it's a pretty safe bet that if you're in special forces, you've been deployed to that region more than once."

She rested her elbow on the table and propped

171

her chin in her palm. When she spoke again, her tone was more subdued. "You know, I can't even imagine being in some of the situations I've read about in the press. The conflicts over there don't follow most of the traditional rules of engagement. Just distinguishing between allies and enemies seems to be a huge challenge."

Lance stopped pursuing the carrot and set his fork down. How had she managed to home in on the very situation that had led to the trauma he'd been dealing with for the past eighteen months?

When the silence lengthened, she set her own fork down too. "I'm sorry. I can see I touched a nerve."

"It's no big deal." He shrugged, but the stiffness in his shoulders negated his denial. "Every soldier over there ran into those kinds of situations on a regular basis."

"But I expect some were worse than others." Her soft, sympathetic voice was filled with compassion, as if she'd looked into his soul and seen the darkness and pain.

"Yeah." He picked up his soda. Took a long swallow.

Once again the room went silent.

After a few moments, she rose and reached for his empty plate, lightening her tone. "Would you like some coffee? I have a few homemade chocolate chip cookies left from my weekend baking binge."

She was dropping the subject. Moving on to dessert he didn't need.

This is your chance to make that fast exit, McGregor. Take it.

Yet for some reason, other words came out.

"That sounds great. Thanks."

As she returned to the kitchen and busied herself with the dessert preparations, Lance frowned and pulled out his phone. Checking messages would buy him a few minutes to regroup.

But instead of reading emails, he saw only a blur of type as he scrolled through the phone log.

Why in sweet heaven had he stayed?

Sure, he liked being with Christy, and that was a fine incentive to hang around—but the spark of attraction between them wasn't why he'd abandoned his original eat-and-exit plan.

The truth was, he'd lingered because her empathetic eyes and kind, caring manner had sucked him in. Tempted him to dredge up all the ugliness he'd buried in the murkiest corner of his heart for the past year and a half. Encouraged him to trust her with secrets he'd shared with no one. To expose his flaws—and the shame he carried—and see if she could dredge up enough compassion to stick with him or turn away in disgust.

There was a danger in following that inclination, though. If she couldn't live with what he'd done, there was very little chance Debbie would be receptive to his story, either . . . or to his plea for forgiveness. Plus, if Christy did distance herself, if she shut the door on the possibility of a personal relationship, where did that leave him?

A flicker of panic sent a spurt of adrenaline racing through him.

"Do you take cream and sugar?" She called the question through the open shelves that separated the kitchen and dining area.

He looked over. A rectangular ceramic plaque on one of the shelves occupied the spot beside her face, the border design representing spring, summer, fall, and winter. He hadn't noticed it while they ate, but now the six words in the center jumped out at him.

To everything there is a season.

It was a quote from the Bible, that much he knew, though the name of the book eluded him.

"Lance?"

He shifted his attention back to her. "Black."

While she retreated to the kitchen, he reread the words. Wasn't there a line in that passage about a time to kill and a time to heal? About mourning and weeping giving way to joy?

Odd that such a quotation would cross his path tonight, just as he was struggling to decide whether to make the leap that could launch a new season in his life.

Could God's hand be in this . . . or was that a stretch?

His heart said the former; his mind, the latter.

Which should he trust?

Lance leaned slightly sideways to watch while Christy poured their coffee. She added a generous portion of cream and a spoonful of sugar to hers. Cutting the blackness. Tempering the bitterness.

The very thing he needed to do with his past.

But if he took the leap, if he trusted her with his secret, would that lead to healing . . . or more regret?

He had no idea.

She opened a tin of cookies and began to arrange them on a plate. Soon she'd rejoin him. He needed to make a decision. Fast.

All at once, her earlier advice echoed in his mind.

"Maybe you should recultivate that habit of prayer you had growing up."

He'd dismissed that notion at the time. With all his baggage, it would surely take more than a few words to reconnect with the God he'd abandoned long ago on some distant battlefield.

On the other hand, what did he have to lose by attempting to reopen the conversation?

For tonight, though, a simple plea would have to suffice.

Lord, please help me with this decision. And if I end up sharing my story with Christy, I ask that you let her listen with an open and compassionate heart.

10

Christy added the last cookie to the plate, replaced the lid on the tin, and blew out a breath. The dinner had gone so well after those first few awkward minutes—why had she ruined it by dwelling on Lance's combat experience, which he obviously didn't want to discuss?

She risked a peek at him. He was checking messages, brow puckered. He hadn't said a word since she'd come into the kitchen.

Not a positive sign.

Maybe he'd down his coffee in a couple of swigs, grab a cookie or two, and hightail it out of here. Why hang around someone who'd put him on the spot twice tonight, first with her prayer before the meal and then by bringing up the Middle East?

The prayer, she didn't regret.

The other . . . big mistake. She'd read enough about the situation in that part of the world to know it left lasting scars on soldiers—physical, psychological . . . or both.

And it was clear Lance bore his share.

Perhaps the best way to salvage the situation would be to introduce some lighter subjects and hope he hung around through dessert.

Balancing the plate of cookies in one hand, she grabbed his mug with the other and rejoined him.

He slid the phone back on his belt as she approached and inspected the cookies. "Are those really homemade?"

"Yes. My mom's secret recipe. They may not be too healthy, but they're great comfort food."

"I'm all for comfort food." He reached for one.

"Let me grab my coffee and some dessert plates and we'll dive in."

"Would you mind bringing the cream too? I'd like to tone down the black tonight after all."

"Coming right up."

She retrieved the items from the kitchen, keeping tabs on him through the shelving. He hadn't bolted—yet—but his posture was tense.

Because you blew it, Christy. Now see if you can fix the damage.

Pasting on a smile, she set the cream and a plate in front of him and took her seat. Time to introduce a safe and innocuous topic, see if she could get those broad shoulders to relax. "So tell me about your furniture shopping expedition tonight. Sounds like you were having loads of fun."

He took a sip of his lightened brew. "Not. In fact, it bumped winter nighttime surveillance down a notch on my top-ten list of least favorite civilian activities."

Interesting how he'd included the word *civilian*. But no way was she touching that.

"I bet your future sister-in-law wasn't happy about being deserted."

"Lisa's a peach—though if you saw her on the job, you'd never know that. She is one tough lady in uniform. You don't get to be a detective with the Chicago PD or a police chief by being soft." He took a sip of coffee, but his cookie lay untouched on the plate. "You don't get to be a Delta Force operator by being soft, either."

She looked at him over the rim of her mug. Did he *want* to talk about his military career now?

"Is that a warning about your character?" She tried for a teasing tone.

"Only if you're a bad guy—and you're neither." He gave her a quick grin and took a small bite of his cookie.

She sipped in silence. Better to let him take the lead. If he wanted to talk about his military career, fine—but she wasn't about to bring it up again.

After a few moments, he set his half-eaten cookie on the plate and wrapped his fingers around his mug. A thread of tension snaked toward her, and she braced for whatever was coming.

"I noticed your plaque." He indicated the shelves behind her.

She blinked.

He wanted to talk about a plaque?

Not what she'd expected, but hey—at least he was talking, not leaving.

"Thanks. My minister gave it to me after my

accident. I wasn't very receptive to his message at first, but in the end I accepted the truth of it. We do have many seasons in our lives—some happier than others. The important thing to remember on winter days is that spring always comes . . . unless we choose to miss it by hibernating in the darkness. Sometimes we have to make the effort to step into the sunshine."

Some indefinable emotion flared in his eyes. "I wouldn't mind letting some sunshine back into my life."

In the silence that followed, the coffeepot sputtered. The automatic ice maker rattled. The heat kicked on with a subtle hum. All everyday, ordinary sounds.

Yet Christy had a feeling his revelation was anything but ordinary or everyday.

Doing her best to maintain a placid expression, she broke off a bite of her cookie. "It sounds like there's a story there."

"There is. One I've never shared with anyone, except in a formal debrief."

Her heart skipped a beat.

Was he suggesting he wanted to share it with her?

He locked gazes with her and answered that unspoken question. "Would you like to hear it?"

She searched those intense blue irises, seeking —and finding—his motivation.

The attraction between them wasn't one way.

He liked her too. A lot, if he was planning to trust her with his biggest secret, despite their short acquaintance.

Cold, blustery wind might be whistling around the corners of her condo, but warmth overflowed in her heart. "I'd be honored."

He pushed his dessert aside and folded his hands on the table. "There's one other thing you need to know first. I've been thinking a lot lately about an incident that happened a year and a half ago, during a mission. I've always known I'd have to deal with that unfinished business before I could move on with my life, but the need never felt urgent—until I met you. I'm sure you can guess why that is."

Whoa.

Lance McGregor's singular focus and let's-get-the-facts-on-the-table-and-deal-with-them style must apply to his personal as well as his professional life.

Could she be as honest?

Gripping her napkin in her lap, she took a deep breath. "I'm thinking it might have something to do with electricity."

One side of his mouth quirked up. "It has everything to do with electricity. The high-voltage kind." The warmth in his eyes added a few degrees to the heat in the room.

Whew.

With an effort, she restrained the urge to fan

herself. "Since we're being candid . . . you know how I implied to Bob Harris that I'd met a new man? I wasn't lying. He's sitting across from me."

"Nice to know." Then he leaned back, his demeanor sobering. "However, I don't mix business and pleasure. It's not only bad policy, it's dangerous. But I'd like to start laying some groundwork for when this is all over, beginning with the incident in my past. You need to know about it before either of us gets too carried away."

A tingle of apprehension vibrated through her fingertips. "That sounds a little ominous."

"It could be. I'm taking a risk by sharing this . . . but you might as well know about the skeletons in my closet up front and decide now whether they change your feelings about me."

She played with the edge of her napkin. From everything she'd observed, Lance McGregor was the real deal—smart, intuitive, honorable, dedicated. But a person's public persona didn't always match their private face. She'd seen plenty of examples of that in the figure skating world.

Still . . . it was hard to believe there was anything this man could tell her that would be a deal breaker.

"I don't expect that to happen, but I appreciate your honesty and consideration." She knitted her fingers together on the table and gave him her full attention.

"I have to warn you, this isn't pretty."

"I didn't think it would be. But I've seen my share of ugly."

"Not like this."

"I think it's too late to back out, don't you?"

He conceded her point with a dip of his head and stared into his mug. "As I told you, most of my military work was classified—including this mission. I can't give you details on dates or locations, but suffice it to say we did a lot of counterterrorism work all over the world that involved snatching insurgency leaders. This particular situation, like most of our missions, was dicey, but it wasn't one of our more dangerous assignments. The guy wasn't all that important and shouldn't have been heavily guarded. Plus, the person on the inside who'd provided the intel was supposed to be an ally."

Shouldn't have been.

Supposed to be.

Those were telling words.

Christy tightened her clasped fingers.

"I was heading up a four-man team. My second-in-command was a buddy from my original training class. Taz. We'd been on a lot of missions together, and over the years we became as close as brothers. I was the best man at his wedding." Lance stopped, and his Adam's apple bobbed. "Our mission that night proceeded according to plan until we got within sight of the walled compound where our target was supposed to be holed up. Then all at once, Taz got cold feet. That had never happened before."

She leaned forward. "What do you mean, cold feet?"

The parallel crevices imbedded in his brow deepened. "He said he had a bad feeling about the mission. No real specifics, other than the place seemed too quiet. There weren't even any barking dogs—and there were always barking dogs. I agreed the silence was suspicious . . . but he also had a pregnant wife at home. I suspected he was overreacting, maybe starting to worry about not being there for his kid."

"That seems like a logical assumption."

"Yeah. Except I didn't have a warm and fuzzy feeling about the situation, either. But I wasn't certain if he'd planted a seed of doubt or if my own instincts were kicking in. Plus, I'd done back-to-back missions and hadn't slept in twenty-four hours. Usually I trusted my gut, but for the first time in my career, I wavered over a command decision."

"Fatigue can muddle thinking."

He dismissed her comment with an impatient wave. "I'd pulled off plenty of missions with less sleep. It shouldn't have made a difference. I did get a read from the two other guys on the team. Neither had any qualms. They just wanted to get in and out ASAP so we'd be back on base for breakfast."

Christy didn't know what was coming, but she had a feeling none of them got their breakfast.

"In the end, I was spooked enough to radio our commander. He assured me the inside source was trustworthy, that the guy was solid and had come through for us on other occasions. Armed with that validation, I dismissed Taz's qualms—and my own—and gave the order to move in."

The coffeepot hissed in the charged silence, and Christy's hand jerked.

Lance didn't seem to notice.

"At first, everything went according to plan. We got into the compound with no resistance—but once we were inside the walls, chaos erupted. Turns out the guy we were after knew all about our plan and had some serious firepower waiting to welcome us. Instead of the guard or two we were expecting, a dozen armed zealots met us. If we hadn't been so well trained and equipped, none of us would have gotten out alive. As it was, one of my guys took a bullet in the leg in the first few seconds."

"What did you do?" Her question came out in a whisper.

"What we were trained to do." His jaw hardened. "We returned fire. Fortunately, the injured guy was able to function, but it was touch and go. We were operating in the dark—literally. And NVGs don't offer much peripheral vision."

Christy ran the acronym through her brain. Came up blank. "What's an NVG?"

"Night vision goggles. We were all wearing them. In the chaos, everyone but Taz missed the guy sneaking up on us. Just as the insurgent lifted his AK-47, Taz put himself between me and the gun and started firing. He took the guy out . . . and got sprayed in the process."

An AK-47 was a machine gun, wasn't it?

And no one survived a head-on assault from a machine gun. Even someone wearing body armor.

A bead of sweat broke out on Lance's forehead, and she was tempted to gently wipe it away. Instead she watched her clenched knuckles turn white.

"As you probably figured out, he didn't make it." Lance's words rasped, and he cleared his throat. "Taz died saving the life of the friend who ignored his reservations and gave the order that sent him to his death."

This time her hand refused to be restrained. It broke free and came to rest on his taut forearm. Yet words failed her. What was there to say in the face of such tragedy?

He turned to her, and the bleakness in his eyes twisted her stomach. "I should have listened to him—and my gut. As the team leader, I had the authority to override command and call off the raid. I chose not to." A spasm tightened his features, and he stopped.

Christy waited, knowing there was more, giving him a chance to regain his composure.

When he continued, the words were scored with self-recrimination. "Here's the worst of it—my mission earlier in the day had been a bust. The guy we were after slipped out right under our noses . . . and I didn't want to come back empty-handed again. I was caught up in that whole macho, elite warrior image. I wanted to redeem myself and return the conquering hero." He blew out a breath, nostrils flaring. "I swore when I got into The Unit I'd never let my ego get out of control, but it happened. And Taz paid the price with his life while I escaped with six stitches." He brushed his fingers over the small jagged scar on his temple.

As his confession hung in the air between them, Christy tried to think of some response. But before she could come up with one, Lance continued in a flat, cold voice. "Those bullets were meant for me, and I should have been the one to die, not him. At least I wouldn't have left behind a pregnant wife and a son who would never know his father."

As his words echoed in the hushed room, she closed her eyes. Lance was right. The story was ugly—and tragic. She couldn't begin to imagine what that young wife must have gone through.

But did Lance deserve the full brunt of blame he'd carried all these months? Yes, he'd been the team leader. Yes, he'd made the call to carry out the mission despite his qualms. Yet he'd checked back with his command, expressed concern. Should he have pushed back? Maybe. Was hisego a factor in the tragedy, as he claimed? Possibly. Special forces command would want operators with strong, confident personalities—and that self-assurance and decisive temperament no doubt worked to their advantage in most situations.

That night had been the exception.

That night, it had sent them into a deathtrap.

"Would you like to hear the end of the story?" Lance's tone was as colorless as his face.

She nodded, afraid to trust her voice.

"We were able to hold them off and radio for help, and once the helos started coming in, the couple of insurgents who were still on their feet made an unsuccessful run for it. My buddy was the only American casualty. The other side didn't fare as well. Let's just say we didn't leave any witnesses behind."

The hard, take-no-prisoners edge to his voice revealed a new side of Lance. It was the voice of a soldier who accepted tough assignments, who carried out deadly missions, who showed no pity for those who opposed him.

It was the voice of a man who did his duty, no matter the cost—and who took full responsibility for the outcome, good or bad.

With trembling fingers, Christy lifted her mug and took a sip.

The brew had turned tepid.

"I shocked you, didn't I?" His features were incised with grief . . . apprehension . . . and perhaps a touch of resignation?

"I don't know if *shock* is the right word." She spoke slowly, struggling to digest everything he'd told her. "Blindsided might be more accurate."

"I wish I could change the ending of that story, Christy. Go back and make a different decision. I would if I could." His anguished words were laced with regret. "But all operators have a certain sense of invincibility, and despite the bad vibes, I was sure four guys from The Unit could best whoever was in that dilapidated compound. It was a bad call."

He stopped. Pressed a finger against a stray crumb on the table. When he lifted it, pulverized powder clung to his skin. "The harsh truth is, a good man died in my place because I let my ego override my instincts. I had the authority to call off the raid, and I didn't. I'll carry that burden of blame for the rest of my life—and I can't fault you if hearing my story is a game changer."

It was a statement, not a question, spoken in a stoic tone. As if he assumed she'd blame him for the death of his friend too.

Did she?

She took another sip of the cooling coffee. There was culpability, certainly, based on his

188

explanation of the events. Yet his remorse was real—and shouldn't that mitigate guilt?

All at once the man beside her started to rise.

"Wait!" She touched his arm.

He paused and looked at her.

Now what?

She went with the first thought that came to mind. "Did your buddy's wife blame you?"

"I don't know."

She frowned. "You've never talked to her?"

"I attended the funeral, but Debbie was too grief-stricken to hold a lucid conversation. I was planning to talk to her before I shipped back out, but on the way home from the burial, she went into premature labor and had to be rushed to the hospital. The emergency didn't get resolved until after I left. I did start a few letters, but they ended up in the trash. I couldn't find the words."

"You found them with me."

"You didn't lose the man you loved."

"No—but you still took a risk sharing the story with me . . . and it paid off."

Caution warred with hope in his eyes. "That incident isn't the best character reference, Christy."

"I don't think the man sitting here is the same man who led his team into the compound that night. I have a feeling this is a new and improved version."

"I'd like to think that's true."

She leaned toward him. "Besides, I have a feeling the old version wasn't as bad as you made him out to be. You were sleep deprived that night, and while you might have thought you were impervious to the effects of fatigue, you probably weren't. I also know you wouldn't have been put in a leadership position with an elite special forces unit if you hadn't demonstrated sound judgment under pressure. I'm not saying your ego didn't get in the way—but how many times in your military career did that same ego, that same confidence, save your life and the lives of others?"

His expression grew pensive. "I suppose that's a valid point."

"Also, I can't begin to imagine the stress of operating in the kind of situations you described. And you did that every day, mission after mission. Who am I to judge the choices you made under such intense pressure? But I'm confident of one thing—you did the best you could under the circumstances that night . . . and that's all anyone can ask."

"The Unit is held to higher standards than anyone else."

"Including God's? Because all he asks is that we do our best."

His half smile held little humor. "Some of the higher-ups have very inflated opinions of themselves—and expect perfection."

"Are you saying you were reprimanded over the outcome?"

"On the contrary. We were commended for cleaning out a nasty den of insurrection in the face of overwhelming odds, despite being set up. But I suspect Debbie would feel differently if she knew the whole story."

Ah. The missing piece. He needed his buddy's wife to absolve him from guilt—or at the very least, forgive him—in order to find closure.

"Maybe it's time you found out."

He picked up his half-eaten cookie and broke off a dangling chocolate chip. "As a matter of fact, I'm considering a quick weekend trip east once this case wraps up. But the truth is, it would be easier to face another walled compound than have a heart-to-heart with Debbie."

"Exposing yourself to physical danger requires a different kind of courage than putting your heart at risk. But if you can do it with me, you can do it with her."

His smile crinkled the skin at the corners of his eyes and produced an endearing dimple. "You're very good at pep talks."

"I should be. I heard a lot of them from coaches during my skating career, and I've given myself plenty over the past few months." She peeked into his mug. "Would you like a warm-up?"

"You've already given me that." He held her gaze for a sizzling, lung-locking moment, then ate the other half of the cookie in one large bite and brushed off his fingers. "I need to go. It's getting late, and I don't want to overstay my welcome."

Not going to happen—but she kept that to herself. There'd been enough soul-baring for one night.

He rose and picked up his plate. "I'll help with the cleanup first, though."

She stood, too, and took the plate from his hand. "There isn't much. Besides, you've had a long day and you still have to drive home. Why don't I take a rain check on that offer?"

"Thanks. And I won't forget. I pay my debts."

A man of honor, through and through—even about the little things.

Nice.

She retrieved his jacket and met him in the hall, holding it up for him to slip his arms through.

"Now that we know our kidnapper is monitoring your movements, I want you to take extra precautions." He tucked the evidence envelopes inside his jacket. "No deserted parking lots at night. If you work late, have someone escort you to your car. No malls after dark. No solitary walks. Okay?"

The present reality crashed back over her, and she wrapped her arms around herself, suppressing a shudder as fear once again began lapping at the edges of her composure.

"Don't worry, I'll be very careful. I'm totally creeped out by this."

"If you see or hear or feel anything that makes you nervous, call me—day or night. Trust your instincts."

"I will."

"Is your phone GPS equipped?"

"Yes, but it's turned off. The guy at the store told me it sucks battery life."

"Turn it on for now. You never know when it might come in handy." He pulled the door open, but instead of leaving, he swiveled back to her. "In case we're being watched, let's make sure our guy continues to believe the boyfriend ruse."

Before she had a chance to react, he wrapped her in his strong arms and pressed her cheek against the scuffed leather of his jacket.

And he didn't let go any too fast.

When at last he pulled back, she couldn't tell if the shivers racing through her were the result of the cold wind whipping in from outside or the adrenaline rush of knowing that this time, there was more to his hug than mere playacting.

"As soon as I have any information from the lab about the DNA from the body, I'll call. Hopefully tomorrow." He turned up the collar of his jacket.

"I'll be waiting to hear."

He hesitated, as if he was as reluctant to leave as she was to see him go. "Thanks for dinner—and for being so understanding."

"Thank *you* for being so honest about us . . . and for trusting me with your story."

"You're easy to trust." With a lift of his hand, he retreated down the sidewalk. Only after he slid into his car did she shut and lock the door. Then she wandered back to the dining room and surveyed the table.

Just two cookies had been taken from the serving plate. Hers lay mostly untouched. Lance's was gone. Both mugs were half full of coffee.

Not much of a dessert party.

Then again, it was hard to get in the mood for sweets while tragedy unfolded.

Yet strangely enough, life felt sweeter than it had in a long while. Despite all her losses, despite the renewed trauma with Ginny, despite the sometimes oppressive quiet of her solitary home, she felt less alone.

Of course, this thing with Lance could peter out. Hormone-charged infatuations didn't always last—and enchanted evenings, falling in love with strangers across crowded rooms, didn't happen in real life. Not in *her* real life, anyway.

But perhaps tonight was the beginning of a new season—for both of them.

She picked up his mug and plate, pausing to reread the plaque the minister had given her while she'd been struggling to decide whether to leave competitive skating behind. How often during the intervening years had she turned to that beautiful passage in Ecclesiastes for hope and comfort and encouragement? And always, she came away renewed and receptive to the promise of brighter days ahead.

Lance had made his intentions clear tonight, and she appreciated his candor. They were too old for the game-playing of adolescent dating. He'd set the stage to see where the potent electricity between them might lead once this case was over and Ginny was safely back—*please, God, let that happen!*

In the meantime, she planned to do exactly what her dinner companion had suggested—be extra careful and watch her back.

Because with a man like Lance waiting in the wings, she didn't want some understudy stepping into her role.

11

"You're in luck, Agent McGregor. I've got a CODIS match for you."

As the crime lab tech in Quantico bypassed a greeting and got straight to business, Lance leaned forward in his desk chair.

They had a hit in the National Missing Person DNA database.

What a great start to a Wednesday.

"Who is it?" He shifted the phone to his other ear and grabbed a pen.

"A woman by the name of Tammy Lee. Do you want the contact information and report number from NamUs?"

Nice of the tech to save him that step. "Sure. Thanks."

He jotted down the information from the National Missing and Unidentified Persons System as the man dictated it. The report had been filed with the St. Louis city cops. Excellent. That would simplify follow-up.

Thirty minutes later, after a quick conversation with the detective who'd handled the case, a fax of the report was printing out.

Mark joined him in the copy room, a sheaf of papers in hand as he headed toward one of the machines. "Anything new on the kidnapping case?"

"Your timing's impeccable. We just got a match on the DNA." Lance retrieved the last page as the report finished printing and filled him in on the ME's call.

"And what does that have to say about Tammy Lee?" Mark waved a hand toward the document as he set his stack of papers in the feeder.

Lance scanned the report. "Age twenty-one, five-six, one-fifteen, long blonde hair, blue eyes. Disappeared the night before the Ginny Reed house fire. Profession is listed as escort."

"A hooker." Mark arched an eyebrow. "Interesting."

"But logical. A lot of those women lose contact with their families, so who would know if they disappeared? Not much chance any of their pimps would file a missing person report and risk prosecution."

"Then who put out the alert?"

"A Brenda Rose. She listed herself as a roommate—and friend."

"Friend for sure. She took a chance by coming forward."

"Yeah. The two of them must have been close."

"She offer any theories about the disappearance?" Mark pulled out a stack of copies and rapped them into alignment.

Lance sped-read the write-up. "She says the night Tammy disappeared, she had an appointment with a guy she'd seen the prior week. They were supposed to connect at a place called the Wild Duck." He shot his colleague a questioning look.

"A hot spot on the East Side. Known as a meeting place for rendezvous of the less genteel kind." Mark removed the rest of his copies from the machine. "Did Brenda leave any contact information?"

"A phone number."

"Good luck with that. Assuming it's legit, odds are the phone's a throwaway and is long gone."

"It's only been two months since the fire. It could still be in service."

"If it's not, some of the vice guys in the city might know her whereabouts."

"A working number would be easier—and faster."

"Who knows? You might get lucky. Keep me in the loop." He stopped in the doorway as he exited. "I know you're still settling in and dealing with a hot case, but don't let the SWAT team drop off your radar."

"I won't." No need to tell him the SWAT team wasn't even *on* his radar.

With a mock salute, Mark disappeared out the door.

Report in hand, Lance returned to his office, pulled out his cell, and weighed it in his hand. Caller ID spoofing program or *67? Both would hide the source of the call if Brenda's pimp happened to be monitoring her phone—but chances were the guy was little league and not all that sophisticated. The *67 strategy should suffice.

Taking his seat, he keyed in the masking code, followed by Brenda's number.

Three rings in, he expected the call to roll to voice mail. Instead, it kept ringing.

Four rings later, a groggy female voice greeted him. " 'Lo."

Lance twisted his wrist. Maybe calling someone in Brenda's profession at eight-thirty in the morning hadn't been the smartest move.

"Brenda Rose?"

"Yeah." A yawn came over the line. "Who's this?"

"Are you alone?"

"Yeah. And I was sound asleep." Irritation sharpened her words. "Who is this?"

"Special Agent Lance McGregor with the FBI. I'm calling in reference to the missing person report you filed two months ago for Tammy Lee."

A gasp came over the line. "Did you find her?"

"I'd prefer to discuss this in person—ASAP. Pick a time and place and I'll meet you."

"Look, I don't want any trouble, okay?" An anxious note crept into her voice. "From you or . . . or anyone else."

Like her pimp.

He changed his tone from crisp to cordial. "Making trouble for you isn't on my agenda. We appreciate that you filed this report. It could help us with more than one case. I just need to ask a few questions."

"Can't you do that by phone?"

Yeah, he could—but it wasn't as informative as looking someone in the eye and watching body language.

"In person is better." Especially since she was the sole connection they had to Ginny's stand-in.

Clues weren't exactly pinging off the walls; he needed to milk this for all it was worth.

"Okay. Fine. Four o'clock. Edy's Ice Cream in Union Station."

Walking distance from his office.

Perfect.

"Watch for the guy in the leather jacket."

"I thought FBI agents always wore suits?" Wariness crept into her voice.

"Not if we want to avoid attracting attention. But I'll be happy to wear my suit if you prefer."

"No, no. That's okay. Low-key is better."

No surprise she'd backpedaled. "See you at four."

"I'll be there." The line went dead.

Slowly Lance replaced the receiver. Hard to say whether she'd show—but if she'd cared enough to put her neck on the line with her pimp by making the report in the first place, she'd probably follow through.

If she didn't?

He had other ways to track her down—and if necessary, he'd use every one.

Nathan opened his eyes. Sniffed.

Something was burning.

He swung his feet to the floor and stood, the mattress creaking as he snatched his jeans from the chair beside the bed.

The old woman must be cooking.

He thrust his legs into the denim, unlocked the door, and raced down the hall to the kitchen.

From the doorway, he took in the scene in one quick sweep.

A faint haze hovered inches below the ceiling. His grandmother was waving her hands to disperse it, like she'd done in Baščaršija Square during their family trip to Sarajevo years ago. That spot had definitely lived up to its Pigeon Square nickname—and she was having no more success getting rid of the smoke than she'd had shooing away the pesky birds.

The apartment would stink all day.

He glared at her. "What did you burn this time?"

At his terse question, she twisted toward him. Gasped. Winced. "Bread." Her reply came out more quaver than word as she gripped her ribs.

He moved beside her, grabbed the charred piece of toast that lay on the counter, and crushed it in his hand, letting the burnt crumbs tumble into the sink. "I do the cooking. You know that. Why didn't you eat some cereal?"

"Gone." She pointed to a box on the counter.

He frowned. Picked it up. Shook it. Hadn't he bought cereal last week?

No, maybe not. His mind had been on more important priorities than grocery shopping lately. They'd run out of milk yesterday too.

Not that he intended to acknowledge his lapse.

Turning, he scowled at her. "Have you been eating more than usual?"

"No, no!" She shrank back, fear darting through her eyes.

"Why didn't you wait for me to make breakfast?"

"I hungar."

So what else was new? She was always hungry.

Still . . . it was after ten. Past breakfast—unless you'd worked the night shift.

His scowl deepened. All these late fill-in hours thanks to Dennis's broken leg were playing havoc with his efforts to monitor Christy's activities. And watching her squirm had been one of the pleasures he'd most looked forward to while making his plans. It wasn't fair that he was missing out on half the fun.

He yanked open a cabinet, reached in, and grabbed a pot. "Sit down. I'll fix you some oatmeal."

The old woman remained motionless.

He took a step toward her. "If you want to eat, sit. Otherwise, you can wait until lunch."

She shuffled to the table and sat.

Better.

She needed to remember who was in charge. He chose what she ate—and who cared if she disliked oatmeal? After stinking up the kitchen, she didn't deserve to be coddled.

"I'll be gone the rest of the day and won't be home till late." He dropped the pot with a loud clatter onto the chipped counter. "Your food will be in the refrigerator. Don't touch anything else. You understand me?"

"Da."

He glowered at her, and she cringed.

"Yes. Yes."

"After all these years, your English is pathetic." He shook some oatmeal into the pot with more force than necessary, added water. "Why do you hang on to the language of a country that treated you like dirt? That killed your husband and daughter-in-law and grandson? That forced you to flee to a foreign land that also treated you like dirt?"

She remained silent.

Banging the pot onto the stove, he watched her flinch. "And how did you and Tata cope with this new country? The respected businessman became a janitor who spent his free time in a drunken stupor and walked in front of a bus on his way home from a bar one night without a thought for the son he left behind. You were no better. Did you ever care that your drinking—and neglect— were the reasons I got carted off to that foster home and was forced to live with strangers who cared more about the government check that came every month than about me?"

He twisted on the burner, watching the fire shoot up around the bottom of the pot. Like he'd watched those flames in November, through his binoculars, listening to the dried-out wood crackle as Ginny Reed's house was consumed.

But the best moment of all had been the screams.

Christy's screams.

And there were more to come.

The old woman coughed, a harsh, grating hack she tried to stifle.

He turned to her. "You didn't understand half of what I said, did you?"

"Yes."

"No, you didn't. But it doesn't matter. I survived, no thanks to you."

Or Christy.

Who knew where he might be if she hadn't abandoned him, like everyone else had?

But she was paying for her betrayal now—just like the old woman.

The oatmeal behind him started to sputter, and he reached for a spoon to stir it. Silence fell in the apartment, which suited him fine. What could Mevlida say in response to his rant, even if she'd understood it? Everything he'd said was true. Thanks to her and Christy, he'd ended up no better than his old man, working a crummy job and living in a mouse-infested apartment. Who wouldn't want to escape a fate like this?

But unlike Tata and Baka, he'd found something better than alcohol to soften the harsh edges of his life, despite the occasional beer he allowed himself.

Nathan picked up the pot, dumped the lumpy oatmeal in a bowl, and set it in front of his grandmother.

She bent over the bowl and began scooping up the thick, unappetizing paste. Milk and sugar would make it more palatable, but she could eat it plain today. He owed her nothing. No kindness, no consideration, no compassion. She should be grateful he'd rescued her from the rehab place after she broke her hip instead of letting her go back to the series of homeless shelters she'd lived in for who knew how long.

Reminding her of that—and tossing out the occasional threat to throw her back out on the street if she started complaining—was all it took to keep her in line.

He dropped the sticky pot in the sink and crossed the room. "Don't forget to clean up after you're finished."

She lifted her head and met his gaze. The abject sorrow in her eyes, the desolation and grief, were profound enough to touch the hardest of hearts.

But they didn't reach his.

Not even close.

On the contrary.

Her misery was like a tonic. It meant he'd accomplished what he'd set out to do when he'd taken her in.

He was in control of her life—and that kind of

power made up for a lot of his other disappointments.

Now he was exerting the same power over Christy. Calling the shots. Throwing her world into turmoil. He didn't have total control yet . . . but he was close.

And once he got it, he intended to enjoy every minute.

No one by the name of Brenda Rose had shown up in any of the databases Lance checked, but he had no problem spotting her the instant she came within sight of the Edy's Ice Cream shop.

Though she'd toned down her working attire, the too-short skirt, calf-hugging boots, mane of blonde hair, and smoky eye makeup broadcast her profession as clearly as a PA announcement.

He remained behind a pillar when she stopped in front of the deserted ice cream shop, scanning the sparse crowd at Union Station. At least she'd shown up. Now he needed her to reveal some helpful piece of information she'd neglected to include in the missing person report.

Once he was confident she hadn't been followed, he stepped out from his concealed position and strolled toward her.

She stopped pacing as soon as she caught sight of him.

"Brenda Rose, I presume." He discreetly offered his creds.

She gave them no more than a quick glance. "You aren't what I expected." Tipping her head, she gave him a brazen once-over. "Are all FBI agents so sexy?"

He ignored that. "Let's sit over there." Indicating a bench off to the side, away from the main concourse, he led the way, waiting until she was seated before claiming the far end.

"A gentleman too. That's nice." She offered him one of her business smiles.

He ignored that as well. "Let's talk about Tammy."

"Did you find her?"

"Yes."

"Is she . . . is she okay?"

"No. I'm sorry. She died the day after she disappeared."

The color drained from her face. "I was afraid of that."

"Why?"

"She would never have taken off without telling me. Everyone knew that—including my . . . boss. He assumed she'd told me her plans, and he tried hard to get me to talk. But I didn't know anything." She hunched forward and picked at the chipped crimson nail polish on her thumb.

Lance studied her. Despite the makeup, she didn't look more than nineteen or twenty. Just a kid who should be going to college and fretting over choosing a major instead of worrying about keeping her pimp happy.

He softened his tone. "My interrogation methods aren't painful."

"That's a nice change." Moisture filmed her eyes as she stroked a yellowish patch of skin on her wrist. "Was Tammy . . . was it murder?"

"That's our conclusion."

Her nostrils flared. "Why would someone do that?"

"To cover up another crime."

"How did she . . . what happened?"

"There was a fire." Close enough. The body had been too badly burned and decayed for the ME to determine cause of death, but most likely fire hadn't taken her life. Odds were she had been dead before it ever started.

A shudder swept over her. "What a terrible way to go. And she was so pretty . . ."

As her words trailed off, Lance angled toward her. "I read the missing person report. I was hoping you could give me a few more details."

"I told that cop everything I know."

"There's nothing in there about Tammy's background or next of kin."

She shrugged. "I don't know much about either."

"I thought you said you were close."

"We were, but we didn't share everything. All I know is she had some problems in high school—

drinking, smoking pot. Her old man was the straight-arrow type, and he threatened to turn her over to the state if she messed up again. When she did, he kept his word—and she ran away. There aren't many options to earn a living when you're fifteen and homeless, if you know what I mean."

Yeah, he knew. The vast majority of teens who ended up on the street got involved in prostitution, drugs, gangs, stealing, pornography—or all of the above.

"I get the picture."

"I figured you would. Look . . ." She leaned closer. "You aren't going to bust me, are you? I stuck my neck out going to the cops and meeting you today."

"That's not why I'm here. I'm only interested in Tammy. Tell me about this guy she was meeting for the second time."

After searching his face, Brenda relaxed back against the bench. "We didn't talk a lot about our customers. Mostly we tried not to think very much about them before, during, or after, you know? But this guy was different. She said he treated her nice, that he wasn't just interested in her body. He asked a bunch of questions about her, like he really cared. She even told him a little about how she ended up on the street, which blew me away."

Their guy was smart. He'd won Tammy's trust and persuaded her to open up. Once she'd told him she was estranged from her family—meaning no relative would know if she went missing—she'd sealed her fate. The killer had found the perfect candidate to make disappear.

Except he hadn't counted on a friend going to the police.

"Did she describe him?"

"Not in a lot of detail. He was medium height, like five-eight or nine, and in good shape—a rarity, believe me."

"What color hair?"

"Black. And he had dark eyes too. She also liked how he talked. Said it was different. Like he wasn't from the Midwest."

That could be helpful.

"What was different about it? Did she describe it as a Southern drawl, a Texas twang, anything like that?"

"No. She said he sounded high class. Spoke real precise. And there was a tiny accent she couldn't place."

Someone who had learned English as a second language, perhaps?

"Did he tell her anything about himself?"

"No. Most guys don't. She was just glad he treated her nice. She was looking forward to seeing him again." Brenda bit her lip. "Do you think he was the guy who killed her?"

"It's a strong possibility. Do you know where they went?"

"No. The first night, he took her to a motel

south of the city. Some place she'd never been to before. She didn't tell me the name, but it sounded like a dive. The walls were real thin, and she said the sheets were frayed at the edges." Brenda shrugged. "She didn't complain, so I guess the company made up for the location. The second time, they met on the East Side."

"At the Wild Duck."

"Yeah. That was in my report. I don't know where they went from there."

"Does your . . . boss know?"

Panic whipped across her face. "No. This was a side job. Tammy picked guys up herself sometimes, even though it was dangerous. She wanted to keep more of the profits from her jobs."

So contacting the pimp would be useless.

Another dead end.

He pulled a card from his pocket and held it out to her. "If you happen to think of anything else that might help us identify this guy, I'd appreciate a call. You can reach me day or night on my cell."

She folded her hands in her lap as she inspected the card. "I can't take that. The wrong person might see it."

He flicked a glance at the fading bruise on her wrist and repocketed the card. "You can always call me at the main FBI number."

"Or on your cell." She recited the number on the card back to him. "I'm good at memorizing."

"I'm impressed."

A cloud passed over her eyes. "About one thing, anyway." She stood and tugged at the hem of her skirt. "I might check in with you in a couple of weeks, see if you found out what happened to Tammy. She may not have been the girl next door, but she sure didn't deserve to end up murdered."

Lance rose too. "Can I buy you an ice-cream cone before you leave?"

She did a double take. "Why?"

Because it's the least I can do to thank you for the risk you took coming forward. Because you seem like you could use a friend. Because I wish I could do more to help young women in your situation.

But he said none of those things.

"Why not?"

She chewed on her lower lip. "Are you having one?"

"Yes."

She eyed the storefront with the tubs of colorful ice cream, then lifted one shoulder. "Okay. Sure."

He followed her over, waiting while she vacillated between butter pecan and double fudge brownie. Finally he stepped in.

"One scoop of each for the lady." He handed the clerk some cash.

"You don't have to buy me a double." Brenda's protest was halfhearted at best.

"It's my pleasure."

Lance ordered his cone, and silence fell while

the woman behind the counter scooped out their selection and handed them each a cone.

Lance dug into his at once.

Brenda followed more slowly, watching him.

Grinning, he waved his paper napkin at her. "Do I have chocolate chips on my chin?"

She gave him a melancholy smile. "No. I was just thinking how nice this feels. How normal. A guy out for ice cream with his girl." She sighed. "Thanks for giving me a few minutes of pretend."

"You could make it real if you wanted to."

"Yeah?" She snorted. "What kind of decent guy would want a girl with a past like mine?"

If there was an upbeat response to that question, it eluded him.

"See what I mean?" She pasted on her professional smile again, tossed her hair, and lifted her cone. "Cheers, Lance McGregor. Now you go back to your world and I'll go back to mine."

With that, she sauntered down the mall toward the exit, hips swaying as she licked her ice cream.

Lance took a few more swipes of his, then pitched it in the trash container before following her out. There wasn't much he could do for the Brenda Roses of the world, short of making this one feel for a brief moment that she had more to offer than their body.

Unfortunately, Tammy Lee's killer understood the power of that approach too—and had used it to manipulate rather than brighten a day.

Thanks to Brenda, however, he had a better feel for who that killer might be: a dark-haired, well-built, medium-height man with a slight accent who might not be American born.

It wasn't much, but every piece of new information helped.

And before this day was over, he intended to run that description by Christy and pass it on to the Rolla agent so he could recontact the subjects he'd interviewed. See if the new information produced any names of possible suspects.

Because a man who fit that description, who'd lured Tammy Lee to her death, was also the man who'd kidnapped Ginny Reed and created the elaborate ruse that continued to baffle him. As Christy had said early on, why would someone go to such effort to disguise a kidnapping with a fire and a fake victim, only to undo all that effort two months later?

The answer to that question would lead them to the kidnapper . . . but so far, none of the few puzzle pieces they'd uncovered were fitting together.

Worst of all, he had a feeling time was running out to complete the picture. That unless they solved this soon, Ginny and Tammy Lee weren't going to be their quarry's only victims.

And as he pushed through the door into the numbing chill of a dark winter evening, that possibility made his blood run cold.

12

"You up for ditching this place for an hour and grabbing some lunch? I have a buy one, get one half price coupon for Ruby Tuesday."

Christy glanced up from her desk as Sarah waved a slip of paper at her from the doorway of the cubicle. "I wish I could, but this is due back at the printer by three o'clock and I'm barely halfway through."

"What is it?"

"The summer youth program proof."

"Already? It's only the end of January."

"We always get them out four months ahead—and I'm behind."

"That's not like you." Her friend entered and dropped into the chair beside the desk. "Then again, nothing's been exactly usual in your world of late, has it? Bob told me about his visitor. When you said last week there'd been a major glitch in your life, you must not have been kidding."

Her friend's tone was conversational, but the slight quiver of hurt tugged at Christy's conscience. "I wanted to tell you about it." She lowered her volume and leaned forward. "But until they figure out what's going on, they thought it would be safer to clue in as few people as possible."

"Of course. I understand."

No, she didn't, based on that glib, too-bright reply. And the last thing Christy wanted to do was lose her best friend over this.

"Look, there's a lot more to this than anyone knows." All at once, pressure built behind her eyes, misting her vision, and she groped for a tissue from the box on her desk.

"Hey." Sarah touched her hand, her tone contrite. "I'm sorry. I didn't mean to come across as miffed. It sounds like you're under plenty of stress without me adding to it."

True. But what harm could there be in sharing a bit of the story?

Christy rose and did a 360 over the tops of the low-walled cubes. The place was deserted. Everyone else must have gone out to lunch.

Perfect.

She sat down and rolled her chair closer to Sarah. "I *am* under a lot of stress. What exactly did Bob tell you?"

"Not a lot. He just said somebody was hassling you. But I didn't understand why the FBI was involved instead of the police."

"Because the investigation isn't about harassment." She dropped her voice to a whisper. "This has to stay between us, okay?"

The other woman nodded.

"The body in my sister's house didn't belong to Ginny."

Sarah's eyes widened. "Oh my word." She breathed, rather than spoke, the shocked phrase. "Who *did* it belong to? And where's your sister?"

Christy hesitated. Should she tell her Lance had called yesterday with an ID on the body?

No.

There were too many details they didn't yet know.

"They're working on those questions now."

"I had no idea something this . . . bizarre . . . was going on." Sarah gripped her hand.

"Bizarre is an appropriate word for it."

"Is there anything I can do to help?"

"Just keep being my friend."

"Count on it. And I won't ask any more questions after this one. Do you feel everything that can be done *is* being done and that the people handling this are competent?"

Christy summoned up a smile. "That's two questions, but the answer to both is yes. The agent who's been assigned to the case is sharp and dedicated. He's on it."

Sarah squinted at her. "Is this the guy you were referring to last week when you said meeting him was good even if the reason wasn't?"

No surprise her romantic friend would remember that.

"Yes."

"Still feel the same?"

"More so."

"Well, that's one positive outcome from this mess, anyway." She stood and tucked the coupon in the pocket of her slacks. "This doesn't expire for a month; we'll use it after things quiet down. Deal?"

"Deal."

"In the meantime, I'll be bending the good Lord's ear about this every day. Keep the faith and don't lose hope."

"Right."

But as Sarah disappeared around the corner of her cube, Christy's lips drooped. Faith she could keep. Hope? Much harder to sustain. The impending sense of doom that had sprouted after the kidnapper's second letter, then mushroomed after Ginny's locket had arrived, continued to swell.

It could just be nerves. She *hoped* it was just nerves. She wanted to believe the notes weren't a hoax, that the kidnapper would, indeed, return Ginny to her in the end. Because losing her sister once had been bad. Losing her twice?

Unthinkable.

And while she prided herself on her fortitude, on hanging tight through all the tough stuff that had happened over the past few months, that could be the blow that might finally make her crumble.

"All right, admit it. You liked your lunch."

Lance pressed the tines of his fork against the

218

minuscule crumbs of coconut cake on his plate, captured one small glob of icing clinging to the edge, and finished off his dessert before responding to Lisa's smug comment.

"It was passable."

"Hah. You scarfed down the grilled sirloin sandwich, demolished the potato salad, and I'm not certain your Evidence Response Team would find enough trace evidence on the plate in front of you to identify your dessert."

He set his fork down and put his napkin to use. Hard to refute facts. The lunch had been decent, even if he *was* the lone guy in the place.

"I'll admit it was better than I . . ." His words trailed off as he caught sight of his brother striding toward the back of the store, where the tearoom was located. "Was Mac planning to join us?"

Lisa frowned and turned in her seat. "No."

The eldest McGregor sibling exchanged only a few words with the hostess before scanning the diners and homing in on them.

At Mac's grim demeanor, Lance's lunch hardened in his stomach.

Something was very wrong.

He was out of his seat and already weaving through the diners as Mac lifted his hand to motion to him.

Bracing himself as he drew close, he clenched his fingers. "What's wrong? Is it Dad?" As far as he knew, his father was doing fine after his mild heart attack six weeks ago—but Mom and Dad didn't tell them everything.

"No." Mac took his arm and propelled him out of the line of traffic, next to a rack of the hand-made kids' clothes the place was noted for. "It's Finn."

The rock in his gut turned to granite.

"Is he . . . ?" He couldn't say the word.

"No, but he's bad. Critical."

His stomach churned, and for a moment he was afraid he was going to lose his lunch.

Mac's fingers tightened on his arm. "Take a deep breath."

He followed his brother's advice until the nausea abated. "What happened?"

"I didn't get a lot of details from Dad. I don't think he has many. The report the Army reps dropped off when they came to inform them was sketchy, at best. But from what I can piece together, Finn's team was fast-roping for an insertion, and an RPG took down the helo. Most of his team didn't make it."

Guys descending on ropes trailing from a helicopter, exposed to enemy fire. Then the helo goes down after taking a hit from a rocket-propelled grenade—maybe on top of them.

It was a miracle there'd been *any* survivors.

"Where is he?"

"Landstuhl. Apparently he's been there since

Tuesday. Once he's stabilized, they're moving him to Walter Reed."

"How soon?"

"I'm trying to get the information now. Dad thought it might be tomorrow."

"I'm going."

"So am I. I checked flights on the drive over. There are several directs to Reagan tomorrow."

Lisa joined them, and while Mac gave her a fast recap, Lance stepped back, angled slightly away, and forced his lungs to keep functioning.

His kid brother was critically wounded.

Maybe dying.

It wasn't computing.

As he struggled to absorb—and accept—the news, one of the handmade kids' outfits caught his eye. A pair of coveralls for a three- or four-year-old, with a parade of animals stitched across the top—elephant, giraffe, monkey. The kind of wildlife you might see on an African safari.

Finn had always wanted to go on one of those.

Now he might never have the chance.

God, please . . . give him that chance! Let him live!

The plea came unbidden, torn from the depths of his soul, an automatic response to a moment of crisis.

Maybe his faith wasn't as anemic as he'd thought.

But he hoped this prayer produced better results

than the last life-and-death appeal he'd made to the almighty, as Taz lay dying in that mud-walled compound in a hostile land.

". . . on what Lance's schedule is like."

At the mention of his name, he tuned back in to the conversation. "What about my schedule?"

Mac shifted toward him. "If Finn's being transported tonight, how soon can you get out of here?"

"Is now soon enough?"

"You might want to check with your boss first. You've been on the job less than a month."

His chin rose a fraction. "I'm going. I'll work it out. I need to see him, even if I can't stay long. What about Mom and Dad?"

"Given Dad's heart issues, they might be stuck in Atlanta. I promised we'd call with regular updates. And I can stay out East for a while if I need to. I've got some vacation accrued."

"That's for your honeymoon."

"Family emergencies take precedence." Lisa linked her arm through Mac's and met her fiancé's gaze. "I'll be happy with a nice long weekend in a cabin in the woods if necessary. We can always hold the trip to Italy for an anniversary."

"No. We'll find a way to make Italy happen too." Mac covered her hand, and the look they exchanged shimmered with warmth. "I waited a long time to find a wife. I'm not about to give up those two weeks in Tuscany with her."

Lance's throat tightened as he watched the two of them, their love so strong and deep and true it was almost palpable.

Funny.

For a guy who'd never given more than a passing thought to settling down, he suddenly found himself envying what they had—and wondering if he might find it with a certain figure skater down the road.

It was the only uplifting prospect on this depressing day.

"Any preferences on flights?" Mac turned his attention back to him.

"The sooner the better, once we have an ETA on Finn."

"I'm working on that. I'll also see if I can tap a few sources for details on what happened."

"I will too—but we might get more information from some of the forums on the net than we will from the brass. I'll do some digging online."

"Let's touch base in a couple of hours."

"Okay. In the meantime, I'll talk to my boss and square things on that end."

"Sounds like a plan. You guys done?" Mac inclined his head toward the tearoom.

"Yeah. Except for the bill." Lance moved back toward the tearoom to retrieve it, but Lisa stopped him with a touch on the arm.

"Taken care of."

"This was supposed to be my treat."

"Another time. Go do what you need to do."

"You picked a good one, you know?" He directed that comment to his brother.

"Yeah. I know." Mac smiled down at Lisa, took her hand, and started toward the exit. "Let's roll."

Lance followed behind, wishing he had a hand to hold too.

Maybe someday.

But for now, he'd do what had to be done solo, as usual—and hope God listened to the prayer of a wayward son to spare Finn's life.

Was anything more boring than a Friday afternoon staff meeting where everyone droned on and on and on and—

Her phone began to vibrate, and Christy eased it out of her pocket to give caller ID a surreptious scan.

Lance.

Two whole days had passed since their last phone conversation, after his meeting with Brenda Lee. Unfortunately, she hadn't been able to suggest anyone for him to follow up with who met the description the woman had given him. Had the agent in Rolla had better luck with Ginny's friends and acquaintances?

It was worth ditching the meeting and risking her boss's ire to find out. As far as she was concerned, this qualified for the man's only-leave-for-emergencies rule.

Trying to be as inconspicuous as possible, she rose and slipped out of the room. Thank goodness she'd managed to claim one of the chairs closest to the door.

As she stepped into the hall, she put the phone to her ear. "Hi."

"Hi back." A serious amount of background noise echoed over the line. "Do you have a minute?"

"Sure." She skirted a day-glow orange warning cone in the hall, where a maintenance guy was working on a section of carpet, and moved off a few feet. "Do you have some news?"

"Not about the case."

She listened without interrupting as he filled her in about his brother, then closed her eyes and propped a shoulder against the wall. "I'm so sorry."

"Thanks." His words came out ragged.

"Is there anything I can do?"

"Pray?"

"That goes without saying."

"Just so you know, I've been bending God's ear too."

"I'm glad, Lance." More than he knew. She wanted to pursue this thing between them once the case was over, but his lapsed faith had been an issue. Yet he'd turned to God in the midst of a crisis. That had to be a positive sign. "When are you leaving?"

"We're getting ready to board a plane now. Mac and I are at the gate."

That explained the hum of noise in the background.

"How long will you be gone?"

"I plan to be back late Sunday night, unless . . ." His voice grated, and he paused for a moment. "We're hoping he'll be stable and I can leave. Mac's planning to stay on for a while after that." He stopped while a boarding announcement was made. "I need to go, but feel free to call me anytime. I'll be answering my cell. For immediate help, though, I want you to contact my colleague, Mark Sanders. He's the ex-HRT operator I told you about. He's up to speed on the case and very competent. If you have a pen and paper, I'll give you his cell number."

"Yes, I do. Go ahead." She unclipped her pen from the notepad and jotted down the digits as he recited them. "Got it. But if the pattern continues, I doubt there will be any developments on my end until early next week."

"I agree. Still, just in case, Mark's on standby."

A final boarding call sounded in the background.

She needed to let the man catch his plane.

The temptation to say "I wish I was there to give you a hug" was strong, the words hovering on the tip of her tongue—but she managed to bite them back. He might have shared a lot with her over chocolate chip cookies the other night, but he'd also made it clear he wanted to keep their relationship professional until the case was over. So she opted for a less personal good-bye.

"You'd better go. I don't want you to miss your plane. Take care of yourself, and let me know how your brother's doing if you get a chance."

"I will." He sounded like he was walking. Fast. "Mark will pick up any slack while I'm gone. Talk to you soon."

The line went dead.

Slowly Christy slid the phone back into her pocket. Rejoining the boring meeting held zero appeal. But there wasn't anything she could do to help Lance or his brother other than pray, and she could do that anywhere. Especially in a boring meeting.

She circled around the guy working on the carpet, which had pulled loose from the baseboard. Too bad all problems couldn't be solved as easily as that one.

But frayed lives were a lot more complicated to fix than a frayed carpet.

And at the moment, her life wasn't the only one that seemed to be unraveling.

13

The man in the bed didn't even look like Finn.

Lance groped for something . . . anything . . . to hang on to as he came to a stop beside his brother's horizontal form in the sterile, antiseptic-smelling hospital room.

He made do with the swivel-armed table that could swing over the bed—which didn't feel any more steady than he felt—and tried to process the disconnects as he gave Finn a swift scan.

Other than the steady, if shallow, rise and fall of his chest, his brother was still as death—and Finn was never motionless.

His complexion was almost as white as the sheet that was pulled up to his neck and the bandage that concealed his auburn hair—and while Finn was fair, he was never ghostly pale.

The skin was stretched taut over his cheek-bones, leaving gaunt, shadowy hollows in his face, making him appear ill and frail—and Finn was never sick or weak.

As for all the pieces of high-tech equipment jammed around the bed, their unnerving beeps and whooshes providing the only sound in the room—were they helping Finn recover . . . or merely keeping him alive?

Across from him, on the other side of the expanse of white sheet, Mac muttered a word he seldom used.

It summed up exactly how he felt too.

"You must be the brothers."

As the voice spoke from the doorway, they turned in unison.

"Brad Owens. I'm handling Finn's case." The white-coated man moved to the foot of the bed, hand extended.

Mac took it first while Lance pried his fingers off the table and hoped his legs didn't fail him once the support was removed.

"The floor supervisor paged me when you arrived. There's a lounge down the hall. Why don't we talk there?"

Leave Finn when they'd just gotten here?

No way.

But as he started to protest, Mac gave him The Look. The one he'd used since they were kids to keep him in line. To remind him to think before he shot off his mouth.

"It might be better to have this discussion in the lounge so we don't disturb Finn—in case he can hear us." Mac emphasized the last six words.

He did the translation.

If Finn is listening and the doc has bad news, hearing it could destroy whatever morale he has left.

Good thing one of their brains was functioning.

With a nod of acquiescence, Lance followed the two of them down the hall.

The doctor launched into his briefing the instant they took their seats. "I'm sure you both have a lot of questions, but let me give you the basics first and save you having to ask some of them. First of all, your brother was one of the lucky ones. I'm told only two men survived the attack. Both of them are here. Finn picked up some shrapnel and suffered a few second-degree burns, but those were dealt with at Landstuhl. His primary injuries at this point are confined to his leg. The fall from the helo did a number on it."

Lance called up a visual of Finn's lower torso from the fast inventory he'd taken. There had been two long mounds under the blanket, the left one much larger than the right, indicating some serious dressing—but at least Finn still had his leg. That was a positive sign.

Wasn't it?

Mac asked the question he didn't want to voice. "How bad is the leg?"

"We're going to do our best to save it, but this is a situation that will require multiple surgeries. Several bones are broken, and his lower right ibia is shattered. Either way, he'll face a long recovery and intense rehab. Best case, he'll make an excellent recovery and go on to lead a very normal life."

Do our best to save it.

Shattered.

Either way.

Lance's heart stuttered as the ominous words resonated in his mind.

Several beats of silence ticked by in the deserted waiting room before Mac leaned forward and clasped his hands between his knees. "Why is his head bandaged?"

"He has a large laceration on his scalp. In and of themselves, that and the shrapnel wounds and burns aren't life-threatening."

The left side of Lance's brain started to kick into gear. "What do you mean, in and of themselves?"

"Your brother suffered injuries beyond the obvious. Blunt force trauma to the abdomen severely damaged his spleen. They removed it at Landstuhl. That injury resulted in rapid and significant internal bleeding, which in turn led to severe shock. During the evacuation from the crash site, he coded."

The bottom fell out of Lance's stomach.

Across from him, Mac sucked in a breath.

Finn's heart had failed.

Their brother had technically died.

"Was there any . . . don't people get brain damage from that?" Lance managed to choke out the words.

"He was resuscitated very quickly. As far as we can tell, there wasn't any neural or organ damage."

As far as they could tell.

231

Not the most comforting response.

Lance swallowed, but his voice still hoarsened on the next question. "Will he be okay without a spleen?"

"Yes. His immune system will be less effective, but other than getting a flu shot every year and pneumonia vaccine, no special treatment is required."

Mac jumped back in. "How soon do you think he'll regain consciousness?"

"He's being heavily medicated for pain, and that's keeping him very drowsy. However, we're tapering off on those drugs. He could wake up anytime. Do you two plan to be around for the next few hours?"

"Yes." They spoke simultaneously.

"Good. I know it's late and you've both spent hours in transit, but I'd like him to see a familiar face when he opens his eyes. Any other questions?"

Mac raised an eyebrow at him. He shook his head.

"Not at the moment."

The physician stood. "There's a recliner in Finn's room. You can take turns grabbing some shut-eye."

Sleep while Finn was in critical condition?

Was he kidding?

Mac rose and took the doctor's extended hand. "Thanks."

At his big brother's nudge, Lance stood, too, and returned the man's shake.

"If you need to speak with me, let one of the nurses know. We're all going to do our very best to help him walk out of here and live a normal life."

Lance watched the man stride away, then turned to Mac. "Not the most upbeat news, huh?"

"It could be worse. They were able to revive him. He still has his leg. There's a reasonable chance he'll pull through with few long-term effects."

Had Mac been listening to the same spiel he'd just heard?

"How did you get such an optimistic spin out of all that?"

"I tuned in to the positives—and I have faith. I can't believe God let him survive a disaster of that magnitude only to destroy the rest of his life." Mac reached over and gripped his arm. Tight. "That's the message we need to communicate to Finn once he's awake, okay? He's going to need all the encouragement and motivation we can offer."

At the very least.

"Got it."

Mac winked and dropped his hand. "Just call up that killer smile you save for pretty girls. Finn needs to see that kind of friendly face."

As Mac headed back to the room, Lance fell in beside him.

Smile, huh?

Tough assignment.

But if it would help Finn, he'd dredge one up. For all the abuse the two of them heaped on their kid brother, nothing would be the same without him. He had to recover.

Mac was right about keeping the faith too—as Christy would surely agree if she was here. They had to believe that if God had brought Finn this far, spared his life when so many others had died, he wasn't going to abandon him now.

As they retraced their steps down the hall, Lance said a silent thank-you for answered prayers and added a plea for the gift of fortitude—for all of them.

Because he had a feeling the trials to come in the days and weeks and months ahead were going to be more daunting than any challenge the McGregor clan had ever faced.

The kidnapper had broken his pattern.

Christy stared at the thin envelope addressed in her sister's hand, tucked in among the gaggle of bills and ads that dominated her mail.

Why had it come on a Saturday instead of the usual Tuesday? Was the kidnapper playing games with her—or was there another, more significant reason he'd mixed things up?

Clutching the mail against her chest, she hurried back inside the condo and shut the door. After locking it behind her, she leaned against it and closed her eyes.

Of all the times for Lance to be gone!

For one fleeting instant she considered calling him. He'd said he'd have his cell and would be available.

But that would be selfish. The man had enough problems without her adding one more. He'd barely arrived at Walter Reed; who knew what he was facing with his brother?

Better to contact his colleague.

She continued to the kitchen, groped through her purse for the slip of paper containing the number she'd jotted down, and placed the call. Mark Sanders answered on the second ring in a crisp, businesslike tone and assured her he'd be over within the hour.

True to his word, thirty-five nerve-wracking minutes later he was knocking at her kitchen door—his suggestion, in case the kidnapper was watching. As he'd pointed out, they didn't want to undermine the boyfriend ruse she and Lance had created.

The guy was sharp, as Lance had said.

He was also tall, lean, and strong-jawed, with a faint hint of silver in his short, neatly trimmed brown hair. In other words, the classic stereotype of a well-groomed, clean-cut FBI agent.

Except for the frayed, paint-spattered jeans and the spot of pink on his jaw.

As she approached the sliding glass door that led to her patio, he held up his ID.

After a quick glance, she flipped the lock and ushered him in out of the cold, gesturing to his attire. "I must have interrupted a home project."

His quick grin produced a tiny dimple. "Nursery. We have a new baby who came a little early and caught us unprepared. We were both handling some demanding cases, and somehow the weeks slipped away."

"Your wife's an agent too?"

"Psychologist."

A power couple.

"Impressive."

"I'll tell Emily you said that. She could use a pick-me-up after being on the night shift with the baby until the wee hours this morning. Mark Sanders, as you saw from my ID." He held out his hand.

She took it, and he gave her fingers a firm squeeze. "Christy Reed."

"Where's the letter?"

So much for chitchat—which was fine with her.

She led him to the counter in silence.

He pulled a pair of latex gloves out of the pocket of his jeans as he eyed the envelope. "The weekend arrival is out of pattern."

Lance had briefed him well. "Yes."

While he removed two folded evidence envelopes from the inside pocket of his jacket, she indicated the knife block off to the side. "Lance always uses one of those to open the envelopes."

He gave her another quick smile. "I came prepared." He removed a pocketknife from his jeans and held it up. "I've never been without one since my Boy Scout days." With a deft flick of his wrist, he slit the top of the envelope and removed the single sheet of paper.

She edged closer to read the message.

Like the others, it was typed—but this one was much shorter.

You will see your sister soon.

She frowned. "That's weird. It almost sounds like he's through communicating."

"Yeah. It does."

"What do you make of it?"

"I'm not sure. In general, developments happen fast in kidnappings, including the ransom terms. This guy waits two months, sends a series of letters, then wraps things up with no demands, no threats, no ultimatums." He slid the two items into evidence envelopes. "Weird is an appropriate word for it."

Christy massaged her temple. "I'm totally confused. I mean, what was the point of all this?"

"Since the typical economic payoff of kidnapping wasn't the goal, we have to consider other motives. A power trip, revenge, vindication. And was Ginny the only intended victim? Playing these games, drawing the kidnapping out over an extended period, has thrown your world into a tailspin too."

"This sounds like a very deliberate strategy to make life as difficult as possible for you."

As Lance's words from the night the second letter arrived echoed in her mind, a shiver ran through her.

"That's kind of what Lance implied early on—and this note seems to support his theory."

"I assume he warned you to be extra careful until we sort this out."

"Yes."

"I'll second that recommendation. In terms of next steps, the lab will have this on Monday, and I'll touch base with Lance today. If this is the kidnapper's last communication, he may play his final card—whatever it is—very soon."

"Do you think . . . is there any chance he might simply let Ginny go?"

"I wouldn't cross anything off the list of possibilities yet." The words were positive, but no encouragement warmed Mark's brown irises. Just the opposite. If Ginny's safe return was even on his list of potential outcomes, it was at the very bottom.

Despite the temperate air being churned out by her furnace, a numbing chill seeped into her pores, penetrating to her core. As bad as the trauma had been so far, she suddenly had a feeling it was about to get a lot uglier.

She linked her fingers in a tight knot. "I appreciate you making a special trip over on a Saturday. And I'm sorry I interrupted your painting project."

"No problem. It'll be waiting for me when I get back. I'll leave the same way I came."

She followed him to the sliding door, thanked him again as he slipped out, then rolled it closed and twisted the lock. A few seconds later, he disappeared around the shrubbery.

Christy had no doubt he'd follow through on everything he'd promised. Mark Sanders seemed like a solid agent—competent, responsive, smart, and buttoned-up.

But he wasn't Lance.

And while she was confident the case was in capable hands, dealing with Mark had neither calmed nor reassured her the way talking to Lance, or being in his company, did.

He alone had the power to create a momentary oasis of peace in her chaotic life.

She crossed to the counter and plucked her cell out of the charger, weighing it in her hand. Would calling him in the midst of his own family crisis really be such a huge imposition?

Of course it would, Christy. That's why he asked Mark to fill in and gave you the man's number. Don't bother him.

The firm reminder from her conscience couldn't be ignored. With a sigh, she dropped the phone back into the device. Lance had said he'd call when he could, and he would.

In the meantime, she needed to sit tight, be careful, and wait for the kidnapper's next move. Mark had suggested it could happen very soon, and that suited her fine. She'd had enough of his games. Whatever was coming, better to get it over with than spend every minute of every day teetering on the edge of a cliff, waiting for the push to come.

But she hoped Lance was back before it did.

14

"Lance! I think he's coming around." Mac shot out of the chair he'd claimed beside Finn's bed.

From his feet-up position in the recliner, Lance pulled himself back from the deep slumber he'd just dropped into after keeping vigil with Mac through the long, dark, endless Friday night.

Swinging his legs to the floor, he rubbed the grit out of his eyes and half staggered across the room.

A groan from Finn as he approached, and the flicker of his brother's eyelids, chased away the last remnants of his sleep.

"I already pressed the call button." Mac didn't take his gaze off Finn.

As Lance joined him beside the bed, Finn blinked. Peered up at them. "What . . ." The single word came out in a croak.

Mac grabbed his hand. "You're at Walter Reed, kid. You're gonna be okay."

"Hey, runt." Lance's voice broke. He cleared his throat and tried again. "You didn't have to go to all this trouble to get our attention, you know."

If either of their comments registered, Finn gave no indication. Instead, panic flared in his glazed eyes and he began to thrash. "Not safe. Go! Go! Take cover!"

Mac held him in place and barked out an order. "Grab his other arm and his good leg."

Lance did as he was told, speaking over his shoulder as a nurse hurried in. "He woke up and went ballistic."

"That's not unusual. They think they're still over there, in the line of fire. Nightmares and hallucinations are common, and the high-powered meds he's been on are contributing to the problem." She went about her work with practiced efficiency, injecting a clear liquid into the IV and checking his vitals. "He'll drop off again in a minute. Next time he wakes up, he should be more lucid. I'll let Dr. Owens know he's talking."

Sixty seconds later, thanks to the spiked IV, Finn's thrashing subsided and his eyelids drifted closed.

"If you guys want to grab some food, you

should have a couple of hours before he wakes up again." She continued attending to Finn.

Lance released his hold on his brother's arm and looked at Mac. "That makes sense." Food might not be at the top of his priority list, but his stomach was sending out a loud SOS. That burger he'd scarfed down last night from the cafeteria was long gone.

"I agree. We'll be back shortly."

The nurse waved them off. "Have a decent breakfast. It will be tougher for you to get away once he's back with us full time."

Lance led the way as they left the room, but when he leaned over in the elevator to punch the button that would take them to the cafeteria, Mac beat him to it and pressed a different number.

"Hey! What are you doing?"

"I want to talk to the other survivor of the helo crash before we eat. His name's Deke Flood and he's two floors up."

Lance squinted at him. "Where did you get that information?"

"I asked one of the nurses to check after you zoned out in the recliner."

He could have done that himself while Mac had taken the first turn sleeping—if he hadn't been so intent on watching Finn's chest rise and fall.

"How bad is he?"

"He lost an arm."

Lance winced. "You sure he's up to talking?"

"I spoke to the floor supervisor. She asked him. He's expecting us."

The elevator pinged, and the doors opened.

"His room is on the right." Mac read the number off the slip of paper he pulled out of his pocket.

Lance let Mac precede him when they arrived. A twentysomething woman looked up from her chair beside the bed, the dark circles under her eyes clear evidence she, too, had spent a long, worried, sleepless night.

"You must be Finn's brothers. I'm Joan."

Lance stared at her girth as she struggled to her feet, his gut twisting.

She had to be eight months pregnant—just as Debbie had been when Taz was killed.

Mac did the introductions, and Lance forced down the bad memories as he gave her cold, shaky hand a squeeze.

"I'll run down the hall and get some juice while you guys talk." She angled toward the guy propped up in the bed, his face marred by contusions, his left arm no more than a stump below the elbow and encased in a thick dressing. "I'll be back in a few minutes, sweetie."

His lips twisted into a lame excuse for a smile. "Don't rush. I'm not going anywhere."

A shadow flitted across her face, but she gamely smiled back before disappearing out the door.

The sandy-haired guy motioned to the two

chairs on his left. "Sit, please. How's Finn?"

Mac took the seat closest to the head of the bed and gave him a quick rundown of Finn's injuries.

When he finished, Deke let out a slow breath. "Is he going to keep his leg?"

"We think so."

"That's good news, anyway. It'd be a lot tougher to lose a leg than an arm. At least I'm right-handed." Once again, he tried for a grin.

There was no easy way to approach the hard stuff, so Lance dived in. "We were hoping you could give us a few more details about what happened."

A shadow darkened Deke's eyes. "I wish I could. But it was pitch black, and it happened fast. The landing area was supposed to have been secured, but as you both know, one guy at night with an RPG and decent aim is all it takes for disaster. One minute we were fast-roping, the next the helo was a ball of fire above us. The next thing I remember, I was on the ground and Finn was putting a tourniquet on my arm. He saved my life, you know. Without him, I'd have bled out by the time help arrived." He swallowed. "And to think he was bleeding worse than I was, only on the inside."

His voice hoarsened, and he reached for the cup of water on the bedside table.

Mac handed it to him, waiting until he finished drinking before asking the next question. "Do you remember anything else?"

"Yeah. It was real quiet after the crash. Too quiet. There should have been moans or calls for help, but there was nothing. I could see from the light of the fire that Finn was dragging himself around on his elbows, trying to check on the rest of the team. Then I noticed this guy in a turban creeping into the crash area, holding a rifle. I tried to reach for my Beretta or a grenade, but I couldn't even lift my good arm at that point."

His features hardened, and he fisted the hand he had left. "All of a sudden, he pulls out a digital camera. He was taking pictures of the kill." Anger and disgust contorted his face as he spat out the words. "I tried again to get to a weapon. He spotted me and lifted his rifle. Finn started screaming at him, and the guy whirled around. A second later, his head was gone."

Deke began to shake, and Mac took the cup from him as the water sloshed close to the edge. "We're sorry to put you through this, but Finn is still out of it and we needed to know what happened."

"Yeah. I get it. I'd do the same thing in your place." His words came out shaky, and he squeezed the sheet in his good hand. "You guys got a hero for a brother, you know. Purple Heart material for sure. That's what I told the brass."

Lance exchanged a look with Mac and saw the same emotion he was feeling reflected in his brother's eyes.

Pride.

Under the most terrifying circumstances, with all the odds stacked against him, their kid brother had done everything—and more—that was expected of an Army Ranger . . . including risking his life to help his teammates and taking out an enemy insurgent, despite his own grievous injuries.

After a lifetime of trying to best his older brothers, the runt had finally succeeded.

He was, indeed, a hero.

"Thanks for telling us all that. It helps to have a picture of what happened." Mac started to rise.

"Wait!"

At the man's urgent command, Mac sat back down. Lance stayed put.

"Look, I don't . . ." Deke stopped. Blew out a breath. "I'm not the kind to tell tales out of school, okay? Me and Finn, we're tight. We trust each other. So I'm taking a risk here. But for the past few months, he's . . . I've been worried about him."

Lance narrowed his eyes.

The past few months.

The same time frame in which he and Mac had noticed a change in Finn.

Maybe they were finally going to get an explanation for it.

"Why?" He leaned forward.

Deke shifted in the bed, wadding the sheet in his hand. "Man, he's gonna hate me if he finds out I told you guys this."

"He won't find out." Mac's tone was resolute. "We'll figure out some way to deal with your information so he doesn't know the source."

"That might be hard to do." Deke exhaled. "But if anyone can come up with a strategy to make that happen, it would be former SEAL and Delta Force operators. And somebody needs to know about this." He tightened his grip on the sheet. "The thing is, I think Finn's got PTSD."

The word Mac had used earlier, when they'd arrived at Finn's bedside, flashed through Lance's mind.

It was as appropriate now as it had been then.

Post-traumatic stress disorder was serious stuff.

Big-time serious stuff.

Mind-mangling stuff.

He did his best to sound calm despite the alarm bells going off in his head. "Why do you think that?"

"He has a bunch of the symptoms. He's got insomnia real bad, and when he does sleep, he thrashes around and sweats like a pig. In our downtime on base, we used to shoot hoops and play a lot of one-on-one, but he lost interest in that and started going off by himself. He always seems on edge too. And he overreacts. Three weeks ago a pot fell in the mess hall kitchen, and he dived for the floor and yelled for everyone to take cover. The guys razzed him about that, and he laughed it off, but all the pieces add up to PTSD."

"When did you first notice this?" Mac's tone was sober, his expression grim.

"Last spring. Right after a recon mission went wrong. Someone in the area got wind of our presence, and before we knew it, we were under fire from the local villagers. It wasn't much of a fight, but there were a few casualties on the other side. One of them came rushing straight at Finn, rifle aimed at his chest. After the skirmish was over, we checked on the dead. Turns out the one Finn shot was a kid. He couldn't have been more than twelve."

Lance closed his eyes. He'd been in similar situations, fighting young boys who should have been playing on the local soccer team, not toting guns.

"I remember him muttering 'What kind of a war is this, where we have to kill children?' " Deke drew a ragged breath. "Something seemed to snap in him that night. He hardly talked for days afterward. The other stuff began to develop over the next few months."

Lance sorted out the timeline in his head. Everything fit with the mini-reunion they'd had in St. Louis last summer, not long after Mac took the job with the St. Louis County PD and moved to the Midwest.

He tightened his grip on the arm of his chair. "Did you ever bring this up to Finn?"

"I tried. He just laughed it off, denied he had any problem."

Not surprising. Most guys in elite units assumed they were above those kinds of issues. Admitting to any sort of weakness was anathema. Sure, stuff like that happened once in a while—but always to the other guy.

That had been his mind-set too.

If it hadn't been, he might have seen the signs sooner in Finn.

Deke spoke again. "I was on the verge of taking my concerns up the chain, but after Finn told me he wasn't re-upping, I thought it might be less of a problem once he was back home."

What?!

Lance sat up straighter.

Finn wasn't re-upping?

Since when?

He turned toward Mac. His big brother appeared to be as surprised by the news as he was.

"You guys didn't know about that?" Deke looked from him to Mac.

"No." Twin furrows creased Mac's brow. "Finn hasn't been that talkative with us over the past few months, either."

"Well, the re-up decision is new. He just told me two weeks ago. But if he does have PTSD, it may not go away so easily after this incident."

He flicked a glance to the stump of his arm.

No kidding.

Mac glanced over at him, and he nodded. It was time to go.

"We appreciate your candor, and we'll honor your confidence." Mac pushed himself to his feet.

"Thanks. Like I said, I don't want to lose Finn's friendship, especially since we're the only ones . . ." His voice choked, and he swiped the back of his hand across his eyes. "Sorry. That tube they jammed down my windpipe during the operation messed up my throat."

Possible.

But trauma—and loss—could also choke a man up.

Lance stood, too, and started toward the door. "We'll get out of your hair and let you rest that throat. Thanks again for filling us in."

"You tell Finn to hang on to his leg, okay?"

Mac paused at the door. "We'll pass that along. Take care of yourself."

Their return trek down the hall was silent. Not until they were in the empty elevator did Lance speak. "Not great news, huh?"

"No."

"We thought something was messing with his head last summer."

"Yeah."

"I didn't expect this, though, did you?"

"No."

A surge of irritation frayed the edges of his already ragged nerves. "This isn't much of a conversation."

The elevator doors opened and Mac exited. "Let's get some food."

Lance left the elevator but moved off to the side and held his ground. "I'm not hungry anymore." That was true, even if his stomach rumbled in protest.

His brother stopped. Turned. Gave him one of the steely-eyed, intimidating stares that worked on most people.

Lance didn't budge.

At last, Mac expelled a breath and strode back. "Look, I know we're both upset, but we have to eat."

"We also need to talk."

"What's there to say? Much as I'd like to think Deke is wrong, I can't dispute his conclusion. We both noticed that Finn's been on edge. That he hasn't been communicating with either of us much in person or by email. That he lost his sense of humor. The signs were there, and we missed them."

Lance's shoulders drooped, and he jammed his hands in his pockets. "Yeah. Me more than you."

His comment hung in the air between them for a moment before Mac responded. "What do you mean?"

Lance forced out the admission. "You know

when we stayed with you last summer, and Finn and I shared that pullout couch in the living room? I sleep like a rock, but the first night his thrashing woke me up. I had to shake him hard to get him to come around, and his T-shirt was soaked with sweat. He claimed he was getting over some kind of bug he'd picked up, and I bought it."

"Maybe he was."

"Except the other nights we were at your place, I went to bed first, and he was already sitting on your deck when I got up the next morning. For all I know, he slept out there to avoid a replay of the nightmare and any questions it might raise. I should have realized he had issues." He wiped a hand down his face. "Maybe I didn't want to realize it. Maybe I wanted to believe the McGregors were invincible."

"Hey." Mac clapped a hand on his shoulder. "Beating ourselves up with should-haves and maybes is a waste of time. We're just going to move forward from here and get Finn the help he needs. Agreed?"

"Yeah." What else could he say?

"Then let's plan our strategy over a real meal. We'll get through this—and so will Finn. Come on."

Mac marched toward the cafeteria, expecting him to follow. To accept any mistakes they'd made and try to fix them instead of wallowing in regret.

As usual, his older brother was right.

The McGregor men weren't quitters. The three of them had overcome plenty of difficulties in the past. This might be the mother of all challenges, but if they stuck together, they'd make it through.

Especially if they took a page from Christy's winning playbook and put God in charge of their team.

Squaring his shoulders, Lance followed Mac, sending a silent thank-you heavenward that his first FBI case had involved a woman who'd steered him back to the Almighty.

And who he suspected was destined to play a role in his life long after the mystery of Ginny Reed's disappearance was solved.

Nathan ran his finger over the curving edge of the pewter Arch on the keychain, looked up at the autographed photo tacked to his bulletin board, and smiled.

Things were going well.

Very well.

Sitting in his cold car near Christy's condo hadn't been a great way to spend his Saturday morning, but watching her come out to retrieve her mail had made all the uncomfortable hours worthwhile. He might not have been able to identify his letter through the binoculars, but her expression had confirmed its arrival. Distress, fear, dread, surprise . . . all the emotions he'd wanted her to feel had been on display for the world to see.

He wrapped his fingers around the cool pewter ornament and squeezed it tight.

Best of all, every one of those emotions would be magnified next week, when his careful months of planning paid off and she found out what her abandonment all those years ago had wrought. That revelation would bring her to her knees.

He could almost taste the . . .

A door creaked open in the hall, and he tuned into the noise. Shuffling steps sounded on the worn carpet. Another door clicked shut.

The old woman had gone to the bathroom.

He set the keychain down and picked up a broken wire hanger, poking at the mouse in the box at his feet through the wire mesh over the top.

Mevlida had been quiet lately. Responding to his comments but never initiating conversations. Staying in her room instead of coming out to watch TV. Was she sick and keeping it to herself? Were her ribs hurt worse than she was letting on?

Possibly.

He'd been clear since she arrived that he couldn't afford a bunch of medical bills. That if her health deteriorated, he'd throw her back on the street.

But she was getting older and more decrepit. One of these days she'd develop some condition that required attention—and he didn't want her talking to anyone who might ask nosey questions about their arrangement.

He jabbed the mouse again.

Once this was over, he'd have to decide what to do about her. The government money, plus having her under his total control, was nice—but that would be less important if he got the promotion at work. And he had a decent chance at it. He knew how to play the game, how to be Mr. Nice Guy when it suited him. His boss liked him. Everyone there did.

Yes, the old woman was a problem—but he could worry about her after he finished carrying out his plan for Christy. For now, he wasn't going to let anything hamper his enjoyment of this long-overdue payoff.

He cornered the mouse, a shiver of anticipation slithering through him as he blocked its frantic efforts to escape. Christy would try to escape too—but she wouldn't be any more successful than this rodent.

It would be just like the day soldiers had destroyed his family—only in reverse.

Because he'd learned his lesson well.

People in power decided who lived and died . . . and now it was his turn to take control.

When he and Christy Reed had their reunion, he'd be calling the shots—and this time around, she wasn't going to ruin his life.

He was going to ruin hers.

15

"That's all we know for now, Mom. Once we talk to Finn, we'll call you back. Try not to worry—and tell Dad the same." Lance glanced down the hall as Mac rounded the corner and walked toward him.

"Worry is part of love. We've fretted over you three before, we'll fret again. That's called being a parent—and we wouldn't have it any other way." Despite the thread of tension running through his mother's words, her voice was strong and determined.

The Rock was living up to the nickname the three of them had bestowed on her two decades ago.

"I need to run." He pushed off from the wall outside his brother's room. "One of us will call you twice a day whether there's news or not."

"And as soon as Finn's able to hold a conversation, you put him on the phone. Day or night. Promise."

"I promise. In the meantime, you two take care of yourselves." They said their good-byes, and as he slid the phone back on his belt, Mac joined him. "Did you find the doctor?"

"Yeah. We had a long talk. He didn't seem

surprised there might be a PTSD issue. Sounds like they see a lot more of that around here than I expected. They'll have Finn evaluated. It will be positioned as routine follow-up after a traumatic battlefield incident, so he'll never know Deke tipped us off. Mom and Dad okay?"

"Worried but hanging in. Also planning to come up in a week."

Mac frowned. "I don't know if Dad should be traveling."

"Try telling that to them. They're determined— and Mom's done her homework, as usual. According to her, it's 692 miles door-to-door. She'll do all the driving, and they'll stop overnight in North Carolina to break up the trip. She's already lined up an apartment two miles from Walter Reed, where they intend to hunker down for the duration . . . or at least until Finn is on the mend."

"Is Dad's doctor okay with all that?"

"She plans to give him her spiel on Monday and get his blessing, then ask for a referral to a cardiologist here. They do have a lot of friends in the area from Dad's State Department stints in Washington. That's a plus. Also, as she pointed out, his second-in-command at the security firm has been handling the business for the past few weeks; no reason he can't handle it for a few more. She's chomping at the bit to get up here."

"That sounds like Mom."

"Hey—for a woman who nurtured a thriving internet graphic design business through years of globe-trotting and raised three hooligans like us in all the far-flung spots around the world where Dad was assigned, this challenge is small potatoes."

Mac rubbed the back of his neck. "I know them coming up here wasn't in the playbook for Dad's recovery, but Finn's going to need some on-site cheerleaders. I can't stay for more than a week or two."

"And I'm wheels-up at eight tomorrow night. But I intend to make a lot of weekend trips."

"Likewise. Still, having Mom on hand takes some of the pressure off."

At the rustle of sheets inside the room, followed by a quiet groan, Lance spun around and dived back in, Mac on his heels.

Finn's eyes were open—and lucid—as they approached.

"Welcome back, runt." Lance tried to call up the smile Mac had requested, but all he could manage was a slight lift of one corner of his mouth.

"Where am I?" Finn encompassed them both in that question.

"Walter Reed." Mac moved to the other side of the bed. "You took a nasty fall from a helicopter."

A spasm of pain tightened Finn's features. "I remember."

"How much?" Lance wrapped his fingers around the railing on the side of the bed.

Finn's expression grew bleak. "Too much. Who else . . . did anyone else make it?"

"Deke. We saw him this morning."

A profound sadness darkened his green irises. "That's it?"

There wasn't any way to sugarcoat the truth, so Lance didn't even try. "Yes."

"I was afraid of that. I tried to check, see if anyone else was breathing. The ones I got to were . . . they were gone."

"You saved Deke's life. Twice. He told us about the tourniquet . . . and the insurgent. Purple Heart stuff—his words, not mine."

Instead of lifting Finn's spirits, as Lance had hoped, the comment had the opposite effect. Moisture gathered in his brother's eyes, and when he spoke, his choked words were laced with futility—and bitterness.

"Right. The big hero, going out in a blaze of glory. Except it didn't work that way. I'm still here."

Finn closed his eyes, and Lance locked gazes with Mac across the bed. Based on his older brother's troubled expression, they'd picked up the same disturbing message.

Their youngest sibling wasn't all that happy he'd survived.

That, too, was consistent with PTSD.

"Hey." Mac clasped his shoulder. "We're glad you *are* still here. Mom and Dad are too. And I expect you to make good on that game of one-on-one you promised me last summer—no excuses."

Finn's Adam's apple convulsed, and he opened his eyes. "Does that mean I still have my leg?"

"Yeah."

"Am I going to keep it?"

"The doctor's optimistic."

"What else is wrong with me?"

Mac gave him a quick rundown of his injuries, leaving the multiple surgeries and rehab until last.

"Sounds like the one-on-one will have to wait a while." Finn smoothed his unsteady fingers over a wrinkle in the sheet.

"A lot of that depends on you." Mac folded his arms.

Lance telegraphed a silent warning to him. Getting Finn back on track—and on his feet— might require some serious prodding and tough love, but given his mental state, it was too soon to implement that tactic.

"Mac and I have your back, though." He tried for an upbeat tone to offset his older brother's harder line. "And Mom and Dad are planning to rent an apartment near here for the duration."

The taut skin over Finn's cheekbones became almost transparent. "So now I've made a mess of everyone else's life too. Great."

"Hey." Lance moved closer—so close he could feel his brother's breath on his chin. At that proximity, Finn was forced to meet his gaze. "This isn't just about you, okay? We're family. We help each other out of messes. And you know what? That's not a burden; it's a blessing. So we'll do our part to get your game with Mac on the calendar, you do your part, and this story's gonna have a happy ending. Got it?"

A tear leaked out of the corner of Finn's eye and trailed down to the pillow.

Oh, man.

And he'd thought Mac was being too tough.

"Hey . . . I didn't mean to—"

A clatter in the hallway interrupted his apology, and Finn's body went rigid. Panic and confusion darted through his eyes as the heart monitor began to beep.

"Take it easy, Finn." Mac gripped his shoulder, his tone gentle and soothing as he pressed the call button. "You're at Walter Reed, remember? A hospital cart ran into the wall." He spoke slowly, enunciating each word. "That's what the noise was. You're safe. We're all safe. Take some deep breaths."

Mac kept talking as their kid brother writhed on the bed, and once the nurse bustled in, Lance moved aside to give her access.

As he clenched his fists and restrained the urge to pound one of them against the wall in helpless frustration, his phone began to vibrate.

Since Mac and the nurse were dealing with Finn, he seized the diversion, stepping back to scan caller ID.

Mark.

His already galloping pulse picked up more speed.

Unless there'd been a development in Christy's case, his colleague wouldn't call—especially on a Saturday.

Waving his phone to attract Mac's attention, he nodded toward the hall and started toward the door, tapping the talk button as he walked. "What's up?"

"You have a minute?"

He checked on the nurse again, who seemed to have the situation under control. "Yeah." He left the room and trekked toward the lounge.

"How's your brother?"

"Conscious, but his leg is in bad shape and he has . . . other issues. Something happen with the kidnapper?"

Lance tucked himself into a quiet corner of the waiting room while Mark gave him a quick recap of the day's events.

"I think the guy's done playing games with letters and is getting ready to make his final move, whatever it is," his colleague concluded. "And I doubt he'll wait long."

"I wish the description Brenda Rose gave me

had resonated with someone in Ginny Reed's circle. We still don't even have a suspect to investigate."

"This guy's done an excellent job covering his tracks, I'll give him that. I'm going to send the latest communique to the lab, but based on past experience, I doubt they'll find anything useful. When are you coming back?"

"Late tomorrow night. In the meantime, I'll give Christy a call."

"I told her she could contact me if necessary—but I can understand why you'd want to stay in touch personally."

Lance ignored the emphasis on the word *personally,* as well as the touch of amusement in his colleague's inflection. "You have anything else?"

A chuckle came over the line. "No comment, huh? Telling. As far as the case goes, you're up to speed."

"Thanks for handling this today."

"Not a problem." The piercing wail of a baby came over the line, and Lance winced, jerking the phone back from his ear. "As you can hear, I'm being summoned. Have a safe trip back, and see you Monday."

For a full minute after Mark broke the connection, Lance remained where he was, analyzing the latest development—and coming to the same conclusion as his fellow agent.

Their guy was poised to make his final move.

Soon.

But despite the kidnapper's promise that a reunion was about to happen, there was a menacing undertone to his note. Every instinct Lance had honed during his tenure in The Unit was sounding a red alert.

Christy was in danger. He knew that, deep in his gut.

And worst of all, there was nothing he could do from nine hundred miles away to protect her.

Christy glided from a flawless double toe loop to a spot-on layback spin to a clean spiral—but none of the textbook-perfect moves were accompanied by the usual heady rush. Nor had the student-free skating session relaxed her.

She might as well call it a night and go home.

Huffing out a sigh, she glided over to the edge of the rink and stepped onto the rubber mat. If skating didn't calm her frayed nerves, nothing would.

Best case, a cup of hot chocolate once she got home would mellow her out enough to induce sleep.

Her cell began to chirp as she sat to unlace her skates, and she fumbled in the pocket of her hoodie. Lance?

But what were the odds he'd be calling at nine thirty—ten thirty eastern—on a Saturday night?

Apparently better than she'd expected, because his name was front and center in the digital display.

Turning away from the crowd of teenagers removing skates and making plans to go out for pizza, she greeted him.

"Did I catch you at a bad time?" His rich baritone voice came over the line, followed by a clunking noise that sounded like a soft-drink vending machine dispensing a can. "I can hear a lot of activity in the background."

"No. I'm at the rink. A bunch of teens are chattering behind me. How's your brother doing?"

"He's awake and talking. His leg's not in great shape, so that will be a long recovery, and he's got a lot of other injuries—but we're hopeful. Mark called me earlier about the latest letter. Anything else happen since you spoke with him?" His words rasped with weariness.

"No. All quiet here. But you sound tired."

"Yeah. I'll have to make up for the sleep I lost once I get back. I plan to fly out tomorrow night and be in the office early Monday. Until then, though, Mark's on standby. You can also call my cell if anything comes up."

"You have too much on your plate out there already without me adding more to it."

"The case is on my mind anyway. And I concur with Mark. I think this guy's about to make his final move. You need to be extra careful and watch your back. Is there someone at the rink who can walk you to your car after you're finished?"

"Yes. There's always a security guard on duty." She scanned the public areas. Spotted Hank. Nice man, but the retired cop had eaten a few too many doughnuts during his career on the force. Not much chance he'd be able to defend her against a guy fit and nimble enough to carry off murder, arson, and kidnapping, then disappear without a trace.

"Use him tonight."

"I will." She fiddled with the lace on her skate. "Now that the kidnapper appears to be winding up his plans, are there any new leads from your end, or are we in a waiting mode?"

"No new leads. We're waiting." His frustration came over the line loud and clear. "This guy's covered his tracks well—but that doesn't mean something won't break, that he won't make a mistake. Don't give up hope."

Easier said than done.

"I'm trying to stay upbeat." It was the best she could offer.

"Good. Because all it takes is one slip, one solid lead, and we could nail him. Now, anything else we should discuss?"

She wished there was. Just listening to his voice calmed her. But he had other, more pressing problems to deal with than her case of nerves.

"No."

"Then I'll head back to Finn's room. Mac and I are taking shifts in the recliner, and it's my turn."

"Will I hear from you Monday?"

"Count on it."

They said their good-byes, and Christy slipped the phone back in her pocket. The teens continued to chatter behind her, their conversation peppered with typical high-school topics—the angst of broken romances, complaints about an English lit assignment, and a spirited discussion about which nearby restaurant had the best deep-dish pizza.

Had her life ever been that uncomplicated?

Simple answer: no. About the age her social life would have kicked in, she'd relocated to Colorado Springs—and Olympic hopefuls didn't have time for dates and dances and pizza outings.

She pulled one skate off, then the other. Wiped the blades dry. Stared through the window at the emptying rink as the session wound down.

In hindsight, it was clear her teen years had been far from normal. Yet she'd never felt as if she was missing out. Skating had been all-consuming. Aside from the hours carved out for schoolwork, it had dominated her every waking thought. She'd pursued her dream with a single-mindedness that left little room for fun, family, or friends—of either gender.

She tucked her skates in the carrying case. Zipped it closed.

Even after she'd left competitive skating, life hadn't slowed down. The pace of the ice show world had been fast, and the nomadic existence hadn't been conducive to lasting friendships. Nor had she had a chance to socialize in college. She'd been too intent on catching up to waste a moment on frivolous activities. And by the time she'd entered the workforce and established her career, the pool of eligible men—eligible by her stan-dards, anyway—had dwindled . . . as Sarah pointed out whenever Christy balked at one of the dates her friend tried to set up for her.

One side of Christy's mouth twitched. Poor Sarah. Despite her best efforts at matchmaking, she'd struck out over and over again. It had been discouraging—for both of them.

Yet just when she'd begun to think that marriage and family had passed her by . . . in the midst of struggling to come to grips with the devastating losses of the past nine months . . . God had sent a ray of hope into her life in the form of a handsome FBI agent.

To everything there is a season.

As always, the Good Book was right.

". . . so cool, and he is so awesome!"

She glanced over her shoulder. Two of the girls had separated themselves from the group of teens, stopping less than three feet from where she sat to have a private conversation. And why not? She was over thirty. Invisible to a teen.

"I think he's going to ask me to the winter ball!" One of the girls gave a muffled squeal.

"I am so jeal!" This petulant comeback from the brunette as she tossed her long mane of hair.

"I still can't believe it! I mean, to think he wants to go out with me . . . this is epic! Whenever he gets close, my heart starts to race like after I run the hundred meter!"

The two girls rejoined the larger group as · it began to drift toward the door, and Christy rose, skates in hand.

Maybe she hadn't missed out on the teen stuff after all.

Maybe she was simply a late bloomer.

Because even though she was twice as old as that girl in the throes of a crush, she felt the same way around Lance.

Too bad her plate was full of a lot of other stuff more important than English lit and pizza. Stuff that couldn't be put on the back burner.

For now, Ginny was her top priority.

And until they figured out what the kidnapper was up to, until she had answers about her sister, until this case was put to rest once and for all . . . romance would have to wait.

If Lance and Mark were right, however, this thing was wrapping up.

Unfortunately, only the kidnapper knew the exact timetable—and agenda.

16

"You mean I'm stuck here overnight?" Lance glowered at the harried agent behind the ticket counter at the airport.

"I'm sorry, sir. The plane has a mechanical issue. I can book you on the first flight out tomorrow morning. It leaves at 6:20 and would get you into St. Louis at 7:25. We can also give you a hotel voucher for tonight."

He shoved his fingers through his hair.

Great. Just great.

Spending Sunday night in Washington was *not* in his plans.

But his dilemma wasn't this woman's fault—and she still had to deal with the angry horde lined up behind him.

Reining in his temper, he rested one elbow on the counter. "Fine. I'll take the early flight and the voucher."

Relief smoothed some of the tension from her features. "Give me a minute."

While her fingers clicked over the keys and he waited for the printer to spit out a new boarding pass, Lance checked his watch. Seven o'clock. If nothing else, he'd get a decent sleep tonight—and he needed the shut-eye. At this rate, he could fall into bed by nine.

Unless you detour to Alexandria.

At the nudge from his conscience, he frowned.

No way.

Visiting Debbie wasn't on his agenda for this trip.

But it could be, now that he had a free evening. Mac was standing watch over Finn, and everything at Walter Reed was as under control as possible. Neither of his brothers needed him at the moment.

Meaning the excuse he'd used all weekend to defer a visit to Debbie didn't exist anymore.

Nevertheless, he wasn't ready to face the garbage he'd been sweeping under the rug for eighteen long months.

"Here you go, sir." The agent handed him a new boarding pass along with a voucher for the hotel. "Sorry for the inconvenience."

She had no idea.

"Thanks." He pocketed the pass and moved aside as the next angry customer braced his hands on the counter and proceeded to give the agent grief.

Should he pay Debbie an impromptu visit?

His temple began to throb as he wrestled with his dilemma. After the numbing fatigue and stress of the past seventy-two hours, his brain seemed incapable of analyzing that question.

A Starbucks caught his eye, and he picked up his carry-on. Maybe a caffeine infusion would jump-start his thinking process.

Once again he joined a long line—but this one moved a lot faster. And after a few slugs of an Americano laced with three shots of espresso, rational thought returned.

He could visit Debbie on a future trip. That was a definite option. He'd be coming back here a lot over the next few months, and he'd waited this long to deal with the situation. A few more weeks wouldn't hurt.

But why put off the inevitable? No matter when he showed up at her door, it was going to be tough. Wouldn't it be better to get it over with and stop procrastinating?

Yes. Go.

Caving to the prod from his conscience, he forced his legs to carry him to ground transportation and lined up yet again.

As he shuffled forward in the cab queue, he started to pull out his phone to call her. Paused. Slid it back into the holder. Better to leave himself some wiggle room. That way, he could change his mind at the last minute if he got cold feet.

Make that *colder* feet. They were already icy.

When his turn for a cab rolled around, he fished Debbie's address out of his wallet. He might not have gone to see her, but he'd kept tabs on her through his contacts in The Unit. Had known within days after she left Fort Bragg six months ago to return to Alexandria, where she had a supportive family.

272

Odd how he'd carried her address with him. As if by doing so, he could fool himself into thinking he was on the verge of going to see her.

Except now he was. In less than thirty minutes, according to the cab driver, they'd be pulling up outside her door.

He used every one of those minutes to try and psyche himself up for the visit. But when the cab halted in front of a modest, two-story duplex with warm light spilling from behind closed shades, he wasn't even close to being ready.

As he watched, a shadow moved past the window.

She was home.

So much for the less-than-noble hope he'd been harboring that she'd be out for the evening—and he could console himself with the excuse that he'd at least made the attempt.

While the driver stopped the meter and gave him the amount, he fought the urge to flee.

"This the right place, buddy?" The cabbie peered at him in the darkness. "It's the only street I know with this name. Did you want to go somewhere else?"

Yeah.

Anywhere but here.

But he needed to do this.

"It's the right place." He dug the money out and handed it over. "I'm going to need a ride to my hotel in about an hour. You want the business?"

"Sure."

"Pick me up at the restaurant on the corner." If Debbie threw him out—a very plausible possibility—he'd need a place that offered shelter from the cold while he waited for his ride.

"You got it."

Lance slid from the cab, hefted his carry-on, and forced himself to walk toward the front door. A gust of frigid wind whipped past, a whorl of tiny ice pellets stinging his exposed skin. An omen of an approaching winter storm, perhaps?

But he was more worried about the storm that might kick up inside the house.

He stepped onto the tiny stoop, took a deep breath, and pressed the bell.

Five seconds later—long before he was ready—she pulled the door open.

In the space of a few heartbeats, he did a rapid assessment.

She looked better than she had at the funeral, when smudged hollows had hung below her lashes and she'd seemed haunted and lost. The shadows were gone now, her demeanor was more alive, and she'd cut her long blonde hair into a flattering shorter style.

Yet she was far thinner than he remembered.

He swallowed and searched for his voice. "Hello, Debbie."

"Lance?" Could her eyes get any wider? "Oh my word, is that really you? Come in, come in."

She angled sideways and swept her arm toward the room behind her.

Holding tight to the handle of his bag, he moved past her, into the living room . . . kitchen . . . dining room. The whole first floor was no more than one large room, with a small galley and tiny eating area at one end.

"What on earth are you doing here? Where have you been? Why didn't you get in touch?" She closed the door and faced him.

"I came tonight to answer all those questions." He gestured toward the living room. "May I?"

"Yes. Of course. I'm sorry . . . I didn't mean to jump all over you. Can I take your coat? Would you like a drink?" She followed him to the center of the room.

"No, thanks. I can't stay long." He hefted his bag. "I was actually on my way out of town, but my flight was cancelled. It seemed like a sign I should pay you a long-overdue visit."

She patted the sofa. "Sit."

After sliding his jacket off, he complied.

She perched on a chair opposite him, confusion replacing the initial warmth that had flooded her eyes. "Long-overdue is an understatement. You fell off the face of the earth after Taz . . . after I lost Taz. I saw you at the funeral, but . . ." She tucked her hair behind her ear. "The three of us had so many good times, and you and Taz were like brothers . . ."

Her gaze flicked toward the table at the far end of the couch, and he glanced over.

A framed photo of him and Taz in the Middle East was front and center. The two of them were grinning and holding a box of brownies Debbie had sent. It wasn't the best shot they'd ever posed for together—but it was the last one.

Taz had died two days later.

The coffee in Lance's stomach curdled.

"I had planned to talk to you after the funeral, but you ended up in the hospital and I had to report back." The excuse sounded pathetic even to *his* ears.

"I know."

Though she fell silent, her eyes asked the question she didn't voice.

But that was eighteen months ago. Where have you been ever since?

The question she did ask, however, tore at his gut. "Did I do something to offend you?"

She thought it was *her* fault he hadn't gotten in touch?

Another wave of guilt crashed over him.

"No. It wasn't anything you did. It was something I did. Or didn't do." He clasped his hands and leaned forward. "I need to tell you about what happened the night Taz . . . the night we were ambushed."

"I know what happened. I had an official briefing."

"You don't know it all."

Now it was her turn to lean forward. "Then tell me."

He did so, sparing himself nothing, laying the blame squarely where it belonged, while she listened in silence.

By the time he finished, his fingers were trembling. "The truth of it is, my pride and ego got in the way. I didn't want to have two failed missions in a row—and Taz paid the price for my bad decision. I should have listened to his doubts."

Faint, parallel crevices etched her brow. "It sounds like you did. You checked with the other guys on the team, and with the base. No one else had any qualms."

"No, but I knew Taz. His instincts had always been spot-on. I was looking for a reason to override them that night, and I latched on to the handiest excuse—impending fatherhood—even though I knew better. Taz would never have let personal issues affect his judgment on a mission."

Debbie studied him for a moment as a tear welled in the corner of her eye. Spilled over. Trailed down her cheek.

She didn't appear to notice.

His stomach twisted, and he braced himself for the lashing he deserved.

"Don't be so sure."

He blinked. Squinted at her. "What do you mean?"

She knitted her fingers together, tight enough to whiten her knuckles. "Did you know he was on the verge of leaving The Unit?"

The curve balls these past few days were coming faster than he could field them.

Taz leave The Unit?

No way.

Delta Force was his life.

But he'd thought the same about Finn and the Rangers too.

Was anything what it seemed anymore?

"I had no idea."

"I'm not surprised he kept that to himself." She sighed and rubbed the bridge of her nose. "You weren't the only one who was beginning to wonder if being a father was compromising his combat judgment, making him too cautious, too risk averse. He told me about a couple of incidents in the month before he died where his hesitation could have had tragic consequences. It didn't, but knowing there would be a next time was eating him up. The last thing he wanted to do was endanger the other operators. Much as he loved Delta Force, he felt he had to get out."

"I can't believe he didn't tell me any of this."

"I can. He was still coming to grips with the decision himself. He hadn't put in the paperwork yet, but he was close." She locked gazes with him. "Here's the thing, Lance. Ever since the night he died, I've been beating myself up. I should have pushed him to get it done. He and I both knew he wasn't at the top of his combat game anymore—and we knew that could be deadly. I could have influenced him. Applied pressure. But I didn't want him to resent me for forcing his hand. Trust me, there's plenty of blame to go around for what happened that night."

As Lance tried to absorb all she'd told him, only the muffled backfire of a passing car and the mournful howl of the wind intruded on the silence.

All these months, Debbie had been dealing with a boatload of guilt too—even if hers was misplaced.

Who'd have predicted he'd end up trying to console *her* tonight?

"Taz wasn't the type to bend to pressure, Debbie. You know that. The few times I tried it, he dug in his heels and got more obstinate."

"A pregnant wife has a lot more leverage."

That could be true.

"I still think you're being too hard on yourself."

"No, I'm not. But I'm not trying to solicit sympathy. I just want you to know I don't blame you for what happened. Taz's ego was as big as yours. If your positions had been reversed, he might have made the same choice you did. He didn't like to fail, either. I knew about the juiced egos when I signed on—and I also knew that without that swagger and self-confidence, you guys wouldn't last a day on the kind of missions you were given. Those big egos were both a blessing and a curse. That night, they worked against you—but so did a lot of other factors."

Before he could respond, a child's cry sounded from upstairs.

Debbie was on her feet instantly. "Josh is teething, and it's playing havoc with his sleep pattern. I need to peek in on him. Would you like to come up?"

Lance stood at once. "Yes."

He followed her up the steps to a nursery illuminated only by the dim light spilling in from the hall. The toddler was sleeping quietly again, sucking on a finger, as Lance paused beside the crib. He had Debbie's blond hair, but the mouth and chin were all Taz.

Part of his buddy lived on in his son.

Pressure built behind Lance's eyes, and the room blurred.

Debbie adjusted the blanket, smoothed the hair back from her son's face, and bent to place a gentle kiss on his forehead. Then she led the way back downstairs.

"He looks like Taz." Lance stopped at the bottom of the steps.

"Yeah." She turned and smiled at him. "He does."

Lance did a sweep of the duplex. It was neat as any home with an eighteen-month-old could be, but the furnishings were basic. "So . . . are you doing okay? Do you need anything?"

"We're solid on the finance front, if that's what you're asking. And I'm learning how to be a single mom. I miss Taz every day—and I always will—but he'd expect me to carry on. So I went back to school to finish the course work for that teaching degree he was always pushing me to wrap up. Josh and I will be fine." She folded her arms and swallowed. "It would be nice, though . . . when he's older . . . if he could hear a few stories about his dad from someone who knew him. Stories I can't tell."

"I'd be honored to do that." Lance shoved his hands in the pockets of his jeans. "Look, I'm sorry I waited so long to visit you. I felt like I'd failed Taz and you and Josh. To be honest, I wasn't sure you'd speak to me once I told you what happened. I'm grateful you didn't throw me out."

Her expression grew pensive. "You know . . . in a way, it's probably better you waited. At the beginning I wasn't thinking clearly. I might have blamed you after hearing your story—because I needed someone else to blame. I couldn't face my own culpability. But time has a way of restoring perspective. Taz was having some judgment issues, and it's possible you were picking those up on some subliminal level. That could have been part of the reason you over-rode him that night."

"But I was wrong. His instincts were sound."

"Did he push back after you decided to proceed?"

"No."

"Then maybe he was questioning his instincts too. Taz wasn't shy about expressing his opinion —and pushing his point of view—as you well know. And second-guessing on a mission—or in life—isn't productive. You guys dealt day in and day out with stuff that gave me nightmares. The stress was immense. I'm not going to throw the first stone by judging the choices you made in such a traumatic situation."

Almost the same sentiment Christy had expressed.

Once more, his vision misted. Eighteen months of angst, all because he hadn't had the courage to face Debbie with the truth and take the consequences. Yet in the end, she'd cut him more slack than he deserved.

He might have left Delta Force, but his stubborn pride and ego obviously needed more work.

If nothing else, tonight was a step in the right direction on that score.

"Thank you for that." He crossed the room to retrieve his carry-on.

"Where are you living these days?"

He pulled a card out of his pocket and held it out to her.

Her eyebrows rose as she scanned the type. "FBI. Impressive. Are you here on business?"

He considered telling her about Finn; decided against it. They'd covered enough heavy stuff for one night. "Family business. A long story I'll tell you on a future visit. But I do have a different story to tell you before I leave."

She tipped her head. "I'm listening."

"Three weeks before the mission that went wrong, Taz and I were at the base, working out. He was trying to convince me to think about settling down—an ongoing campaign of his. I told him to give me one good reason why, and I'll never forget what he said. 'Because when you meet the right woman, it's like putting on 3-D glasses at a movie. All of a sudden you realize how flat and one dimensional your life's been. That's what my life was like before I met Debbie.'" Lance hung on to his composure by a thread. "Taz wasn't exactly a poetic guy, but that stuck with me. Even before he died, I'd planned to share it with you the next time we met."

Her eyes shimmered. "Thank you for telling me now."

He set his bag on the floor and held out his arms. She didn't hesitate to move into them.

"He was a good man, Debbie." His words roughened, but he didn't care—or try to hide his emotion. "I miss him every day too."

For a long moment they held each other, and

when at last he released her and picked up his bag, she pulled a tissue out of her pocket. "Don't be a stranger, okay?"

"I'll be making regular trips to DC for a while. Why don't you and I and Josh have dinner the next time I'm in town?"

"Dinner with an eighteen-month-old?" She gave him a watery smile. "You may regret that offer."

"I don't think so." He opened the door.

"In that case, you're on." She peered past him, into the darkness. "Do you have a car?"

"No. The cab's meeting me at the restaurant down the street."

A gust of wind whistled around the corner of the duplex, ice crystals glittering in the air as they spun past the porch light. "It's too cold to be walking."

"It's not far." He lifted a hand. "Take care, and I'll be in touch."

She watched from the door until he paused at the sidewalk for a final wave, then disappeared inside as he set off down the street. She was right. It was too cold to be walking. The wind was bitter. Under other circumstances, he might regret having to make this trek.

But the warmth in his heart, the new lightness in his soul, the sudden uptick in his spirits insulated him from the winter chill.

Spring might be weeks away, but with Finn out

of immediate danger, the situation with Debbie resolved, and a beautiful woman waiting in St. Louis—who'd done for his life what Taz had always said Debbie did for his—the seasons had already changed in his heart.

The one cloud hovering on the horizon was the kidnapping case.

However, if he and Mark were correct in their assessment, that was about to wrap up.

And once he touched down in St. Louis tomorrow morning, he intended to do everything in his power to make certain it wrapped up in their favor—not the kidnapper's.

17

Smothering a yawn, Lance exited the Jetway, pulled out his phone, and began scrolling through messages. Good. Only a few had come in during the flight from Washington, and none appeared to be urgent. They could all wait until he got to the office and fortified himself with some caffeine . . .

His finger paused on an email from an unfamiliar name.

Leanne Drury.

He checked the subject line—and jolted to a stop.

Missing Person ID.

Another passenger bumped him from behind, and with a mumbled apology he moved out of the surging horde.

In his short tenure with the Bureau, he'd affixed his name to only one missing person report.

The one he'd entered in the National Missing Person DNA Database and NamUs.

The one for Ginny Reed.

Even before he opened the email, he knew this wasn't the kind of news he needed after a crack-of-dawn wake-up call, a bumpy two-hour plane ride back to St. Louis, and the sub-zero wind chill waiting for him once he stepped outside the terminal.

Bracing himself, he double clicked on the subject line and homed in on the sender's address.

Memphis PD.

The message was short and clipped.

We have a DNA match on a body found in the Mississippi River on January 2. NamUs case #327465. Name Ginny Reed. Medical examiner's report attached. Cause of death inconclusive due to advanced state of decomposition. Call if you need more info. Please advise disposition of remains.

Stifling a word he rarely used, Lance exhaled. They'd been hoping for a new development in the Ginny Reed case—but this wasn't what he'd had in mind.

He ducked into an empty gate area and dropped into a chair to mull over the news.

Despite the kidnapper's efforts to convince them Ginny was alive, she'd been dead long before he sent his first note.

What kind of sick game was this guy playing? Why was he torturing Christy, reviving her hope weeks after she'd buried her sister, stringing her along?

Could this whole thing be about Christy, after all, as he'd speculated early on?

Mind racing, he clicked on the Shelby County ME's report. The autopsy had been done at the Regional Forensic Center in Memphis, and a fast read confirmed the detective's summation. The nude body had been in bad shape. Both feet and one hand were missing—not inconsistent with a body left to decay in water. The remains had been spotted by a fisherman, half submerged among a pile of debris and driftwood. No apparent cause of death could be determined.

Yet Ginny Reed had been murdered, no question about it.

Lance wiped a hand down his face, pulled himself to his feet, and started walking toward the bus that would take him to the long-term parking lot. He needed to get to the office. Talk this through with Mark and his boss. Decide on next steps.

But first he had to deliver a devastating piece of news that would once again upend Christy's world.

Christy braked as the light turned yellow and glanced at the digital clock on the dashboard. Naturally she'd hit every light on a day she was running late. At this rate, there was no way she'd make it to her desk by eight thirty. But after staring at the ceiling for most of the night, then thrashing through the little slumber she'd managed to eke out as dawn lightened the sky, it wasn't surprising she'd fallen into an oblivious stupor and slept through the alarm.

Too bad she hadn't indulged in some hot chocolate again last night. It had relaxed her enough Saturday to coax her into sleep.

Or maybe her mellow state that night had been due more to her phone conversation with Lance at the rink.

The light changed, and she accelerated. At least he'd be back today, and . . .

From within her purse, her phone began to chirp.

Keeping tabs on the traffic, she groped for it, skimming caller ID as she pulled it out.

Huh.

Had Lance somehow known she was thinking about him?

No. That was silly. More like wishful thinking on *her* part.

Smiling nonetheless, she put the phone to her ear and maneuvered around a woman who was trying to brush on mascara while she drove.

"Good morning. Are you back?"

"Yes. Are you at work?"

"Not yet. I'm running late—but I should be there in ten minutes if the stoplights cooperate. Are you at the office?"

"No. On the bus, heading for the long-term parking lot." A subtle strain stiffened his words.

She frowned. Had his brother taken a turn for the worse?

"Is everything all right with Finn?"

"Yeah. Listen . . . I need to talk to you, but not at your office."

Bad vibes snaked through the line, and her stomach clenched. "What's wrong?"

"Let's do this in person, okay?"

He didn't deny there was a problem.

"Lance . . . tell me." Her lungs locked, and her fingers tightened on the wheel.

"I'll swing into the parking lot at the rec center and call you from my car. I can be there in twenty minutes." A swish and a clatter sounded in the background. The bus door opening?

Another light changed from yellow to red in front of her, and she slammed on her brakes. "I have a meeting at nine thirty."

"This won't take long. I'm getting in my car now."

"Fine." It was clear he wasn't going to tell her anything by phone. "I'll wait for your call."

She finished the drive on autopilot, then huddled in her cubicle, phone close at hand. She tried to read a stack of parent evaluations for the family star-searching party they'd held a week ago in conjunction with the St. Louis Astronomical Society, but not a single word registered. All she could think about was Lance's impromptu visit.

Something had happened since they'd last talked, that much she knew—and it wasn't good.

Beyond that, she was at a loss.

By the time her phone finally began to vibrate, the bagel she'd scarfed down as she dashed out the door of her condo had turned into a hard lump of dough in her stomach.

She pressed the phone to her ear, heart banging against her rib cage. "You're here?"

"Yes."

"I'll be right out."

Without bothering to grab her coat, she tore down the hall.

"Whoa! Where's the fire?" Sarah gripped her arms as she careened around a corner and almost mowed down her friend.

"Lance is in the parking lot. I have to talk to him." Her words came out in a breathless rush.

Sarah's grin faded. "What's going on?"

"I don't know—but I'm about to find out."

She pulled free and took off again.

"Hey . . . I'll be here when you get back!"

Christy waved over her shoulder in acknowledgment and pushed through the main door. She spotted Lance's black Cruze at once and jogged toward it, dodging the large piles of snow that hadn't yet melted since the last storm.

The passenger door opened as she approached, and she slid into the warm interior. At her first glimpse of Lance's grim demeanor, her pulse skittered.

"I have some news." He reached over and folded her hand in his, sympathy softening the strong planes of his face.

And then she knew.

The breath whooshed out of her lungs.

"Ginny's dead, isn't she?" Her words came out dull. Shell-shocked.

A muscle flexed in his jaw. "Yes."

She closed her eyes. Tight. All those weeks of mourning, followed by weeks of hope . . . only to end up exactly where she'd been before.

God, why? Why would you do this to me?

Hard as she listened, no answer came.

"I'm so sorry." Lance's concerned voice, the comforting brush of his thumb over the back of her hand, barely registered.

A tear spilled out, but she didn't care. "Tell me."

She listened as he spoke, trying to take in the words, to make sense of the bizarre development, to accept the reality that this time, her sister was really dead. There would be no more false hope.

When he finished, she gripped his hand tighter and searched his eyes, seeking answers she knew he didn't have. "Why would someone do this?"

"I don't know, but we're not dealing with a rational person, that's more clear than ever. I'm going to have some of my colleagues weigh in on this as soon as I get back to the office."

"What about . . . Ginny?"

"I assume you want the remains . . . her body . . . brought back here?"

"Yes."

"I'll let the Memphis PD know—and I can help coordinate the transfer." He leaned closer and gently wiped away a tear with the pad of his thumb. "Do you want me to drive you home?"

"No. I . . . there's nothing for me to do there. And my car's here. I'd rather . . . go through the motions of the day." She drew in a shaky breath. Blinked to clear her vision. "Ever since we realized the kidnapper took that photo of Ginny right after the fire, a cloud of dread has been hanging over my head. Part of me was prepared for bad news . . . but I could never quite extinguish that tiny flicker of hope, you know?" Her voice choked, and she groped in her pocket for a tissue. "I just don't get why someone would put me through all this."

"I'm back to thinking this guy was targeting you as well as your sister."

"But like I've said all along, we don't have any enemies. Certainly no common enemies."

Lance's features hardened. "There's an enemy out there somewhere—and we're going to find him." He cranked up the heat, studying her. "Are you sure you don't want to go home?"

"Yes. But I do want you to get back to work so you can find this guy." She groped for the handle of the door . . . but when she tried to tug her hand free, he held tight.

"Do you know what I'd like to do right now?"

She angled back toward him, and despite the swirl of confusion muddling her thinking, she had no problem deciphering the emotion in his eyes.

He wanted to pull her into his arms and hold her until the world steadied.

Not possible, of course. Lance was too much of a pro to get that personal in the middle of a case. Especially in a public parking lot.

But knowing that was what he wanted to do gave her more comfort than he'd ever know.

"Yeah, I think I do. Hold that thought, okay?"

"I intend to." With a final squeeze of her fingers, he released her and shifted into drive. "I'll drop you at the door. You're not dressed for this weather."

True. Her black slacks and thin wool sweater weren't made to withstand winter temperatures.

The instant he stopped in front of the entrance,

she pushed open her door. "Thank you for delivering the news in person."

"I'm sorry I had to deliver it at all."

With a nod, she slid out before she broke down again, hurrying inside as he drove away.

Sarah was waiting in one of the chairs in the lobby, and she rose as Christy pushed through the door in a gust of cold air. After a quick scan of her face, she took her arm and propelled her down the hall.

"While you were outside, I cased the offices. Matt's out of town on a ski trip with his family. We can talk there."

Once they were inside the rec center manager's office, Sarah closed the door and faced her. "You don't have to tell me anything if you don't want to, but you look like you're about to fold. I just want you to know I'm here if you need me."

Her vision blurred. She might not have any family left, but she had Sarah—and Lance. Both valued friends she'd be relying on heavily in the weeks to come.

"They found Ginny's body." She managed to choke out the words.

Sarah's face went slack. "Where?"

"Memphis. In the r-river."

Some of the color drained from Sarah's face. "Are they certain?"

"Yeah. They got a DNA match."

"So . . . what's going on? None of this makes sense."

"Tell me about it." Christy dropped onto the edge of Matt's desk and rubbed her arms as a chill swept over her. "They're trying to sort it out. And until they do, this has to stay between us."

"My lips are sealed." Sarah squeezed her hand. "You want me to drive you home?"

"Lance made the same offer."

"Good man."

Yeah, he was.

"No. I'll end up brooding if I'm by myself. I'd rather let work distract me."

"Will you at least come to dinner tonight?"

"I appreciate the offer, but let me see how I'm feeling by this afternoon. You know I love your family, but I might not be up for a . . . lively . . . meal."

"You mean noisy and rowdy. Yeah, I see your point. I'll tell you what. Why don't I call you later and you can decide then if you're in the mood for a meal in the Marshall household? In the meantime, keep hanging in."

She pushed off from the desk, the simple movement requiring more effort than she expected. "I don't have much choice."

"Yes, you do. You could fall apart. After all you've been through these past few months, I'm surprised you haven't. But Olympic athletes must be made of tougher stuff than the rest of us. You need me, you call. Got it?"

"Got it."

They parted in the hall, and as Christy walked back to her cube, Sarah's comment echoed in her head.

It was possible Olympic athletes were made of tougher stuff—but if that was true, she'd lost her edge.

Because she was a heartbeat away from caving.

"This guy's got an agenda that has nothing to do with Ginny Reed. We need to switch gears and look closer at the sister."

As Steve Preston echoed the conclusion he'd already reached, Lance glanced over at Mark. Based on his expression, his fellow agent appeared to be on the same page.

"The question is, what is it?" Mark crossed an ankle over his knee.

"It's more than harassment or psychological torture." Lance tightened his grip on the arm of his chair. "No one goes to all the trouble this guy did just to play a sick joke. He has bigger plans for Christy Reed. Are we in a position to offer any protection?"

"No. Not our purview." Steve's response confirmed what Lance already knew: the FBI only provided security for the attorney general and FBI director. "I reviewed the background file you gave me. What's the story on her parents?"

"They were killed in a car accident about nine months ago. Her mother died in the crash. Her father lingered for a couple of months in a coma but never regained consciousness."

"The whole family wiped out in the space of six months." Steve fixed him with an intent look. "Seem a little suspicious to you?"

"Yes." Lance leaned forward. He'd had the exact same thought after the locket arrived with the two Xed out pictures of her parents. "But I reviewed the accident report, and it was straight-forward. They were returning home on a rural road from a potluck church supper they'd attended with Ginny in Chandler. The skid marks suggested her father tried to avoid something on the road and slid out of control. The sheriff concluded it was an animal, probably a deer. They have a significant number of deer-related accidents on that road each year."

"Was it raining that night?"

"No."

"You talk to the deputy who filed the report or the tech who analyzed the skid marks?"

Lance shifted his weight, once more feeling as if the word *rookie* was stamped across his forehead. "No."

"Do it. That whole scenario smells, given all that's happened since." Steve rested his elbows on his desk and steepled his fingers. "Let's keep the discovery of the body under wraps for now. No need to let the kidnapper know we're on to his scam."

At least he'd taken care of that piece of business. "I already passed that on to Memphis."

"You need any more help with this besides Mark?"

"Not yet." Truth be told, he didn't even need Mark at the moment. It wasn't as if they were scrambling to investigate dozens of leads.

"When this does start to heat up, let me know." Steve picked up his phone. "And keep me apprised of any developments."

End of meeting.

Lance followed Mark out and down the hall, where his colleague ducked into an empty conference room and motioned him in. "Don't beat yourself up about the parents. I wouldn't have done more than review the sheriff's report, either, unless I spotted a red flag."

Weird how Mark could read him so well. He was usually better at keeping his thoughts—and emotions—to himself.

His colleague grinned. "HRT, Delta Force. We're both cut from the same cloth. I'd be second-guessing myself if I was in your shoes too. I do agree the timing is suspicious, but I bet the sheriff's report is clean. If, by chance, our guy was involved in that accident, he didn't leave a trace—which seems to be his MO."

"Steve's right, though. Talking to the deputy won't hurt. If I decide to take a run out to the accident site, you want to go along?"

"Sure, if nothing else is hopping. Keep me in the loop." With a lift of his hand, Mark strolled down the hall.

Once back at his desk, Lance pulled the accident report out of the case file and reread it. One-car accident, speed about forty-five mph. The car had tumbled into a ravine after skidding out of control in a rural area around nine thirty—well after sundown. No alcohol had been involved, based on BAC tests done on Christy's father. In fact, no drugs of any kind had been found in his system.

Nothing jumped out at him on a second pass, either.

He found the responding deputy's phone number at the bottom of the report, tapped it in his phone, and leaned back. The man answered on the second ring.

"Deputy Meyer, this is Special Agent Lance McGregor with the St. Louis FBI office. Do you have a minute?"

A moment of silence ticked by. In all likelihood, a rural Missouri sheriff's department didn't get a lot of calls from the FBI.

"Uh, sure. What can I do for you?"

"I'm interested in an accident that occurred on May 14." He gave the man the location and the particulars. "You filed the report."

"Yes, I remember that one. Sad case."

"The report appears to be fairly straightforward, but I'm wondering if there's anything you might have noticed that didn't get into the official document."

"Such as?" There was a wary edge to the question. As if the guy thought he was impugning his competence.

Not the best way to build rapport—and get information.

He switched to a conversational tone. "Well, I've filed my share of reports, and I know they don't allow room for interpretation or conjecture. How long have you been in law enforcement?"

"Eighteen years."

"That's a lot of experience. I expect your seasoned eye might notice details that aren't appropriate for a facts-only official report but could offer some insight into a case. That's the kind of input I'm looking for. Was there anything that struck you as odd or gave you pause that night?"

"Are you thinking this wasn't an accident?"

That question called for a combination of diplomacy and evasion.

"We're investigating it in conjunction with another case. This particular situation isn't our main interest."

Despite his sidestep, the answer seemed to satisfy the deputy.

"I can't say there was anything in particular about the accident itself that raised an eyebrow. It had all the markings of a deer dodge—and we see a lot of those around here. All the facts are in the report." He stopped, and Lance waited him out. "I do remember thinking what a shame it was the deer picked that spot to cross."

Lance's antennas went up. "Why?"

"Well, they were coming from the monthly potluck church supper they always attended with their daughter, headed back to St. Louis."

An event they always attended? That nuance hadn't shown up in the report. If their guy had been watching them, he would have picked up that pattern—and could have used it to suit his purposes.

"I can figure the route they were taking," the deputy continued. "Been over it plenty of times myself. Just two lanes, but a nice, easy drive. If you ran off the road in most places, you'd end up in a cornfield or wedged up against a tree. About the only stretch that's dangerous is the very spot the accident occurred. There's a limestone bluff on one side and a sharp drop on the other. Fifty, sixty feet I'd estimate. Plus a nasty curve. No guardrail, either. Not enough traffic to warrant one—though it would have helped that night. I remember thinking it was bad luck they lost control at that very spot."

Bad luck—or a well-orchestrated accident?

Given their guy's attention to detail and his demonstrated ability to carry out a complicated operation, Lance was beginning to suspect the reactive squad supervisor's instincts were correct and it was the latter.

But how did you send a car careening out of control without leaving any trace?

Or was there a trace no one had noticed because they'd too quickly nailed a deer as the culprit?

If so, was it still there?

"Anything else, Agent McGregor?"

"No. You've been very helpful."

"Glad to be of service. You need anything else, give me a call."

"I'll do that."

After ending the call, Lance leaned back in his chair. There wasn't any rush to investigate the so-called accident. It had happened in the middle of nowhere, so there were no witnesses except the ubiquitous deer that populated rural Missouri. And even if he stumbled upon an indication of foul play, it wasn't likely to help them identify Ginny's kidnapper.

He'd rather spend his day hanging around Christy. Waiting for the guy's next move. Watching her back. Could he think of an excuse his boss would buy to pay her another visit . . .

"You have anything hot to do on the kidnapping in the next couple of hours?" Mark stopped outside his office, Special Agent Nick Bradley on his heels. Both their demeanors were serious.

"Nothing that can't wait if you've got an urgent issue."

"Steve wants every free agent in the conference room. Stat. A tip came in on the most-wanted line at Headquarters. Sounds like one of our top ten could be lurking in this area." He called the final sentence over his shoulder as he picked up his pace again.

So much for staying close to Christy.

But if nothing else, in his off hours he intended to play the boyfriend part as much as possible.

18

Somewhere far away, a bell was ringing.

Pulling herself back from the exhausted slumber that had felled her after a night of pillow punching, followed by frenzied cleaning, followed by more pillow punching, Christy groped for the alarm clock and jabbed the shutoff button.

Five more minutes. That's all she needed. Just five more—

The ringing started again.

What the . . . ?

She pried her eyelids open and peered at the clock. Six forty-five? Her alarm wasn't scheduled to go off until seven.

Another ring—followed by a rush of adrenaline—brought her fully awake.

Someone was calling on her landline.

She threw back the covers, scrambled out of bed, and dashed for the kitchen. Maybe there was news, and Lance had tried to call her on the cell she'd left beside her bed. If she'd slept through the alarm yesterday, she could very well have slept through the chirp of her cell. He could be trying to reach her on her home phone.

By the time she grabbed it out of the charger, her answering machine had already kicked in.

"Hello?" She stopped the recorded message as she issued the breathless greeting.

"Christy Reed?" An unfamiliar woman's voice.

"Yes?"

"Sorry to disturb you so early, but I wanted to catch you before you left for work. This is Regina Devereaux with the *Post-Dispatch*. I'm following up on a story that came over the wire about the discovery of your sister's body in Memphis. I hoped you might answer a few questions."

Christy stared at her spotless kitchen—one of the few positive results of her restless night—and scrambled to process the unwelcome turn of events.

A reporter was calling about Ginny. The news was on the wire service. This woman wanted to write an article about it for the *Post* . . . where the kidnapper could see it.

Her stomach twisted.

This was bad.

Very bad.

Lance wanted to keep the news about Ginny under wraps. And during his brief call last night in the middle of a manhunt that had required all FBI hands on deck, he'd assured her the Memphis police were on board with that plan.

So how had the story leaked?

"Ms. Reed?"

Heart banging against her ribs, she pushed her tangled hair back from her face. She needed to talk to Lance. Now. Before she said a word to any reporter.

"This isn't a convenient time."

"I only need a quote or two." The woman's tone was pleasant but determined. "I'm sure the discovery was quite a shock. Did you have any idea the woman who died in the house fire wasn't your sister?"

"I'm sorry. I have no comment. Good-bye." She punched the end button.

The instant she got the dial tone, she called Lance's cell number.

Two rings in, he answered, sounding as groggy as she'd felt after her own phone had jolted her awake. The man had probably been up half the night too, chasing the high-profile criminal he'd alluded to during their quick conversation.

"Lance, it's Christy. Sorry if I woke you, but I just had a call from a reporter at the *Post*. She said there's a story about Ginny on the wire service." Despite her attempt to remain calm, her voice hitched on the last word.

A few seconds ticked by. When he responded, he sounded 100 percent alert—and angry. "The leak wasn't on our end. I'll call Memphis, but the damage is done. What did you tell her?"

"No comment."

"Good—although that may not stop the story from running. Who was the reporter?"

She gave him the woman's name.

"I'll see what I can find out about her. If we're lucky, she's not the go-getter type, and if a story does run, it will be a single paragraph buried somewhere in a back section."

"She sounded very determined."

"That figures." Lance sighed. "Give me an hour. If she calls back, stick with no comment. Go about your normal activities, and if she shows up in person, don't let her badger you into talking, no matter how persistent she is."

The sick feeling in the pit of her stomach intensified. "This is a disaster, isn't it? If the kidnapper knows we're on to him, he could disappear. We'll never catch him."

"Let's not jump to conclusions. Our guy has an agenda. After all the effort he's put into this, I'm not certain he'll give up so close to the last act. He may alter his plans, though. Let me call you back after I have more facts. We'll get this guy no matter what, Christy."

The steel in his voice bolstered her spirits. "I'm counting on that. Talk to you soon."

Long after the line went dead, her fingers remained clenched around the phone. Perhaps fate would be kind, as Lance had suggested. The reporter might not pursue the story or, if she did, it might run as a small paragraph in some obscure part of the paper where the kidnapper would never notice it.

Yet as she dropped the phone back into the charger, her hopes dimmed.

So far, all the luck had been on the kidnapper's side.

And she had an ominous feeling that pattern wasn't going to change anytime soon.

Lance slammed down his desk phone, banged a drawer shut, and blew out a breath.

"That doesn't sound positive."

He turned to find Mark eying him from the doorway of his cube.

"It's not." He filled him in as he paced, watching the man's countenance change from curious to concerned to seriously worried. "According to Officer Drury in Memphis, a reporter from the local paper got the scoop from a newbie in the media relations group before the instruction to keep this quiet was passed along. The media guy assumed once next-of-kin had been notified, he was free to talk to the press. A brief article ran in the Memphis paper this morning and was picked up by the wire."

"Does the PR guy still have a job?" Mark's eyes thinned.

"He wouldn't under my watch. But the real question at this point is what's our guy going to do if he finds out we're on to him?"

"You could try convincing the *Post* reporter to hold off on the story."

"I could—but if she finds out the FBI is involved, that might make her more eager to get a scoop. I ran some intel. She's an up-and-coming investigative reporter who's starting to win some prestigious awards. Her bio describes her as tenacious and fearless."

"Ambitious too, I'm thinking." Mark braced one shoulder against the wall.

"Goes without saying."

"The kidnapper might not be watching the papers."

"That's what I'm hoping. But if this went out on the wire, there could be national interest. It's an unusual case, and some sharp-eyed print or broadcast reporter will see the feature potential." Lance raked his fingers through his hair.

"Let's hope we get the kidnapper first."

"Amen to that."

"On a brighter note, at least you won't be pulled away for any more top ten tracking duty. Scuttlebutt says he's on the run again. If he was here, we apparently missed him." Mark straightened up. "The last sighting was in Columbia."

"Fine with me. That will give me a chance to run down to the accident site and scout around. Still up for a road trip?"

"If you can wait until this afternoon. I need to tie up a few loose ends this morning."

"No problem." It wasn't as if whatever they might find on the country road where Christy's parents had been fatally injured was going to ID their guy, anyway—but it was better than sitting around waiting for the kidnapper's next move. "We can grab a burger on the way."

"I'll swing by about twelve thirty. While I'm out, I'll stop by my house and change." Mark flipped his tie. "Not the best attire for a winter walk in the country." With that, he disappeared down the hall.

Lance dropped into his desk chair and faced his computer. Outdoor reconnaissance wasn't his favorite way to spend a frigid January afternoon, but it beat doing nothing.

And *nothing* was an appropriate word for the Ginny Reed kidnapping. His first case with the Bureau, and he was batting zero. Three weeks in, and all he had was a vague description of the probable killer.

In other words, their guy was still calling the shots.

Even worse, there was now a strong chance he'd find out they knew his elaborate ruse was a sham.

Lance rocked back in his chair and played with his mouse, watching the cursor zip around the screen as he pondered the potential fall-out.

Most of the scenarios that strobed through his mind weren't encouraging—but in light of what they knew about their quarry, was there a chance the news leak could work to their advantage?

His hand stilled.

Maybe.

This guy was a planner. He'd pulled off a mind-blowing deception because he'd had time to plot it out in meticulous detail—and the whole scheme hinged on making Christy believe her sister was alive. If he heard about the discovery, he'd have to modify his plans on the fly.

And people often made mistakes when they rushed.

Lance exhaled. That positive spin was a long shot—but he chose to believe it was possible.

Otherwise, barring a mistake, this guy could win the game he was playing—meaning Christy would lose.

An outcome Lance didn't intend to accept professionally . . . or personally.

···

Nathan stretched, adjusted his pillow, and opened his eyes to find sunlight streaming in his window —a rare luxury on a weekday morning. Sleeping in was a definite benefit to the night shift work he'd had to pick up after Dennis broke his leg. In truth, other than the rotten timing in terms of his plans for Christy, he preferred having the deserted building almost to himself. No pretense to keep up, no forced smiles, no idle chitchat, no bosses looking over his shoulder.

But you didn't get promotions working alone at night. That took face time.

He knew all about the games people played.

Swinging his legs to the floor, he homed in on the photo of Christy on the bulletin board, a quiver of excitement zipping through him.

This was the week.

In three days, twelve hours—after she finished with her second student at the rink Friday night —he'd be waiting. And he'd keep the promise he made to her in his last note. Before morning dawned, she'd see her sister again . . . assuming all those platitudes she'd spouted years ago about being reunited with loved ones in death happened to be true.

He snorted.

Good luck with that.

If there was a God, he'd distanced himself from his creation long ago. As far as Nathan could see, humans were on their own. You lived. You died. In between, you tried to survive. The world was a chaotic, survival-of-the-fittest struggle. The powerful prospered; the weak suffered. That was how nature worked.

He rose and strolled over to the photo, barely glancing at the mutilated mouse on the desk as he picked up the paring knife beside it. Instead, he focused on Christy in her glittery skating out-fit, arms raised over her head in a triumphant posture, chin high, eyes sparkling as she smiled at the camera.

At him.

Smiling back, he tightened his grip on the knife.

Raised his arm.

And drove the blade straight into her heart.

Lance had no problem finding the accident scene. The sheriff's report detailed the location, but tire skids also marked the spot.

He put on his flashers and eased as far as possible onto the minuscule shoulder. The rural route was quiet on this cold Tuesday afternoon; partially blocking the road shouldn't be an issue.

"Ready?" He tugged on a pair of gloves and turned up the collar of his sheepskin-lined jacket, glad he'd followed Mark's lead and made a quick trip home to change before they set out.

His colleague pulled on a ski hat and opened his

door. "Yeah. Boots on the ground is always the best way to get the lay of the land."

Lance slid out of the car, walked over to where the skid marks began, and assessed the terrain. "The deputy was right about this being the worst possible location to lose control." He indicated the steep drop-off and the curve ahead.

"Also fishy." Mark shaded his eyes against the sun and inspected the area.

"Why don't we walk the road first, down the middle. You work the right side, I'll take the left. Then we'll retrace our steps from the shoulders."

"Makes sense."

They followed the skid marks from their beginning, to the fishtails as Christy's father struggled for control, to where the black tracks ended at the edge of the precipice.

Lance stepped to the lip and looked down. He'd seen the photos of the accident, knew where the car had come to rest. But even without the photos, the crushed and broken limbs, naked in the middle of winter, marked the spot.

"I'm surprised either of them survived." Beside him, Mark surveyed the steep drop-off.

"I bet our guy was too—assuming he was responsible. And if he was, he was also probably sweating bullets in case Christy's father regained consciousness."

Mark folded his arms. "I don't know. Unless he left something at the scene to identify himself or showed himself to her parents—which is doubtful —he may not have cared if one of them survived. In fact, he might have hoped for that outcome. That way, Christy would have had to watch a beloved, seriously impaired parent suffer."

"That's sick."

"Fits what we know about this guy, though."

True.

Lance flexed his fingers to keep the circulation moving. Despite his thermal gloves, bitter air was seeping in. "You see anything on our walk down?"

"No."

"Me, neither. Let's try the shoulders."

They moved back toward the car, attention fixed on the ground, then repeated the walk several times, scrutinizing the shrubs and trees on the sides of the road.

"I think this was a bust." Mark tugged his cap down further over his ears as the wind picked up.

Much as he hated to admit it, Lance agreed.

"Before we head out, let's regroup for a minute in the car. While we warm up, we can do some brainstorming now that we've seen the place."

Mark shot him a skeptical look but didn't argue.

Once back in his seat, Lance cranked up the heater, tugged off his gloves, and examined the scene through the windshield. "If you wanted to send a car out of control on this road and leave no trace, how would you do it?"

"We already know he's savvy with GPS. He could have put a device on their car, followed their progress on a cell phone, and known when they'd arrive at this spot."

"Right. And the deputy said they attended that church dinner every month with Ginny, so there was a pattern."

"In other words, our guy could pick his night and lay in wait. The real question is what could he quickly put on the road—and get rid of just as fast—in case another car showed up? All without leaving a trace?"

"And without risking his own neck—which leaves jumping in front of the car to startle them out of the equation." Lance examined the skid marks again.

"It would have to be an object that appeared suddenly at eye level to be most effective."

"Like a deer darting across the road . . . caught in the beam of headlights on a dark night and disappearing without a trace an instant later, leaving chaos in its wake."

"Yeah. The sudden appearance is key. If the driver had seen it from a distance, he could have slowed down well in advance."

"I wonder if he had some sort of object rigged to drop from above as the car approached?" Lance leaned forward and examined the trees through the windshield, then shook his head. "Scratch that. The trees on top of the limestone bluff are too high, and the ones growing on the sides of the cliff are too low."

"Maybe whatever it was didn't drop from above. Some of the trees clinging to the side of the bluff are tall enough to climb, and on a dark night, in full spring foliage, the branches would have provided excellent cover for our guy while he waited to pull an object onto the road as the car approached."

"Like what?"

"I have no idea. All I'm saying is the scenario isn't that far out in left field. If he was willing to stage a fire with a fake victim, I don't think this challenge would be beyond him."

"Yeah."

"You know, it almost seems as if he has a vendetta against the whole Reed family." Mark angled toward him. "Either that, or he has a serious gripe against Christy and has gone above and beyond making her pay for whatever she did to him."

"I don't buy the family vendetta premise. All of their background checks came back squeaky clean. One family member might have an unknown enemy, but not all of them."

"Since Christy is the only one left standing, my money's on her."

Lance's grip tightened on the wheel. "How could she have made an enemy this evil without realizing it?"

"That, my friend, is the question of the day—and we're not going to find the answer here. You ready to head back?"

No, he wasn't. Now that he'd visited the scene and driven the presumed route, he was more certain than ever the location of the so-called accident wasn't coincidence. They might not have found anything to prove that theory, but his gut told him the evidence was here if they'd known what to look for.

"I guess so." He unbuttoned his coat, put the car in gear, and pulled back onto the road.

"You're coming back, aren't you?"

Did his colleague have a sixth sense or what?

"I might."

"If it was my case, I would too. Loose ends bother me. You planning to tell Christy about our speculation that this wasn't an accident?"

"No. She's got enough to deal with at the moment. Besides, even if we're right, it doesn't change anything. Bottom line, her parents are gone. If you come up with any other theories about the accident, let me know."

"Will do . . . although I have a feeling this case will break wide open before you get around to making another trip out here."

So did he. They were still working on the killer's timetable, and he'd already suggested the end was in sight.

The best they could hope for was that whether

or not the news story about Ginny appeared in the St. Louis paper, their guy would somehow stumble and make a mistake that would give them the lead they desperately needed.

Soon.

Because while there were lots of unknowns in this case, Lance was certain of one thing.

They were running out of time.

19

"No!"

As Neven's furious bellow boomed through the apartment, Mevlida jerked toward the door of her bedroom, fingers tightening on the book of prayers clutched in her hand.

A chair clattered, as if it had been kicked or knocked over.

What on earth . . . ?

Neven never raised his voice or was violent in noisy ways. His anger was always cold. Quiet. Controlled.

A cabinet door banged, shaking the walls.

A roller shade clattered.

Glass shattered.

Quivering, Mevlida stared at her closed door. Who knew what had triggered tonight's rage? But no matter the cause, one outcome was guaranteed.

Her life would become even more miserable.

Because whenever Neven was unhappy, he took it out on her.

Footsteps stomped down the hall, and she cringed as he approached her door—but he kept going, muttering words she couldn't understand.

She cocked her ear, listening as he inserted the key into the lock on his door. A few seconds later, the slam reverberated through the apartment. Though muffled noises continued to penetrate the thin walls, they offered no clue what he was up to.

Ten minutes later, his door opened again. She tensed—but he continued down the hall, toward the living room.

The front door opened.

Banged.

Quiet descended.

For the next thirty minutes, Mevlida remained perched on the edge of her chair. Waiting. Listening. Trembling.

Finally, prodded by a gnawing hunger, she gathered up her courage and pushed herself to her feet. She needed to eat, and who knew when Neven would return? Sometimes after a bad day, he'd leave without a word and not come back until long after she'd gone to bed.

But she knew where he went on those nights. Bars had a distinctive odor that clung to skin and hair and clothing. Not that he ever over-indulged in alcohol, as she and his father had.

Neven was stronger about that, no matter his emotional state. But he wasn't above a drink now and then to celebrate—or lament.

Based on his mood tonight, he had a lot of lamenting to do.

She needed to eat dinner before he returned or she might not get any food until morning.

After setting the book of prayers on her bed, she crept across her room and cracked the door—in case he'd snuck back in. He'd done that to her once, jumping out as she entered the kitchen. Her hand had twitched for hours afterward.

All was quiet tonight, however.

Pushing her walker ahead of her, she shuffled down the hall and stopped at the kitchen door. The roller shade that had snapped had been pulled back down, but the chair remained on its side, and shards of glass lay on the floor below a gouge in the wall.

She surveyed the counter and table. No dinner had been prepared for her, and she dare not cook herself. There were consequences for that. Cereal would have to do—again. At least he'd restocked the pantry over the weekend.

As she passed the table, she glanced at the folded-back newspaper Neven had retrieved from a trash can at work, as usual. After all these years, the words were still hieroglyphics to her.

But the photo—it seemed familiar.

Moving close, she peered at the image.

It was the girl in the photo on the bulletin board in Neven's room. The skater.

This was a different picture, but the shot was similar enough to leave no doubt about her identity. She was dressed in one of those little skating outfits, arms outstretched as she glided toward the camera on one foot, her other leg raised in the air behind her.

There was another photo beside it, of a different girl. That one she didn't recognize—but the family resemblance was clear. Were the two sisters?

She examined the third photo, taken near a river. Emergency vehicles were in the foreground.

Had something happened to those girls?

What connection did Neven have to them?

And why had this story incited his fury?

Hunger evaporating, Mevlida swiveled toward the clock. That local news program Neven sometimes watched while he ate dinner should be on about now—and spoken words were easier to understand than the written language. Perhaps there would be a story about the skater.

She turned on the small TV that sat in the corner on the counter, found the news channel, and leaned on her walker as the woman broadcaster with the perfect hair and makeup spoke to the nice-looking man seated beside her.

Pictures of a school, a police car, the airport zipped across the screen as they bounced from story to story. No mention of the lovely skater.

Just as she was about to give up, though, a photo of her on the ice appeared behind the news duo.

Mevlida listened intently, trying to decipher their rapid-fire delivery, but only managed to pick out every few words as scenes of a fire played on the screen, followed by the same photo of the second girl that was in the paper.

Fire. Wrong. Dead. Sister. Those words she could distinguish.

Were the two pretty girls dead?

But no . . . some footage showing an older, distraught version of the skater began to run. The camera was in her face as she grabbed mail from a box, pushed past the reporter, and hurried away to disappear through a door.

The skater must be alive.

For now.

Her forehead began to throb, and Mevlida lifted a shaking hand to massage her temple. She needed one of those blue pills. Too bad she hadn't taken several the night she'd found Neven's door unlocked. Now she'd have to suffer until morning.

Unless . . .

Was it possible that in his rage, he might have forgotten to lock the door again? He *had* left in a hurry—and as best she could recall, the key hadn't rattled in the lock.

It couldn't hurt to check.

Gripping the walker, she slowly retraced her steps to his door. Paused. Listened. No sound of him returning—but he didn't usually stay out late on weeknights. He could come through the door at any moment.

She needed to move fast.

Summoning up her courage, she lifted her hand. Grasped the knob. Twisted.

Her eyes widened as the door opened. Unlocked twice in two weeks.

If nothing else tonight, she would have some relief for her headache—and she'd take a few extra pills to stash in her room too.

After pushing the door wide, she listened once again. All clear. Gripping the walker, she maneuvered it into the room and toward the desk as fast as she could. She should be able to get in and out in three minutes if . . .

Za ime boga!

She gasped, heart stumbling as she gaped at the picture of the skater.

There was a knife stuck through her chest.

An icy chill swept over her despite the wool sweater she was never without in the tepid apartment.

Her gaze dropped to the mutilated mouse on top of the desk.

Lifted again to the pretty skater.

Dead.

That single word, and the images from the news stories, surged through her mind.

Somehow, Neven was involved in all of that.

The fire, the river, the distress on that young woman's face as the camera got too close.

And she was in danger.

Mevlida knew that as surely as she knew she couldn't stand by and let an innocent person be harmed. Maybe she hadn't been able to save Mihad or Daris or Sonja . . . or even Neven's father . . . but she had to try to help this young woman. To warn her.

Because difficult as it was to accept, something inside her grandson was broken—and for whatever reason, he was intent on destroying the woman in the picture.

But what could she do?

Her chin quivered as she looked from the stabbed photo to the dead mouse. If she called the police, they would probably dismiss her story. She had no proof. No command of the language to communicate her concerns. No words to make anyone grasp what Neven was capable of if they *could* understand her.

The pounding in her head intensified, and she fumbled for the bottle of pills. Shook out eight. Retreated to the hall, closing the door carefully behind her.

Only after she'd taken four of the tablets and the throbbing subsided did she allow herself to think through the problem.

If she did call the police . . . if she did find a way to communicate with them . . . if they did believe there was cause for concern and began investigating . . . Neven would be livid. And even if they *didn't* believe her, he would be furious. He hated dealing with anyone connected to the government.

No matter the outcome, if she called the authorities her life wouldn't be worth living.

The minutes ticked by as she wrestled with the dilemma, fingers clenched around the handle of the walker—until, all at once, a solution popped into her head. One so bold, so daring, her lungs froze.

No.

That was crazy.

She shook her head, trying to erase the idea from her mind. She didn't have the courage to carry out such an audacious plan.

But if she didn't, that skater could end up dead—at her grandson's hands.

And the blood would be on hers as well.

Trembling, she slowly lowered herself into the chair where she spent hours with her book of prayers—the only thing that offered her comfort these days. She picked up the well-thumbed volume, caressed the worn cover . . . and faced the truth.

Neven had no conscience. No respect for life. No humanity.

Perhaps he never had.

If that skater had offended him in some way,

he could have decided she must die—and he would have no compunction about carrying out such a sentence. Her solution might be the only way to stop whatever evil intent dwelt in his heart . . . and she could carry it out tomorrow, while he was at work. It would be finished long before he arrived home.

But was that the best course of action?

Oh, Mihad, what should I do?

How she longed to see her dear husband, take his strong hand, hear his wise voice! No matter what crisis had befallen them during their marriage, he'd remained calm and clear-thinking. What would he say about her plan?

She strained, trying to hear even a soft, distant yes or no.

No guidance came.

Yet she did hear the echo of a gentle encouragement he'd offered her long ago.

When one has hope and love, all things are possible, pile moje.

She replayed the words in her mind, savoring the memory of his kind, soothing tone as he'd spoken them, his hands cupping her face in the loving gesture that never failed to make her throat ache with tenderness.

Might they be the answer to her dilemma?

Mevlida looked up, into the shadows, as some creature scuttled through the darkness above the ceiling. There was no hope or love left in her life. Nor any possibility of stopping Neven's plan, whatever it was, on her own. That would require the intervention of people with power and authority.

She knew no one who fit that description.

Yet she did know one person who would understand her message and make sure it reached the proper authorities.

With unsteady fingers, she paged through her book of prayers until she found the card she'd tucked inside two years ago. Turned it over and read the scrawled note.

"If you ever need anything, don't hesitate to get in touch."

She'd never expected to contact Jasna again. Finding Neven had seemed like the answer to her prayers, and he'd been so kind in those first weeks. She'd almost thrown the card away.

Lucky she hadn't.

Setting the book aside, she braced for the pain in her ribs, then struggled to her feet. Once she caught her breath, she shuffled over to her nightstand. Pulled out a tablet and a pen. Returned to her chair and eased back down. Most of her plan she could implement tomorrow—if her courage held—but this part she could do tonight.

She positioned the pen over the paper, tilted the tablet toward the light beside her chair, and began to write.

All the while praying her desperate effort to prevent a tragedy wouldn't be in vain.

Christy peeked through the peephole, verified the identity of her visitor, and pulled the door open just enough to admit him.

After squeezing through the gap, Lance nudged the door shut with his shoulder and scrutinized her. "Tough day."

"Yeah." So tough it took every ounce of her willpower to keep from throwing herself into his arms.

He jammed his hands in his pockets as if he was fighting the same impulse. "The coast is clear right now, or I would have come in the back way."

"It was hard to tell in the dark. That's why I only cracked the door. I hoped once the camera guy got that shot of me at the mailbox he'd back off, but the crew was still hanging around when the sun set. Have a seat." She backed away to give him access to the living room, where the cozy, flickering gas logs helped dispel some of the tension that had been dogging her since Sarah appeared in her office this morning bearing the blood-pressure-spiking, page-three story in the *Post*, complete with photos.

So much for any hope the kidnapper might miss the news.

"I can't stay long." As he spoke, he moved into the living room and claimed a spot on the couch.

"I'm helping Mark out with a gang-related case, and I need to follow up on a lead tonight."

She sat beside him. "It's after seven."

"Welcome to life as an FBI agent. Anything else happen since you phoned me about the news crew outside?"

"No." She twisted her fingers into a tight ball. "I'm assuming the kidnapper has gotten wind of this by now."

"That would be a safe bet. However, I'm convinced he's too close to the payoff to simply walk away."

Christy frowned. "And the payoff is . . . ?"

"I wish I knew—but it involves you. At this point I think we can conclude the fire and kidnapping were orchestrated to wreak havoc in your life. He can't be happy Ginny's body was found, and he may lie low for a while to regroup, but I doubt we've heard the last from him. This guy has an agenda."

Despite the warmth wafting toward her from the fire, the room suddenly felt cold. "Don't you think he'll be a lot more careful now that he knows law enforcement is involved?"

"Yes. But on the plus side, once a story like this breaks, new leads tend to surface. Tips get phoned in to our hotline. Most won't amount to anything, but we only need a couple legit ones to give us some traction."

"And in the meantime?"

"Starting tomorrow, we'll release new details to the press every day. The existence of the notes, the names of the towns they were mailed from, the description we got from Brenda Rose. There's no sense keeping any of that under wraps anymore." He pulled his phone off his belt, scanned it, and frowned. "This is my brother from Walter Reed. Give me a minute."

As he rose and walked back toward the foyer, Christy scooted closer to the fire, trying to give him some privacy. But though he angled away and spoke in a low voice, bits and pieces of the conversation drifted toward her.

"What are they giving him for that? . . . How long will he be in there? . . . Did you tell Mom and Dad?" Lance ran his fingers through his hair. "Yeah, but not till late Friday . . . Unless you think I should come sooner?"

That didn't sound good.

"That makes sense. You getting any sleep?" A soft chuckle. "That sounds like Mom." Then he stiffened. "Where'd you hear that? . . . Yeah, it broke here today too . . . Long story . . . Coping." He dropped his volume a few more decibels. "Very funny." Christy had a feeling they were talking about her. "Call me with an update early tomorrow . . . Yeah, you too."

Lance slid the phone onto his belt, waited a moment, and swiveled back to her.

"Is there a problem with your brother?" No

sense pretending she hadn't picked up his part of the conversation.

He returned to the couch but didn't sit.

That must mean he was leaving.

She stifled a surge of disappointment.

"He's got an infection in his leg, and his temperature spiked to 104. They moved him into the ICU while they pump him full of antibiotics."

She rose, once more tempted to walk into his arms—this time to comfort rather than be comforted. Again, she held back. "I'm sorry."

"Thanks. But he's young and strong. The doctors are hopeful this is nothing more than a slight detour on his road to recovery. That's what we're praying for, anyway." He wiped a hand down his face. The dicey situation with his brother and the kidnapping—not to mention the long hours he'd been putting in on other cases— had chiseled lines beside his eyes and at the corners of his mouth. "By the way, Mac saw the story about Ginny online today while he was surfing the net. I figured it would go national at some point."

Wonderful.

She wrapped her arms around her body. "What if the press shows up again?"

"Stick with no comment." He twisted his wrist and frowned at his watch. "I need to run. Will you be all right by yourself?"

No.

She wanted him to stay within arm's reach until they caught this maniac.

But that wasn't going to happen. The man was already stretched too thin, and he had more work to do tonight. She needed to suck it up.

Pasting on a smile, she lifted her chin and tried to look stronger than she felt. "Yes. I have solid doors and first-class locks."

"But no security system."

Her smiled dimmed. "I've never needed one."

You do now.

He didn't voice that comment, but the sudden thinning of his lips communicated the message loud and clear.

"Keep your cell close at hand. Don't venture into dark parking lots alone. Stay alert in public. And call me if anything—and I mean anything— makes you nervous."

She gave a mock salute, trying to lighten the suddenly tense atmosphere. "Aye, aye, sir."

Too bad her quip wavered.

The twin crevices on his brow deepened. For a moment she thought he was going to comment, but instead he walked toward the door and checked the peephole. "All clear, as far as I can tell."

Swallowing, she tried to psyche herself up for his departure. "Thanks for stopping by. I know you're busy."

She expected him to reach for the knob.

Instead, he turned, tugged her close, and wrapped her in his arms. "I know this isn't protocol, but somehow a handshake doesn't seem appropriate." His husky words were muffled against her hair.

Closing her eyes, she held on tight and inhaled the masculine scent of his aftershave as the steady beat of his heart vibrated beside her ear, beneath the worn leather.

"I wish you didn't have to go." The admission was out before she could stop it.

"I wish I didn't, either." Exhaling, he slowly extricated himself. "But I'm only—and always—just a phone call away. Remember that, okay?"

Her breath hitched as he lifted his hand and brushed his thumb across her cheek. "Okay."

"Lock the door behind me. I'll wait until I hear it click." With that, he slipped outside.

She did as he'd asked, following his progress down the walk through the peephole's distorted view of the world.

Kind of like the warped way the kidnapper must perceive life.

A shudder rippled through her, the feeling of safety she'd enjoyed in Lance's arms evaporating as fast as breath on a frosty night.

He was convinced she was this sicko's primary target—and more and more, she was finding that difficult to refute.

Yet if that was true . . .

Stomach knotting, she gritted her teeth and accepted the hard reality.

If that was true, Ginny had died because of her.

Collapsing onto the sofa, she dropped her face into her hands.

Dear God, how was she supposed to live with that?

Trust in the Lord with all your heart.

The line from Proverbs echoed in her mind, and she let it resonate, drawing comfort from the advice. Difficult as it was to follow, she had to believe God saw the big picture. Had to believe that with him, all things were possible.

She also had to trust in Lance and the FBI. They were doing their best to track down the kidnapper, to make sense of events that defied logic. They were pros—and one of these days, they'd find a lead that would put this evil man in their cross hairs.

Until then, she needed to stay calm, be careful—and pray the monster who'd taken her sister's life gave them the time they needed to find that lead.

The boyfriend hadn't stayed long tonight.

Unless he wasn't a boyfriend.

Nathan squinted at the tall guy as he slid into the black Cruze in front of Christy Reed's condo. Could he be a cop?

Except cops didn't get cozy with their customers.

Still . . .

He narrowed his eyes as he studied her closed door. The police wouldn't have been able to identify Ginny Reed's body without DNA samples or dental records. Had Christy gone to the authorities, despite his warning? Told them about the letters and filed a missing person report?

Or was there another explanation for the ID?

Whatever the reason, if the body had waited another week to surface, the ID wouldn't have mattered. His grand scheme would have been completed.

Nathan drummed his fingers on the wheel as the guy pulled away from the curb. Maybe he *was* a cop. After all, he'd only begun showing up in the past few weeks. Sure, it was possible Christy had simply met someone new, that it was all coincidence—but coincidences were suspicious. Just because this guy didn't dress or act like a cop didn't mean he wasn't one. Appearances and behavior could be deceptive.

He watched the taillights travel down the street. Should he follow?

No. What was the point? Whether or not he was a cop, the police were involved. Either way, he needed to be extra careful going forward.

The taillights disappeared, and Nathan lifted the coffee from the cup holder. Took a sip. Very little buzz remained from the three beers he'd downed in quick succession after storming out of the apartment. Three was the perfect number, enough to take the edge off without muddling his thinking. And he needed clear thinking from here on out, especially with the cops crawling all over this thing.

He took another sip, letting the hot java sluice down and warm his insides. Having cops in the picture wasn't ideal, but he should be fine. There was nothing to tie him to Ginny Reed's death or to her sister. He'd left no tracks. Nor would he. He knew how to be careful.

Juggling the coffee cup, he started the engine. No need to hang around here. Christy was safe for tonight.

But not for much longer.

He put the car in gear and pulled away from the curb. He might have to alter his plans and timing slightly, thanks to this glitch—but the end result would be the same.

Christy Reed would die.

Sooner rather than later.

20

Clutching the letter, Mevlida leaned on her walker and peered out the front window of the apartment. Where was the mail carrier? He always delivered to the row of boxes outside their door by one o'clock, and it was already . . . she strained to read the clock on the living room wall . . . one thirty.

She bit her lip. He could have taken the day off—but Thursday was an odd choice for that. Too early for what her grandson called a three-day weekend.

Or maybe he was sick. A lot of people had the flu, according to Neven.

Bad news, either way. The substitutes always came at unpredictable times, often late in the day—after Neven was home. If no one showed up soon, she'd have to wait until tomorrow.

And one more day might be too late.

Her heart skipped a beat. Whatever Neven's plan, he could already be . . .

The familiar red, white, and blue truck turned the corner.

She let out a shaky breath, the envelope crinkling in her fingers. No need to delay after all.

Yet on the heels of relief came panic. Once she gave the man this letter, there was no going back.

But what if she couldn't find the courage to complete the last step?

A shudder quivered through her, and she pulled her sweater tighter against the chilling doubts swirling around her.

What choice did she have, though? She'd examined the options, debated the pros and cons through the long, sleepless night, and this was the best solution. The one she was certain Mihad would have chosen had he been in her place. It would send the message that needed to be sent— and protect her from Neven's wrath.

Yes.

She could do this.

She *would* do this.

Pressing her lips together, she shuffled to the front door. Thank goodness the apartment was on the first floor, near the mail slots for all the units.

As soon as she heard the man approach, she twisted the knob and peeked out.

He looked over and smiled. "Afternoon, ma'am."

She pulled the door wider, maneuvered her walker halfway out, and lifted the envelope, displaying the address she'd carefully copied from the card tucked in her book of prayers.

"You want to mail that?" He moved closer.

She didn't understand every word, but based on his inflection, she was confident he understood her message.

"Yes." She held out the envelope.

As he took it, she reached into her pocket, pointed to the empty upper right corner of the envelope, then extended her palm to display a selection of coins.

The man smiled again, his demeanor friendly, his eyes kind as he rooted through the change. After selecting several coins, he indicated the stamp on one of the envelopes he was delivering, pointed to her envelope, and nodded. "I'll take care of this for you."

English might be difficult for her, but she was certain he knew what she wanted and would send her letter on its way.

"Tank you."

"My pleasure. Now you'd better get inside where it's warm. You could catch pneumonia out here." He did a shooing motion toward the door and playacted a shiver.

Such a nice man, to be concerned about her health.

If only her own grandson was as considerate.

Fighting back tears, she retreated a step. Watched him tuck the envelope into his sack. Hesitated on the threshold.

She could still take the letter back.

Be strong, Mevlida! Make Mihad proud.

Gripping the handles of the walker, she wrestled down her fear.

The man finished sliding the mail into the slots. "Have a nice day, ma'am." With a jaunty salute, he turned and walked back to his truck. A few seconds later the red, white, and blue van pulled away from the curb and disappeared around a bend.

It was done.

Mevlida slowly closed the door against the frigid wind—but the cold remained in her heart. Never, in all her seventy-eight years, had her courage been tested in this way. Yes, she and her son and grandson had left everything they'd known behind when they'd escaped to this country—but there had been no choice. Staying in her cherished homeland had no longer been possible. As for all the loved ones she'd lost . . . that, too, had been beyond her control. And living with Neven . . . where else could she have gone, except back to a homeless shelter?

But this decision was hers. A difficult one, yes—but hers. She had taken the initiative, let her voice be heard. For once, she would not be a victim.

And now it was time for the final step.

A bead of sweat trickled down her temple. The room tilted. Her legs threatened to buckle.

No!

She would not weaken!

This was a matter of life and death.

Tightening her grip on the walker, she lifted her chin and set off down the hall to seal her fate.

Nathan tossed the newspaper on the kitchen table, grabbed a beer, and surveyed the contents of the refrigerator.

Odd.

The old woman hadn't eaten the bowl of chili he'd left her for lunch.

Then again, she'd never been a fan of the bean-based dish.

He opened the freezer and took a quick inventory. She liked the stuffed cabbage rolls in tomato sauce. They reminded her of the sarma she'd enjoyed in the old country. Why not surprise her and heat it up for tonight? It was important to keep her off-balance, throw in enough kindness to give her hope life might get better.

As if.

He pulled out the package, removed the serving container, and threw it in the microwave. What a disgusting dish . . . but he could put up with the smell for one night. Besides, the aroma of the barbecue takeout he'd picked up on the way home would overpower it.

Taking a pull from his beer, he walked down the hall and knocked on her door. "Dinner will be ready in five minutes."

No response.

The can crinkled beneath his fingers. She knew better than to ignore him.

It was possible she was asleep, though. She took to her bed more often these days, especially since she'd fallen and hurt her ribs. Plus, her hearing was starting to go. Soon he'd have to shout if he wanted to communicate with her.

Another reason to end their arrangement once he was finished with Christy.

He knocked harder. "Wake up in there!"

More silence.

Mashing his lips together, he twisted the knob. This is what he got for showing her some courtesy, for knocking instead of barging in. Well, she'd hear about . . .

As he pushed the door open and took in the scene, the air whooshed out of his lungs.

No!

This couldn't be!

She wouldn't do this to him!

But as the reality sank in, as his fingers tightened on the can and sent a geyser of beer spurting through the tab, as the consequences of her actions began to register, he fumbled for the doorframe to steady himself.

The meek old woman had abandoned him in the end, just like all the others—leaving him with a cluster bomb of trouble.

And unless he did some damage control—fast —his plans for Christy would have to be put on ice.

Perhaps for a very long time.

"I still can't believe you talked me into a second trip out here." Mark pulled on the same ski hat he'd worn during their previous excursion to the cliffside accident site.

Stifling a yawn, Lance did a U-turn, eased as far off the road as possible, and put on his flashers. "I didn't exactly have to twist your arm. It was either this or the Monday morning staff meeting. You made the wise choice." He dropped the keys into the pocket of his jacket and scanned the terrain. "Like I said on the ride down, your idea about something being pulled across the road makes sense. Eye level would be most effective."

"And you think there would still be some evidence of that months later, as careful as this guy's been to cover his tracks?" Mark sent him a skeptical look.

"It's possible." Barely.

But they didn't need two naysayers on this reconnaissance mission.

Besides, he hadn't been any more keen to attend a boring meeting than his colleague.

Mark didn't comment on his optimistic response. Instead, he inspected the sides of the deserted road. "Eye level means it had to be tallish and not very heavy or it would have been too difficult to maneuver fast."

"Right."

"So you're thinking our guy connected it to a wire or rope and positioned it on one side of the road, then pulled it across from the other side once the car got close."

The more his colleague talked, the less feasible the idea sounded.

"Maybe." He sized up the road. There was no place on the minuscule shoulder cliffside to conceal anything large, and the bluff sloped directly up from the tiny shoulder on the other.

But they were here now, and he wasn't leaving without another look.

Turning up the collar of his coat, he gestured to the skid marks in front of them. "Given the narrow road and the lack of traffic, let's assume Christy's father was using his high beams that night. So he's seeing three to four hundred feet ahead at best. Speed might have been forty, given the darkness and curves. That puts stopping distance at about a hundred and fifty feet, not factoring in brake lag, the time from touching to full depression, lock up, or reduced reaction speed due to age."

Mark arched an eyebrow. "Do you know those numbers off the top of your head or did you do some homework?"

"I'd like to claim the former—but that would be a lie."

"An honest man."

He studied the road again. "I'm estimating the distance from the beginning of the skid marks to the point where the car went over the edge is only about a hundred feet."

"Meaning the object appeared suddenly, sixty or seventy feet in front of the car, close to the cliff—and our guy hoped Christy's father would fishtail out of control and go over before he could stop."

"That's my hypothesis."

"So we need to take a lot closer look at the

shoulder for the last eighty or so feet of skid marks." Mark pushed open his door. "Let's do it."

Lance stepped out into the blustery wind and called over the roof of the car. "You want to take the cliffside?"

"Sure." Mark pulled on a pair of gloves.

For the next quarter hour they scrutinized the ground, the bushes, the trees as they paced off the route—and with each minute that ticked by, Lance grew more pessimistic. This had been a long shot from the get-go.

Besides, even if they found some validation for their theory, it wasn't likely to help them ID the perpetrator. At best, it could verify the man had a bigger agenda, that the fire and kidnapping were part of a larger, more diabolical plan. But what they really needed was a solid lead that would help them—

"Lance!"

He stopped and turned. Mark had gotten up close and personal with a cedar tree poking above the cliff, parting the dense boughs to examine the trunk.

Lance crossed the road. "What have you got?"

Keeping the branches spread apart, he backed off and tipped his head.

Lance leaned in closer. "I don't see anyth . . ."

A metallic glint caught his eye as Mark gave the tree a slight shake, and he frowned. Looked again. A thin band of some sort of reflective material was tied around the trunk, one loose length fluttering in the breeze. "How did you manage to spot that? And what is it?"

"The wind picked up as I was passing, and I saw the reflection." Mark caught the loose end of the half-inch-wide shiny strip. "This was peeking out of the branches. A second earlier or later, I'd never have spotted it. It looks like VHS tape to me."

VHS tape tied to a tree in the middle of nowhere.

This had to be relevant—but how?

Lance stuck his hands on his hips. "You have any idea how this might be related to the case?"

"As a matter of fact, I do." Mark let the branches snap back into place and folded his arms. "One night when I was a kid, we were driving home late from some family event. Halfway down our street, my dad slammed on the brakes. I looked out the front window and saw what appeared to be a wire stretched across the road at windshield height. My mom screamed. I remember covering my head. The car skidded. The wire got closer. We passed it—and nothing happened."

"Let me guess." Lance fingered the end of the tape sticking out of the tree as he did a quick analysis. "The headlights caught the tape and illuminated it, making you think it was a wire."

"Yep—and it scared us to death. The skid marks were on our street for months . . . and if the night had been rainy, we'd have ended up wrapped around one of the big oak trees that lined the sidewalk. Turns out a couple of teenagers thought it would be a funny practical joke."

Lance angled back toward the road. "This placement is too perfect to be coincidental."

"Agreed."

"Our guy could have waited here until GPS told him Christy's parents were getting close, laid the tape on the road, and tucked himself in by that tree." He pointed to another dense cedar on the bluff side of the road. "All he had to do was watch for their headlights, wait for the right moment, and pull the tape taut."

So simple—yet so deadly.

"That would do the trick." Mark shifted sideways as another gust of wind whipped past.

"Then he just gathered up his tape and high-tailed it to wherever he'd parked his car."

"I'm surprised he left any souvenirs, though."

"Maybe another car came along, or he thought the tape would stay hidden in the branches."

"Possible. I would never have noticed it if the sun hadn't hit it."

"Well, we were due for a break. Let me get an evidence bag."

"Hey." Mark grabbed his arm. "Don't hold your breath for prints. This guy isn't sloppy—and without fingerprints or witnesses, there's no way we can pin this on him."

Like he didn't know that.

"True—but is there any doubt in your mind this is related to the accident?"

"No."

"Me, neither. And leaving it behind was a mistake. If our guy made one, he may make more. That's my positive takeaway from this. Give me a minute."

With that, Lance jogged toward the car—praying their man would, indeed, make another error.

Soon.

Because he was now absolutely certain Ginny's killer had also taken the lives of Christy's parents.

And he had a feeling the man had one final victim to cross off his list.

"So how are you holding up after Saturday?" Sarah gave a perfunctory knock on the edge of Christy's cube wall, then took the chair beside the desk and set a Panera bag near the keyboard.

"Okay."

Liar, liar.

Burying her sister a second time had been the hardest thing she'd ever done.

Sarah scrutinized her. "Not buying. You look like you haven't slept in two days."

Probably because she hadn't.

"I'll catch up. Listen . . ." She cocooned Sarah's hand in hers. "Thank you again for coming. I know how busy your weekends are."

"Never too busy to be there for a friend. But between the minister and your FBI agent, you didn't need me."

"Yes, I did. You've been the one steady person in my life through all these nightmare months. Your presence meant the world to me."

Sarah sniffed and swiped at the corner of her eye. "Keep that up, I'm going to have to raid your tissue box. And speaking of your FBI agent—I approve. He struck me as a keeper."

"I agree."

"From what I observed, the feeling is mutual." Sarah slid the bag closer to her. "In case you didn't eat breakfast, I picked up one of those asiago bagels you like. Not the healthiest way to start the week—but comfort food has a place."

"You're a great friend, you know that?"

"You'd do the same for me if the situation was reversed." She sighed and shook her head. "But we could do with a little less tragedy around this place, that's for sure. Did you hear about Nathan?"

Christy ran the name through her mind and came up blank. "Nathan who?"

"You might not know him. He's been on the maintenance crew less than a year, and he usually handles outside stuff. But you may have seen him filling in here and there since Dennis broke his leg. I know he was working on some carpet issues around the conference room about a week ago."

"Oh yeah. I know who you mean." Not much about the guy had registered beyond dark hair and muscular arms. She'd been too busy trying to absorb Lance's news about his brother. "What happened to him?"

"Not him. His grandmother." Sarah glanced around, leaned closer, and dropped her volume another few decibels. "She lived with him, and the scuttlebutt is he came home from work on Thursday and found her hanging in her bedroom. She killed herself."

Shock reverberated through Christy. "That's terrible!"

"Yeah. Apparently she's from some country in eastern Europe and didn't speak much English. He took her in after she broke her hip and was left somewhat disabled. I heard she was his only relative, so I imagine they were very close. He must be devastated."

"I wonder why she would take her life?"

Sarah shrugged. "From what I hear, her health has been deteriorating. Chronic pain, with no hope of getting better, can lead to depression. I can't begin to imagine what Nathan is going through."

"Yeah." All these months, she'd been so wrapped up in her own problems she'd forgotten other people were facing personal crises too. "Is anyone taking up a collection for flowers?"

"No flowers. There's no visitation. He had her cremated after the coroner released the body, and I think there's a private graveside service tomorrow. But a card is circulating, and people are contributing toward a donation to the literacy council. Nathan told his boss his grandmother had always wanted to learn the language but was never able to master it."

"I need to track the card down. I'd like to contribute."

"You have enough going on without worrying about anyone else. You don't even know him."

"We may have spoken. I've talked to a few of the maintenance guys over the past year. Besides, that doesn't matter. If he has no family left, it might raise his spirits to see a lot of names on that card."

Sarah pushed the Panera bag toward her. "Moments like this remind me why we're friends. Now eat."

"I will. And moments like this"—she patted the bag—"remind *me* why we're friends." Her phone began to ring, and she checked caller ID. "It's Lance."

"I'm out of here." Sarah rose. "Catch you later."

As her friend disappeared out the door, Christy swiveled away from the hall, picked up the phone, and greeted him. "Thank you again for delaying your flight to Washington so you could be there Saturday—and for helping to expedite the arrangements with Memphis."

"I wish I could have done more. No one

should have to bury someone they love twice."

At the warmth and compassion in his voice, her throat tightened. "Having you and Sarah and my minister there helped. How's your brother?"

"Fever's down. They moved him out of ICU right before I caught the red-eye back last night."

"That's good news—but you must be dead on your feet."

"I've gotten by with less sleep."

She ran a finger over the edge of the Panera bag. "I don't suppose there's anything new."

The infinitesimal hesitation before he responded raised her antennas. "No new leads on the kidnapping, unfortunately."

Maybe not . . . but he had some kind of news.

"What aren't you telling me?"

Another tiny pause. "We've been doing some digging, but we haven't found anything directly pertinent to your sister."

More dodging—not his usual modus operandi. Why?

As if sensing her question, he spoke again. "I'll tell you what. I'll give you a complete briefing next time we get together."

"When will that be?"

"As soon as I can find a legitimate excuse to pay you a visit."

"I like that answer."

"I hoped you would. How are you coping at work today?"

She inched the bag closer. "Sarah stopped by a few minutes ago to ask the same question and drop off one of my favorite treats from Panera. It helps a lot to know people care."

"Count on it."

Silence.

She waited him out.

"You know . . . I just thought of a reason to pay you a visit. If I can arrange my schedule, would you be available for lunch? I could grab some sandwiches, run by, and bring you up to speed. Is there a quiet corner at the rec center we could claim?"

Quiet corners were hard to come by, but she wasn't about to pass up a chance to see Lance.

"I'll find one. Call me if you can swing it and I'll meet you in the lobby."

"Sounds like a plan. See you soon."

The line went dead, and Christy dropped the phone into the cradle. Slowly leaned back in her chair.

What news might he be bringing her that he couldn't relay over the phone?

A twinge of unease scuttled through her, and despite the bagel inches away and the grumble in her stomach, her appetite ebbed. She might not yet know Lance well, but she was already learning to pick up his subtle signals.

And those signals were warning her that whatever he was going to share would once again tip her world off its axis.

21

"Whenever you're ready to arrange burial, we'll be happy to assist." The funeral director reverently placed the urn containing the old woman's ashes on the polished wood of his desk.

Nathan eyed the $279 cedar box. What a waste of money. The bamboo urn for thirty bucks would have been good enough, but a heartbroken, distraught grandson wouldn't go low end—and he needed to keep up that pretense here, as he had at work . . . and with the cops who'd nosed around the apartment, asking questions. But forking over 975 bucks for the expensive bronze job this guy had tried peddling?

Fat chance.

"Thank you." He picked up the urn. The thing couldn't weigh more than five pounds. All that was left of the troublesome old woman.

Good riddance.

But it would have been a lot simpler if she'd died in her sleep.

"Do you have any timing in mind for a final interment?"

Nathan swallowed past his disgust. The man's oozing sympathy was nothing but an act. All he cared about was padding the bottom line. Man, what a racket! Who knew death was so profitable? The prices on the fee schedule for a traditional funeral could have paid for a first-class trip to Tahiti—and he was about as likely to traipse off to the South Pacific as he was to invest one extra dime to maintain the charade of loving grandson.

"No. Not yet." He stroked the urn and blinked, laying the grieving-grandson act on thick. "Letting go of Gram would be too hard right now."

When he sniffed, the funeral director discreetly passed him a tissue from the handy box on his desk. "I understand. It takes time to adjust to a sudden loss. But we're here whenever you're ready." He pulled a card out of a silver holder and passed that over as well. "Feel free to call at any hour. My home number is on the card too. Don't hesitate to use it. We like to be available 24/7 to our clients."

"Thank you." Nathan slid the card into the pocket of his jacket and pulled out an envelope. "That should cover all the expenses." Almost a thousand bucks to burn a body. What a racket.

The man hesitated. "We'd be more than happy to send you an invoice."

"Gram taught me to pay my bills immediately." A lie, but the slimy death broker needed no further urging to take the envelope and slip it into a desk drawer.

"There are many excellent lessons to be earned from the older generation. Let me walk you out." The man started to rise.

"No need. I know the way." The faster he could get out of this rook joint, the better. "Thank you again for your help."

"Of course. And again, please accept my condolences on your loss."

Nathan dipped his head, pushed through the door of the office, and hurried toward the exit. The place reeked of death—and greed.

Once outside, he lifted his face toward the sun and drew in a lungful of the cold, crisp air.

Much better.

Shoving the urn under his arm, he pulled out the guy's card, ripped it into tiny pieces, and hurled it into the wind. The nightmare was over—and despite the hassle, the old woman's death had ended up causing nothing more than a brief postponement of his plans rather than a major delay.

Plus, one positive had come out of all this. He'd been able to use the bereavement leave from work to finalize his plans for Christy—and he had one more free day tomorrow. The day he'd told his boss he'd set aside for a private burial.

He opened the car door, slid behind the wheel, and dumped the urn onto the passenger seat.

Private burial?

Ha.

He had better things to do with his Tuesday. Far better.

And they all involved Christy.

Smiling, he fitted the key in the ignition—but as he spared the wooden box one more look, his mouth flattened. Who'd have guessed the old woman would cost him not only a ton of aggravation but some serious money?

Money.

Hmm.

He started the engine, put the car in gear, and accelerated toward the exit.

Maybe once this annoying snag blew over, he'd dump the ashes in the trash—and see if there was a market for used urns on eBay.

Lance pulled up in front of Christy's condo, cut the engine, grabbed the bag of sandwiches he'd picked up at the deli by the office—and hesitated.

Was it a mistake to tell her about the discovery he and Mark had made on the country road?

Maybe.

Based on her colorless face as he'd stood beside her in the cemetery on Saturday while the minister echoed the same words he would have said less than three months ago, she was close to caving.

One more blow might push her over the edge.

Yet she needed to fully understand the extent of the evil they were up against. This guy had orchestrated the deaths of her entire family—and

357

every instinct Lance had honed during his years in The Unit told him she was now in his sights. The man's plans might have been temporarily derailed by the discovery of Ginny's body, but he'd be back to finish the job he'd started—meaning Christy needed to be more vigilant than ever.

Bringing her up to speed was the right thing to do . . . and better here than at her office. The spur-of-the-moment lunch suggestion had been a mistake—one he'd rectified within the hour. He needed to break this news away from the public eye, where she could crumble in private.

Sack in hand, he covered the short walk to her door in a few long strides.

She pulled it open before he could ring the bell—looking better than she had Saturday at the interment, but still too pale.

And tonight's news wasn't going to restore her color.

"Hi. I've been watching for you." She stepped back and motioned him in.

He slipped past her and hefted the bag. "In the kitchen?"

"Yes." She fell in behind him. "What would you like to drink?"

"Any kind of soda is fine."

"Go ahead and have a seat while I grab it."

He unpacked the bag as she moved about the kitchen. "I got turkey and chicken salad. I hoped you'd like one of those."

"Both, actually." She smiled at him across the counter that separated the kitchen and dining area. "Want to split?"

"I'm game."

Before she joined him, he'd unwrapped the two sandwiches, divided them between the plates she'd already set out, and opened the containers of pasta salad and coleslaw he'd added to the mix.

"Hot food would be better on a cold night." He sent her an apologetic glance.

"Cold food travels better in the winter—and I love sandwiches." She set their glasses on the table and took her seat. "This looks great."

"It's from a favorite lunch spot of my colleagues."

She picked up the chicken salad croissant, took a bite, chewed. "Mmm. Excellent choice. So what news brings you out on this frosty night?" Though her tone was conversational, she wasn't able to hide the underlying thread of tension.

The bite of turkey he'd just swallowed stuck halfway down, and he grabbed his can of soda. No surprise she hadn't waited until after dinner to broach the reason for this get-together. The former Olympic athlete was a let's-put-the-information-on-the-table-and-deal-with-it kind of woman.

But he'd hoped she'd down some of her dinner first—because he doubted she'd feel like eating after he shared his news.

He set his sandwich back on the plate, took a

long swig, and groped for some sort of gentle lead-in.

"This isn't good, is it?" Her voice was controlled and even, but an erratic pulse throbbed in the hollow of her throat, above the vee of her dark green cardigan.

"No."

She scrutinized him. "Short of you telling me our guy has disappeared off the face of the earth and the FBI is closing the case, I'm at a loss as to what bad news you could be bringing."

He tried again to think of a way to soften the blow.

Failed.

Instead, he reached for her hand.

Her gaze flicked down to their joined fingers. Lifted to his. Panic flitted through her eyes as she wrapped the fingers of her free hand around the edge of the table. "This is really bad, isn't it?"

"Yeah." He took a steadying breath. "It's about your parents."

She wrinkled her forehead. "My parents?"

"Mark and I have been digging into their accident."

"Why?"

"In light of everything that's happened, it wasn't sitting right." He tightened his grip on her cold fingers as he delivered the bombshell. "We can't prove it at the moment. We may never be able to prove it. But Mark and I are convinced your parents' accident wasn't an accident."

She stared at him as she absorbed the news, the silence broken only by the keening of the wind as it whipped past the corner of the house and the wail of a distant siren.

He knew the instant she realized she was the link in all the deaths in her family. . . that she was the reason they'd been killed. Anguish flooded her jade-hued irises, so deep, so profound, so pain-filled it stabbed his gut with the physical intensity of a knife thrust.

"No." She shook her head, the tortured denial a broken whisper as she searched his face. "You must be wrong."

"I wish I was—but all the evidence points in that direction."

"Tell me."

He did as she asked, giving her all the details of their search—and their conclusions.

By the time he finished, all the color had drained from her complexion and her eyes were glazed with shock. "So it's true. Everything that's happened is my fault. They all died because of me."

Tremors began rippling through her, and he squeezed her hand, forcing her to look at him. "No, it's not your fault. This guy's mind is twisted. He's blown whatever you did to incur his wrath out of all proportion. The fact that you weren't able to come up with one single enemy when we first discussed this proves that. I know you better now, so I also know you would never intentionally do anything to hurt anyone. This lowlife has a warped view of the world. What happened is not your fault."

"It feels l-like it is. And the end result is the same. My family is still g-gone, and . . ." Her voice choked, and the moisture in her eyes spilled over.

Lance grabbed one of the paper napkins that had come with their dinner and dabbed gently at her tears. "We're going to catch this guy, okay? And he'll pay the price for what he did." Small consolation in the face of such devastating loss —but it was the best he could promise.

"That won't bring back Mom and Dad or Ginny."

No, it wouldn't—and nothing he could say or do would change that reality.

But there was one other consolation he could offer.

Rising, he pulled her to her feet and wrapped her in his arms. Forget FBI protocol. Forget keeping personal and professional behavior separate. Forget every rule he'd ever followed about avoiding romance during a mission—or a case.

For this moment, he was going to play one part and one part only—a guy falling in love with a remarkable woman whose heart was breaking. If he couldn't take the hurt away, restore her family, put joy back in her soul, he could at least let her know she could count on him not just tonight but in the dark days and months to come.

She clung to him, sobs wracking her slender body, and he rested his cheek against her soft hair as he reread the quote from Ecclesiastes. As far as he was concerned, Christy's season of weeping and mourning had gone on far too long.

Not until her tears began to taper off did he speak. "We'll get through this together. I'm here—and I'll be here going forward. Things will get better. You need to keep believing that."

"It's hard right now." Her anguished words were muffled against his chest.

"I know. Sometimes the darkness can overwhelm—and blind. When that happens, it's easy to get lost. I've been there—and it's not a pretty place. Don't get lost, Christy. Hang on to the faith that's sustained you all these years. It will get you through this."

She didn't respond.

Way to go, McGregor. Who are you to offer pious platitudes after abandoning God? She has every right to resent your advice, tell you to—

She pulled back and lifted her chin to look at him. "Thanks for that reminder."

He listened for sarcasm but heard only sincerity. Still . . . best to be cautious. "I may not be the best person to give that advice."

"You're the perfect person. You've been through the fire. You watched your best friend die and have carried a load of guilt for eighteen months. Now you're dealing with your brother's injuries. If you found your way back to God through all that, you're more than qualified to offer advice."

"I hope it helps you as much as yours helped me."

Her eyes clouded. "When did I give you advice?"

"After I told you about Taz. You suggested it might be time Debbie heard my side of the story. I visited her while I was in Washington last weekend, and putting everything on the table did help. My somewhat awkward attempts to reconnect with the Almighty have too. Life looks a lot different through the lens of faith. I'd forgotten that." He searched her eyes. The glassy shock was fading, but the bleakness remained—as did the shakes. "Why don't we sit by the fire for a while?"

"I'm sure you have places to go and things to do." But she didn't pull back from his arms.

"They can wait." He walked her into the living room, urged her down onto the couch, then nodded toward the kitchen. "I'll put away the food. We can eat later."

Lance quickly relegated the meal to the fridge and returned to Christy. When he put his arm around her and tugged her close, she dropped her head to his shoulder, as if it was the most natural thing to do despite their short acquaintance.

A positive omen for the future—he hoped.

She didn't talk much for the next forty-five minutes, and he didn't push her. People dealt with bad news in different ways. If she needed a sympathetic ear in the days ahead, he'd make himself available.

Before he left, he did manage to coax her into eating some of the food, and by the time she walked him to the foyer, a trace of color had returned to her face.

Too bad he had to ratchet up the tension again.

He turned at the door. "Call me if you want to talk later—or anytime."

"You already have a lot of stuff on your plate with your brother."

"There's plenty of room left for you—including the issue of your safety. If the Bureau had the resources, I'd put a bodyguard on you 24/7."

She wrapped her arms around herself. "If you're trying to scare me, it's working."

"Not scare you. Put you on alert. Red alert. I don't know what this guy's plans are for you, but I guarantee they're not pleasant."

She tucked her hair behind her ear. "Maybe he's already accomplished what he set out to do. Maybe he just wanted to make my life miserable. Take away everyone I cared about so I'd have to spend the rest of my life mourning them

—and missing them. That's possible, isn't it?"

He hated to burst her bubble, but they needed to face the grim reality. "It might have been—except for his last note. Now that we know Ginny's dead, his 'you will see your sister soon' message has a lethal undertone."

The little color that had seeped into her complexion leached out. "So what should I do?"

"Take all the precautions we've already talked about. Be attentive and stay in public areas when you're out and about. This condo is my biggest concern."

"If it makes you feel any better, I'm having a security system installed tomorrow."

That was the best news he'd had all day.

"Smart move—with or without this situation. In today's world, it pays to be prudent and take precautions. From our standpoint, we'll continue to release information to the media. We've had a few calls, none of which have been helpful. But that could change at any moment." He forced himself to reach for the doorknob instead of her. "I'll call you in the morning."

"Use my cell. I'll be here while they install the security system."

"Got it." Not trusting his hands, he kept one on the knob and the other wrapped around his keys while he leaned close to brush his lips over her forehead. "Lock up behind me."

Then he beat a hasty retreat before he caved and

snuck a taste of the lush mouth that had been tempting him since the first day at Panera when she'd shared her story.

That fantasy stayed with him for several blocks . . . until a harsher reality intruded.

He had a tail.

Adrenaline spiking, he kept one eye on the distant headlights in the rearview mirror and one on the road. Had the car been with him since he pulled out of Christy's street?

Must have been. None of his other cases merited a tail.

This had to be their guy.

After pulling the Bureau radio microphone off its clip from under the seat, he signaled and turned left at the next corner.

Twenty seconds later, the car behind him made a left too.

Bingo.

He identified himself to the FBI dispatcher with a few clipped words. "Get the police dispatcher on the line. I've got a tail I need identified. Have the cop pull him over on some pretext and fill out a field interview report. I'll need a copy of that ASAP and—"

Lance stifled a curse as he caught sight of a police cruiser approaching in the rearview mirror behind the car trailing him, lights flashing and sirens screaming.

Too soon to be his cop.

The headlights he'd been watching took a sharp right and disappeared.

He hissed out a word that would make his mother cringe. Even if he executed a high-speed U turn, there was no way he could catch up with the guy before he blended into traffic.

Could the timing have been any worse?

"Agent McGregor? Are you there?"

"Yeah." He wiped a hand down his face. "Scratch the request. Our guy got spooked and took off."

Ending the call, he pulled aside to let the police car race past, adrenaline still pinging. Their guy had been almost close enough to spit on, yet Lance didn't even have a make on the car.

But he had picked up one important piece of intel: the killer wasn't lying as low as they'd expected after the news about Ginny broke. He was keeping tabs on Christy in person, not just via the GPS device on her car.

Hands clamped on the wheel, Lance pulled back into traffic. The security system she was having installed tomorrow was a plus. In fact, after tonight, he'd have pushed hard for that if she hadn't already made the decision herself.

No matter how effective it was, though, there were too many other places she was vulnerable. To keep her safe, they either needed to step up their game or get a rock-solid lead.

Preferably both.

22

Nathan took a sip of coffee and padded down the hall to his room. He could get used to sleeping until noon on weekdays. Too bad he didn't have any more ailing relatives; bereavement leave was a nice job perk.

He stopped beside the laptop on his desk, pulled up the GPS monitor on Christy's car—and frowned.

Why was she at home instead of work?

She never missed work.

And what about her Tuesday night skating student? Had she cancelled that commitment too?

Tapping one finger against his mug, he began to pace.

This was bad.

If she didn't go to work, all the plans he'd made for tonight would have to be rescheduled, all the prep he'd done yesterday dismantled. And what if the weather changed? Today was perfect —twenty-five degrees and no precipitation— exactly what his plan required. It might be a long while before he had such perfect conditions again.

Should he drive by her house, scout around a little?

The jarring strobe of flashing lights and the

scream of the siren from last night replayed in his brain, and his hand jerked, sloshing his coffee.

No. Bad idea. That incident had jacked up his adrenaline so high he hadn't been able to get to sleep for hours.

His own fault, though. Following Christy's boyfriend had been dumb. It didn't matter whether he was a cop or not; the plan was set. He should have driven straight home, as usual. And there was no reason to risk another visit. He was too close to finishing this to take any chances. If Christy didn't . . .

Wait.

He stopped. Peered at the monitor. Hurried over.

Yes!

Her car was moving.

Keeping his gaze on the screen, he lowered himself into his desk chair and followed her progress. It looked promising. She drove the same route to work every day, and other than a short detour—also predictable—to Panera on occasion, she never deviated from her routine.

He took a sip of coffee. Christy was such a creature of habit. And she was disciplined. Focused. Single-minded in pursuit of her goals. All excellent qualities for an Olympic athlete.

But not so great when they ruined lives in the process.

It was her quest for gold that had spelled his doom.

His fingers tightened on the mug. Maybe she didn't understand how her abandonment had ruined his life. But she would. Soon.

Her car continued to travel in the usual direction, and when it stopped in the parking lot at the rec center, he exhaled.

Things were back on track.

And in less than eight hours, the games would begin—only four days later than planned, despite the curve Mevlida had thrown him.

Nathan took another sip of coffee. He'd have to make a thermosful for tonight. Keeping the cold at bay would be a challenge—but the outcome would be well worth any discomfort.

He rose, stretched and wandered toward the hall, pausing outside the old woman's room.

The shredded blanket and sheets she'd cut into strips to fashion into a rope lay in a heap on the floor, and the chair she'd kicked out from under her was still on its side. Otherwise, the room looked the same as it had since they'd moved here eighteen months ago—tidy, clean, and sparse.

Her book of prayers caught his eye, and he smirked. A lot of good her faith had done her. In the end, when she'd been alone and desperate, her god had abandoned her.

He crossed to the book and thumbed through the pages. The detectives had done the same—searching for a farewell note, they'd claimed. But she'd written no note. He'd checked before he'd called the police.

His grandmother had departed life mute.

The pages fell open to the business card the cops had asked about. Jasna Baljić. The do-gooder nurse at the rehab center who'd tracked him down with the help of some Legal Aid attorney she knew, after the old woman fell. A call from a lawyer had spooked him enough to respond— and the allure of monthly government checks had been too tempting to pass up. But the pittance hadn't ended up being worth the aggravation. Lucky for her, the rush he got from controlling her life had compensated for the hassles or she'd have been back on the streets within weeks.

He tossed the book back onto the table. At least the tragedy, as the police and his boss called it, hadn't caused a major delay in his plans for Christy, as he'd feared.

From the threshold of the room, he took one more look around, shook his head, and shut the door.

Mevlida Terzic's death had been as meaningless as her life.

"Afternoon, Jasna. You've got quite a handful there."

As the mailman grinned and hefted his sack, Jasna bounced a fussy Ben on her hip and kept a firm grip on Lana's hand while her daughter did an impromptu dance. You'd think three-year-olds who'd missed their nap would be out of energy by four o'clock.

Not this one.

She tightened her grip on the straining fingers. "You could say that."

"You coming or going?"

"Going—unfortunately. I just swung by from work to pick up the kids. I think this one's got an ear infection"—she hefted Ben—"and I'm trying to get to the pediatrician's office before they close."

"Tough schedule, after putting in a full shift at the hospital."

"Yeah. Any other day, my mom would stay and keep an eye on Lana, but she's not feeling well—and my husband's going straight from work to his night class at the university." She lifted one shoulder. "What can you do?"

"You have my sympathy. Would you like me to put your mail in the slot?" He dug some envelopes out of his bag and waved them toward the front door of the four-family flat.

"Thanks. That would be great. I don't need to go through it until—Lana!"

Jasna watched in dismay as the little girl jumped for the handful of mail, knocking it from the man's hand. It arced through the air and scattered across the frozen ground.

"I'm so sorry." She released Lana's hand and

leaned down to her level. "Stay right here, young lady. Don't move a muscle." After issuing the stern warning, she bent to help the man collect the letters, bills, and ads.

He grabbed for a shiny flyer that was fluttering in the wind. "No worries. I've dropped plenty of mail myself. Better than losing my bag while being chased by a dog, let me tell you. Been there, done that too."

Jasna reached for the last letter, pausing as she read the return address.

Why would her former employer be contacting her?

"Want me to add that to the stack for the slot?" The mailman motioned toward the envelope in her hand.

"No, I'll take this one with me. Sorry again."

"Like I said, all in a day's work." When her chastened daughter peeked up at him, he leaned down and patted her head. "Can I see that pretty smile again?"

She gave him a tremulous one as a single tear quivered on her eyelash.

"Much better. Smiles make the sun shine even on cold days like this." He straightened up and, with a wink, continued toward the mail slots on the doors of the flat.

Jasna weighed the envelope in her hand, then tucked it into her purse and took Lana's hand. Whatever was inside would have to keep until she got to the waiting room and had a minute to sit. Besides, she'd been gone from that facility for more than a year.

How urgent could the letter be?

"I've got a call from a woman who claims to have information that's relevant to the Ginny Reed case."

Lance juggled the phone against his ear, one arm in the sleeve of his topcoat as the receptionist relayed the news.

So much for trying to get out of the office before six for once.

Then again, maybe he would. This would most likely turn out to be a bust, as had the other half dozen tips that had come in on the hotline today after they'd reissued the description of the suspect Brenda had given him.

"Did you get a name?"

"Yes. Jasna Baljić."

Good. The caller had been willing to identify herself. That was a step up from a couple of the anonymous tips that had produced nothing but wild goose chases.

"You want the spelling on that?"

At Sharon's prompt, he shrugged out of his coat and sat back in his desk chair. "Yeah. Go ahead." He copied it down as she spelled it out. "Does she have an accent?"

"Slight. Bosnian, I presume. You're too new to

know, but St. Louis has a very large Bosnian community. The largest in the US, as a matter of fact. A lot of them live down around Bevo Mill . . . south city."

An ethnic group with members who could have dark hair and eyes, depending on their ancestry, and who might speak with the hint of an accent.

This could be a real lead.

"Got it. Let me talk to her."

The line clicked. "Ma'am, I'm putting you through to Agent McGregor." Another click as Sharon cut her connection.

Lance leaned forward in his chair. "This is Agent McGregor. I understand you have some information that might be useful to us in the Ginny Reed case."

"I'm not sure—it may be. I'm a nurse, and I got a letter today from a former patient. It's very . . . disturbing. Especially the last few lines." The distress in her voice was palpable.

Mark passed by his cube, and Lance waved the other agent in.

"What did she say?"

"That she hoped I could convince the authorities to pay attention to her concerns so her death wouldn't be in vain."

Mark dropped into the chair beside the desk.

"How is that relevant to the Ginny Reed case?"

"That line isn't—but it upset me. It sounds like she . . . like she was planning to take her life or thought someone was going to kill her. I tried to call her, but the number I had is out of service."

Maybe this wasn't going anywhere after all.

Lance sat back in his chair, striving for patience. "Ms. Baljić, I understand why you'd be upset by a comment like that—but my first concern is the Ginny Reed case. Did she say something specific about that?"

"Not about Ginny Reed. Her sister, Christy. The one that's been on the news and in the papers the past week or so."

Lance straightened up. "Go on."

"She said her grandson has a photo of Christy Reed in his room—with a knife stuck through the heart. He was also very angry when the news came out about her sister's body being found."

His adrenaline started pumping. "Are you in a position to fax me a copy of that letter?"

"It's in Bosnian."

That figured.

"But I could type up a translation for you."

Perfect.

"That would be very helpful. While you're doing that, I'll drive over to pick up the original and talk with you in person. What's your address?"

He jotted it down as she recited it. Sharon had pegged it. The woman lived in the Bevo Mill neighborhood.

377

"I can be there in fifteen or twenty minutes. I'll also need to get in touch with the woman who wrote the letter and her grandson. Do you have names and addresses for them?"

"Only names. There was no return address on the envelope. The last I heard, she was living with her grandson—but I think they must have moved, since the phone number isn't in service anymore. I helped find her grandson for her when she was in rehab because she had nowhere to go after she was released. They'd been estranged for years."

"Go ahead and give me the names and we'll track down an address for him."

Again, he jotted as she spoke, writing the unusual names in block letters so he wouldn't have to second-guess his scribbles later.

"The grandson had switched to an Americanized name, but I can't recall what it was. Mevlida always called him Neven. I'm sorry."

"We can track that down too. Expect me shortly."

"All right. But could you check on Mevlida? I have a bad feeling about the end of the letter. It sounds so . . . desperate. I think she could be in danger—or that something bad has already happened to her."

"I'm going to put a call in to the police as soon as we hang up. I'll let you know what I find out. And thank you for contacting us with this."

"Once you read Mevlida's letter, you'll know

I had no choice. She was very worried about that skater."

So was he.

"Okay. I'll see you in a few minutes." He dropped the phone back into the cradle and swiveled toward Mark.

The other man narrowed his eyes. "Why do I get the feeling you're about to pull me into night duty?"

"It's your choice—but I think we have a serious lead." Lance filled him in on the conversation, then pulled his cell off his belt. "I'm going to call my brother and find out if this Mevlida crossed paths with County homicide—or ended up with the ME. I'm also going to call Christy, see if this guy's name rings any bells. Plus, I need some intel run on Neven Terzic. If you want to get home to Emily and that new baby, though, I understand. I can tag someone else for this."

Mark folded his arms. "It does happen to be my night for baby duty—but the situation could heat up fast if this guy ends up being a serious suspect."

"True." Lance stood and put his coat on. Unless he'd totally misjudged the former HRT operator and SWAT team leader, Mark wasn't about to pass up any potential action—or case payoff.

"I'm in." The other man stood too. "I'll make it up to Emily. Maybe treat her to a facial next weekend. She likes those but never goes on her own. Claims they're too self-indulgent, believe it or not. Want me to run the intel while you pay your source a visit?"

"That's what I had in mind. Keep me in the loop."

"You got it."

While Mark disappeared down the hall, Lance pressed Christy's speed-dial number. Hopefully she'd recognize the name Jasna had given him—and remember some incident that would help them get a handle on why he might have targeted her.

But even if she didn't, his gut told him this guy could be their man. That he might have fixated on her for reasons clear only to him.

The best news? If he was the culprit, Christy would be safe as soon as they found him.

Because once Neven Terzic was under serious suspicion, he'd also be under serious investigation—and surveillance.

And with the FBI hovering over his shoulder, there was no way he'd be able to carry out whatever he had planned for a certain Olympic skater.

"Excellent, Natalie. I think that was the best layback spin you've ever done." Christy glided to a stop next to her Tuesday night student in the center of the ice.

The thirteen-year-old grinned up at her. "My

hips felt right for once. They were really underneath me, and I hung back and exhaled once I was in position, like you said."

"I could tell. The spin was freer and easier. Your free leg position was also spot on—and you kept your shoulders level. You've been practicing."

"And watching those videos you gave me."

"Good girl. Why don't you try it once more? Then we'll move on to the footwork sequence we've been building. I want to add some twizzles tonight."

As Natalie pushed off to set up for the spin, Christy's phone began to vibrate against her hip.

Keeping an eye on her student, she quashed her guilt and eased the cell discreetly out of her pocket. Yes, she was breaking one of her hard and fast rules. And no, taking calls during lessons wasn't fair to her students. But she had a lot going on in her life right now, and what if this was Lance? He might have news.

You're rationalizing, Christy. You're checking because you hope it's him and want to hear his voice.

Busted.

With a sigh of capitulation, she glanced at the screen.

It *was* him.

Spirits lifting, she put the phone to her ear, and they exchanged greetings.

But his next comment made her heart stumble.

"We've had a credible lead. I need to ask you a few questions."

Natalie finished the spin and looked her way. Christy lifted a finger to signal that she needed a minute. "I'm with a student. Can this wait?"

"Not long. Where are you in the lesson?"

"I've got another thirty-five minutes. Let me give her a few things to work on while we talk." She pressed the mute button and skated over to Natalie. "Nice job on the spin."

The girl gave her a puzzled look. "I fell out of it."

Great.

Natalie was so not getting her money's worth tonight. She'd have to give her some extra time in the next session.

"Sorry. My mind wandered for a minute. Why don't you practice your footwork sequence while I take this call? I'll get back to you as fast as I can."

"Sure." The girl shrugged and skated off.

Christy glided over to the edge of the rink and stepped onto the mat, phone pressed to her ear. "I've got a few minutes now."

"I can save the specifics for later, but my main question is whether you know a Neven Terzic."

The name echoed in her memory, pulling up a fuzzy image of a skinny, dark-eyed boy.

"Yes, I think so. I believe he was the boy who came to our high school the last semester I was there before I went to Colorado." She spoke slowly, pulling the details from the recesses of her memory. "He was from some Slavic country, near as I can recall, and spoke very little English. Why?"

"He may be our man. Is there any reason he might have a grudge against you?"

"No. I hardly knew him." She dug deeper, unearthing memories that hadn't seen the light in seventeen years. "I do remember feeling sorry for him. A lot of the kids made fun of him because he wore odd clothes and his hair was shaggy. Plus, he couldn't communicate very well. He needed help to assimilate to American culture, and neither the school nor the students did much to make him feel welcome. I got the impression the foster family he'd just gone to live with wasn't all that caring, either."

"How about you? Did you have any altercations with him?"

"No. Just the opposite. I tried to include him in a few events and sat with him at lunch on occasion. I can't imagine he'd have any reason to wish me ill. If anything, I would have expected him to be grateful." She watched a tiny skater topple and pull his friend down with him as a dull ache began to throb in her temples. "Why do you think it's him? I mean, I haven't seen him in ages. And why would he wait all these years to seek revenge if he did have some reason to hate me?"

"I don't have the answers to those questions—but getting them is my top priority. I'm on my way to follow up with the woman who called in the lead. Once I have more information, I'll be back in touch. Are you going straight home after you finish there?"

"Yes."

"Good. Have the guard walk you to your car."

"That was my plan."

"Stick with it. I'll be in touch later. Now I'll let you get back to your lesson."

As the line went dead, Christy pushed the end button and slipped the phone back into her pocket.

Neven Terzic.

She shook her head.

Why would that lost young man have targeted her in such a vicious way?

Natalie waved at her from center ice, reminding her she still had another half hour of lesson ahead, and Christy moved back toward the rink. She'd try her best to give the girl her full attention, but she had a feeling this session was going to be a total loss. How could she concentrate after Lance's bombshell that a person she hadn't seen in almost two decades, a person she'd gone out of her way to be kind to, might be gunning for her?

It didn't make sense.

Then again, since the night her parents went off

the edge of a cliff, she'd felt as if she was living in the twilight zone. Her life had been one bizarre event after another.

All orchestrated by Neven Terzic?

And if so, why?

As she joined Natalie at center ice and continued the lesson on autopilot, no answers came to mind.

But if this lead did turn out to be legit, Lance might be on the verge of getting some. Closure could be at hand.

For the first time in weeks, the knot in her stomach eased.

Maybe this nightmare was about to end.

23

Lance pulled up to the curb, set the brake, and blew out a frustrated breath.

Of all nights for his brother to be off the grid.

What was he doing that was so important he couldn't return an urgent call or text?

Reining in his aggravation, Lance slid from the car. He'd give Mac ten more minutes to respond to his abbreviated voice mail and more detailed follow-up text. If he didn't hear from him, he'd ask Mark to contact County.

But Mac would get him answers faster.

As he approached the door to Jasna's flat, a child's muffled wail greeted him.

Sounded like he wasn't the only one who was frustrated tonight.

He leaned forward and pressed the bell.

After twenty seconds ticked by with no response, he pressed it again.

Half a minute later, the door swung open. A harried-looking woman stood on the other side, the howling toddler in her arms. The kid's ear-piercing wails stopped long enough for the tyke to give him a fast once-over, then resumed with renewed gusto as he grabbed fistfuls of the woman's hair and began tugging.

"Ben . . . no! Stop! That hurts Mommy." She tried without success to lean away from her squirming son. "Agent McGregor?"

"Yes." He extended his credentials.

She gave them no more than a cursory glance. "Come in. This one has an ear infection"—she inclined her head toward the toddler—"and he's very cranky. Make yourself comfortable in the living room while I try to calm him down." She closed the door behind him and vanished into the recesses of the house.

As Lance took a seat in the sole chair not covered with toys, a solemn little girl peeked at him from around the door where her mother had disappeared.

He smiled. "Hi there."

No change of expression. No smile. No shy dip of the chin.

The child just continued to stare at him, statue-like.

So much for his attempt to make friends. A smile was the only trick in his bag for kids.

But he had a feeling Christy would have won the little girl over in a heartbeat. An innate warmth and caring flowed out of her like—

"Lana! I started the video. Come back and watch it with Ben."

The youngster backed away and disappeared as music kicked in from the rear of the flat.

Doing his best to set aside thoughts of Christy, he rechecked his messages while he waited for Jasna.

Yes!

A text had come in from Mac, clipped and to the point.

Checking. Stand by.

At least he'd have an answer to his question about Mevlida soon.

Jasna returned, an envelope and sheet of paper in her hand. She handed him both and tossed aside a doll to open up a spot on the couch. "Sorry for the noise and mess. It's been one of those days."

"No problem. Give me a minute while I read this."

Dear Jasna,

I do not wish to complicate your life, but I have no one else to turn to. I hope you will find a way to give this information to people who can stop my grandson from whatever he is planning to do. I beg you to try, because I am very much afraid tragedy will follow if you don't.

I have talked with you about Neven—but I have not told you everything. It pains me to admit this, but here is the truth—he was always a different boy, even before we left our homeland. Often uncaring, sometimes cruel. And the atrocities that happened in our country, the brutality he witnessed that no boy should ever see, I fear they killed whatever small measure of kindness might have been in his heart. I have come to believe they also twisted his mind. He does not see the world the way other people do.

When you found him for me two years ago, I was hopeful he and I could make a new start. He was kind in the beginning . . . but that changed quickly, and he has made my life very difficult ever since.

I thought it was only me he wished to punish, for letting the state take him after his father died—but now I worry that others have also angered him. Especially an ice-skater named Christy Reed.

Lance read the description of what the woman had found in her grandson's room. The signed picture of Christy with the knife thrust into it. The old group photo that included her and Terzic. The remains of a tortured mouse.

Guns.

Add in Mevlida's account of his reaction to the newspaper article after Ginny's body had surfaced, as well as her description of his personality, and it was obvious they were dealing with a very disturbed mind.

This guy had all the earmarks of a psychopath.

In other words, he was a perfect candidate to be Christy's tormentor.

And based on the woman's closing lines, Jasna's worry about Mevlida wasn't misplaced.

By the time you get this, I will be with my beloved husband. It is not the end I intended, but it is for the best. Neven's anger is too difficult to bear. I have wondered every day these past few months if I will live to see the next morning. Now there is no uncertainty. I know the end is coming.

My dear Jasna, I thank you again for all your kindnesses during my illness. Please forgive me for this burden I have placed on you. But I beg you, do not let my attempt to help that young woman be in vain.

When Lance looked up, Jasna leaned forward, her features taut. "You see why I had to call you."

"Yes." He indicated the return address on the envelope. "Why did she send the letter there?"

"That's where I worked when we met. They forwarded it. As you can see from the postmark, she mailed it Thursday. Five days ago. I hope it's not too late—for Mevlida or that skater."

"I talked to the skater less than an hour ago. She's fine. I also have a call in to the County police about Mevlida, and a colleague is tracking down her grandson's address as we speak." He pulled out a notebook. "What can you tell me about him?"

"Not much. We only exchanged a few words twice—the first time he came to see Mevlida, and the day he picked her up."

"Give me your impression."

She picked up the doll beside her and held it tight against her chest. "To be honest, he scared me a little. He smiled and was solicitous toward Mevlida, but his eyes . . ." She shivered. "They seemed cold and callous. His smile never reached them. That's one of the reasons I gave Mevlida my card. I had a feeling living with him might not turn out as rosy as she hoped."

"You said he and his grandmother were estranged. Do you know why?"

"Yes. I was the only one at the facility who spoke Bosnian, and Mevlida knew very little English, so we often talked. She didn't give me a lot of background, but she did share a few details.

She and her son and grandson sought refuge in America about the same time my family did— after the Srebrenica genocide. Do you know about that?"

Lance scrolled through his memory, pulling up what he could remember about the two-decade-old tragedy. "Bits and pieces. Thousands of Bosnians were massacred, as I recall."

"Yes. I was very young and don't remember much, but my parents and grandparents still speak of it with horror . . . on the rare occasion they speak of it at all. Thousands of people were killed—including women, children, and elderly— in hundreds of villages. Soldiers would pick people out of the crowd and execute them or take them away. Women were violated in public. Homes were ransacked and set on fire. Men of military age were executed and buried in mass graves. My uncle was among them." Her breath hitched, and she swallowed. "Mevlida lost her husband, daughter-in-law, and her other grand-son during that terrible time."

Lance didn't want to appear indifferent to the old trauma Jasna had described from her home-land, but he needed her help to prevent another tragedy from happening here. Now. "Why were she and Neven estranged?"

"Both she and her son began to drink once they arrived here. To forget the horror, she told me. After her son was hit—and killed—by a bus, she began to drink more. Eventually Neven's neglect was reported to the authorities, and they put him in a foster home. I got the impression it was a very bad experience, and he blamed her for it. He ended up running away, and the two of them didn't reconnect until an attorney I know tracked him down after she fell and broke her hip. At that point, she was destitute and living in a homeless shelter. After we were able to get some public assistance for her, Neven took her in."

Along with her checks.

Jasna's implication was clear.

Another wail came from the kitchen, and she vaulted to her feet. "I'll be right back."

"No problem. I need a minute to think through everything you've told me."

While she retreated to the kitchen, Lance weighed the letter in his hand, his mind racing.

You didn't have to be a psychologist to realize Neven Terzic had serious mental issues. Exacerbated by his traumatic experiences in Bosnia, perhaps, but based on Mevlida's letter, it sounded as if he'd already been troubled. Considering his long estrangement from her, he was also a man who held grudges. Plus, he'd made the older woman's life miserable once he'd taken her in—as punishment for past transgressions, no doubt.

What transgression had Christy committed that—in Terzic's mind—deserved the kind of punishment he'd meted out?

His phone began to vibrate, and he pulled it out, moving to the tiny foyer as he spoke to Mac. "It's about time."

A beat of silence. "Hello to you too."

He ignored the mild annoyance in his brother's tone. "I don't have time for niceties tonight." Soft jazz music played in the background, accompanied by the tinkle of glasses and a soft buzz of conversation. "Where are you?"

"Not that it's relevant, but I'm having a long-delayed night out with my fiancée. Your messages came in while we were making a toast and discussing our wedding plans."

"Oh." No wonder his brother sounded peeved. "Sorry to interrupt, but my case heated up."

"So I gathered. I made a couple of calls after I got your text. Since we're dispensing with niceties, I'll cut to the chase. Mevlida Terzic is dead."

The bottom dropped out of Lance's stomach. "When? What happened?"

"Her grandson found her body hanging in her room on Thursday evening."

The same day she'd written the letter to Jasna.

And Terzic hadn't been implicated. Otherwise, he wouldn't have been tailing *anyone* last night.

"Suicide?"

"That was the conclusion—but you should talk to Mitch."

It took a second for Lance to place the name. "The SEAL buddy who got you the gig at County?"

393

"Yeah. He did the investigation and has some interesting insights. He started to brief me, but I figured it would be better if you spoke to him directly."

"And left you free to spend your evening with Lisa instead of talking shop."

"That too."

Hard to fault Mac's priorities.

"You have his number handy?" He dug out his pen again and jotted down the digits as Mac recited them.

"He's expecting your call." Mac's next words were muffled. Something about oysters. He must really be splurging tonight. "You need anything else?"

"Yeah. A solution to this case."

"Can't help you there—but it sounds like you're making serious headway."

"I hope so. Enjoy the rest of your evening, and give my apologies to Lisa."

"Will do. Good luck."

He'd take all the luck fate was willing to hand out. But in light of this guy's ability to elude the law, he'd need a whole lot more than that to nail him.

As he slipped the phone back onto his belt, he heard Jasna return behind him. Passing on the news that her suspicions had been warranted wasn't going to be easy—and he couldn't stick around to hold her hand . . . figuratively speaking.

He needed to call Mitch for details on Mevlida's death and see what Mark had dug up on Terzic.

Because this guy was a ticking bomb.

And every instinct he'd developed during his Delta days told him they were running out of time.

Fast.

Christy swung into her driveway, pulled around to the rear of the condo . . . and mashed down the brake.

Of all nights for a tree limb to fall and block the garage door.

She huffed out a breath and gave the adjacent maple tree the evil eye. It had been dropping branches for months—as she'd told the condo association on several occasions.

Too bad their promise to take care of the dead wood had never materialized.

And too bad the wind hadn't picked a more convenient time to wrench that sucker free. Like a Saturday morning in spring instead of a windy, dark winter weeknight.

Could she leave her car here and worry about moving the limb in the morning?

Twisting her neck, she scrutinized the wind-tossed tree.

Nope.

Another limb could come hurtling down any minute—and she didn't need to add car damage to her list of problems.

Bracing herself for the sub-freezing temperature, she pushed her door open, slid out from behind the wheel, and hustled over to the branch. Not as big as she'd thought at first; it wouldn't take much effort to drag it off to the side. The maintenance crew could dispose of it tomorrow.

She took a firm grip on the thickest part and began to haul it across the asphalt.

Halfway to her destination, she froze as prickles rose on the back of her neck.

Someone was close.

Too close.

Lungs locking, she dropped the limb and started to swing around.

She only made it halfway.

Before she even caught a glimpse of the person lurking in the shadows, a hand clamped over her mouth. Hard. Her attacker yanked, and she lost her balance as he began dragging her backward.

Adrenaline pumping, she kicked. Flailed. Wiggled. Bucked.

Nothing fazed him. His grip remained firm, his rock-solid hand muffling her attempt to scream.

Not until he reached the back of her car did he reposition his hand.

Now it also covered her nose—cutting off her air supply.

Another wave of panic crashed over her. Energized by a second burst of adrenaline, she struggled to twist her head. Loosen his grip. Suck in one tiny breath of air.

She failed on all three counts.

Five seconds passed. Ten. The edges of the shadowy world began to merge into a dark tapestry. Detail disappeared. Shapes blurred. Her arms and legs lost their strength.

He was going to suffocate her—and she was powerless to stop him.

But as she hovered on the brink of blackness, he suddenly removed his hand.

As blessed air flowed into her lungs, her eyes widened. Why would he . . .

Before the question fully formed, she had her answer.

He whipped her around.

Gripped her shoulder.

And punched her in the stomach.

Pain exploded in her midsection, and she dropped to her knees. Doubled over. Once more she fought against waves of darkness.

No!

Don't pass out!

If you can't stand up, scream!

She dragged in a breath, refilling her lungs. He might have the upper hand physically, but she had her vocal cords. Surely someone would hear her and come to her aid. Or call the police.

The instant she opened her mouth, however, he slapped duct tape across it. Spun her around.

Secured her wrists behind her back with another length of tape he must have precut. Yanked her to her feet.

He'd rendered her mute and helpless in less than fifteen seconds.

Except for her legs.

Panic spiking, she kicked out at him. Hard.

When her boot connected with flesh, her attacker spat out a curse. Tightening his grip, he lifted her and dumped her into the trunk.

The lid slammed.

Ten seconds later, before she could catch her breath, the car began to move.

No!

Rolling onto her back, she began kicking the lid.

The car swerved sharply, and she crashed against the side of the trunk, banging her head.

A second attempt produced the same result.

Bracing herself against the side of the trunk with her feet, she faced the hard truth.

Her life was in the hands of the man who'd sent her parents over the edge of a cliff to their deaths.

Who'd burned her sister's house to the ground.

Who'd killed an innocent woman to cover up Ginny's abduction, then murdered her sister and thrown her body in the river.

If it was Neven Terzic behind the wheel, the frightened, insecure boy she'd stood up for against more than one bully had become a calculating, cold-blooded killer who'd carried out his ambitious plan with flawless precision.

And there was no reason to think he'd begin making mistakes.

Except . . . Lance knew who he was now—assuming Neven *was* their man. FBI agents were already on his trail. They'd pursue this round the clock—more so once they realized both she and Neven were missing. Lance could be trying to call her right now, and when she didn't answer, he'd know she was in trouble. The former Delta Force operator would be all over this, with every resource of the Bureau at his disposal.

The car swerved again, tossing her against the unforgiving side of the trunk.

But how would they ever determine where Neven was taking her?

Wait!

Her cell was in her pocket! The FBI could use the GPS in the phone to track her!

Thank God Lance had suggested she activate the tracking feature.

She twisted her bound arms and reached for it.

Came up empty.

Frowned.

Had the cell fallen out when Neven threw her in the trunk?

She began to grope around—then froze as memory came surging back.

Halfway home from the rec center, she'd

transferred it to her gym bag because it had been digging into her hip.

It was now sitting beside her abductor on the front seat—and given the man's thoroughness, he'd surely checked through the contents for a phone and shut it off.

The cell would be of no help.

But there was GPS on her car too, thanks to Neven himself. Might he have overlooked that, or simply ignored it since he didn't think anyone knew about it?

Her momentary hope dimmed. Not likely, given how thorough he'd been all along.

So how would Lance find her?

No answer materialized . . . and with every jarring mile that passed, Christy's spirits spiraled downward.

Fighting despair, she closed her eyes and turned to the source of hope and strength she'd relied on during the past difficult year.

God, please guide Lance in his search. Let the authorities figure this out in time. And give me strength to fight this battle too. To do whatever I have to do to survive.

As she finished the prayer, she clenched her fists and stared into the darkness. No matter the outcome, God would be with her. She believed that. She did.

But she hoped he also sent in reinforcements.

Because no matter how hard she tried to thwart

this madman's plans, she doubted this was a battle she'd be able to win alone.

Lance pulled out his phone as a teary-eyed Jasna closed the door behind him.

Less than half a minute later, Mitch Morgan was on the line.

"Mac said you'd be calling to talk about the Mevlida Terzic case."

"Yes." Once again, soft music played in the background, and a woman spoke, her words indistinguishable.

Was everyone except him enjoying a peaceful, romantic night?

He tamped down his irritation. "Sorry to interrupt your evening."

"No problem. My wife and I are just watching an old movie. How can I help you?"

"Mac said you investigated the death. Can you run me through your impressions of the scene and of Neven Terzic?"

A moment of silence. "You do know he goes by Nathan Turner."

No—but Mark would have found that information by now.

"We knew he'd Americanized his name. What else do you have?"

"I'll give you the official verdict first. Suicide, not homicide. There was no indication anyone else was involved in the death. We did take a second look after the medical examiner found significant bruising on the woman's torso, plus a cracked rib—but those injuries predated the death."

"How did Terz—Turner—explain that?"

"He said his grandmother had fallen a few weeks ago and had never complained about injuries. She was also slightly malnourished. According to him, she'd been eating less in recent weeks. We had no grounds to dispute those claims. The body was released, and the case was closed."

A subtle inflection put Lance on alert. "You weren't happy about that outcome."

"Off the record—no."

"Why?" He slid behind the wheel and pulled out his notebook again.

"Turner struck me as a user. Gut feel—but I trust my gut. He played the part of the shocked and grieving grandson well, but my money says it was an act. I'm not suggesting he had anything directly to do with the woman's death, but I could see how this guy might get pleasure out of making her life miserable. His words and behavior were appropriate; his eyes weren't. They were cold as some of the terrorists' I tangled with in the Middle East."

Jasna had noticed the same thing.

He needed to talk to this guy.

Now.

"Did you get a chance to nose around his place?"

"Yeah. We asked, and he was very cooperative. We did a walk-through. Nothing suspicious."

"He could have stashed anything incriminating before he called you."

"That thought did cross my mind."

Lance ignored the wry note in Morgan's voice. "Did you see any guns?"

"No. Why?"

"He has two."

"Then they were hidden."

"I'm going to run by there. Can you give me the address?" He wrote it down as the other man recited it.

"I take it he's connected with some case you're investigating."

"That's our suspicion."

"If he is, I hope you nail him. He may not be legally culpable for his grandmother's death, but I'm convinced he played a role in it."

"I think we're on the same page." A call-waiting tone sounded, and he checked the display. Mark. "Thanks for the information."

"Let me know if you need anything else."

He ended the call and switched to Mark, filling him in on his conversations with Christy, Jasna, and Morgan.

"You've covered a lot of ground already. I found the name change too. He made it legal when he was twenty-one. He's now thirty-two. He came to the US at fifteen and was naturalized two years later. But here's the most interesting piece of information—he and Christy Reed work at the same facility. He's been there about a year."

Since three months before her parents were ambushed.

The timing was too perfect to be coincidental.

Christy might even know him—as Nathan, not Neven. Seventeen years after their adolescent acquaintance, it was possible his appearance had changed dramatically.

"I'm thinking he recognized her but she didn't recognize him." Lance gave voice to the scenario taking shape in his mind. "Crossing paths with her might have reignited his grudge. Maybe he decided this was a second chance to get retribution for whatever she did to incur his wrath."

"Seems plausible. What's your plan?"

He started the engine and put the car in gear. "I'm heading to Neven's apartment. I'll call Christy en route and fill her in. You want to meet me at his place?"

"Sure. How are you positioning the visit?"

"I'm going to be honest—to a point. Tell him we had a tip on the Ginny Reed case and we're following up. No details. I just want to sniff out the place, see how cooperative he is, and put him on alert we're watching him."

"That could backfire, you know. If you force

his hand, he might accelerate whatever plans he has for Christy."

Like he hadn't thought of that.

"That's possible. Or it could make him nervous, slow him down. I'm hoping he'll lay low long enough for us to dig up some evidence that will put him at the scenes of the crimes. I also plan to get a warrant for his computer ASAP. Unless he's some kind of technical genius, our people will be able to verify if he's the one who's been following the GPS tracking device on Christy's car."

"Okay. I'm on my way. Our ETA should be about the same."

The instant the line went dead, Lance punched Christy's speed-dial number. He wanted her locked in her condo, alarm set, until he escorted her to work tomorrow morning.

After three rings, the phone rolled to voice mail.

Apprehension prickled his nerve endings.

She should be home by now—but she might be in the bathroom . . . or retrieving her mail.

He left a message and continued toward Neven's.

Five minutes later, when she hadn't returned his call, he tried again.

Still no answer.

He switched to her landline.

No answer.

He punched in Mark's number and skipped the

greeting. "Christy's not answering. I'm diverting to swing by her place first. Why don't you continue to Terzic's, see if there's any sign he's at home?"

"Will do."

Lance tossed the cell onto the passenger seat, swung onto the entrance ramp for I-44, and floored it. Yes, there could be a reasonable explanation for her lack of response.

But after all he'd found out about Terzic in the past ninety minutes, he had a stomach-churning feeling the real explanation was far more sinister.

24

The road wasn't smooth anymore.

Bad sign.

Whatever their destination, they could be getting close.

Using her feet to brace against the jostling motion of the car, Christy forced herself to take slow, steady breaths. If she panicked, she had no chance of outmaneuvering her abductor. She needed to keep her wits about her, think clearly.

But how could she strategize when she had no idea what was coming?

One thing for sure, though—time was her friend. The longer she delayed whatever end he had in mind for her, the longer she'd have to discern his intent and come up with a plan . . . and the longer Lance and the FBI would have to find her.

If Neven was behind this, she might be able to get him to talk. Encourage him to tell her why he'd gone to extreme lengths to exact punishment. Someone who'd planned such meticulous crimes might want to brag . . . or even gloat . . . about them—and she was his only possible audience, barring a confession to law enforcement.

She doubted that was on his agenda.

If trying to engage him in conversation didn't work, maybe she could . . .

Her lungs froze.

The car was stopping.

A new swell of panic crashed over her. Should she scrap her previous ideas and kick out at him when he opened the trunk? But if she did, would he finish her off on the spot?

A car door opened. The Mazda shifted. A door shut.

She was out of time.

Every muscle taut, her gaze flew to the top of the trunk lid. With so little information to go on, she'd have to play this by ear. Trust her instincts.

And pray she made the right choices in the critical moments to come.

Christy's car wasn't here.

Lowering his flashlight, Lance stepped back

from the small window in her condo's rear-entry garage.

Not good.

His phone began to vibrate, and Mark's name appeared on the screen.

He punched the talk button. "She's not here. What do you have?"

"Terzic's MIA too. His apartment was dark when I pulled up, and no one answered the door. But his car's here. I got his plate number and matched it up to a Civic in the lot. Then I knocked on a couple of doors. One neighbor saw him leaving about an hour and a half ago—on foot, with a backpack."

Lance's pulse spiked. "I'm going to call in a BOLO alert on Christy's car and see if our tech agents can get a GPS fix on her cell. I'm also going to look around here for any evidence she made it home. I could use another set of eyes."

"I'm on my way."

As Lance dealt with the BOLO alert and passed on Christy's cell information to the office, he walked around her property. Through a side window, he could see the red light on the new security keypad by the back door. Activated. Her mail was still in the box. A UPS sticker was stuck to her front door.

He had the office track down the securityguard at the rink, who confirmed he'd walked Christy to her car and watched her pull out of the lot.

So what had happened between there and here?

Just as he received the news that there was no signal from her phone, Mark pulled up.

Lance continued the conversation as he went to meet the other agent. "Keep monitoring it in case a signal does come through." A long shot . . . but possible. Christy would know he'd be trying to pinpoint her location. If she got the chance, she'd turn the cell on. They only needed a brief window to lock in on her. "Call me if you get a fix."

"Find anything?" Mark tapped his flashlight against his palm and did a quick visual sweep.

Lance slid the phone back onto his belt. "Nothing in the front or on the sides. I want to scout around the back some more."

"Let's do it."

Once they began a circuit at the rear of the condo, it didn't take Lance long to spot the branch—or the remnants of a trail of twigs across the driveway that appeared to have been hastily brushed aside.

"Mark! Over here."

The other agent joined him. His colleague sized up the situation in one glance and came to the same conclusion Lance had already reached. "A branch blocking the entrance to her garage—a simple but effective ploy to get her out of the car."

"Yeah." Lance peered at the asphalt, then directed his flashlight at two faint parallel tracks.

The bottom fell out of his stomach.

"Heels." He looked over at Mark. "Someone dragged Christy. I bet she ended up in her own trunk."

The other man's features hardened. "Trunks are bad places. I almost lost Emily in one."

Lance reached for his phone. "I'm gonna get an evidence response tech out here. If there's anything linking Terzic to whatever happened in this driveway, I want it found."

A light came on in the adjacent condo while he punched in the number, and a moment later the door cracked open. A sixtyish man peered out, his expression wary. "Can I help you two gentlemen?"

Leaving Mark to deal with him, Lance turned aside and walked several yards away.

By the time he finished the call, Mark was back. "That saves us knocking on one door—which I assume is the next step."

"Yeah. I'm going to ask County for some manpower to help us with the door-to-door stuff. Did that guy offer anything?" Lance slid his phone onto his belt.

"An ETA for Christy. He saw her car pull in at 6:45 while he was getting his mail."

"Did he see it leave?"

"No."

"We need to find out if anyone else did. I also want to get into Terzic's apartment with one of our computer techs. There's a chance he didn't deactivate the GPS unit he put on Christy's car. Why would he, if he thought no one knew what he was up to?"

"I don't think he'd be that sloppy—but it's worth a shot. Why don't I call for the cop backup here and get another agent on site to coordinate the door-to-door while you check in with Steve?"

The reactive squad supervisor.

His boss.

Right.

He owed him an update.

Man, getting used to the whole chain-of-command rigmarole was a bear. The authority to act on his own initiative had been one of the best parts of being in The Unit.

"My next call." He pulled his phone back out.

"You might want to get him working on warrants too. We've got exigent circumstances on our side for tracking Christy's GPS and a warrantless entry at Terzic's, but we at least need to get the paperwork in process."

"Right." He knew that—but red tape rankled . . . and he had a feeling it always would after the freedom of Delta. "I'll make my calls while I head over to Terzic's. I'll also see if our office can track someone down who will let us in at the apartment. You want to hang around here and brief the local cops until we have another agent on site?"

"Yeah. I'll join you as soon as I can. If you aren't already in, I have a pick gun in the car."

Lance arched an eyebrow. "You carry a pick gun?"

"You'd be surprised how often it comes in handy—even on SWAT missions. It may be more dramatic to kick down a door or shoot out a lock, but it's a lot safer to use a pick."

Smart thinking.

Working on a SWAT team under the former HRT operator's leadership could be interesting . . . if he ever wanted to consider it.

"Okay. I'll see you at Terzic's." Lance took off at a jog for his car, already dialing Steve's number.

If fate was kind, one of Christy's neighbors had seen some helpful detail—or the GPS unit on her car was still working.

But given their track record so far with this case, the odds of getting a break weren't comforting.

Another shiver convulsed Christy as she curled into a ball in the frigid trunk, her shakes fed by equal parts fear and cold.

Where was her abductor?

The car had stopped . . . how long ago? Ten minutes? Half an hour? Impossible to tell. Each second felt like an eternity.

But he'd been gone a while.

Why was he waiting to open the trunk?

She shifted her position, trying to relieve the ache in her stomach. There was a reason for the delay. This guy was meticulous. He had an agenda —and a timetable. He'd be back to finish her off as soon as that item came up on his checklist. If he'd simply wanted her dead, he could have accomplished that in the driveway with a simple knife thrust.

Given the elaborate lengths he'd gone to with her parents and Ginny, he'd surely thought up some creative way for her to die—and it wasn't going to be quick and easy. If she was the payoff, the finale, he'd probably saved the—

She tensed.

Outside sounds were muffled, but that faint snapping of twigs could—

All at once, a key was inserted in the lock on the trunk.

A heartbeat later, the lid swung up.

Instantly, a bright light blinded her.

She turned her head aside, but he grabbed her face in a vise-like grip and forced it back, toward the searing beam.

"Look at me."

She slitted her eyes, but the light was too bright.

"I said look at me!" His grip tightened, the pressure crushing her cheekbones.

A tear leaked out of her eye.

He released her face, and the light became a bit less intense. "Tears? Excellent. I like to see you cry—and you did it very well at all the funerals. I think Ginny's service was the best. The first one, anyway."

The man's cold, amused words sucked the life out of her tears, replacing them with terror.

He'd been there, at all the funerals? Watching the people he'd killed be buried, gloating over her pain?

Sick, sick, sick.

Fighting back a wave of nausea, she forced herself to squint into the light until a murky shape emerged out of the darkness. Her abductor appeared to be of medium height. And lean, despite the insulated outerwear he wore. She already knew he was strong. His face was too shadowed to see clearly, even if he hadn't been wearing a ski mask . . . but what was that on his head?

A miner's helmet?

He altered his position slightly. The light moved with him, reducing the glare long enough for her to confirm the source of illumination.

Ingenious.

The helmet left his hands free and kept her in the dark—literally.

This guy was every bit as smart as they'd feared.

"You aren't going to cry after all? Disappointing . . . but I can wait. There'll be more tears later. Lots more."

His accent was faint but detectable if you were listening for it.

Meaning this was the guy who'd killed her sister. The one the prostitute had told Lance about.

But was it Neven?

He leaned closer, and she shrank back, trying to tuck herself into a crevice in the trunk, out of his reach.

It didn't work. He grabbed her leg, pulled her forward, and hoisted her out, setting her on the ground in one fast, fluid motion.

The world tilted, and his hand shot out to steady her. "No fainting, Christy. I need you upright until after the performance."

She blinked.

Performance?

What on earth was he talking about?

"Start walking. That way." He pointed behind her.

She twisted her neck. They were in a small clearing in the middle of the woods, surrounded by darkness.

Where was she supposed to walk?

"Move."

Something hard rammed her between the shoulder blades, and she stumbled forward. Turned back.

The barrel of a pistol was aimed at her heart.

And while she'd never seen one in real life, that appendage on the end looked like a silencer.

Her lungs deflated.

"I'm not going to shoot you . . . if you follow my instructions. That's very important, Christy. People who don't follow my instructions make me angry. I do things that aren't very nice when I'm angry."

Like run people off cliffs. Burn down houses. Throw bodies in the river.

She swiveled back and started walking, praying her shaky legs would continue to support her.

Don't make him mad, Christy. Buy time. Look for an opportunity to outsmart him. The longer you can stall, the better the chance you'll live to see morning.

She kept looping those instructions through her mind as she lurched over the frozen, uneven terrain and into the woods, walking as slowly as she dared. Every second she bought herself could matter in the end.

Though her masked abductor was silent behind her—as if he was accustomed to moving noiselessly through the forest—his malevolent presence was almost palpable. Somehow she sensed this was a man who was used to tracking his prey undetected. A hunter, perhaps.

But on this trip, he wasn't after animals.

He was after her.

And unless she figured out a way to outwit him fast, he was going to bag his ultimate trophy before this night was over.

The apartment manager was waiting when Lance arrived at Terzic's address.

That was one plus to being part of a large,

collaborative organization. He might be used to handling his own details as a Delta Force operator, but the FBI support staff was great at getting ducks in a row so he could do his job.

Lance displayed his badge as the man introduced himself. "You know I need to get into Nathan Turner's apartment."

"Yes. Your people called." The man held up a key and pointed to a door that faced the open-air breezeway between two buildings. "That's it. The woman I spoke with said a warrant was in progress?"

"Yes." Or it would be soon, based on his conversation with Steve. "But we're dealing with a life-and-death situation here. We don't need to wait for the paperwork to show up."

"That's what the woman said."

The man led the way down the breezeway, fitted the key in the lock, and pushed the door open.

"Thanks." Lance entered and pulled on a pair of latex gloves. "I'm expecting two more agents. They'll be here shortly."

"I'll keep an eye out for them."

As the man pulled the door shut behind him, Lance flicked on the overhead light, positioned himself in the middle of the living room, and did a quick 360. The carpet had seen better days, the woodwork was chipped, the furnishings were low-end. But the place was clean and tidy.

It was also impersonal. There was nothing in

this room that offered any deep insights into the occupants. Nor did it contain any electronics other than a TV.

He bypassed the kitchen, stopping on the threshold only long enough to scan the counter-tops for a computer.

Again, nothing.

He passed the door to the hall bathroom. Paused and flicked on the light in the bedroom on the right. Took a quick inventory.

A bundle of ripped bedclothes on the floor. Several ceiling tiles askew, an overturned chair beneath one tile that exposed a pipe. Pink quilt crumpled on the bed. Framed black-and-white photo on the nightstand of a long-ago bride and groom.

This was the room where Mevlida had died.

Terzic's computer wouldn't be here.

He continued to the last door on the left. Felt around for a light switch. Flipped it on.

Pay dirt.

A laptop rested on top of a desk in the far corner.

Lance crossed the room in four long strides—and came face-to-face with the photo of Christy that Mevlida had described. Terzic must have stashed it before calling the cops after she killed herself, then restored it to the center of the bulletin board above the computer once they left—complete with the knife through the heart.

His own heart stuttered as he stared at it.

Mevlida's worry hadn't been misplaced.

Evil intent permeated this room.

Reining in his terror, he opened the laptop and booted it up. He was no computer genius, but he knew a few basics about the inner workings of a lot of different pieces of electronic equipment. It was possible he could locate a GPS feed while he waited for the tech specialist.

Because he knew one thing with deadly clarity.

They were running out of time.

25

"Turn right."

Christy peered ahead into the woods. Her abductor had doused the light on his miner's helmet, and the path—if there was one—was pitch black.

She pushed through some brambles. Stumbled. Went down on one knee.

That earned her another prod in the back.

"Keep going. We're almost there."

Not the news she wanted to hear.

Struggling to keep her balance, she hauled herself to her feet and continued. As far as she could tell, they were in the middle of nowhere. No lights peeked through the trees suggesting a house in the distance, and no sounds save the

occasional eerie hoot of an owl broke the stillness.

Even if she had the use of her voice, there was a
strong possibility no one was close enough to
hear her screams.

So what options did that leave her, short of
the unlikely chance she could overpower her
abductor?

None—or at least none that had presented
themselves yet.

But one might at any moment. There was still
hope.

She had to keep believing that.

The terrain began to slope down, and she picked
her way through the barren winter underbrush,
edging around the drifts of snow that hadn't
melted during the brief thaw after the last storm,
trying without much success to avoid the sharp
branches that clawed at her calves through the
thin leggings she reserved for indoor skating.

After a couple dozen yards, the terrain leveled
again and she emerged into a small clearing just
as the moon peeked out from behind the clouds.

No, scratch that. It wasn't a clearing.

The open area in the hollow was a frozen lake,
forty or fifty feet in diameter.

"Over there." At the fringe of her peripheral
vision, the hand with the silenced gun waved to
her right.

She twisted that direction. Two folding chairs

were set up at the edge of the lake. The carrying case for her skates rested beside one of them— along with her gym bag.

Her gym bag!

Yes!

Unless he'd removed it, her phone was close at hand—and by now, Lance would be searching for her. Since he was the one who'd told her to activate the GPS, the FBI would be watching for a signal.

Wouldn't they?

She quashed down the sudden pang of doubt. Of course they would. Lance was the kind of guy who covered all the bases.

Now all she had to do was find a way to turn on the phone. Even a brief signal could have a huge impact on the outcome of this night.

"Sit in the chair that's farthest away."

She had thirty feet to come up with a plan as they skirted the edge of the frozen lake toward their destination. Twenty seconds if she dragged out the trip as long as she dared.

Think, Christy! Think!

Five seconds later, an idea began to take shape in her mind. It wasn't great, and it might not work, but it was the best her stressed-out brain could come up with in the short window she had.

Clenching her icy fingers, she waited until she was a few feet away from the chair. Then allowed her steps to falter. After staggering the remaining distance to the chair, she sank down and leaned forward.

Neven—or whoever he was—turned on the light attached to his helmet and aimed it at her face. "What's wrong?"

Inhaling loud and hard through her nose, she rolled her eyes as far back as she could and swayed in her chair.

"Hey!" He grabbed her shoulder. "What's wrong with you?"

She toed the gym bag and nodded toward it frantically. In the blinding light, she couldn't see his features. But he sounded alarmed—just as she'd hoped. He'd come too far to let her collapse during the closing act of his grand plan . . . if he could help it.

Please, God, let him buy this charade!

A few seconds passed. She increased the pace of her breathing—but if he didn't respond soon, she was going to hyperventilate and pass out for real.

All at once, he reached down, ripped the duct tape off her mouth, and got in her face, the searing light bright and hot. She lowered her eyelids halfway. "You make one sound, you're dead. Got it?"

She gave a weak nod.

"Now tell me what's wrong."

"Asthma." She gasped out the word and toed her gym bag again. "Medicine."

He snatched up the bag, backed away, and began to root through it. "Where?"

This wasn't working.

She needed the bag in *her* hands.

She gave him a panicked look—no acting required—and breathed more harshly through her mouth, pretending she couldn't speak.

Please . . . let him think I'm too desperate for air to be thinking about an escape plan! And please let him not know that if I really had asthma, I'd have an inhaler, not pills.

He hesitated—then pulled out a knife and cut the binding on her wrists.

Thank you, God!

She plunged her hands in the bag, giving the performance of her life as she rooted frantically through the contents until her fingers closed over the phone.

Yes!

With one hand she felt for the on button and pressed hard. With the other she grasped the two Zyrtec she always carried in an inside pocket in case her mild allergies flared up and grabbed her bottle of water.

Her abductor watched while she put the tablets on her tongue and took a long gulp. She continued to wheeze as he repositioned his chair a few feet away, extinguished the light, and sat. His gaze—and the barrel of the gun—never wavered from her. But on the plus side, he apparently didn't know enough about asthma to realize pills were no substitute for an inhaler.

"You've got ten minutes to recover. Then we start."

Start what?

She didn't ask.

Yet as she looked across the darkness that separated them, toward the face hidden behind the ski mask, she knew the end was approaching.

At least the SOS had been sent.

Now she could only pray someone was listening.

"We picked up a signal from the cell and we have a location."

As the news from the tech agent came over the line, Lance groped in his pocket for a pen. "Where?"

"Middle of nowhere, as far as I can tell. Near Cedar Hill."

He ran the St. Louis suburbs through his mind. The name didn't match any of them.

"Where is that?"

"About forty minutes south of the city. Less if you burn rubber. The signal is coming from just southeast of the LaBarque Creek Conservation Area."

"Is it moving?"

"No."

"Keep watching. Give me the exact location." He jotted it down as the man relayed the information.

"That last is a county two-laner," the man concluded. "Since it won't get you to the exact location, there must be a private road leading off from there—or else she trekked through the countryside."

Mark appeared in the doorway of Terzic's bedroom, followed by the FBI computer expert. He motioned them both in.

"Keep tracking her phone. Home in on my cell too. You can guide us in once we get there. Also, find the owner of the property. I need to talk to him or her ASAP. Email me and Mark Sanders a topographic map as well and see if you can determine whether there are any houses nearby. Call me immediately if the location changes."

He rose from his spot in front of Terzic's laptop and filled in the new arrivals. "I still need you to check out his computer." He signaled the expert to take his place in front of the screen. "If the GPS on her car is transmitting, that would be great—but I'm not holding my breath. I mostly need you to find out whether this computer has been tracking it."

"That shouldn't take long to verify." The guy went to work.

"Let's move." Lance motioned Mark to follow him out.

"We can make Cedar Hill in thirty minutes from here." Voice clipped, Mark pulled out his phone as they exited Terzic's apartment. "Let's take my Suburban. I've got my SWAT gear in the back. I also want my sniper and spotter onsite ASAP, and the rest of the team as fast as they can get there. You drive while I get all that rolling and talk to Steve."

Lance stifled a surge of irritation as they jogged toward the SUV. This was his case, and he should be in charge until the higher-ups arrived.

On the other hand, Mark had a lot more FBI and SWAT team experience than he did.

Keep your mouth shut, McGregor. Let the man run the show. This is about saving Christy's life, not protecting your ego.

Mark finished the first call as they arrived at the SUV and grabbed Lance's arm. "I know what you're thinking—and for the record, I'm not taking over your case. But I've been through this drill a few more times than you have, and there's a life hanging in the balance. We don't want to take any chances."

"Already processed and accepted."

Mark scrutinized him. Gave a curt—and what appeared to be approving—nod. "Let's go."

Lance slid behind the wheel. "Should we get the local police or sheriff's department to set up a loose perimeter in case our guy starts traveling?"

"Not advisable in this situation." Mark punched some numbers into his phone. "I don't know the players in that area, and if they did anything to tip this guy off, he could go ballistic. We'll be there in half an hour—almost as fast as they could get people into position." He pressed the phone to his ear, continuing their conversation while he waited for the call to go through. "Take I-270 to Gravois and head south. That'll get us within a few miles of our target."

Lance put the SUV in gear and raced for the highway. If him acting as driver would expedite this operation, he'd rise to the occasion—and get them there even faster than Mark expected.

Maybe too fast, based on his colleague's grab for the dash as he took the entrance ramp onto I-270 at speeds far exceeding the posted limit.

To the man's credit, though, he didn't comment —or miss a beat in his phone exchange.

Lance floored it once they were on the highway, weaving around the traffic as he tuned into the one-sided conversation. Mark gave clipped directions to the SWAT team members, then briefed Steve. No words were wasted. His summary of the situation was concise, his assessment of the situation spot on, his logistics and tactical discussion reasoned and thorough.

This guy knew his stuff—and that was a huge plus. Events could unfold fast once they got on the scene. Terzic had only a brief window until Christy was missed. If she wasn't at work tomorrow, an alarm would be raised. He needed this to be over tonight so he could go about his normal business in the morning, the picture of innocence and concern as the news spread at the rec center.

Besides, once a search was underway, the guy was too smart to risk detection by stashing Christy somewhere alive and making a return visit.

Before this night was over, she'd be dead and disposed of.

And where better to take care of both than in the middle of the woods?

While Mark continued to deal with the logistics, Lance pressed harder on the accelerator—all the while praying that whatever Terzic had in store for Christy, he'd play it out late into the night.

As for Christy, if she'd managed to turn on her phone, she'd also be doing her best to buy them some time to arrive, assess the situation—and initiate a rescue effort.

And they'd need every second she could eke out.

"Your ten minutes are up."

Christy's heart skipped a beat as she watched the man seated a few feet from her. He hadn't moved a muscle since she'd taken the pills. Just sat and observed her from behind his mask.

A cold wind whistled past, and she rubbed her arms, her teeth chattering in the subfreezing temperatures.

Stall! Stall! Stall!

"I need some more water."

He hesitated, then gestured to the bottle protruding from her gym bag. "Help yourself."

She reached for it, her numb fingers balking as she tried to close them around the plastic. Once she had the cap off, she sipped the cold liquid. More than she wanted of it. Any ploy to eat up a few more seconds.

"I never saw asthma mentioned in articles about you."

The man's comment came out of nowhere—but conversation was useful. It would buy her more time.

"I never t-talked about my health in p-public. But leaf mold and c-cold can trigger asthma attacks." All true—though not for her.

"You sound fine now."

"M-medicine helps."

"Good. Because we're ready to begin." He rose, towering over her. "First, a couple of rules. If you scream, the gag goes back on. Besides, you'd be wasting your effort. The closest farmhouse is two miles away, and no one's going to be out walking in the woods on a cold night. I won't hesitate to use this"—he waved the revolver at her—"if you get out of line. Silencers aren't really silent, but they mask the sound well enough in isolated areas like this. Understood?"

She nodded. Gripped her hands in her lap. *Keep him talking.*

"Would you at least tell me why you're doing this?"

"Because you deserve it."

"Why? I don't even know you—do I?" Best not to clue him in that she suspected his identity. Not yet, anyway.

Silence stretched between them again, broken only by the rustling of the few desiccated, decaying leaves that clung to the winter-ravaged trees.

Just when she thought he was going to ignore her, he returned to his seat. Took off his helmet and placed it on the ground. Flipped on the light and aimed it to provide a dim circle of illumination between them. Then he stripped off his ski mask.

His face was still in shadows, but it took Christy no more than a few moments to recognize him.

Her jaw went slack.

Nathan Turner, the maintenance guy from work, was her abductor? The man who'd days ago lost the beloved grandmother he'd welcomed into his home after she became infirm? The same guy who'd been repairing the carpet outside the conference room. Who'd been in the hall the night she'd dropped her gym bag while searching for her cell to take Lance's first phone call. Who'd been mopping in the rec center lobby that day Bob had flagged her down.

The killer wasn't Neven Terzic after all.

Or was it?

She squinted, trying to scrutinize his features in the shadowy light. To reconcile this black-eyed, lean-cheeked man with the gangly teen who'd crossed her path for those few brief weeks.

With his hint of an accent, it could be him.

"Neven?"

"Give the lady a gold star. But it's Nathan now."

So the tip Lance had received earlier tonight had been correct.

Yet it made no more sense now than when he'd told her his suspicions.

"I don't understand." She tried to suppress a shiver. "I was your friend."

Even in the dim light, she could see his features tighten. Feel the sudden waves of anger radiating off him. "Friends don't abandon friends."

She frowned. "I don't know what you're talking about."

He began to jiggle his foot. "You misled me. You made me think you cared. Then you left, just like everyone else in my life who pretended I mattered to them." He pulled out a keychain and dangled it in front of her. "Do you remember this?"

As the pewter Arch swayed before her, a fuzzy memory sharpened. "I gave you that to welcome you to St. Louis."

"And I carried it with me everywhere for a whole year. Until I finally realized you were never going to answer the letters I sent you in care of that ice rink in Colorado Springs where you went to train. One each week for the first three weeks you were gone."

"I never got any letters from you."

He snorted. "Right."

"Look, I wasn't even officially training at the rink the first six weeks I was there. We were too busy getting acclimated. The rink didn't know who I was yet—and hundreds of skaters train there."

Her eyes were growing accustomed to the light now, and she was able to pick up more details in his expression . . . including a hint of doubt.

But all at once, his features hardened again. "You could be lying."

"I'm not."

"So you say—but it doesn't matter. You could have contacted me. Asked how I was doing. Stayed in touch. And you didn't."

"I hardly knew you."

"That's a lie!" His posture stiffened, and his dark irises began to smolder. "We were *friends*. We ate lunch together. You invited me to events at school. You talked to me in the hall. You stood up for me when people made fun of my hair and clothes and accent."

"But . . . but I didn't really know you. I was just being kind."

"That's not true! Only friends give each other

presents!" He thrust the keychain in her face again. "You know what else you gave me? Hope that things could be better, that not everyone I met would make fun of me. You made me think I could have a successful life here."

"You could have."

He leaned closer, the miner's light throwing macabre shadows on his face. "No, I couldn't. Do you know what it was like at that school after you left? They treated me like dirt! Filth! That's why I dropped out. Why I ended up no better than my old man—a maintenance guy who cleans up other people's messes. But if you'd stayed being my friend, I could have been much more. I *deserved* to be more. To be powerful and in control. You ruined everything when you abandoned me."

Christy stared at him, trying to formulate a response. A defense. An explanation.

No words came to her.

Even if they had, though, the man glaring at her from across the faint circle of light wasn't going to listen to reason. His mind was past that.

Way past.

If Neven could view their history rationally, he'd realize that the hand of friendship she'd extended for a few brief weeks during her last year at the high school had been a simple act of kindness, not a commitment. They'd been casual acquaintances, nothing more. Those were the facts.

But he'd twisted them. Reshaped them to cast her as a scapegoat for his unrealized dreams.

And he'd killed to exact revenge. Was planning to kill again.

Soon.

Unless she continued to stall.

Keep him talking.

She swallowed. "Why did you wait all these years to come after me?"

"I had other issues to deal with after you left. A new life to create out of the ashes. But then there you were, a few yards down the hall, my first week on the job at the rec center. It was like fate was offering me a chance to finally make you pay for what you did. How could I pass up that opportunity?" He gave her a malevolent sneer. "And I've had a lot of fun these past few months carrying out my plans for your family. Making you cry."

Fun?!

Murdering people was fun?

Watching people suffer was fun?

Christy's stomach heaved. "My parents and my sister were innocent. How could you kill them just to get back at m-me?"

"Innocence is a matter of perspective—and they were a means to an end. A way to hurt you. This was always about you, Christy. From the very beginning. You were the target."

Lance's conclusion had been correct.

Her family had died because of her.

Bile rose in her throat, and she retched.

"Feeling ill? How nice." Neven's smile broadened. "Watching you suffer is always a high point of my day."

This guy wasn't just sick; he was a psychopath with no conscience or moral compass. It would be futile to plead for mercy with a man like this. Compassion wasn't part of his DNA.

Her only chance was to appeal to his self-interest.

She swallowed past her nausea. Inhaled a lungful of cold air. "You're taking a big risk. You aren't going to get away with another murder."

"It's not going to look like a murder. You've had a tough year, Christy. You lost your parents in a tragic car accident, your sister died in a house fire—or so you thought. Your emotional state would understandably be shaky. Anyone could suffer depression after such back-to-back tragedies. When your car is found near a bridge, people will suspect you jumped—and there'll be nothing to prove otherwise. Only you and I will know the truth."

"You're going to throw me in the river like you did Ginny?" The horror of it reduced her voice to a whisper.

"It worked once; it'll work again."

She tried to slow her breathing, but the frequency of the short puffs of vapor in front of her face mocked her effort. "The police will find evidence of you in my car, or of me in the trunk."

He rose, and her lungs froze.

Her abductor was about done talking.

"I know all about trace evidence. I watch cop shows on TV. They won't find anything from me in the car—why do you think I'm wearing this"—he swept a hand down his thermal coveralls—"and that?" He pointed with a gloved finger to the ski mask that had covered his hair and face. "I plan to vacuum the trunk, but you're right . . . they might figure out you were in there if they're thorough. So what? There won't be any connection to me. Now put your skates on."

She blinked at the abrupt change of topic. "What?"

"You're going to skate for me, Christy. A private exhibition by an Olympic athlete, just for me. Also a farewell performance. Move!" He gestured with the gun to her skate bag.

Fingers trembling, she picked up her bag, trying to sort through her chaotic thoughts. Putting on the skates would limit her mobility off the ice. She could run in them, but not far and not fast—assuming she got the chance to run at all. And that was a leap. With a gun aimed at her, trying to make a break for the woods in skates *or* boots would be suicide.

For now, it might be better to simply give him the show he wanted. Keep him entertained long enough for the FBI to get some agents here.

She needed to make this the performance of her life.

Because if she didn't, her life would be over before help could arrive.

26

By the time Mark finished his final logistics call—to put a paramedic team on standby—Lance had been barreling south for twenty minutes.

"I've got a sniper who lives out this way. He'll beat us there and scout out a staging area." Mark holstered his phone. "My spotter should arrive before us too. The rest of the team members will assemble as fast as they can get there and wait at the staging area for instructions."

"Do you think one of the ASACs will come out?" Lance hadn't had a lot of dealings with either of the assistant special agents in charge of the St. Louis office, and while they were probably competent, he'd rather have a known quantity like Steve or Mark calling the shots.

"It this drags on too long, one of them will. But I doubt that's going to happen. This is our show until Steve gets here—which could be a while. He's busy lining up a flyover and thermal scan in case we need aerial surveillance, and he's getting a hostage negotiator on the road in the unlikely event we end up talking to the guy. He's also going to alert County and muster some of their SWAT people for backup."

Lance's phone began to vibrate, and he yanked it off his belt. The name of the agent tracking Christy's phone appeared on the screen.

"McGregor. What do you have?"

"The signal's still stationary. I've got Jack Ramsey, the owner of the property, on hold. I ran a quick background check, and he looks clean. Retired businessman, on several charitable boards, no problems with the law. He owns about four hundred acres. As far as I can tell, there aren't any houses in the immediate vicinity of the signal I'm monitoring. I emailed the topographic map."

Another agent who didn't waste words.

Good.

"Thanks. Go ahead and put Ramsey through." After the handoff, Lance introduced himself and got straight to business. "Mr. Ramsey, are you acquainted with a man by the name of either Neven Terzic or Nathan Turner?"

"Definitely not anyone named Neven, but the other name does ring a bell. Can you give me some context?"

"He works in maintenance." Lance named the municipal recreation facility.

"Ah, now it clicks. Yes, a pleasant young man. I have a membership in the gym there, and he stopped to help me with a flat tire in the parking lot last winter."

"Is there any reason he might be on the property you own near Cedar Hill?"

"It's possible. I've spoken with him on several occasions since the tire incident, and when I found out we shared a love of hunting, I invited him to use my land. Seemed like a more tangible expression of gratitude than a mere thank-you. I bought the parcel as an investment many years ago and only go down now and then to hunt myself. Less often these days. I know he's taken me up on the offer more than once. What's the problem?"

"We need to speak with him, and we believe he's on your property. We're en route there now. Are there any structures on the land?"

"Only a deer blind in a tree on the west side of the pond."

"Any nearby neighbors?"

"A few farmhouses, but none close to the perimeter of my land. I back up to a conservation area, so it's very isolated."

Great.

"Any special geographic features or information about the terrain that might be helpful?" Lance swerved around a slow-moving car that shouldn't be in the fast lane, glowering at the oblivious driver as he rocketed past.

"It's hilly, heavily wooded, with a small pond.

The ground is rough and not easy to navigate. I put in a gravel drive from the county road not long after I bought the acreage, and one of my neighbors uses his brush hog to keep the forest from encroaching. It goes in about two hundred yards to a wide turnaround. The rest of the land is unimproved, except for the deer blind."

Mark touched his arm and pointed to an exit sign in the distance, then pulled out his own phone.

"Any open areas?" Lance set a diagonal route across the lanes of traffic. The topographic map would tell them that, but the more detail they could get from someone who'd been there, the better.

"Just the pond, which is a bit east of the center, and a field on the southern end."

"Okay. That's all I need for now. We'd appreciate it if you'd remain available for the next few hours in case we have questions once we arrive."

"No problem. Let me give you my direct cell number."

"Hold one sec." Lance pantomimed for Mark to get out his pen and repeated the number as Ramsey recited it. "Thanks. We may be in touch again."

Mark finished his call a moment later. "We've got a barn as a staging area. It's on the other side of the road from Ramsey's property, not far from the gravel drive he mentioned. Our ETA is about six minutes from the exit."

"Get our guy in the office back on the line. Have him guide us in while you pull up the topographic map on my phone." Lance handed him his cell and zoomed down the exit ramp.

With Mark's phone on speaker, Lance followed the directions as they were relayed while his colleague studied the topographic map.

"Where on the property are you putting the cell signal?" Mark directed the question at his phone during a lull in the driving instructions.

"Very slightly east of center."

Lance looked over at his passenger. "Ramsey said there was a lake in that area. How far in are we talking?"

Mark lifted the cell closer to his face. "Hard to calculate on a tiny screen."

"I can help you with that." The other agent's voice came over the other phone. "Using the county road as a starting point, about half a mile."

Half a mile in the dark over rough terrain—and sound would carry in the quiet of the country. They'd have to tread carefully to avoid alerting Terzic to their presence—and that kind of slow approach ate up precious time.

Not ideal.

"Stand by. We'll be back in touch as we move in." Mark ended the call and leaned forward,

441

peering through the windshield. "The barn should be up ahead on the right. I have some extra cold-weather gear in back you can use."

"Thanks." For more than the gear. The tactical part of this operation would be handled by the SWAT team, and as the leader, Mark had every right to restrict the fieldwork to his own people. Lance would have pushed back if he'd tried to exclude him—but that wasn't a battle he'd have relished.

"The team's arriving." Mark pointed out the dim outlines of three vehicles clustered next to a large structure. "Let's get this show on the road."

Lance mashed down the gas pedal, adrenaline surging. Christy was nearby—and she'd be working hard to delay Neven's plan. Olympic athletes didn't give up. She'd fight to win.

Unless she couldn't.

Unless Neven had already . . .

He gritted his teeth and crushed that thought.

Not going there.

Christy would be fine.

She had to be.

For despite their short acquaintance . . . despite his attempt to maintain a professional distance during the case . . . despite the inappropriate-ness of taking a personal interest in a subject . . . he was falling in love with the Olympic skater.

Fast.

And losing her wasn't an option.

• • •

Christy took as long as she dared lacing up her skates, shoving her icy fingers into a pair of gloves, and pulling on the fleece-lined hoodie she'd insisted was necessary to keep another asthma attack at bay in the cold weather.

But finally Neven ran out of patience.

"That's enough. Get on the ice."

She pushed herself to her feet, praying her shaky legs would hold her up, and surveyed the murky surface. "I can't skate in the dark. I need to watch for debris, see where the edges are."

"Don't worry about that. Move out to the center."

Every muscle taut, she stepped onto the ice and glided into the night, melting into the obscuring gloom.

Hmm.

Maybe the darkness was a plus.

Neven's helmet would illuminate her while she was on this side of the pond . . . but the head lamp wasn't likely to shed much light on the far side. She squinted across the frozen surface. Those were cedar trees over there, weren't they? The dense foliage would hide her if she could skate to that edge, hop off the ice, and get behind them. If she could tug her skates off fast, she might be able to . . .

All at once, the pond lit up.

She stopped abruptly in a spray of ice. Spun back toward the chairs.

Two spotlights, suspended from trees, were aimed toward the frozen surface. They were powered by a generator, based on the faint hum thrumming through the stillness. Neither was super bright, but the circles of light pooled on the pond provided sufficient illumination to let her see where she was skating.

And to let Neven keep tabs on her location no matter where she was on the ice.

Meaning if she tried to make a run for it, he'd shoot her before she got five feet.

Her sudden surge of hope deflated.

"You're used to spotlights, aren't you, Christy? I wanted you to feel at home for this performance."

He'd extinguished the light on his miner's helmet and pulled the ski mask back over his face. In his black jumpsuit, he was nothing more than a shadow at the edge of the pond as he walked to one of the chairs and sat.

All at once, quiet music filled the air.

It was one of the pieces she'd often skated to in exhibitions.

"I did some research, as you can see. Thisshould sound very familiar—and I have plenty more. Now skate. The way you did in that TV special."

"That . . . that was fourteen years ago. I don't have those skills anymore."

"I'm sure you can improvise some interesting routines."

444

Stall some more.

"I need to w-warm up first."

"Oh, that's right. They always have a warm-up at competitions, don't they? I'll give you five minutes—because you'll want to do your best tonight. The longer you can skate . . . and keep me entertained . . . the longer you stay alive."

She already knew that.

But hearing it put into words sent a chill straight to her heart.

Every muscle quivering, she pushed off on the rough surface—and promptly sprawled on the ice as some piece of debris snagged her skate.

"Not an impressive opening, Christy. I'm disappointed."

She stood again. "Lake skating is d-difficult." Despite a herculean effort to sound calm and in control, fear and cold conspired against her. No matter how hard she tried, she couldn't stop her teeth from chattering. "The wind roughens the surface, and there are t-twigs and leaves frozen into the ice."

"Deal with it . . . unless you want to give up already?" The shadow began to rise.

She pushed off in panic, her movements jerky.

His laugh followed her, the sound evil and inhuman.

But at least he sat back down.

"You have four minutes of warm-up left."

You can do this, Christy. Focus on the skating

. . . and on coming up with a plan to thwart him. The ice is your world, not his. Use it to your advantage.

Repeating that pep talk over and over in her mind, she began to execute a series of simple 3 turns and mohawks. The easy moves left her mind free to strategize—and pray for inspiration.

And she needed to do both. At this point, she couldn't count on the FBI arriving in time, no matter how hard Lance was pushing them. Neven's exact schedule for the rest of the evening might be a mystery, but she knew one thing with absolute certainty.

The clock on her life was ticking into the final minutes.

Lance finished fastening his Kevlar vest while Mark secured his earpiece and wrapped up with the SWAT team assembled in the barn, using the rough property map he'd hand-sketched.

"To recap: Brett, you and Kurt stick close together. I want sniper and spotter tight in case a window opens. We may only get one chance at this. Go in slightly north of the pond. Nick, circle in from the east. You guys"—Mark indicated two other SWAT team members who'd arrived— "fan out and close in from the west. Lance and I will stick together and go in from the south. We need to cover the half mile fast but quiet. Communicate anything you see that may be helpful. Be aware of where the other agents are at all times so we don't get into a cross-fire scenario. If you're unsure, verify by radio. Otherwise, maintain silence. Let's do this."

The men filed out of the barn, black clothing and black balaclavas merging with the night, their NVGs guiding them through the darkness. Once they reached the end of the short gravel road, they melted into the darkness like shadows in shade.

Without an earpiece, Lance wasn't privy to any conversation taking place, but as far as he could tell, no one was talking. Mark was mute as he advanced through the underbrush with a silent stealth he must have honed during his HRT days. On his heels, Lance was just as quiet. When your life depended on perfecting covert approaches, you learned the skill fast.

A third of a mile in, Lance slowed.

Was that . . . music?

He touched Mark's arm, and the other man angled toward him.

The almost inaudible melody was vaguely familiar. Where had he heard that before . . .

Clair de Lune.

It was the piece Mac had teased him about that day in his apartment, after he'd thought the title was a woman's name.

"Do you hear that?" He pitched his voice so low Mark had to lean toward him to pick up the words.

"Yeah. Any idea what's going on?"

"Christy used that music for one of her competitive routines, and it's coming from the vicinity of the pond. A natural ice rink. Our guy could be making her skate. He's sick enough to pull a stunt like that."

Mark spoke into his voice-activated mike, filling in the rest of the team. "Move in slowly until we get a visual." He paused. "That fits. Let us know when you have something in sight." Mark turned to him. "Kurt's picking up a slight glow in the vicinity of the lake."

"He must have some lights set up. Pretty risky for a guy who's been very careful up till now."

"Not if he knows the area is secluded and is convinced he isn't on anyone's radar. Plus, even the most adept lawbreakers can become lax and cocky once they've gotten away with a few crimes. In any case, the light will work to our advantage. Let's take this last stretch slow and easy."

Lance fell in behind him in silence, his heart prodding him to run while his brain said creep.

Better that Mark was leading this show after all—because he wasn't certain which would have won.

Sixty seconds later, he spotted the faint glow through the trees.

Mark stopped. Touched his earpiece. "Keep looking. Check out the blind. Everyone else, find a concealed position as close as you can get to the pond." He shifted toward him. "Kurt can see the ice. Christy's skating. There are two chairs at the edge of the pond—but no sign of Terzic."

Christy's skating.

As Mark's words registered, Lance grasped a tree trunk to steady himself.

She was okay.

But that could change in a heartbeat if they didn't find Terzic fast.

His nerve endings began to buzz. "He's watching the show from somewhere—and odds are he has a gun trained on her."

Breathe, McGregor.

"I think that's a safe bet." Mark sounded cool. Calm. Controlled. The way you were supposed to sound on a high-stakes mission. The way he'd always sounded on missions where lives hung in the balance.

Until tonight.

"You want to hang back here while we finish this?"

The fact that Mark had picked up on his nerves didn't surprise him. The guy was a pro at reading people. He had to be, with his background. And his question wasn't unexpected. Had their positions been reversed, Lance would have ordered Mark to stay back. No option. By giving him a choice, Mark was expressing confidence he could get a handle on his emotions and do the job.

And he could.

He would.

"No. I'm in this to the finish." His reply came out strong, confident, and steady.

"Okay. Let's work our way in."

Lance followed the SWAT team leader, wincing with every snap of a dead twig. Ending this was going to be dicey even with the element of surprise on their side. Tipping off Terzic to their presence before they were ready could be disastrous.

The faint glow was easier to discern as they approached, though it was still subdued, and when Mark stopped to motion him forward, he saw why.

The pond was in a small, bowl-shaped depression, the woods rising like a natural amphitheater around it.

But it was Christy who drew his focus. She was skating, as Kurt had said, her motions stiffer than he recalled from the long-ago tapes he'd watched.

Understandable, given the circumstances.

"Kurt spotted the deer blind, but he's not seeing any movement." Mark pointed across the frozen surface as he pulled out a pair of night-vision binoculars and handed them over. "I don't, either. Take a look."

Lance aimed them toward the area, giving his eyes a few seconds to adjust. "Nothing."

"If he's in the blind, he's staying very still."

"He might have heard us."

"Let's hope not. That's a complication we don't need." Mark spoke into the mike. "Brett and Kurt, find a spot that gives you an optimal line of sight to the pond in general. Everyone else, find a concealed position and scan for our target. He's here somewhere, and until we get a fix on his position, we wait."

Mark began to move again, easing down, taking care to make as little noise as possible.

As Christy continued to skate, Lance followed him down—doing his best to curb his frustration. He had no quarrel with the SWAT team leader's waiting strategy. In Mark's position, he would have made the same call.

But Christy was so close. A hundred feet away when she glided by on this side of the pond— yet there wasn't a thing he could do to help her except wait. Try to spot Terzic. Stay quiet.

And pray they pinpointed Terzic's location before he tired of Christy's skating and stopped the show.

Permanently.

27

Her legs were getting tired.

Her fingers were growing numb.

Her body was beginning to shake from the cold.

She wasn't going to be able to keep skating much longer.

And once she stopped, it was over.

Pressure built behind Christy's eyes, and her vision blurred. She stumbled. Caught her balance.

Don't cry! That will only give Neven more pleasure, and that's the last thing you want to do. Right?

Right.

She needed to stay strong. Hang on to her control.

Opening and closing her fingers to stimulate circulation, she glided around a twig embedded in the ice and forced herself to face reality.

The FBI either wasn't tracking her cell after all, or if they were, they weren't going to get here fast enough.

Before she succumbed to cold and fatigue, she needed to play her final card. The one she'd dreamed up while going through her skating moves on autopilot, when her skate blade had sliced through a dead leaf caught in the ice and she'd realized she *did* have a weapon.

Skate blades could cut.

Toe picks were sharp.

Up close they could both do serious damage.

Pulse accelerating, she glided into a spiral, examining the perimeter as she circled the pond on one leg, the frigid air stinging her face. Still no sign of Neven. Why had he left his ringside seat . . . and why hadn't he returned? Was he watching her from the shadows? Was he getting into position for a kill shot—or just trying to fluster her with his absence? Would he respond as she hoped after she laid her trap to lure him onto the ice . . . or simply shoot her and be done with it?

But if he killed her here, he'd have to carry her back through the woods to the car. That would be far too much trouble . . . wouldn't it?

Maybe not. Who knew how his brain worked?

If she didn't try this, though, she'd be dead soon anyway.

Better to go down fighting.

She made one more circuit of the pond. Neven remained MIA. Was there a remote possibility he wasn't watching? That she had a window of opportunity to skate off the ice and disappear behind those cedar trees?

No.

This show was for him, and he wouldn't want to

miss any of it after going to such great lengths to set it up. He was there, in the darkness, enjoying every minute of the command performance. Waiting for her to drop. Relishing the idea of literally bringing her to her knees.

Well, she wasn't going to give him that chance.

Heart pounding, she finished the spiral, furtively worked off one glove, and picked up speed.

Now!

She set up for a double axel. Jumped. Rotated in the air.

And as she prepared to land, she lifted her hand and took the final step to make the ruse seem authentic—praying that if Neven fell for it, the ending of this story would be far different than the one he had planned.

Lance watched Christy leap, rotate—and fall hard on the unforgiving surface. She crumpled into a heap and skidded across the ice, coming to rest near the center of the pond.

And she didn't get up.

As she lay there still as death, every muscle in his body tensed.

Mark's vise-like fingers tightened on his arm. "Don't move!" The hissed words were soft but terse.

Fisting his hands, Lance wrestled his instinctive spring-into-action response into submission. His colleague was right. Neven was out there somewhere. If they exposed their position now and the man panicked, the situation could go south very fast.

"This might draw him out." Mark loosened his grip, inspected the perimeter of the lake with his NVGs, then spoke into the mike. "Everyone hold. Keep a sharp eye out for our target."

Lance lifted the night-vision binoculars again. The tremor in his fingers was a new experience on a mission . . . but he'd never been trying to save the life of a woman he was falling in love with, either.

As he zoomed in on her motionless form, he sucked in a breath. Despite the green NV hue, he had no problem spotting the growing, dark pool on the ice beside her temple.

"She's bleeding!"

"I saw that." Mark's voice remained calm. "There's a paramedic team waiting at the barn by now."

A lot of good that did them. Christy needed medical help here. Now.

He forced his lungs to keep working and scrutinized her face. It appeared the blood on the ice was coming from a gash on her temple. She must have hit her head hard or she wouldn't be . . .

He blinked.

Looked again.

Had her eyelash flickered?

He skimmed the rest of her body. One hand was curled into a fist—and she appeared to be breathing fast. Not typical symptoms of unconsciousness. The blood was real, but . . . could she have fallen on purpose?

His brain began firing. "Mark, I think the fall might be a trick to lure Terzic onto the ice." He recapped what he'd noticed. "Getting him onto her territory would help level the playing field, give her a fighting chance."

The other agent studied Christy. "You think she'd actually try a stunt like that?"

"Without question. You don't get to be an Olympic athlete without taking calculated risks —and fighting to win."

Silence while Mark mulled that over.

"I guess it's not outside the realm of possibility. Let's see if it works."

As Mark filled in the rest of the team and gave another set of instructions, Lance continued to watch Christy. If this was an act, she was doing a stellar job. Despite the cold that must be seeping through her leggings and inadequate jacket, she wasn't moving a muscle. Her willpower and discipline had to be off the chart.

Either that, or she was really hurt.

Whichever it was, though, her fall was going to force Terzic to react. This drama was about to end.

One way or the other.

• • •

An accident wasn't part of his plan.

From his perch in the deer blind, Terzic glared down at Christy. She'd warned him the surface was too rough for skating, and the several hard falls she'd taken in the past half hour were proof of that. Still, watching her get bruised and battered had been a plus from his perspective.

But it would have been nice to have another thirty minutes of fun before he ended the show.

That didn't appear to be in the cards, however. Not with that blood on her forehead. And if she was dizzy once she came to, getting her back to the car through the woods was going to be a bear. It would also take longer than he'd planned.

He needed to wrap this up.

Shifting carefully in the confined space, he scanned the area around the perimeter of the pond. All was quiet.

Nevertheless, he hesitated.

Was it possible those breaking twigs that had sent him scurrying for the cover of the deer blind had been caused by humans rather than a roving deer or raccoon? Or was he overreacting?

Surely it had to be the latter. No one suspected he had Christy—or knew where he was on this cold night.

Yet something didn't feel right.

Better to test the waters before he ventured into the open.

He felt around until his fingers closed over a half-empty box of ammunition on the floor. Tucking himself close to the rear wall, he lobbed it through an opening, putting as much muscle behind the throw as possible.

A few seconds later, it crashed into the undergrowth in the distance.

Then he waited.

And watched.

"Our guys on the west side are checking it out. It could be a deer."

As Mark relayed the gist of his radio transmission, Lance tried to rein in his impatience. "Too coincidental with Christy's fall."

"I'm inclined to agree. But let's wait for a report. If it was a deer, our target will be spooked too. He'll be on edge and jittery."

That made two of them.

Two eternal minutes later, Mark pressed a finger to his ear. "Copy. Kurt and Brett, get where you need to be." He swiveled around. "No sign of an animal, but while our guys were investigating the noise, they think they saw a movement in the deer blind."

Knowing Terzic's position was good; the position itself wasn't.

"That spot gives him a direct line of sight to Christy. He finds out we're here, he could pull the trigger—and blind shots by us might not take care of him fast enough to stop a fatal bullet from finding her." Lance motioned toward the north side of the pond. "Those chairs and generator are outside the circle of light. If we could turn off the generator, that would give us a window to get her out of harm's way."

"You're assuming he doesn't have NVGs."

"Yeah, I am. But if he does have them, I doubt he was wearing them for the show."

"The show's over."

"Look . . ." Lance did the quick mental fact-sort he'd perfected in Delta Force. "Why bother with NVGs if you're going to light up the pond? They restrict peripheral vision, and unless you're used to wearing them, they're annoying. If he illumi-nated that"—he gestured to the pond—"I'm betting he used a flashlight on their walk through the woods."

"There's a lot hinging on that bet."

As if he didn't know that.

"Do you have any other ideas about how to flush him out? Christy's bleeding, and if she doesn't already have hypothermia, she'll get it fast lying on that ice. If Terzic hasn't come out on his own by now, do you really think he's going to? He must be spooked already, and if that was a deer in the brush rather than an attempt on his part to draw *us* out, he's going to be more cautious than ever. Since we can assume he plans to kill Christy anyway, he can wait for hours to see if we make a move. She can't."

His logic was hard to refute—but Mark had nailed it. If he'd called this wrong, if Terzic had NVGs, this could backfire.

Big time.

But doing nothing wouldn't be an option much longer, given Christy's perilous position.

"I'm assuming you want to use the window of darkness before Terzic snaps on his flashlight—or whatever light source he has—to grab Christy."

"Yes. Once I have her, we can take cover behind those cedar trees." He motioned toward the small cluster of dense evergreens at the edge of the pond.

"After you cross the slippery ice."

"I played hockey. I've been around ice." Years ago . . . but he left that unsaid.

"On skates."

Lance gave the SWAT team leader a steady look. "I can do this, Mark. I was involved in dozens of high-stakes rescues in The Unit. I know how to evaluate risk and develop a strategy to minimize it."

Three long seconds crawled by.

"Okay. Given the circumstances, it's not a bad option, and I think it could work—assuming our target isn't wearing NVGs. I'll get the guys set. How much time do you need to get into position?"

"Five minutes."

"We'll cover you as best we can if Terzic gets

trigger happy once the lights go out. Good luck."

"Thanks."

But as he slipped away and began to descend toward the pond, Lance knew they'd need a whole lot more than luck to pull off this operation without bloodshed.

No one was here except him and Christy. She hadn't stirred—nor had anyone else since he'd thrown the box of bullets into the woods.

He just had a case of nerves.

Neven fingered his pistol and exhaled. Being a little jittery was understandable in the final stage of a brilliant plan that had accomplished exactly what he'd intended without creating so much as a blip on the radar of law enforcement. It was a perfect example of his organization and planning skills—and a perfect example of why he should have been so much more than a maintenance man. He was management material.

Too bad he couldn't put this whole operation on a résumé. It would certainly be impressive.

Smirking at the thought of listing such an item under the heading of accomplishments, he edged toward the ladder and took one last look at Christy from his elevated perch. Still motionless. Too bad. He wouldn't mind watching her stagger to her feet and wobble through another few spins and jumps.

On the plus side, though, the temperature was

dropping fast—and an early end to the show would allow him to get to the best part of the evening sooner.

The part where he ended the life of the woman who'd ruined his.

Adrenaline surging, he started to lower his legs to the ladder.

Suddenly, the night went pitch black.

What the . . . ?

He scrambled back into the blind, wedged himself in a corner, and peered through a crack. The generator had plenty of fuel. There should have been more than . . .

A movement on the ice caught his eye, and he homed in on it. A shadow on the surface was scooting toward the trees on the side of the pond.

Christy!

She was trying to get away!

Neven's mouth hardened as a surge of anger swept over him. No way.

He lifted his gun, steadied his arm, and took aim.

28

Christy was fighting him.

Hard.

She punched. She kicked. She scratched.

His cheek began to smart as her fingernails raked across it.

Yes!

Her fall had been a fake, just as he'd suspected. She wasn't hurt.

"Christy—it's Lance." He grappled with her flailing arms, easily restraining her as he slid them both toward the cover of the cedar trees. The darkness would only give them an advantage until Terzic's eyes adjusted or he flashed a light at them. They had a few seconds, at best. "Work with me."

She froze. Emitted a shuddering sob. Then she began pushing with her skate blades, propelling them even faster across the ice.

Once at the edge, he swept her into his arms, rose to a crouch, and dove into the small cluster of cedar trees. After setting her on the ground, he pulled out his Glock. "Are you hurt?" He scanned the perimeter of the lake as he whispered the question, wanting to cradle her in his arms and check for himself but doing instead what duty required.

"N-no."

"Stay quiet."

She was shaking—badly—as she huddled beside him, and though she didn't say a word, the chattering of her teeth echoed in the silent woods. They needed to fix that.

He dug for his wallet. If she clenched her teeth around . . .

The chattering stopped.

He flicked her a quick glance.

She'd stuck her glove-encased finger between her teeth.

What a trooper.

Again resisting the impulse to touch her, he went back to scrutinizing the perimeter. That's what a pro did.

But once this was over and FBI Special Agent McGregor was off duty, Lance intended to wrap her in his arms and hold on tight.

For a very long time.

As Christy disappeared into the small cluster of cedar trees at the edge of the pond, Neven lowered his gun.

Better not to shoot. Despite the silencer, it would give away his position. Besides, it didn't matter that she'd managed to get off the ice. In her injured state, wearing skates, how far could she run? He could easily catch up to her.

The real problem was the person who'd turned off the generator. Whoever that was could be watching for him to make a move. He couldn't show himself until . . .

"Mr. Terzic, FBI. We know you're in the deer blind. Come down and raise your hands above your head. You're surrounded by agents. Let's talk about this so no one gets hurt."

FBI?!

No!

Impossible!

No one knew about his plans. No one!

"Mr. Terzic, come down now. Agent Bradley, are you in position?"

"Yes." A second voice, off to the right.

A wave of panic, of suffocating helplessness, crashed over him, the same way it had the day his brother had been killed in the street and his mother had been dragged off by soldiers. Even if he'd been willing to risk his own neck, there hadn't been anything he could have done to help them. The soldiers had been in control in that faraway place.

But he was supposed to be in control here.

Except his biggest bargaining chip had just disappeared into the undergrowth.

He sucked in a harsh breath as the nauseating reality crashed over him.

Giving himself up, however, was not an option. They'd put him behind bars like some animal. Other people would be in control. They'd tell him what to do every day for the rest of his life. He'd never again have power or . . .

"This is your last chance, Mr. Terzic. Agent Perez, are you in position?"

"Yes."

Another new voice, this one from behind him.

He swung around. Stared at the blank wall at the back of the blind.

Last chance? No way. He knew these woods.

They didn't. If he could elude them, he'd disappear, start over like he had the day Neven Terzic had died and Nathan Turner had been born. He was good at starting over. Good at taking control.

And he could regain control of this situation.

Jaw set, he grasped his pistol, scooted over to the ladder, and plunged into the underbrush at the base of the blind. The agents wouldn't be this close. They didn't know what kind of weapons he had, and they wouldn't risk their lives by closing in too fast. They might have night vision equipment, but the woods were dense. It would be hard for them to get a decent shot at him. The odds were in his favor as long as he kept weaving around the trees and ducking and bobbing and . . .

All at once, his foot plunged into a hole and he pitched forward, his gun flying into the darkness as he went down hard. The air whooshed out of his lungs.

As he struggled to breathe, the rustle of dead leaves told him he wasn't alone even before a steel-hard voice spoke.

"It's over, Terzic. Make one move, I won't hesitate to pull this trigger."

The man's cold, deadly tone told him the threat wasn't idle.

An instant later, bright lights were aimed into his eyes, blinding him.

"Face down on the ground. Arms behind you, palms up. Now!"

There were at least four agents on hand . . . and all of them would have weapons. Resisting would be suicide—and he wasn't about to take the cowardly way out, like the old woman had.

So for now he'd have to go along with them. But lots of people broke out of jail. He could be one of them. He knew how to bide his time and plan. This wasn't the end—no matter what they thought. He was too smart for that.

Slowly he complied with the order.

A moment later his wrists were cuffed and he was pulled to his feet.

Squinting in the light, he looked around. Several men in assault gear were watching him— including the one who was helping Christy slide her arms into a jacket. As the guy bent and lifted her into his arms, he peered at the man's face.

It was the guy she'd been hanging around with these past few weeks.

So the boyfriend was a cop after all. No, worse than a cop. An FBI agent.

Anger began to churn in his gut. She'd defied him from the beginning. Ignored his directives and gone to the authorities after that first letter. She'd betrayed him just as she had all those years ago in high school.

But still . . . he'd covered his tracks. They

shouldn't have been able to figure out he was the one behind the letters—or the fire at her sister's house.

"Let's get out of here. You want to alert the paramedics?" The tall guy holding Christy spoke to another agent.

"Already done. They're waiting at the turn-around."

Someone urged him forward from behind. "Start walking."

"Wait!" Neven held his ground, trying to quash the new surge of panic that was short-circuiting his brain. "Who told you about . . . how did you know about this?"

The agent holding Christy tossed the response over his shoulder as he walked away. "Your grandmother sent a letter."

What?

The helpless, meek old woman had turned in her own flesh and blood?

Her *grandson?*

She might have abandoned him once before, but that hadn't been intentional. This was worse. Much worse.

This was a betrayal.

More ruthless, even, than Christy's.

"Move."

Someone prodded him from behind again, and he stumbled forward, rage scouring his stomach as he silently cursed her.

It was a good thing Mevlida Terzic was already dead.

Because if she wasn't, he'd kill her.

Christy snuggled deeper into the blessed warmth. Shifted her position slightly to ease the tingle in her legs and the lingering ache in her stomach. Sighed, suspended somewhere between sleep and wakefulness.

Mmm.

It was so safe and peaceful and perfect here. She could stay like this forever . . .

"Morning, sleepyhead."

As the husky masculine voice spoke close to her ear, her eyelids flew open and she blinked, trying to orient herself.

She was on her couch. Pale light was peeking in at the edges of her blinds. Flames were flickering in her fireplace. And she was cuddled up next to Lance . . . whose weary eyes and stubbled chin told her he'd been beside her, keeping vigil while she slept, since they'd arrived home from the ER at three in the morning.

She willed the last vestiges of sleep to disperse and tried to pry herself away from his side.

"Uh-uh." He held fast. "I've been waiting all night to do this. My patience is gone."

Then, without giving her a chance to anticipate or prepare or get nervous, he dipped his head and gave her a kiss that was tender, careful, and restrained . . . but also simmering with a barely leashed passion, a promise of things to come, that set her heart racing.

When at last he drew back, she let out a slow, unsteady breath. "That was some first kiss."

"And way overdue." He cleared the hoarseness from his throat. "I lied a minute ago. I've been waiting much longer than all night to do that. And there'll be a lot more of those once you're back to normal. How are you feeling?"

"Swept off my feet?" She smiled up at him.

"Nice to hear. But I was referring to your physical condition." His own smile faded as he searched her face. "I wish you'd spent a few more hours in the hospital. You're too pale."

"I'm fine, Lance. A bad chill that didn't qualify even as mild hypothermia, a few assorted bruises, and a touch of frostbite. The hot chocolate you fixed after we got back was much more effective than another warmed IV. Not to mention the body heat you provided." She snuggled closer. "You can warm me up anytime."

He tipped his head. "Are you flirting with me?"

"Maybe. That's allowed now that the case is over, isn't it?"

"Allowed—and encouraged." A yawn snuck up on him. "Sorry."

The man's dead on his feet, Christy. Send him home.

She squelched her selfish impulses—the ones

clamoring for her to urge him to stay. "Don't apologize. You need to get some sleep."

"I have to admit, a few hours of shut-eye would be welcome. Will you be okay here by yourself?"

"Yes. I plan to spend a large part of the day planted in front of the fire. Staying warm is my top priority—along with giving thanks that this whole nightmare is over." She crimped the afghan in her fingers and released a shaky breath. "I still can't believe how this played out. That Neven was behind it. I tried so hard to be nice to him in high school, and he repaid me by destroying my family?" A shudder rippled through her.

Lance twined his fingers with hers, the warmth of his touch taking the edge off her soul-deep chill. "Psychopaths aren't wired to react like rational, compassionate human beings, Christy. But he won't have a chance to hurt anyone else ever again." He stroked one finger along the edge of the bandage slanted across her temple. "Speaking of hurting, this is nasty. I can't believe you gouged out a chunk of skin with your fingernails on purpose. It was almost deep enough to need stitches."

She lifted one shoulder. "I thought blood would make the ruse more realistic. I wanted Neven to believe I was really injured so he'd come out on the ice."

"I can't speak for him, but it freaked *me* out."

"I'm sorry for that. And for this." She laid a hand next to the scratch she'd inflicted on his cheek.

He covered her fingers with his. "Don't be. Having you go ballistic was the answer to a prayer. I knew then you'd faked the fall." He yawned again, his expression rueful. "I must be getting soft—or old. I used to be able to go a lot longer than this without getting tired."

"Lance McGregor. Soft. Old." She pretended to ponder that. "Nope. Not computing. But high-stakes drama can be draining, especially if there's emotional involvement."

"Guilty on that score—and not ashamed to admit it. Shall I demonstrate the extent of my involvement?" He waggled his eyebrows.

She chuckled. "Later. Right now, you need to sleep. I'll walk you to the door." She stood and held out her hand.

He took it without further protest—confirming how tired he was.

Once in the foyer, he turned to her. "After I sleep and shower, I'm going to be hungry. Do you think you'll be up for dinner tonight?"

"Yes."

He grinned. "A decisive woman. I like that."

"I learned long ago that when you have your sights set on gold, you can't be tentative." She rested her hands against his solid chest, the steady beat of his heart beneath her fingers the most comforting reassurance the nightmare was over. "And you, Lance McGregor, are gold."

His blue eyes softened, the tender look sending a tingle to her fingertips that had nothing to do with the aftereffects of frostbite. "I think that may be the nicest thing anyone has ever said to me." He took her hands and folded them in his. "While we're setting up dates, hold February 14 for me too, okay?"

"Valentine's Day?" She tilted her head and smiled. "Funny. You don't strike me as the sentimental type."

"I never was before. You bring out the romantic in me. Shall we consider it a date?"

"I'll pencil it in."

"Write it in ink." He looped his arms around her waist. "In fact, write me in every day for as far out as your calendar goes—because I have plans for us. An exclusive arrangement, in fact. Interested?"

"Just show me where to sign."

"Why don't we seal the deal in a more personal way?"

He bent toward her, and she rose on tiptoes to meet him, this man who had entered her world in the midst of tragedy, who'd fought to find the answers she needed, who'd salvaged her battered heart and helped her believe that better days were ahead.

His lips closed over hers then, and as joy chased away the darkness, she knew her season of weeping and mourning was at last drawing to a close. For with Lance by her side, she would find healing—and hope.

And on one bright tomorrow in the not-too-distant future, it would be her time to laugh—and to love.

Epilogue

Five Months Later

"Nervous?" Lance popped a chip in his mouth and grinned at Christy. Rhetorical question. She'd been as antsy as a kid waiting to see Santa Claus since she'd arrived at his apartment ten minutes ago.

She wiped her palms down her shorts and adjusted the plastic wrap covering the oversized bowl of potato salad she'd made for his family's Fourth of July shindig.

"Do I look nervous?"

"A tad." He picked up another chip. "But you also look gorgeous. Nice outfit." He gave her hemp sandals, white shorts, and soft blue top a leisurely—and appreciative—perusal.

"Meeting the family is a big deal." She smoothed a hand over her wavy hair, pulled back for the occasion with a red, white, and blue ribbon.

"You'll love my parents—and they'll love you. You already know Mac, and if you like him, you'll like the runt."

The tension in her features dissipated slightly. "I'm glad Finn was able to come."

"Me too. I think Mac and Lisa's wedding gave him the incentive to buckle down with the physical therapy. That, and the invitation to share best man duties with me on Saturday."

"How did he seem when you stopped at Mac's last night to say hi after your SWAT callout?"

"Okay. Better than okay, actually. He's thinner than he should be, but his eyes aren't as haunted as they were a few months back, and he's walking great. He still has a slight limp, but it's a lot less noticeable than it was a few weeks ago when I flew up to see him."

"His recovery has been amazing."

"I agree, given the initial prognosis."

"I think prayer had a lot to do with it."

"No arguments there."

"I'm glad he decided to stick around St. Louis for the rest of his recovery too. Being near family will help."

"Yeah. It took a little arm twisting by me and Mac, but Finn finally caved after we promised not to hover. Like we have time to do that, anyway." He plucked another chip from the bag in his hands.

She cocked her head. "You heard my excuse for being nervous. What's yours?"

His hand froze in midair. "I'm not nervous."

"Ha. You only stuff your face with empty calories when you're worried or stressed or hyper. What's up?"

The lady had him pegged.

Not surprising, since they'd spent every spare minute of their free time together over the past five months.

Dropping the chip back in the bag, he bought himself a few seconds by crimping the top and brushing some wayward grains of salt off his T-shirt.

Punt . . . or be honest?

He shoved his hands into the pockets of his jeans. Touched the gold band tucked in one corner. His plan to steal away with her once the fireworks started tonight at Lisa's house and propose under a canopy of sparkling lights had sounded romantic in theory.

But they'd have more privacy here—and there'd be no pesky mosquitoes to contend with, like there would be out in the country. Plus, he'd be able to see her clearly. To watch the reaction in those amazing green eyes. To kiss her in the air-conditioned comfort of his apartment.

With the mercury expected to hover in the mid-nineties by dinner, the latter was no small consideration.

"Lance?" She sent him a curious glance.

He waved a hand toward the couch. The one

that had been on back order for months and had arrived yesterday after Lisa began badgering the store. He couldn't have cared less about the delay . . . but since it was the only piece of furniture in the place that could accommodate two people, the timing seemed providential. "Let's sit for a minute."

Distress tightened her features, and she clenched her fingers. "Are you about to give me some bad news?"

"No. Sorry. I didn't mean to scare you." He took her hand and tugged her onto the couch beside him. "You've had enough bad news to last a lifetime. This is just the opposite—I hope."

She exhaled. "Now it's my turn to apologize. I didn't mean to overreact."

"You had reason to." He stroked a finger across the faint white line on her temple, the only visible remnant of the horror she'd faced that cold February night. It was fading—but slowly . . . like her traumatic memories.

"Things are getting better, though." She sent him a reassuring smile. "The nightmares are diminishing, and I'm sleeping better. I consider that great progress. Now tell me your news."

The ball was back in his court.

His palms grew damp, and he could feel beads of sweat breaking out on his forehead.

Had the air conditioner in here stopped working?

She squeezed his fingers. "Are you sure everything's all right?"

Just do it, McGregor. You've conducted raids in enemy territory, led high-risk rescue operations, and put your life on the line during dozens of missions. This should be easy.

Except it wasn't.

Because something a lot more important than his physical life hinged on the outcome of these next few minutes.

Christy's expression grew speculative, and one side of her mouth twitched. "Would you like me to guess what this is about?"

Man, he was blowing this big time if she was offering to preempt him.

"No. I'm getting to it." He fished around in the pocket of his jeans again. Closed his fingers around the ring and pulled it out. Took a deep breath.

Her gaze dropped to his white knuckles for a moment. Lifted.

He swallowed, trying to remember the script he'd been practicing for weeks. "I want you to know these past few months have been the best in my life."

"Mine too."

Those little gold flecks in her jade irises began to glitter, like they always did when she was excited—and, as usual, he lost his train of thought. Hard as he tried, he couldn't remember a word of the rest of his speech.

A wave of panic washed over him. Could he backpedal? Revert to the fireworks plan so he could practice his spiel some more?

He studied her expectant face.

No.

He was too far in to bail.

He'd have to improvise.

Tightening his grip on her fingers, he plunged in. "So . . . here's the thing. I never thought a lot about getting married. It was always a step I assumed I'd take someday, when life slowed down. Except it never did . . . and someday never came. To be honest, I didn't worry much about that. I figured if it was meant to be, the right woman would eventually come along."

Keep breathing, McGregor.

"Then one day, out of the blue, she did. And odd as it may sound, I knew almost from the moment we met that you were the one. These past few months of getting to know one another have only reinforced what I realized from the very beginning." With one final squeeze of the ring, he opened his fingers to reveal the marquis-shaped diamond.

Christy let out a small gasp—of delight, he hoped.

One of them started to tremble.

Maybe they both did.

"As my brothers would be the first to tell you, I'm not great with words. But here's the simple truth—I love you with all my heart, and I always will. I want to spend every day of the rest of my life with you. I want to sit with you on a porch and watch our children play. I want to wake up next to you each morning and go to sleep each night with you beside me. I want to grow old in your arms. You are the best gift God ever gave me, and I'll try as hard as I can to be the kind of husband he'll look at on judgment day and say, well done, good and faithful servant. So Christy . . . will you marry me?"

Her eyes began to shimmer, and her answer came out in a whisper—but with no hesitation. "Yes."

He slipped the ring on her finger—and though the fireworks planned for tonight wouldn't begin for hours, sparklers and pinwheels and rockets set off a joyous celebration in his heart.

She stared at the stone for another few seconds before lifting her chin. "It's beautiful, Lance."

"I'd have bought you the Hope diamond if I could."

"I don't need flashy jewelry. Just your love."

"You've got that—for always."

"And you have mine. All those things you said . . . I feel exactly the same way. You bring joy and sunshine to my days, and I can't imagine the rest of my life without you." She touched the ring, blinked away her tears, and gave him a solemn look. "But I do have one question."

He braced at her serious tone. "Okay. Shoot—metaphorically speaking."

"You're not going to change your mind and become a priest, are you?"

A chuckle bubbled up from deep in his chest, erupting into a hearty laugh. "Not a chance."

Grinning, she scooted closer and draped her arms around his neck. "Actions speak louder than words."

"Oh, trust me. I have lots of action in mind." He tugged her even closer, until their lips were a breath apart. "Gold medal quality."

Her eyes twinkled into his. "Then let the games begin."

And with no further discussion, they did.

Acknowledgments

Suspense books require a great deal of research, and I am indebted to the following people for their generous assistance with *Thin Ice*.

FBI veteran Tom Becker, now chief of police in Frontenac, Missouri, who answered the countless questions that arose over the many months it took to write this book. Thank you for your speed and thoroughness. Your input gave this book its polish of authenticity.

Captain Ed Nestor from the Chesterfield, Missouri, Police Department, my first law enforcement contact. Thank you for connecting me to amazing sources, who in turn led me to other sources. The incredible network I now have started with you!

I'd also like to thank the following:

The superlative team at Revell. I look forward to doing many more books with you.

My mom and dad—my first fans! God smiled on me the day he made you my parents.

The readers who enjoy my books. Because of you, I get to tell stories for a living . . . and I give thanks for you every day.

And finally, my husband, Tom. The memories of the happy times we've shared are among my greatest treasures.

About the Author

Irene Hannon is a bestselling, award-winning author who took the publishing world by storm at the tender age of ten with a sparkling piece of fiction that received national attention.

Okay . . . maybe that's a slight exaggeration. But she *was* one of the honorees in a complete-the-story contest conducted by a national children's magazine. And she likes to think of that as her "official" fiction-writing debut!

Since then, she has written more than fifty contemporary romance and romantic suspense novels. Irene is a seven-time finalist and three-time winner of the RITA award—the "Oscar" of romantic fiction—from Romance Writers of America. She is also a member of that organization's elite Hall of Fame. Her books have been honored with a National Readers' Choice award, three HOLT medallions, a Daphne du Maurier award, a Retailers Choice award, two Booksellers' Best awards, a Carol award, and two Reviewers' Choice awards from *RT Book Reviews* magazine. In addition, she is a two-time Christy award finalist.

Irene, who holds a BA in psychology and an MA in journalism, juggled two careers for many

485

years until she gave up her executive corporate communications position with a Fortune 500 company to write full-time. She is happy to say she has no regrets! As she points out, leaving behind the rush-hour commute, corporate politics, and a relentless BlackBerry that never slept was no sacrifice.

A trained vocalist, Irene has sung the leading role in numerous community musical theater productions and is also a soloist at her church.

When not otherwise occupied, she and her husband enjoy traveling, Saturday mornings at their favorite coffee shop, and spending time with family. They make their home in Missouri.

To learn more about Irene and her books, visit www.irenehannon.com. She is also active on Facebook and Twitter.

Center Point Large Print
600 Brooks Road / PO Box 1
Thorndike, ME 04986-0001 USA

(207) 568-3717

US & Canada:
1 800 929-9108
www.centerpointlargeprint.com